AFTER DEATH

DERRICK LACOMBE

ISBN:0991458303
ISBN-13: 978-0-9914583-0-1

Edited by Monique Happy Editorial Services
Copyeditors: Monique Happy & Tracey Fitzgerald Rose
http://www.moniquehappy.com

Cover art: Todd Schmidt

Manufactured and produced
in the United States of America.

For information regarding special discounts for bulk purchases,
please contact Derrick LaCombe

A special dedication to my wife, whose patience and love allowed me to complete this novel.

A special thanks to proofreaders, Brian, Kim, and Vicki. Confidence builders!

AFTER DEATH

Prologue:

The Mayan High Priest stood on the temple's ceremonial platform, a colorful headdress of feathers sprouting from his skull. His robe was made from the spotted skins of the sacred jaguar; skillful painting repeated the pattern on his face. Thus adorned and ready for the task at hand, he gestured for the prisoner to be brought forward and laid atop the altar. The large group of people gathered below watched with desperate anticipation.

The captive man, body painted blue, struggled against the jungle vines which bound his wrists. Prodded forward by the High Priest's guards, he moved strangely, snarling and mumbling indecipherable phrases. His fingers were splayed, rigid and pointing like miniature spears. The flesh of his left ankle scraped across rough stone, but he did not cry out in pain.

Impassive, the High Priest watched as guards forced the prisoner onto the sacrificial altar. As he approached the prone captive, the High Priest chanted. The excitement of the crowd intensified, becoming nearly palpable. At the head of the altar the High Priest raised an obsidian blade high into the air. Sunlight glinted off of its razor edge. Thousands of people at the base of the temple cheered, frenzied with anticipation.

A practiced showman, the High Priest knew it was time and did exactly what the people wanted: he thrust the blade into the prisoner's chest. The chest cavity burst open, and the High Priest plunged one of his hands through the rib cage. Blood mixed with air, creating a froth that bubbled around the edges of the wound. When the fevered pitch of the crowd reached its peak, the High Priest quickly twisted his hand and ripped out the still-beating heart.

A moment passed as the onlookers laughed and sang. Suddenly, the body of the sacrificed captive writhed. The guards stood back in terror. How could the body continue to move? They knelt before the curiosity and bowed their heads, too afraid to speak. Talk of the happening spread through the crowd like wildfire.

The High Priest looked at the body and gestured for silence. Pressured to perform a more brutal ritual, he hefted a large obsidian axe and shook it above his head. The massive crowd roared, near hysteria. This sacrifice would free them from several years of drought. They screamed their pleas as they motioned for a decapitation. Silencing the crowd once more, the High Priest whipped the axe through the air, severing the skull from the body.

The prisoner finally lay limp on the bloodied altar. Never had the High Priest seen such an event, and he hoped it would bring good fortune to his people. The crowd's response was deafening as he lifted the painted, bloodied head by its hair and tossed it down the steps. The head rolled and bounced as the crowd rushed in, every person vying to be the first to hold it. Each time the head was lifted into the air and passed around, the thirsty believers pumped their fists in rage. Blood and bits of viscera dripped down upon them.

Again, the High Priest lifted the axe over his head and shook it vigorously. He chanted another oath, but his words were drowned out by the roaring of the people. They had gotten what they wanted. The sacrifice had been made and the Gods appeased. Rain would come soon. The guards rose from their knees and bowed to the High Priest.

Belize Jungle, 1635 Hours; Team One:

"I'm done ... and satisfied! Let's wrap this photo shoot up, head back to camp," Angela said, tossing her hair behind her shoulders. "I'm exhausted."

Kimball flashed his sweet eyes and pleaded, "C'mon, just one more pic?" But he already knew what she'd say, and hurriedly climbed atop a stone to reach an unfamiliar hieroglyphic.

Angela hoped he could feel her rolling her eyes and sarcastically replied, "Always just one more! Fine, one more, but hurry! I really am tired."

Kimball replied as if he had just seen a crashed U.F.O. "These glyphs ... they're gonna defy the archeological record!"

Angela finally gave in, showing her true fascination and stepping forward with a charmed grin. "I know. Who knew the Mayans were into Bio, too? Maybe there's something to the legend after all."

Kimball, finally satisfied with the angle of the shot, said, "Okay, I got it ... and it's a very nice pic! Ya' wanna see it?" When he turned around, Angela was already near the cave's exit.

Underwhelmed and frustrated again, Angela called over her shoulder. "Later, later! Let's get out of here. We'll miss our chopper."

Belize Jungle, 1635 Hours; Team Two:

A quarter of a mile away, Max was as happy as a pig in mud. Maneuvering his bulk, he leaned forward, sweating and squinting. He got within inches of the specimen and said to Phoenix, "This fungus growth ... it's odd!" Pushing his eyeglasses further up the bridge of his nose, he continued, "I don't think I've seen anything like it. Sporaton will think they've died and gone to heaven!" Max reached to swat an ant that had clamped down on his ankle.

Phoenix was wearing a battered Texas Rangers baseball cap with the brim turned backward. He looked at Max and sardonically replied, "Yeah, right; it's freakin' awesome! The mysteries we'll unlock with this discovery." Exhausted by the oppressive heat, Phoenix rested against the wall of the cavern. Taking a deep breath, he glanced at his watch. "Dude! I just got some of that nasty fungus on my forearm. This place is ticking me off! I'm ready for some ribs." Phoenix grabbed a small towel emblazoned with the Sporaton logo, wiped the fungus off, then threw it toward his bag, unconcerned when it landed on Max's gear instead.

Oblivious to Phoenix's rant, Max leaned over to take the specimen, asking his much younger companion, "Can you help me with this?" Max tweezed the segment loose, and placed it onto a wet sponge.

"I'm coming," Phoenix replied, already walking over to Max. He squatted next to the growth and tilted a test tube. Max folded the wet sponge and placed it into the container. Before he could retrieve more, he slapped at another ant that had crawled up to the bend of his elbow. The ant sailed through the air and landed atop the fungus.

Max continued on to the second specimen, but a third ant latched onto his finger. The stout doctor flicked at the bothersome insect, but it was firmly attached. He looked at it and shouted, "You nasty little bugger!"

The ant's pincers had firm hold of Max's skin. He stared at the squirming ant, briefly tempted to just yank it off. Instead, he waited and watched curiously as the ant, coated with specks of fungus, moved about in a cartoonish manner, a bit like a drunkard. After a few moments, Max tugged at the ant. He was successful in removing the main body of the ant, but the head and its mandibles stayed firmly attached. He had to remove the head by using his field tweezers. A small drop of blood welled and fell from his finger. Max stuck his sore forefinger into his mouth and sucked on it to stop the bleeding.

Phoenix laughed and said, "That's nasty, man! That ant had it out for you."

Max merely grunted and wiped his finger on his pants, grimacing at the light red streak left behind. Then he motioned to Phoenix that he was ready to go.

The two men packed their gear and headed for the cavern's exit. Phoenix looked down and noticed a long ant trail leaving, too, with insect carcasses twice the size of the ants carrying them. A few of the soldier ants had herded some of the spastic ants away from the others. *Curious.* Phoenix believed that ants were strange little insects, anyway.

Without looking, Max asked, "You say something, Phoenix?"

Phoenix shrugged his shoulders and replied, "Nah! Let's get outta here."

Base Camp, 1645 Hours:

Phan's team patiently waited for the other Sporaton members to return. After a week of sweating it out in the jungle, they were upbeat as they milled about the remnants of the camp. The chopper flight out of Belize would be there soon. Most of Phan's crew chatted about the discoveries of the past week or talked about home-cooked meals. Some of the team members, however, were graduate students and had already pulled out their laptops, using remaining battery power to pore over research data.

Chac, a pony-tailed Mayan and an expert in deciphering hieroglyphics, had begun the preliminary task of examining some of the photographs for the men. A native of Belize, he was working on contract with the Sporaton crew. Studying the images on the computer screen, Chac said to Phan, "Some of these glyphs are very different from the others I have studied."

Dusting off his old, floppy hat, Phan asked, "What do you mean?"

Chac clicked his way to a photo and answered, "Well, for one, the tone of the glyphs seems to be more somber, darker than I've seen."

Phan leaned closer to the screen and studied the high-definition picture. To him, it looked like a scene from a nightmare. He replied, "I don't know anything about deciphering these. But I'll take your word for it."

Chac continued, "It's very curious. Notice here, and here," he motioned. As Chac pointed, Phan noticed that the Mayan's hands were tattooed with glyphs

Scraping the mud from his boots, Phan said, "I see. It's like a puzzle."

Chac was silent for a moment, pondering. His tone was emphatic when he said, "There may be something to this. We need to study it in its entirety. In fact, my government needs to set aside funds for the area to be studied as one entity. There are hidden structures under the jungle foliage, and we need to uncover them."

Phan nodded his head. "Perhaps Sporaton will be back and able to help you with your goal."

An excited shout came from one of the students. "Look, here come the rest!" The members of Phan's team cheered.

Phan smiled and exclaimed, "And here comes the chopper!"

Chartered Flight, 1815 Hours:

Most of the team members remained animated during the short helicopter hop to a small airstrip where a Sporaton company plane awaited them. After an hour or so, however, things were different. The scientists' moods began to sour. Some of the crew were sweaty and fidgety, and had cranked up their air vents; others did their best to ignore their own physical problems and chatted quietly with their fellow team members.

Phoenix hated the stale air of the cabin and took in shallow breaths. As he listened to music with his headphones, he glanced around, worried about his teammates. Most seemed uncomfortable or agitated. Phoenix decided they must be feeling the post-expedition blues. Everyone loved being in the field; this sort of mild depression happened all the time. It was akin to disembarking from a cruise ship after seven days of adventure. Phoenix internally shrugged, closed his eyes and relaxed into his seat.

Texas Airport, 0100 Hours:

Back home on a Texas airfield, Phoenix noticed that everyone had phones out. They were already starting to call off from work. He watched with furrowed brows as his co-workers fumbled with the bright screens. *He* felt great after the nap he'd caught, but these guys looked like they were drunk, instead of just tired from their expedition.

Sick of the packaged MREs they'd had the entire week, Phoenix milled about, looking for any volunteers to go with him for breakfast. He shouted out to get a taker or two. "Who wants to get breakfast?" No actual replies; only mumbles and moans. *No one manning up,* he thought. Since he was the youngest of the scientists, he was accustomed to the usual non-replies. He heckled his teammates as they walked away. "Sorry you boys can't hang with the big dog! I'll see you all tomorrow." Phoenix received the usual halfhearted grunts and the backs of hands as the Sporaton scientists clambered into cars.

***

Oscar stood shakily between two cars and almost vomited into his hands. He said to Jim, who looked just as ill, "I think I have the flu. I've already left a message and called off for tomorrow. That's sure gonna tick off Billings, but I really feel sick."

Jim stopped at the back bumper of his car and replied, "Yeah, I feel the same way. Maybe it's a jungle bug; I've dealt with them before. This one sure seems to have hit quickly, though." He reached out and weakly clapped Oscar on the shoulder. "Well, I'll see you later."

Oscar eased into his car, his muscles exhausted. Once he had his seat belt on, he started the ignition and turned on the radio. *Good ol' Texas Swing.* He sighed and watched as the rest of the crew drove out of the parking lot for their homes, but he was so tired he decided to lay his head back for a few minutes.

Alone, he whispered, "Just a quick nap."

Baron, Texas:

The small town of Baron, Texas prided itself on hard work. Located near the convergence of Highways 70 and 256 in northern Texas, Baron was one of the few places left in Texas where half of the population could trace its lineage back to "Old Texas." The town marker greeted passersby with a declaration: *We're Proud to be American TEXANS.*

Baron had become a town when one Lord Baron struck oil on his sprawling ranch. The small population swelled as Lord Baron provided jobs that were rapidly filled by nearby ranch hands. Dozens of workers populated his land within a few short years, prompting the Lord to turn his homestead into a town. Over the generations that followed, Baron evolved into a thriving, proud community.

That pride was still displayed during an annual celebration that helped citizens trace their ancestry back one hundred and fifty-five years. Each year the town council sponsored a booth where an expert would trace a citizen's heritage for free. There was one catch: If you wanted a printed book, it would cost twenty dollars. The multi-term mayor's extra campaign funds paid for kids to have their faces painted.

Free barbecue was provided courtesy of Big Texas Roadhouse. The owner of the joint, "Big Tex," considered it a way to give back to the community for supporting him and making him a success. The town of Baron was now known for turning out the best barbecue in the Lone Star State. Plenty of other barbecue restaurants claimed that they had the world's best, but Big Texas Roadhouse reigned supreme. Big Tex also had a brisk mail order business, shipping cases of his twenty-four ounce bottles of sauce to addresses all over the world. Ever since he'd launched his web page, he'd sold two hundred and fifty bottles a week.

The newest company, Sporaton, was hailed as a "hero" company. It was the first high-tech business in the newly developed "bio-zone." The company provided the town with an infusion of cash and youth, but also benefited from tax incentives and perks. Scientists from around the world began to move to Baron in the weeks leading up to the grand opening. Their paychecks provided a much needed boost to the economy. At first, the scientists seemed nerdy and odd to the blue-collar locals. Of course, the variety of non-southern accents did not help. The Sporaton employees finally achieved some acceptance and started to blend in nicely as the locals took advantage of the free computer-fixes and advice.

Sporaton Lab, 0800 Hours:

Phoenix adjusted his baseball cap and walked through the door, feeling energized and antsy. He immediately caught sight of Professor Harrington, who hurried over and asked anxiously, "Where is everyone? Let's get this debriefing started."

As soon as everyone had staggered in and taken seats, Professor Harrington got down to business. "Well, did you discover anything new?"

Phoenix grinned and replied in a teasing voice, "Maybe … just maybe … a new fungus species!"

Unable to hold back his excitement, the lanky Harrington blurted out, "Well, spill the beans, Phoenix! What did it look like?"

"It's fleshy looking, with stalks growing from it. And when we cut it open, it let out a strange, musty odor. But you know what was really interesting? A carpenter ant bit Max, and actually drew blood. As for the rest, it will have to wait until tomorrow. I can't say anything more!"

Harrington, obviously frustrated, pleaded, "C'mon, tell me everything! *I'm* your boss, not Bob!"

Phoenix held his ground. "No siree! You know how Bob is. He'll be ticked, and I don't wanna hear it from him. You'll just have to wait until tomorrow." He walked over to his cubicle, chuckling quietly.

Max's Home, 1730 Hours:

Irritated and home later than she'd planned, Sandy called out for Max but heard no reply. She tossed her purse onto the sofa and again yelled, "MAX! Quit playing with your fungus – I'm home." She walked into the kitchen, flipped on the evening news, and donned an apron sporting a whimsical armadillo design. As she turned on the faucet, she yelled out "MAX!" once more. Over the sounds of running water and the television, she didn't hear the slow, awkward approach of her husband.

The grotesque zombie moved against the strain of rigor mortis, causing its stiffened joints to pop and crunch. Its skin was ashen green, and its eyes were black and bulging. It approached Sandy from behind.

She finally heard the shuffling noise; Max coming to give her a peck on the cheek, no doubt. When Sandy turned for the affectionate gesture, she found herself face to face with the hideous zombie. Its distorted face was dominated by terrifying jaws that snapped open and closed, again and again. Gurgling sounds came from its tortured mouth, and black, slimy spittle flew onto Sandy's face.

She was dumbstruck, a deer in the headlights. The fear and confusion came crashing in. *Is this thing the man I left this morning?* Sandy screamed and tried to dodge the arms that swiped at her head. She stumbled backward and slipped, falling hard onto the ceramic floor. As the zombie lunged for her, she screamed, "NO! MAX!"

Phan's Home (Max's Next Door Neighbor):

The zombie continued to bite off chunks of scalp from its victim's head. Blood decorated the wall and puddled around the body. The victim had slumped in a kneeling position, one arm twisted behind his head. Screams intensified from the others inside the home, causing the zombie to rise from its meal and stumble outside in a state of agitation.

It abruptly froze; its brain quivered within and then exploded. Chunks of skull and grey matter splattered a nearby porch window. Silhouetted by the setting sun, dark blood pumped from exposed cerebral arteries, and the zombie fell to the ground.

Phan's Home, 1800 Hours:

Ahn pumped the shotgun and paused a moment, trying to still his trembling hands. When he could wait no longer, he pulled the trigger; an explosion of fire and buckshot decimated his target. What had been his father's head now lay splattered in pieces along the hallway. Chunks of brain matter dripped from the ceiling. Pulverized viscera became a grotesque parody of modern art, clinging to a gold-leafed mirror.

The remnants of the corpse lay contorted, partially draped over a table. Ahn threw his shotgun down and stood next to his father's mangled body. He was taken back to his twelfth birthday, nearly a year past – the day his father had given him the gun and told Ahn that he was now a man. Ahn looked down with tears in his eyes and cried, "I'm so sorry, Father!" With the sleeve of his shirt he wiped tears and streaks of blood from his face, then stepped forward and strode past his mother's corpse. Though he had done what needed to be done, he was overwhelmed with terrible sorrow. He stopped to look back at her

9

body, whispering, "Mom." The word hung in the air. Ahn's young eyes emptied as he turned from the gory scene to find his sisters.

Ahn's sisters were older than him, but were completely hysterical. They cried and vomited as they ran past the hallway to get out of the house. Ahn caught up with them in the front yard, and used the pink, bejeweled cell phone they shared to call 911. Upset in a way he had never experienced, he could barely control his fingers as he struggled with the smart phone's touchscreen. He entered the numbers and waited for an answer.

"911 Operator. State your emergency, please."

Ahn held his emotions in check as he said, "My name is Ahn. I live at 142 Spur Street. I just blew my father's head off."

The 911 operator asked, "Please repeat? I'm not sure I heard you correctly. Do you need an ambulance?"

Ahn replied without emotion. "Yes."

Big Texas Road House, 1900 Hours:

Phoenix was so hungry that he literally salivated as he daydreamed about the baby-back ribs he loved. He left work and headed straight for the Big Texas Road House, the restaurant with the best ribs in Texas. They were juicy, fall-off-the-bone good, and the barbeque sauce was a blue-ribbon award winner. Big Tex had once told him he wanted to somehow get the sauce featured on a cable food channel, but to keep that a secret for now. Phoenix didn't argue, since Big Tex was a lumbering giant of a man. He was a friendly and lovable teddy bear, but still someone you knew not to mess with.

People drove from all over the North Texas panhandle (and beyond) to eat the lip-smacking ribs glazed with the secret sauce, and since Sporaton's arrival in town, Phoenix had become a regular. Big Tex knew he'd been off on one of his expeditions, and as his favorite customer walked through the door he could tell he was a hungry man. Before Phoenix even had a chance to settle in for a chat with his favorite bartender, the baby-backs had already been ordered for him. Being a regular customer had its perks.

In his bellowing voice, Big Tex yelled out, "Hey, it's good to see you, my man! How was the trip south of the border?"

"Well, if you wanna know the truth, Big Tex ... it was the same as always. Find fungus, take samples of fungus, and bring fungus back for more study. Cha-ching!"

Big Tex grinned. "It all sounds really interesting, dude. Glad you're home!" He patted Phoenix hard on the back and headed off to chat up another customer.

Phoenix's attention wandered back to the beauty behind the bar. He locked on to her hazel eyes and winked, then said, "I'm so happy to see you I could eat you up. Do you have anything for me?"

Betsy Ann was now familiar with his old line and replied, "You know the two-step isn't for me. I'm a one-stepping' kinda girl!" She winked back and poured a draft beer. Phoenix took his brew in mock defeat and started to make his rounds.

The bar was especially crowded because it was a Friday night. Phoenix thought it was the best bar he'd ever visited. Indeed, a wrought iron sign spelled it out for everyone that walked in: *"Best of the West."* Phoenix surveyed the familiar surroundings. Posters advertising live bands lined one wall, and a karaoke stage was tucked against another. A woman with a pixie haircut rode a mechanical bull in the center of the room, doing Olympic-caliber backbends to attract attention. She was the closest thing to being a professional mechanical-bull rider that there was. Big Tex had recruited her from New Orleans' world famous Bourbon Street. Men and women were lined up to take turns for five bucks a pop.

Phoenix, beer mug in hand, walked over to the bull line and high-fived all of the people he knew as they welcomed him back. One of the ladies, noticing that his hat still held the pungent smell of the tropics, said, "Oooh, I love the smell of a jungle man!"

Phoenix took his hat off, bowed, and grinned as he said, "Well then, I'll see you in a little while."

He meandered over to the karaoke side of the bar, and as luck would have it, he was able to jump into the rotation and sing right away. His favorite song was *"Wanted Dead or Alive"* by Bon Jovi, and he loved how he was always able to get some sort of audience participation whenever he sang it. They cheered him on, and after entertaining the crowd, he high-fived everyone with their hands out. Rejuvenated, Phoenix put his empty mug down and went to find his dinner.

Phan's Home, Approximately 2200 Hours:

The police questioned Ahn in his living room, but the officers went easy on him. They didn't perform the usual "good cop, bad cop" theatrics, as they found it impossible to believe his version of the story.

They figured the truth would come out the next day, when he was interrogated at the station.

His terrified sisters verified everything that Ahn had said, but the police knew that siblings always tended to defend one other when things went horribly wrong. The girls were shaken but sincere; still, the officers maintained their suspicions. As they left the crime scene, Ahn looked back over his shoulder and saw the coroner's technicians carry out a body bag. His parents were both small of stature, and he wondered if it was his mother or father in the bag. As Ahn ushered his sisters into Uncle Si's car, they tried to look back, but he shielded their view.

Uncle Si's Home, 2300 Hours:

The ride to Uncle Si's home was short, just about a ten minute drive. Ahn sat calmly during the trip. His sisters trembled and held each other. Upon arrival at the modest, one-story home, Aunt Si already had the porch light turned on. The home sat in a quiet cul-de-sac, and the light silhouetted a plastic drinking well in the front yard. As soon as their uncle pulled into the driveway, Aunt Si ushered them inside before the nosy neighbors could become suspicious. With urgency in her voice, she half-whispered, "Hurry inside children."

The sisters sat at the kitchen table as their aunt warmed up some leftover Pho. As it was heating, Uncle Si led Ahn to the spare bathroom to wash the blood from his face and arms. Ahn showered and put on clean clothes. A glance in the mirror revealed a normal pre-teen. Ahn saw a stranger.

Ahn sat back down at the kitchen table after his shower, dazed and shell-shocked. The girls fidgeted but ate their soup. Aunt Si was anxious for a full explanation, but her husband wanted to wait until morning to give the children some breathing room. His brother and sister-in-law were dead — that was a fact — but he knew the boy could not have done it maliciously. He was a good kid, a straight 'A' student. Aunt Si had already called to excuse herself and her husband from work the following day, knowing that they would have to prepare for a funeral and handle the emotional needs of the children. The five family members sat silently, the slurping of soup the only occasional sound.

Aunt Si checked Ahn's temperature before he went to bed. The old-fashioned mercury thermometer showed 99.9 degrees. She went back into the kitchen and mixed a Vietnamese herbal concoction to help relieve Ahn's fever. The girls were given an herbal version to relax them. The children taken care of, husband and wife sat down in the living room and discussed the funeral arrangements that needed to be made. He would have to create an altar according to cultural rules, and she would have to buy special incense and make all of the necessary phone calls.

***

Early the next morning, the doorbell rang. Ahn's friend, Ben, stood there uneasily. Aunt Si had called him over to comfort Ahn before her nephew would be taken to the police station for questioning. She pointed down the hallway and told Ben, "Just be yourself. Don't ask questions." The girls were still in bed, and she let them sleep. She knew they had to rest. *They're been through a lot*, she thought.

Uncle Si mowed the lawn before the Texas heat made it too hot for him to do so. There was going to be a double funeral; everything had to be in order. The relatives would have to be fed and possibly housed, as was their custom. He would also have to help his wife in the kitchen. It would be a very busy week.

Ben stood quietly at the doorway of the darkened guest bedroom. He looked toward the computer where Ahn could usually be found, but did not see him. Then he heard the blanket rustle. He whispered, "Hey, Ahn?" but there was no response. He slowly tiptoed in, careful not to knock anything over. He plopped down in the swivel chair at the computer desk with his back to his friend's bed. Ben surfed the internet for their favorite websites, occasionally saying things like, "Hey dude, this is so funny. Come see this," or "Dude, this car is hot." Ahn never answered. He didn't make a sound.

Outside, Uncle Si continued to mow the lawn. As he pushed the mower along the fence line, he went through his mental checklist of what needed to be done. He was happy to get the lawn done early, but was already sweating bullets. It would not be long before the news spread to all of their relatives. They would begin arriving soon.

Aunt Si turned on the morning news, sat in her favorite chair and sipped a cup of herbal tea to clear her mind. She loved her herbs and could name each one growing in her planters, along with their associated healing properties. She especially loved making medicinal teas. Uncle Si had been her guinea pig on many occasions (whether he liked it or not), but he didn't really mind, as they usually worked well.

She heard faint scratching, scraping noises coming from the guest bedroom where the girls slept, but ignored them. The warm tea felt good going down. Aunt Si closed her eyes. Her nerves slowly calmed in preparation for the telephone calls that she needed to make.

Meanwhile, Ben still surfed the web with his back to the bed. Ahn started to mumble and stir a bit. Ben clicked the mouse and said, "Dude, you gotta see this one. It's so funny!" He was trying everything he could to distract his friend from what had happened the night before. He was just about to turn around in frustration when a hot chick in a bikini popped up on the screen. "Oh, man! You have to see this!"

The zombie awkwardly removed the blanket from its body. The light of the computer screen cast an eerie glow on its head and face, which was now slightly distorted and greenish in color. Ben heard the mattress squeak and waited for his buddy to join him so they could rate the lingerie models on the screen together. The zombie started to rise from the bed just as he said, "Dude, this babe is hot, come see!" Ben continued to click on page after page of sexy models, mesmerized. He also cranked up some rap music, because he knew that Ahn hated it. If that didn't get him up, nothing would. As the music pumped at jet-engine decibels, Ben bobbed his head and rapped the lyrics.

The zombie, features twisted and black eyes locked on Ben, moved closer. It lifted its arm and then swung hard at the back of the bopping head. Ben's skull shattered as his neck twisted. Chunks of bone, blond hair still attached, flew with such force that they were embedded in the drywall. Blood sprayed like a geyser, soaking the speakers and silencing the rap. What was left of Ben's head lay slumped over the computer keyboard. He never knew what hit him.

Aunt Si quietly watched the morning news, but she was angry inside. Her husband's brother and sister-in-law had been murdered by that boy. Even though she had not heard his version of what had happened, she believed the worst. *That boy should be locked up, and made to drink one of my special herbal brews.* She closed her eyes and rubbed her temples. The morning news was too much for her to take; the tea had been too weak and had not calmed her after all. She would need a stronger concoction.

The taller female zombie pushed open the bedroom door; the other followed closely. Shoulder to shoulder, they moved toward the kitchen. They were no longer lovely; their hair was matted in oozing clumps and starting to fall out, revealing small scalp polyps. They held hands so tightly that their fingers had swollen and twisted together. They walked on legs that were oddly bent, flexed like those on a plastic toy pony.

Aunt Si opened her eyes when an herbal supplement commercial came on. At the same time, she heard a commotion in the kitchen, and strained her neck to see if it was the girls. *They must be getting into something they shouldn't.* When the noise continued, she called out their names but received no answer. She waited a few more seconds, then got up and strode toward the kitchen.

In the hallway, she noticed that her favorite herb planter had been knocked over, and muttered angrily, "I'm gonna get those girls." She stalked past the fallen planter with her arms stiffened at her sides, then turned the corner and refocused her eyes in the bright kitchen.

She froze on the spot. The horrific sight of the two hideous zombies, her nieces, was overwhelming. She tried to turn around and run, but her legs would not obey. The zombies moved together and tackled her with clumsy intensity. Their once-pretty faces had become hideous masks, their black eyes glaring as they clawed strips of flesh from Aunt Si's body. She cried out a pitiful "Help!" as the zombies assuaged their hunger pains. As her body was quickly ravaged and her blood spread across the tile floor, her last thoughts were for Ahn. He was right … and she had been so wrong.

Wiping sweat from his brow, Uncle Si shut the lawnmower down. His mouth was parched and he desperately needed a drink of water. As he entered the house through the kitchen door, he saw a vision of horror that would have made most people immediately turn and flee; instead, he ran for his rifle locker. The zombies followed, but before they reached Uncle Si, one of their heads exploded from the sound of the locker door being slammed open against the wall. Its brains slowly dribbled down the screen of the television set.

The other shuffled forward, its hand ripping at the back of Uncle Si's tee shirt. He cried out and shoved the zombie back, trying to make sense of what was happening. A slightly smaller zombie rounded the corner: Ahn, or what used to be his nephew. Uncle Si fought through the terror and retrieved a shotgun, struggling to load it with trembling hands. The two zombies latched onto his arms and pulled, and he crashed to the ground, shotgun shells scattering across the floor.

With tears in his eyes, he crawled toward what was left of his wife, the zombies clinging doggedly to his back. They took bite after bite out of him, stripping his flesh to the bone. He convulsed in pain, but struggled forward. His last thoughts were for his love. As he reached for the nearest part of his dead wife's body, his final thought was a whispered *I love you.* The zombies chewed and slashed. Two glistening pools of blood merged on the cold tile floor.

Phoenix's Apartment:

Pulling into his driveway after a long night at Big Tex's joint, Phoenix was as happy as a lark. He'd partied with two sexy blondes, and as luck would have it, they were still with him. One of them was wearing his baseball cap backward and a tee shirt emblazoned with the words "Men are Bigger in Texas." The other glanced at him seductively, still wearing her wet t-shirt with the word 'BIG' written over one breast, and 'TEX' over the other. He escorted them up the wooden stairs and into the house. As he went into the kitchen for a bottle opener, he said over his shoulder, "Make yourselves at home, girls."

Missy (she of the backward hat) ran her fingers through the long pony-tail hanging over her shoulder and replied, "We sure will."

The wet t-shirt contest winner said, "I'm cold. I'm gonna take this shirt off. Can you get me something warm to wear?" She lifted her shirt high above her head, revealing her voluptuous breasts.

Phoenix nodded his head and said, "Now we're talking. I'll get that shirt right away." She giggled, suggesting he didn't need to hurry.

He got Miss Wet T-Shirt one of his thinner undershirts to wear, and the three sat for a while, flirting and drinking beer. As the girls started to wind down, Phoenix decided to tell a few of his famous one-liners, and the girls laughed so hard that their breasts jiggled under their scanty tops. He knew it was now or never, and he led them to the bedroom. After a week in the jungle, this night was going to be very special.

Professor Harrington, Flight 1622:

Professor Harrington boarded the flight for Hong Kong, delighted to be representing Sporaton's newest breakthroughs at this important international convention. He wasn't feeling so great, but he walked right past the signage outlining the international rules about flying while feeling ill or having a fever. He had waited a whole year for this event, and thought of it as a working vacation. No way would he miss it!

Once Harrington was aboard the plane, he struggled through the aisle with his carry-on luggage. As he pulled it along, he brushed against multiple people, politely apologizing for bumping into them. They could see the excitement on his face, and all smiled and murmured some version of "No problem, mister!" He continued down the aisle, and finally found his seat in the row directly behind the wing of the plane.

The jumbo jet accelerated and was airborne. The trip would be long, so Harrington unbuckled his seat belt and asked the stewardess for a couple of Tylenol tablets.

The stewardess peered at him, batted her eyes, and asked, "Is this because of a fever, sir?"

"No," he lied. "I just have a headache." Although he did indeed feel feverish, he assured himself that it was just a little inconvenience. He'd feel much better after the Tylenol and a long nap.

"Okay, I'll be right back," she said, and walked to the attendants' station at the back of the plane.

Angela's Apartment:

Angela was single and lived alone. She was quite a bookworm, and always had a good novel or electronic pad close at hand. She enjoyed her private time lost in good stories, and for the most part, preferred it that way. She was alone with her favorite love story when her heart stopped beating.

She wobbled to her feet, her reflection in the window revealing the hideous zombie she had become. She lurched across the room to the sliding glass doors and crashed through them, shards of glass slicing into her flesh. Strips of bloodied skin and muscle hung from her face and arms, and her auburn hair became drenched in dark blood. She wavered in place, then awkwardly and slowly made her way along the narrow side alley.

Mrs. Krauss was bent over her garden bed, using a spade to turn over and aerate the soil. She noticed a shadow on the brick wall in front of her, and realized someone was standing directly behind her. She turned and looked up, but the sun's glare hid her visitor's face. She shifted slightly to get a better look, but it was already too late. The zombie swung an arm and connected with her jaw. Unable to utter a single word, Mrs. Krauss swung the spade at the zombie and sliced through its abdomen. The small-statured zombie grabbed her by the throat and lifted her up. The stomach slash had done nothing to stop the assault, so Mrs. Krauss frantically lifted the spade and stabbed it deep into the zombie's shoulder, but the attacker still held on tightly.

Mrs. Krauss struggled violently to get free as the zombie took a massive bite out of her neck. Her body convulsed and she thrashed from side to side. Blood from her carotid artery pulsed in sprays upon her petunias, like an intermittent water sprinkler. Her body suffered several more bites to the face and temple before she hit the dirt, crushing her beloved flowers. A small ceramic sign near her detached eyeball declared, "Gardening is fun!"

The zombie continued through the neighborhood on its indiscriminate path of destruction. Twenty-year-old Joe lay under his classic '57, tightening a bolt as he waited for a special order part to be delivered. It was the last thing he needed before he could get the car up and running. He heard someone enter the garage and shouted, "Just leave it on the chair." The delivery man did not reply, and Joe assumed he had done as he was asked.

As the zombie lurched forward, leaned down, and snatched him by the ankles, Joe dropped his wrench and let out a yelp. The zombie pulled upward and Joe's shins were scraped raw by the underside of the bumper. Startled and in pain, he kicked at the hands, but the zombie tightened its grip and yanked him out from under the Ford. Joe's music player fell from the hood of the car and shattered, the rock classics abruptly halting. Joe yelled, "What the hell!" He painfully got to his feet.

A zombie stood in front of him. Even as he screamed, Joe was aware that he sounded like a little girl. "Oh my God, lady!" he yelled as he reached for a tool from atop the hood of the car. He swung at the zombie's head, connecting with its temple. The blow scraped off skin and muscle down to the skull, but the zombie merely moved in closer. It latched onto his head with both hands and bit off his right ear. Then it bit again, deeper, revealing grey brain matter. Joe fell to the ground from the agony of the crushing bite, writhing in pain and shock. The zombie dropped to its knees and began to feast.

After a few minutes, the blood-saturated zombie stood up. Bits of human tissue covered its lips. Bulging jaw muscles and the uncontrollable urge to bite caused its mouth to repeatedly open and shut with an audible snap.

The zombie rambled on down the street and happened upon a woman hanging her linens to dry. It moved unsteadily towards her between the hanging sheets, coming closer as she placed another clothespin on the line. She saw the awkward movement of someone walking through her freshly cleaned linens and called out, "Hello … who's there?" The zombie emerged from behind a thick comforter and the woman screamed.

The entire world seemed to slow as she watched the zombie's head burst from her piercing screams. Brain matter and chunks of cranium splattered both the woman and her freshly-laundered comforter. The spray of arterial blood from the neck stump left colorful linear patterns on the sheets. The woman gagged and spit out the gore that had landed in her mouth, then fell to the ground, screaming hysterically. After a few moments, she regained her composure somewhat, pulled her cell phone from her pocket and dialed 911.

Within minutes, several squad cars arrived at the woman's home. After questioning the woman and reviewing the scene, the officers could see that no identifiable weapon had been used to cause such severe trauma to the nearly headless corpse. They were puzzled by the spade that was still imbedded in its shoulder, but the woman denied that it was her doing. The severity of the head wound was such that the officers knew there was no way a lone spade could have been the cause of death.

The officers escorted the woman away from the scene and into her home. A female officer volunteered to assist the woman to the bathroom to clean up. Still shaking, the woman watched as water mixed with blood and tissue fragments spiraled down the drain. She dazedly hoped that the larger fragments would not clog her sink. Once she was done cleaning herself up, the officers allowed her to call her husband. When he answered, she tearfully blurted out, "Come home now, there's been an accident," and handed the phone to a nearby officer.

The county coroner arrived quickly, and had no problem pronouncing the victim dead. He was, however, fascinated by the mysterious spade wound and the overall condition of the corpse. As the coroner's technicians loaded the body into a bag, dark blood dripped into one of the tech's shoes. The technician exclaimed in typical Texas drawl, "Hot cactus! Blood just got into one of my shoes!"

The other technician laughed derisively. "I told you to wear shoe covers." The bloodied tech shrugged his shoulders and continued to push the gurney. They loaded the body into the old county van and hurried to the morgue to get it stored in one of the refrigeration units. It was already smelly, and they didn't want to deal with it any longer than they had to.

After the police finished interrogating the woman, they sat in the cruiser and filled out their electronic reports. The female officer asked her senior partner, "What do you think happened?"

He continued to type the report. "I don't know. But whatever the circumstances, the damage was far too severe to have been done by that woman."

The female officer responded, "I think I agree with you on this one. It's gotta be a first!"

Kimball's Home:

The body of Kimball's wife lay near the staircase. Her son's tiny corpse lay on the last step. Laura had put up a fierce fight defending her young son.

When the zombie had begun its assault, she'd barreled into it from the rear and slammed it into a wall, knocking it off-balance. She ran quickly to grab a meat cleaver from the kitchen, but by the time she got back it already had her son cornered. The little boy screamed, his voice piercing. "Daddy? No, Daddy! No!"

Laura didn't know what had happened to her husband and didn't have time to care. Her maternal instinct took over. She jumped onto the back of what used to be Kimball. It grabbed her and flung her to the ground. Her sanity was strained to its breaking point as she cried and pleaded for him to stop. She couldn't understand why her husband was doing this. Scrambling to her feet, she raised the meat cleaver and hacked at the arm closest to her son. She figured he could probably survive that blow, if he somehow snapped out of this terrible madness. The razor-sharp edge of the cleaver landed on the zombie's upper arm; as the lower chunk of the arm fell, she caught a glimpse of shattered bone. The exposed muscle and a shredded sleeve momentarily captured her attention, her mind a gory wonderland as she wondered how she would ever be able to clean the hopelessly stained shirt. Blood sprayed onto a photograph on the wall, a picture of an ancient pyramid. The dark wetness seemed to drip surreally down the pyramid's steps. The severed arm fell on top of her son's shoulder in such a way that it almost appeared to give him a hug. Laura realized she was going into shock.

The deformed thing that had once been her husband spun around and grabbed her arm as she raised the cleaver for another blow. It bared its teeth and bit down viciously. Laura let loose an agonized scream. A large section of her deltoid muscle was in the zombie's mouth. The little boy beat at his daddy's legs like a toddler with a toy drum. Laura wrenched her mangled arm from its grasp and tried to break away, to divert the zombie up the staircase and away from her son, but it had her trapped.

It tore mercilessly through her flesh. Her face contorted in agony and she let loose scream after piercing scream as her power to fight back rapidly drained. Her son yelled "Mommy ... Mommy!" Laura turned for a last look at him as the zombie clamped its jaws onto her neck, slicing through her jugular. Warm blood shot out over the staircase and sprayed the floor below. As the darkness closed in around her, her last breath was for her son. "Run!"

The terrified boy peed in his pants. He turned and stumbled over the zombie's fallen arm. He kicked at it and said, "Bad Daddy!" Having never been exposed to violence of any kind, he could not will his tiny feet to move. He was terrified and confused. Why was Daddy acting this way?

The zombie, covered in blood, approached with snapping jaws and picked the boy up by the shoulders. In his final plea, the boy softly said, "Daddy?" The zombie's mouth clamped down on his throat; a fountain of blood bathed the child. The zombie dropped the boy's lifeless, rag doll body and staggered into the street.

Professor Harrington, Flight 1622:

Professor Harrington was becoming increasingly fidgety. The Tylenol he had asked for at the beginning of the flight hadn't come yet, and he was burning up with fever. Jeannette, the stewardess, finally retrieved the medicine from the galley and made her way back down the aisle. She gave him a stern look as she handed him the pills, and tried not to touch him in the exchange. She clucked to herself. *That'll let him know I knew he was sick and boarded the plane against regs.* He had not been truthful, and as a result could give everyone else on the plane whatever it was he had. He diverted his eyes as he took the pills from her palm, and their hands brushed briefly. She wanted to isolate him, just in case, but there wasn't an available isolation seat to put him in. *Maybe I'll get legislation started. All international flights should have an iso seat aboard.* For the time being, though, she was unable to do anything about it. They were airborne, and that was that.

Harrington got up to go to the lavatory and noticed that his legs were a bit wobbly, even though there was no air turbulence. He also had a hard time lifting his feet. As he made his way down the aisle, he put his hands on the seat tops of his fellow passengers to help keep his balance. People glared at him grumpily, but he didn't really care. Once in the lavatory, he looked himself over in the mirror and saw a terrible mess. His eyes were glazed with fever, and he looked like he had been punched in the face. He realized, much too late, that he should have stayed home. *Perhaps if I take it easy for a bit, I'll be alright for the conference.* He made his way back to his seat and redirected the air conditioning vent directly onto his head. He closed his eyes and took a nap.

Phan's Crew Members:

The zombie staggered through the gates that opened to Doc Bob's ranch. Inside the sprawling home, Bob's family lay slaughtered among the rustic twig decor. Their bodies, tangled in macabre death positions, looked as though they were meant to be part of the twisted designs. Bullet holes pocked the walls throughout the house. Several victims were disemboweled, their intestines stretched out along the leather sofa like party garland. It was an unbelievable sea of carnage.

The zombie's final victim was pressed hard against the barbed wire fence, nearly decapitated. A baseball bat was still clutched in his hand. He had left a mark on the zombie before dying; it was hopping and could not control its twisted left leg, which seemed to be dislocated at the hip socket. It slowly moved down Ranch Road, foot dragging into the dirt and leaving behind a channel highlighted by puffs of dust. Bullet holes riddled its body, except for its grotesque head. It garbled out unintelligible sounds as it repeatedly snapped its jaws at the air like a rabid animal.

Jack, Bob's nearest neighbor, sipped coffee by the open door of his truck as he took in the beauty of the distant mountains and thought about going into town. He had never been blessed with good hearing and was oblivious to the sound of the zombie as it approached.

The zombie attacked with a sudden and brutal intensity, trapping Jack inside the pickup truck. Jack, a strong man, fought back without pause, but the zombie's strength was double his own. He was totally overwhelmed, and grabbed desperately for his dashboard knife. He plunged it into the zombie's chest and cracked its breastbone. Unfazed by the counter-attack, the zombie bit into Jack's forehead. Arterial blood spewed across the windshield.

Jack pushed the zombie off and tried to reach the other door, but couldn't get it open. Again he thrust his knife at the zombie, sinking the blade into its ribcage. Jack swiftly pulled the knife out and tried to plunge it into the thing's head, but the blade only scraped the corner of its face and removed cheek muscle while it bit and gnawed at his wrist. Jack screamed for his life; the zombie snarled, "Rrrag-ga," as it grasped Jack's head between its hands. It squeezed the skull and bit hungrily into a warm neck.

Jack felt his pounding heart begin to slow and his fight or flight response began to fade. He focused the last flickers of his awareness on the horrible thing's face. "Bob? Why?" The zombie backed out of the truck, then gulped down the last bits of its terrible meal before limping along Ranch Road.

Out for her morning run, Susie saw a man in the distance and could tell that he was injured. His atypical gait caused his right shoulder to pivot back and forth, while his left leg, Gestapo style, propelled forward stiffly. *Probably someone I know. Better try to help.* It would definitely mess up her morning jog, but it was the Texas thing to do. As Susie ran closer, she realized that the injury was severe.

The zombie stopped and wavered in place. Susie ran so fast that she was upon him in a flash before stopping in her tracks. The horrific sight of the man's injuries made her want to run, vomit, or scream in fear, but it was obvious that he needed her help. She put her hand on his shoulder gently and looked into his eyes, asking, "Mister, are you okay?" The zombie whipped its arm forward like a slingshot and connected hard with Susie's pretty face. The blow ripped a long gash across her cheek and knocked out several of her teeth. The sudden pain almost caused her to black out. Dazed, she managed to grab the zombie's arm, knowing instinctively that she had to stop him from hitting her again – but in her confused state, she didn't realize the full extent of the danger she was facing. The zombie stretched its mouth open before swiftly locking its jaws onto Susie's face.

Baron Community Hospital:

All around Baron, the citizens were becoming infected. First they trickled into the hospital's emergency room at a slow pace, over the course of several hours. Then they began arriving at an alarming rate. Some were brought in by loved ones or friends, and others drove themselves. One of the family members was overheard saying that it was a weird time of year to be getting the flu.

Emergency 911 responders were bombarded by people complaining that their loved ones or neighbors were going insane and trying to bite them. When asked to describe what they meant, all callers repeated the same description to the operator: the affected had a distorted, bulging face, and a freakish amount of strength, enough to break bones.

The emergency room at Baron Hospital was packed to capacity. Seeing the severity of the latest incoming victim's wounds, Patty, the triage nurse, hurried the man into a treatment room ahead of other patients, even though many had already been waiting for hours. She asked, "Sir, what is your name?"

He grimaced and replied, "Oscar."

"What kind of animal assaulted you, Oscar?"

He gritted his teeth from the pain. "It wasn't an animal!"

Another nurse came in. "Oscar, we need to start an IV. Can you let me see your arm?"

He lowered the arm that he had been guarding and replied, "Sure. No problem."

The nurse applied a blue tourniquet and thumped his wrist to raise a vein, then wiped his arm with an alcohol prep pad. She inserted the intravenous needle, secured it to his skin with tape, and connected it to a bag of fluids. Oscar had been motionless throughout the procedure. After a short time, however, he looked up and started to shake.

Together, Patty and the trauma doctor cut Oscar's shirt from his body. He had severe bite wounds on his shoulder and arm. Each bite had removed varying degrees of skin, fat, and muscle. After completing his assessment, the doctor said, "This was a human assault. Look at the bite patterns and the bruising." Patty nodded her head in agreement, and the doctor gave an order for antiseptic cleaners and various bandage supplies.

An orderly retrieved the supplies from the storage cabinet, and the doctor stitched the minor wounds and packed the deeper ones with moist gauze. He looked at his patient's pupils worriedly and said, "This was just a quick fix. This guy is going to need emergency surgery. Call the general surgeon and the on-call surgical crew." Patty was already on the move.

"Right away, doctor."

The second nurse, Jill, asked Oscar if he was allergic to anything. He swallowed hard, trying to will his pain away, then replied, "No ma'am." He angrily added, "It was a freak! It came out of nowhere!"

Jill brushed the hair off of Oscar's forehead and asked the doctor, "Can we give him something? He's suffering."

The doctor replied, "Give him four milligrams of morphine, IV."

Patty already had it prepared and pushed the drug. She asked, "Do you know who did this to you?"

Beginning to feel some relief from the dose of morphine, Oscar replied, "Its head … it wasn't normal."

Patty tried again. "Do you know who did this to you?" She received no response as the morphine took full effect and Oscar drifted off to sleep.

A few minutes later, the transport orderly pushed a gurney into the room. "I'm ready to take the patient to surgery." The triage nurse finished taping the last of the dressings and replied,

"We're finishing up here. Just a sec."

Not long after, the housekeeping crew was paged. They were given the job of cleaning and disinfecting everything that Oscar had touched. As the two-man team cleaned, the older worker noticed that his partner wasn't wearing gloves. He said, "Hey man, ya know you gotta wear gloves. Why don't you put some on?"

Embarrassed, the newly-hired worker replied, "Sorry bro. Will do." He grabbed a pair of exam gloves and snapped them on.

After the duo finished with the treatment room, they went for a break in the cafeteria. The first thing they did when they walked through the turnstile was ogle the cashier to get her attention. She was brunette and good looking, and was ringing up another customer as they grabbed their snacks and got in line.

"Gonna ask her on a date this time?" the young guy queried.

His buddy smiled. "Sure thing. This is gonna be my day."

These two had become regulars, and sometimes Carla flirted back with them. They came in almost every day, hoping for a date, but never had any luck when it came to Carla, who was waiting for a handsome doctor to sweep her off her feet. Their favorite moment was when the money changed hands. Despite standing beneath the air conditioning vent all day, her hands were always very warm. Now, standing face to face with his fantasy woman, the older janitor could barely open his mouth. In a quiet voice he said, "We should hook up for the movies Friday night."

Carla replied with a wink and a smile. "Maybe next week!"

After nearly dropping his change, he said, "I'm gonna hold you to that," and walked away. His buddy walked out with him, saying, "You know she's just messin' with you."

Baron, Infection After Infection:

The coroner arrived at the dead man's home. The technicians pulled out a collapsible gurney and pushed it over to the car in the driveway, ready to transport the headless body from the front seat. Gerry peeked inside the window, then looked at his partner. He asked, "Man, what's going on in Baron?"

Juan shrugged his shoulders and laughed as he replied, "I don't know…maybe it's in the water! They've been getting reports from all over town."

Before Juan even finished the sentence, Gerry had already begun thinking about what needed to be done. "Call our friend who specializes in this kind of mess. I'm not dealing with it. By the way…maybe you're right about the water. Don't drink any."

Juan pointed and replied after gulping down soda, "Yeah, the reservoir is right over there." Gerry responded sarcastically,

"Yeah, I know where it is." Juan ignored his sarcasm dialed the specialist, but got no answer. He looked back at Gerry. "Nothing."

Gerry sighed. "Well, we're gonna have to clean it up after all." The two men retrieved the body parts and put them in plastic bags. They next selected their cleaning tools and entered the car. Despite being careful, they couldn't avoid contact with the remains. Blood soaked through the white bunny suits they wore and saturated their knees. Spongy brain matter dripped down from the ceiling and landed on the backs of their necks. "Dude, this is so nasty," Gerry yelled out. He did not like this part of the job at all, but the town had a contract with the Coroner's Office for this type of clean-up work. Gerry scooped up the fragments with a plastic kiddie shovel and said, "It smells like this thing died days ago, instead of just a few hours." Then he added, "Did you notice how much rigor mortis has set into the body parts?"

"Yeah, I know," said Juan. "Strange."

Baron Police Station:

The police station had only two cells, and they were typically used to hold misdemeanor offenders. The newest lockup was a drunken repeat-offender who had become so agitated that the on-duty officer had to do something about it.

Officer Caldwell heard the racket coming from the cell. He swallowed the last bite of his fish taco, beating a pesky fly to his treat. A tiny dribble of sauce fell from the corner of his lips and he wiped his chin clean, irritated that it hadn't ended up in his mouth. He got up and strolled toward the noisy cell. He dragged his baton across the bars in the darkened room to get the prisoner's attention, then peered in, waiting for a response. The man had become entangled in his blanket. Caldwell sighed. *Another drunk confused about his surroundings.*

The man got up from the cot and thrashed around the cell like a bull in a china shop. Caldwell decided to ignore the station protocol.

He had already read the arrest report; the prisoner was only there for public intoxication and disorderly conduct. In the morning he would just pay the fine and be discharged after he slept it off. Routine!

Officer Caldwell unlocked the cell and entered quickly. He pulled the blanket off of the prisoner. To his horror, he saw that the man had greenish-tinged skin. Small lumps pulsed on the top and sides of his head, and his face sagged on the right side. Caldwell gaped. *Oh my GOD, he's having a stroke or something!* In the next heartbeat, the zombie struck him hard on the left side of his head. The blow was so powerful that it ripped his ear off; it flew onto the concrete floor. Caldwell tumbled to the ground. His head was spinning from the force of the impact, and he knew he was in trouble. Dazed and disoriented, he un-holstered his pistol and yelled for help. At eye level with his now-detached ear, he mumbled, "Oh crap!" The prisoner in the next cell, who had been arrested for a family quarrel, was not fond of Caldwell and wanted to see him get a taste of his own medicine. He banged on the cell bars to distract the other officer.

***

Officer Shane felt ill, but did what he had always done: took two aspirin, kissed his wife, and went to work. As he pulled out of the driveway in his take-home patrol car, he radioed dispatch that he was on duty again. The department was operating under budget cuts; the town council had let go several men from the force. Though he was an eighteen-year veteran, Shane was forced to fill in the gaps with required overtime. It sucked, but he did like the extra cash. It also meant he would not have to work lousy details, or write trumped-up traffic tickets. He hated secret quotas. As he accelerated away from the house, he wondered what his neighbor had done to merit being murdered.

Throughout the night, Officer Shane had become sicker and weaker. He tried to keep a positive outlook and repeated to himself, "A few more hours, just a few more hours, and I'll be home." He pulled into the parking lot of Jenny's Tex Mart, and called in for a break. He looked into the rearview mirror, saw the dark circles under his watery eyes, and thought, *Looking great.* Barely able to keep his eyes open, he decided to grab a cat nap. To get comfortable, he took off his hat, and noticed while doing so that he was having trouble moving his arms. They felt a little stiff, especially in the elbow areas. The two-way radio buzz annoyed him, so he turned it low for the break – a department no-no. He was ticked off about catching whatever bug he apparently had.

The only unusual thing that had happened recently was his neighbor's murder. Shane had visited the scene. He did not recall that he had brushed against a small trace of blood splatter.

***

Officer Caldwell tried to avoid the zombie's second lunge, but he was in shock and moving slowly. Jaws chomping hungrily, it bit him viciously on the upper shoulder. Caldwell fired his pistol directly into the thing's chest, and could not understand why the prisoner would not go down. Round after round hit the zombie in its stomach, chest and upper arms, to no effect. Arms outstretched, it struck again. The weapon flew from Caldwell's hand as he fought to regain control. As he reached for the pistol, the zombie jumped on top of him. He could feel his head being savaged by teeth. The thing bit into his neck, crushing his windpipe. He heard a high-pitched, hollow tone, and then blacked out.

The backup officer ran toward the detention area with his weapon drawn. He gazed into the cell where Caldwell lay stretched across the floor, but it was too late. He had no idea what had happened, but he could tell his partner was dead by seeing the amount of blood that streaked the cinderblock walls. The prisoner squatted over the dead officer. His face no longer looked even remotely human. As the zombie looked up, bits of scalp and hair fell from its mouth, and it simply stared at him. The prisoner in the other cell had quieted down, sensing that something had gone terribly wrong. The backup officer discharged his weapon, and the 9mm rounds struck the zombie in the torso, neck and head. It collapsed into a heap.

Alarmed by the second volley of weapons fire, the front desk officer bolted from his station and entered the small detention area. There was so much blood; he couldn't make sense of it. The backup officer was as still as a statue at the cell entrance. The desk officer called his name, but there was no response. Moving further into the cell area, the desk officer realized that the drunken man had assaulted Caldwell, and the responding officer had fired his weapon in self-defense. He called out his partner's name again.

***

When Officer Shane awoke, it was about ten after midnight, but it did not matter. He felt woozy and needed to check in so he could go to bed. He drove the patrol car back to the station, having a hard time staying focused on the road. He radioed dispatch to say that he was very sick, but only heard static. His head pounded as hard as his heart. Through his pain, he thought in fragments, *Not looking good for me.*

As he approached the station, he went into cardiac arrest and white-knuckled the steering wheel. His leg and foot seized up, causing him to floor the accelerator. The patrol car slammed full force into the station's front entrance. The white airbag deployed and forced Shane back against his seat. The lucky horseshoe that hung above the doorway went flying, hitting the opposite wall with a clang. The steel door, window frames, dry wall and furniture were propelled through the air, raining down where the desk officer had just been sitting. Bruised, disheveled and bleeding, Shane, now a zombie, moaned and spat out blood. The powder from the airbag covered his head, creating an eerily ghost-like effect. The zombie stumbled out of the wrecked car.

The desk officer heard the loud crash in the front lobby and ran to investigate. *Geez, what now?!* He couldn't believe his eyes. The zombie emerged from the debris and dust, moving just fast enough to catch him off-guard. It ripped into his chest, then pulled his head backward and twisted hard. His neck muscles stretched and tore, and with a quick snap, his spinal cord was ripped in two. He saw a luminescent tunnel and floated to it. The zombie clawed its way into his balding head, and began to devour his brain.

A custodian ran to the reception area, and picked up the two-way radio. He yelled, "Mayday, mayday! We need help at the station. We're under attack!" He listened for a reply, but only heard radio static. The zombie moved toward him. He was shaking with fear, but saw the officer's pistol and dove for it. The zombie grabbed him and began pulling him backward. The custodian twisted around and placed the pistol directly under the zombie's chin, pulling the trigger repeatedly. Brain fragments, teeth and hair flew into the air, splattering everything.

The prisoner in the back yelled out, "Hey man, let me out of this cell right now! I didn't do anything wrong!"

Dueling Dude Ranch:

A sign posted on the gate exclaimed, "Welcome to Baron Ranch." The ranch was tailor-made for those who wanted the adventure of the Old West in a safe and controlled environment. If you were here, you had probably responded to a brochure mailed to prospective clients in the Dallas area. The ranch was described as a respite for city slickers, and could house twenty tourists looking for real cowboy adventures. The guests welcomed this week by the ranch's owner, Mr. Akin, were on the younger side; they would be nicknamed 'dudes' and 'dudettes'. They would be taught the basics of cattle roping, handling a six shooter, and cooking an authentic campfire meal complete with cowboy coffee. The big money-maker was the action photos, which provided an extra thousand bucks a week in sales. Six shooters were kept under lock and key in case anyone felt like getting rowdy. After seven days, certificates were handed out to all the guests proclaiming that they were now certified cowboys and cowgirls. The dudes and dudettes would go home happy and brag about their week; their word-of-mouth was the best advertising by far. Coveted full-time positions were worked by a few local cowboys who made their living solely on the ranch. A few older folks were thrown into the mix to corral the youngsters when needed. Volunteers who wanted to embrace the cowboy lifestyle manned various part-time positions for a little extra adventure.

The Honolulu Ranch, a mile down the road, was Mr. Akin's closest competition. It housed eighty tourists and was always filled to capacity. Full-time staff worked over five hundred head of cattle in addition to their tourist duties. The big draw was the cowboy luau at the end of each week; the cowboys were required to swap their authentic gear for Hawaiian shirts and leis for the day.

Steven, the newest ranch hand, loved to dress like an old-time cowboy. In his spurs and checkered shirt, he was the epitome of a Hollywood western icon. At the end of the week, since he was the low man on the totem pole, he was sent into town for a much-needed resupply. He knew if he got his errands done quickly he could slip into Big Texas Roadhouse for a rack of lip-smacking baby-backs before returning to the ranch. Those ribs were his one luxury, and he didn't mind splurging once in a while.

That evening at the roadhouse, he exchanged high fives with Phoenix. As he leaned against the barn wall later that night feeling desperately ill, he had no idea that it was that brief encounter with Phoenix that had infected him. Steven was miserable and feverish, and chewed on a single strand of straw to help sooth himself; he couldn't afford health insurance. Exhausted, and with a belly full of ribs, he curled up in the barn and took a nap. The minutes ticked away until he was not Steven anymore.

The zombie stumbled to its feet shakily, the picture of someone recently thrown from a bull. Each foot pounded into the dirt as the zombie lumbered through the barn. The stabled horses whinnied and neighed as the zombie passed them. Its jaws stretched open, and it made horrid moaning noises as it shuffled along drunkenly and made its way toward the guest bunkhouses.

Though his job was to keep an eye out for rogue coyotes prowling in the wee hours, the graveyard-shift watchman snored peacefully. The dimming flame of the antique oil lantern and the lullaby of crickets had coaxed him to sleep. He made soft snoring sounds, as oblivious and content as a baby.

With a sudden vicious fury, he was jerked from slumber. Someone was squeezing his head. The watchman tried to convince himself that he was still dreaming; the man in front of him was a nightmare of horrible disfigurements. One of its hands wrapped around his face, while the other pulled his head closer to its mouth. The flame in the oil lamp flickered and failed as the young, strong zombie twisted and yanked the watchman's head off. Covered in bright red blood, the zombie gorged on the shredded flesh of the neck stump, then continued on.

The insatiable zombie happened upon a lip-locked couple making out behind a tractor. They were oblivious to the impending danger until it ripped a handful of hair from each of their heads. As they screamed in horror and pain, the zombie slammed their skulls together with crushing force. Their mangled bodies dropped, pulpy remnants of skulls smeared against a tractor tire.

The sounds of loud music drew the zombie's attention next; it easily forced its way through the nearby bunkhouse door. It struck a startled Lacy as she lay in her bunk. She screamed as it clawed its way through her abdomen and tossed her intestines to the ground. The other women in the bunkhouse were paralyzed with fear as they watched the zombie lift a chunk of Lacy's liver and consume it noisily. One woman broke through her terror and attacked the zombie, shrieking hysterically and beating at it with her bare hands. It turned and speared a fist into her gut.

The men and women in the nearby bunkhouses heard screams and ran to help. As they entered the building through the wreckage of the door, they came face-to-face with the horrific sight of the cowboy zombie, intent on his feast. Several people ran to retrieve their pistols, which the ranch's policies allowed them to keep. They fired on the zombie, riddling it with bullets, sending it to its death in the hail of gunfire.

The owner of the Honolulu Ranch, Kalani, jumped out of bed and dressed so quickly that he didn't even have time to button his favorite

Hawaiian shirt. His belly jiggled as he hurried to the porch, where he was met by Jake, his foreman.

Jake grabbed both of his shoulders, looked him in the eyes and said, "It's not good, Kalani. It's Steven! He went crazy. He started to eat someone!" Kalani knew that Jake was a pretty serious and steady guy; he wouldn't make up a crazy story like this. Kalani understood immediately that they were now in full crisis mode and would have to work hard to calm the guests down and restore order. His reputation was riding on it.

All of the guests remaining in the bunkhouses were escorted into the big house, where they stood in a state of collective shock. In his most sympathetic and soft-spoken voice, Kalani said, "Ladies and gentlemen, come and get something to eat. It'll help calm you." He immediately went to the kitchen to put together some snacks, motioning for Jake to help out.

When he returned with the tray of food, he noticed that the expressions of the women ranged from disbelief to disgust as they contemplated eating after what they had witnessed. Since no one else was interested in the food, and because he was nervous, Kalani picked up a pineapple slice and stuffed it into his mouth. He pulled Jake to the side of the buffet table and whispered, "So tell me what happened!"

Jake explained, "Steven went crazy on one of our guests. She died from massive wounds. Some of the guests had to shoot him to get him to stop."

Kalani replied, "We have to call the Sheriff."

One of the male guests overheard the conversation and commented, "He wasn't normal, man. It took so many bullets to take him out ... The dude looked like a zombie." The other guests nodded their heads in agreement.

Jake added, "Several people said that the thing had super-human strength. They couldn't get it off of her."

Kalani thought about it for a moment and asked, "Well, if he wasn't human, what was he?"

Jake threw his hands in the air and replied, "Don't know, boss." Both of them pondered for a moment what had caused Steven to go crazy like that.

The women huddled together in the sprawling room to comfort one another, while the men stood around and talked about the attack. Kalani asked Jake to call 911 and tell them what had happened while he sat with the guests.

Jake picked up the phone and called the police station directly. He didn't know the person who answered the phone, but he sounded panic-stricken. The man muttered, "We're in a state of emergency, and it might be a while before we can get someone out there. Cover and refrigerate the bodies." Jake heard terrified screams in the background, and then the phone went dead in his hand. He hung up and cupped his hands atop his head.

After everyone had calmed down a bit, Kalani asked the guests to transfer their personal items into the main house. They would spend the night there and be returned to their vehicles in the morning. When the shaken guests regrouped, they spread out blankets and pillows on the wooden floor and settled in quietly. The tenuous peace was short-lived, however. With no other directions or options, the ranch hands carried Lacy's body and the zombie's corpse into the main house, maneuvering them toward the large walk-in cooler. Several of the women sobbed inconsolably, while others stumbled outside and vomited. Fighting back the night's stresses, Kalani grabbed a skewer of cold pork and shoveled it into his mouth like he was a sword swallower.

Big Texas Roadhouse; Back Apartment:

Big Tex felt sorry for Betsy Ann. The way she'd described it earlier, her migraine had been like having her brain slowly twisted into a knot. She hadn't been her spritely self, so he'd let her go home early.

Betsy Ann lived in the apartment right behind the restaurant. Sometimes her "brain-drains" went on for several days; she just needed a dark, quiet room to sleep it off. With no money for expensive prescription medicines, she put on her most comfortable pink pajamas, crawled into bed, and pulled the blankets over her head.

It was late when Jay, dressed in his "Everybody's A Big Tex" tee shirt, propped the back door of the restaurant open with an empty beer keg. He thought about how lucky he'd been that his boss had given him a break. He'd just been to court for fighting, but had sworn to the judge that the altercation was not his fault. The judge went easy on him since juvenile detention was already overcrowded, and sent him back to Big Tex instead. Big Tex told him all he needed was a little discipline, some better boxing moves, and truckloads of dishes to wash so he could work off some of that energy.

In and out of the propped door Jay went, wishing that his shift was over. He started to wonder if he had really been given a break, but knew he could have just as easily been sent to a juvenile detention center. He thought about the party he had been invited to, and couldn't wait to finish work and head over there. The large metal garbage cans scraped the ground as he dragged them to the pick-up area. He positioned them just the way Big Tex had told him to and went back for more.

Betsy Ann's sexy pink pajama top was covered in dark, viscous ooze. Her neck muscles were enlarged, double their normal size, and pulsating. The little that remained of her beautiful auburn hair was a matted mess. Her lips were pulled back, showing festering gums and grinding gray teeth. The zombie she had become shouldered its way through the apartment door. It mumbled "Zaaa-gra!" as it descended the stairs and staggered out into the dusty night air.

The zombie's clumsy movements hindered its speed, but it managed to make its way toward the clanging trash cans. Jay was on his way back inside to get the last can. He accidentally dropped his ear buds as he tried to readjust them, and bent over to pick them up. His hair fell across his face, but out the corner of his eye he caught a glimpse of someone's bare feet. He recognized the ankle bracelet and started to rise, slowly taking in the sight of his favorite coworker. As he completed his scan, a lump rose in his throat and he could barely speak.

"Betsy Ann?" Jay took in the full horror of the zombie and couldn't believe what he saw. For an instant, he thought it was another of Big Tex's jokes. Then the pink-clad thing lunged at him, jaws gaping.

The Old Man Didn't Know What to Do:

Old man Higgins heard the sound of the garbage cans being dragged around and decided to check in on Jay. He rubbed his aching hip, then slowly rose from his hiding spot and found a chink in the fence to peek through. He pushed back the brim of his old Cavalry hat and put his eye to the hole in the fence boards. A nearby street lamp cast a yellowish glow, elongating two people's shadows. Higgins could not quite make out their features. He took off his eyeglasses and cleaned them with a little spit and shirt tail, then slid them back onto his nose. Again, the old man peered between the fence boards. In a dry, tired voice, he whispered, "Is that you, Jay?"

Straddling Jay:

Jay ducked as the zombie grabbed for him. He swept its legs, knocking it to the ground – a skill recently taught by a kickboxing buddy. The zombie fell flat onto its back, but so did Jay as he lost his balance, still clumsy with the maneuver. As the zombie started to rise, Jay rolled over and grabbed a nearby two-by-four. The zombie reached for him again, latched onto his leg, and swiftly crushed his shin. Jay yelled out from the excruciating pain. The zombie's strength shocked him as it pulled him closer to its frantically snapping mouth. *This can't be real.* Now in a panic, Jay smashed the board over the thing's head with every ounce of strength he had, but it kept coming, its mouth now level with his crotch. He screamed, "Oh no, you don't!" and pulled at the remaining strands of the zombie's hair to lift its head, but the hair ripped away from the scalp, leaving him with no leverage. Terrified, he jammed his thumb into a completely blackened and puffy eye, then recoiled. Jay's thumb was coated with blood and the gelatinous goop that now oozed from the zombie's socket.

Undaunted, the zombie advanced again, forcing Jay onto his back. As it viciously clawed a ragged hole in his stomach, all he could think was, *Why isn't it stopping?* The putrid abomination straddled his chest and bit him again and again with a mechanical power. A large chunk of skull was soon missing near Jay's temple. His brain, exposed to the air, immediately swelled like a sponge submerged in water. The zombie began to feast on the protruding grey matter, and when it was satiated, lifted its polyp-covered head and stood up. It stepped on Jay's broken face and staggered toward the noisy bar, its mouth and chin still caked with brain fragments.

Old Man Higgins:

Old Man Higgins shuddered involuntarily. At eighty-six years old, he'd slowed down some, but was even slower these past few weeks thanks to hip surgery. He'd witnessed the gruesome carnage from his vantage behind the fence, and knew there was nothing he could have done about it, but the shock and distress brought flashbacks of the horrors he had seen during the war. He held himself in check as best he could and whispered, "Poor Jay."

On the move, Higgins stumbled along. Favoring his sore hip, he got all the way to Pecos Road before remembering that his bag of baby-back ribs was still in its hiding spot. He scratched thoughtfully at his unshaven chin, but better judgment prevailed. *Better leave 'em.* He looked left and then right. Right would take him to the center of town; left would take him out to the ranches. He started limping his way to the left. *At least I'll be fed by the nice fella out there.*

The Honolulu Ranch, 8 AM:

Driven by the wind, tumbleweeds bounced and rolled, migrating across the ranch. They wound up piled against a barbed wire fence, a desolate backdrop as dozens of zombies stumbled from the main house in a gruesome herd. The twisted bodies heaved and shambled forward as they sought out human flesh, jaws snapping.

Ranch cook Bubba was vigorously swinging the antique bell clapper to announce breakfast when he noticed the commotion. Several zombies had zeroed in on the clanging bell and were headed his way. When he panicked and tried to outrun them, he tripped and wound up cornered with his back against the water-well. He attempted to rise and face his attackers, but was quickly pummeled back to the ground. With one eye in the dirt and the other eye looking up toward the group of horrible zombies, he used the only defense he could muster: tucking himself into a fetal position, a tactic generally used for bear attacks. Bubba was easily quartered, butchered as they ripped him apart one limb at a time.

Ranch hand Garrett heard the ghoulish mob approaching and dug into his pocket for his few remaining bullets. Backed into the screen door of a bunkhouse, he flipped open the cylinder of his six-shooter and carefully reloaded the chambers. As the last round was inserted, Garrett felt someone touch the screen at his back and quickly turned. He could not believe his eyes; a zombie stood there, convulsing violently. Garrett scanned the zombie's face and noticed that a bullet had passed through its cheek. Its forehead was enlarged, but the misshapen head had narrowed at the chin, creating an overall shape akin to a guitar pick. With a start of recognition, Garrett cried, "No! Not you, Earl!" The zombie stumbled hard into the screen and left behind a mask-like impression of viscera. Garrett pulled the trigger. The left side of the zombie's head exploded as it crumpled to the floor.

A young female zombie stepped woodenly onto the bunkhouse front porch, just a few feet from Garrett. The horrifying sight made him gasp. He pulled the trigger of the pistol, but he was shaking so much from a burst of adrenaline that the round went wild. To conserve ammo, he advanced on the zombie, planning to smash its head in with the pearl-handled pistol. Unfortunately, the heel of his boot caught the edge of an uplifted board and he tripped toward the thing. It reached its arm out as if to catch him and ripped a claw-like hand into the muscles at the back of his neck. It wrapped its muscular arm around his head, pulling Garrett down as it dropped to its knees. It vigorously gnawed at his scalp until a massive hole opened in his skull, exposing his brain. Trapped in the zombie's arms, Garrett lost consciousness as his blood pooled and dripped through the cracks of the floorboards.

***

Jed, a tourist, zigzagged in and out of the zombies, shooting at anything that came close. Some of these things had been his close friends; they'd joined him in helping out in the bunkhouse the night before. Their faces were now transformed into something only a very warped mind could have envisioned. Jed soon realized that body shots were doing nothing to stop the zombies, and ran to a small utility building to hide. He picked up the shovel he found in one corner, figuring he could use the business end of it for protection when his ammo ran out. Through a small gap between the doorframe and door, he glimpsed several zombies heading in his direction. He fired at the closest, the smell of gunpowder permeated the air.

Most of the shambling zombies milling outside the building were only ten to twenty feet away. Jed put his hand in his shirt pocket and counted three remaining rounds. He shook his head and whispered, "Dang it." A shiver raced up and down his spine, like someone had put an ice cube down his shirt. He was in big trouble and knew it. He leaned his full two hundred and twenty pounds against the rough wooden door, gained control of his breathing, and waited. As expected, he felt their weight push against the door. He pushed back with all of his might. Bloodied fingers squeezed through various cracks and holes in the door as the zombies struggled to gain entry. Jed dug in with his boots, and pushed back hard. The door bulged awkwardly.

A zombie moaned in the darkness of the room. The zombies outside began forcing their arms and legs through a gap they'd created. Jed fired the pistol into the darkness, rapidly emptying the chambers. One of the bullets struck the zombie between the eyes and it fell forward into the light. The sound of the gun firing in the enclosed space made Jed's ears ring. In a daze, he loaded the last three rounds as the wooden door splintered behind him and zombies poured into the small room. One zombie grabbed his arm while another grabbed him by the leg. He shot the one that held his leg pointblank in the head. A third hand grabbed his hair and yanked him backward. He fired the weapon behind him, trying desperately to free himself. Fully in the grasp of the remaining zombies, and with only one round left in the chamber, he muttered, "Shit." Jed pressed the pistol's barrel under his chin and pulled the trigger.

***

Mary was frightened beyond belief. She didn't want to hear the story of the attack repeated yet again, and backed away from the others, leaning against the meat cooler. She remembered that the thing that had once been her friend Lacy was inside. Distraught and irrational, she opened the door and nervously entered. She leaned over and pulled the blanket away from the face of the first body. What was left of the head looked like nothing more than a clump of ground meat. It was the zombie that had murdered her friend. She swallowed hard, dropped the blanket and backed up slowly to where Lacy lay. As she turned to face her, she thought she saw movement. *Am I imagining this? Oh my God! Lacy's alive! Oh my God!* She quickly pulled the blanket from Lacy's face, ready to give her friend the biggest hug ever, but discovered that the once-beautiful countenance was now a horrid vision of mangled flesh and dark blood.

The zombie's eyes popped open. It grabbed Mary by the arm and pulled her down, its jaws opening as if unhinged. Mary screamed and used her free hand to punch and beat at the hideous thing, but it held her in a death grip and merely pulled her closer to its hungry mouth. As the thing chomped down, Mary could feel its teeth grind against her skull. She tried to dig her heels into the floor and back away, but slipped repeatedly on the thin layer of ice that coated the floor. Her skull was ripped opened by the powerful force of the zombie's bite. As the zombie crushed the bone of her skull, she felt a sensation of coolness enter her head, and realized she was not going to get away. *How could my friend do this to me?* Blood poured from her wound and down her face, dripping from the lashes of her closed eyes. One by one, images of her loved ones flashed through her mind. As Mary rose above her body, she saw the trauma that she had endured and felt at peace. She watched as others entered the cooler, and understood everything as gunshots were fired into the zombie's head.

Baron Ranch, 8 AM:

Most people at the Baron ranch woke to the voice of the comical cook. He shouted, "Wakie-wakie, eggs and bakie!" Even if his silly jokes did not, the wonderful smells of fried eggs, bacon, and ham got everyone up. As the men and women made their way to the outdoor breakfast area, they chatted about their newly acquired skills. Today they would be given the certificates of accomplishment that they could brag about back home. The ranch's staff had already set up the show corral and firing range, complete with bleacher seating and award tables.

Baron Community Hospital, 8 AM:

Rico swiped his badge for the morning shift, then moved aside to let Frank get to the time clock. He said, "I hope today goes by fast. I have a hot date tonight."

Frank swiped his badge and replied, "Yeah, like *you* can get a hot date."

Rico shrugged his shoulders. "C'mon man, you know I'm a smoothie. I have the moves that women want!" He moonwalked backward to prove his point.

Frank rolled his eyes. "For the record, I saw you trip over your own feet yesterday." He shoved open the door to the locker room and Rico followed. They each entered codes into the scrub dispenser and got their uniforms for the day. *Baron Community Hospital, Team Players,* was embroidered above the pocket.

Rico fantasized about working on an interstellar hospital ship. The winding hallways and corridors always made him feel that way. He imagined his grueling shifts as part of a life-or-death mission in deep space. As he was waiting for Frank and daydreaming about the day's adventure, he caught sight of someone sprawled in a nearby chair. "Hey Frank, check out this dude. He don't look so good."

The two friends approached the man in the chair. Rico asked, "Hey buddy, you alright?" There was no reply.

Frank repeated, "Hey dude, you okay?" Again, no response. They looked at each other and knew they would have to actually shake the guy.

Rico stepped back. "You know this dude?"

Frank backed up and replied, "Vaguely. He was hired a couple of years before me."

Rico pointed at him and said, "Good, then you get to shake him first."

Frank held his hands in the air in surrender. "Man, why I gotta do everything?" He walked over and gently shook the man's shoulder.

The zombie stiffened. Its eyes popped open and it gurgled, "Rarrrgra!" It punctuated the utterance with a right hook that smashed into Frank's face. Frank flew backward and crashed into a locker.

Rico shouted, "Oh crap! You didn't do that to my boy!" He reached for the zombie's arm, but it grabbed him and bit into his hand. Rico yanked his hand back, holding it up like a torch. He screamed as severed arteries spurted blood into the air. Three of his fingers had been amputated at the last knuckle and were dangling from the mouth of the maniac.

Frank stood and charged at the zombie, intending to punch it in the face. It opened its jaw just as his fist was about to connect; his hand ended up buried deeply in its huge mouth. The zombie bit down with unbelievable force. Frank pulled back, the horror of his bloody stump causing him to scream until his throat was raw. Blood sprayed everywhere, spattering both Rico and the maniac in the face. The zombie grabbed Frank by the shoulders and lifted him, pinning him against the lockers with his legs dangling. Rico made a fist with his injured hand and tucked it into his pocket, then rammed his shoulder hard into the zombie's back. All three went down in a heap.

***

Doctor Eagle Feather, on call in the emergency room, looked at his wrist watch and muttered, "Sorry Doc, 8:00 a.m.; gotta take this call." He opened the door and ducked into the call room, even though Dr. Coleman had posted a large sign that stated: DO NOT AWAKEN! He wondered how the good doctor could sleep so long on such an uncomfortable bed. He quietly sat down and answered his phone, murmuring in a low voice. He ended the call and sat quietly for a few seconds, enjoying the peace and quiet until his phone rang again. The ringtone mimicked a soaring eagle's shriek, and worked well when he needed to wake up for those three a.m. emergencies.

The zombie lay motionless on the bed until the double shriek of the phone agitated it into awareness. Its brain swelled as it rose from the supine position. It lumbered toward Doctor Eagle Feather. With ferocious intensity, it attacked the doctor from behind. It grabbed the hand that held the cell phone and pulled backward until the phone fell to the ground and the arm snapped. Doctor Eagle Feather turned to find a hideous parody of Thaddeus Coleman standing behind him, ready to attack again. In severe pain and unable to use his right arm, he bolted for the door, but the zombie leapt onto the back of the tall doctor and started to bite his head and neck. He yelled, "Have you gone mad?" The zombie bit down on the back of his head and ripped the ponytail from his scalp. His phone continued to shriek and vibrate along the floor as it was kicked around like a hockey puck. The doctor screamed for help, but the room was designed to be soundproof. No one heard his screams.

***

The zombie was slightly hunched over as it stepped into the emergency room. For the first few seconds, no one noticed the horror. Looking up from her chart, a nearby nurse let loose a terrified scream. The zombie grabbed her as she tried to run past, using her momentum to swing her toward its gaping mouth. It bit into her face, removing her lips, teeth and tongue in one bite. Others ran to her aid, but were also attacked by the crazed zombie. The unit secretary dialed code black to activate the emergency strobe lights and alert security.

Less than a minute later, security guards arrived to find the room full of bloody carnage. The zombie had bitten and maimed an additional ten people before shambling off. Officer Chad felt for his gun out of habit, remembering too late the hospital's policy: *No weapons allowed on the premises.* He scanned the area and could see that the families and patients able to walk had cowered into any corner that they could find. Several of the nurses shushed Chad as the zombie shuffled down the corridor just beyond a wall. Officer Chad squatted and duck-walked forward, intending to ambush the zombie.

Nearby, a patient in cardiac arrest flat-lined. The continuous high-pitched tone of the heart monitor attracted the zombie. It lurched toward the patient, digging its fingers into his eyes and ripping his skull open before focusing on the exposed brain.

Chad saw his chance and rushed at the zombie. He hit it across the shoulders with his telescoping club, but it had no effect. He shouted to his partner, "Call 911!" The partner dialed the number hurriedly, but no one answered.

Blood and Milk:

Alicia's face was red and sweaty. The dark circles around her eyes made her look like a raccoon. She was confused, nervous, and excited all at the same time. Her mother was going to meet her in the maternity ward very shortly, according to a well laid out plan. The hospital's strobe lights flashed on and off, but she was not at all worried as she entered the labor and delivery unit. The registered nurse on duty whispered to the nurse's aide, "She's a sweet mom, and delivering her first baby … maybe a ten pounder." She smiled at Alicia and said, "Right this way, honey."

The nurse led Alicia to a waiting wheelchair, and made a mental note to chart her slightly awkward gait. She was rolled into a combination exam and birthing room, and was helped into a hospital gown and onto the bed. The nurse hooked her up to a fetal monitoring device and EKG leads, and performed some very brief range-of-motion exercises on her legs, mentally noting that her joints were stiff. She asked, "Is anyone meeting you here, honey?"

Alicia stared at the ceiling, taking a deep breath as she felt a contraction hit. "My mom is on her way!"

The nurse was happy that the young mother-to-be had someone to be by her side for the most important day of her life. She replied in a soothing voice, "Okay, honey that's great. Now I have to put your legs up in these stirrups for a pelvic exam." Alicia moaned as another hard contraction started. When the nurse finished her examination of Alicia, she said, "Oh, honey. You're going to be delivering any time now – you're fully dilated! How much longer before your mom arrives?"

Alisha let out a long, deep groan from the ongoing contraction, then said, "About ten or fifteen minutes!"

The nurse tried to lighten the mood. "Don't go anywhere, honey. I have to call your doctor."

Alisha tried to smile, but knew something just wasn't right. She didn't know how to describe what she was feeling to the nurse, so she nodded her head.

"I won't!"

Ear Buds:

The zombie had Chad cornered next to a supply cabinet. It lunged but missed because Chad was able to sidestep the thrust of its arm. With its other arm, the zombie reached out and clawed through Chad's six-pack abs from hip to hip. Chad looked at his gut, watching his intestines unravel before his eyes. He dropped to his knees and scooted back against the wall, trying to push his guts back into his abdomen. The zombie followed, lifting Chad by his head and violently twisting until his spine snapped. The zombie dropped him; Chad landed face-down in his own wet mass of sprawling intestines.

***

The housekeeper's ear buds blasted out loud Indie music, blocking out the moans of the zombie that stood in front of his tall cart. He didn't see the zombie until the cart was flipped over. His first thought was that he'd been the victim of a bad practical joke. He didn't recoil from the horrible zombie when it lunged at him. *Man, that's a really good mask!* He reached out his hands to unmask the prankster. "Game over!" he laughed, just before the zombie grabbed him and lifted him off his feet. One bite later and a lung was exposed. The zombie plunged its face into the gaping chest cavity and chewed out the upper lobe of the lung. The housekeeper fell dead at the zombie's feet, ear buds still blasting music. The zombie resumed its meandering walk through the halls of the hospital.

Momma:

After fifteen minutes alone in the room, Alicia felt as though her legs had turned into heavy concrete, ready to crush the stirrups they were strapped in. Hearing another mother's screams, she was thankful for a moment that her contractions were not yet that bad. She thought she heard her nurse scream at the woman, and whispered to herself, "How rude!" Then she was overtaken by another contraction.

After a few more minutes, Alicia called out for someone to assist her; she had several questions and was getting nervous. She panicked when her heart monitor faded from a steady, even beep, to a very rapid beep, and then back to normal. She had become faint and lightheaded and yelled as loudly as she could for help, but no one showed up. Just then she heard muted voices in the hall and shouted, "Is that you, Mom?" There was no reply. Contraction after contraction made her feel as if she were being ripped apart. Nothing made any sense to her. Between contractions, she yelled, "Nurse? Mom? Doctor?" She turned her head to the side to watch the fetal monitor. She saw that her contractions were spiking off of the chart. Another contraction twisted deep inside of her pelvis, and she arched her back in a full-body spasm, while continuing to yell, "Oh GOD, Mommy, nurse, please help me!"

Make It Count:

The zombie continued its macabre jaunt down the hallway. Fatty tissue and bone fragments smeared its face. It wandered into an employee break room full of nurses. Nurse Ann was the first to see it enter and screamed, alerting the rest of the chatty nurses. A rookie nurse vomited at the sight of the blood-saturated zombie. Nurse Hathaway screamed, "Oh my GOD ... Ann ... do something!"

The zombie swung its fist at Nurse Ann, but she sidestepped to the right and backed into a refrigerator. Another nurse threw a pair of scissors at the thing, but they bounced off of its body. Nurse Beth tried to scoot past the zombie, but it turned quickly and grabbed her. It bit into her upper arm, shredding it completely. Muscle fibers hung like strands of string cheese, and Beth collapsed from the shock of the bite. She bled out rapidly as her inert body blocked the door.

Nurse Ann picked up a chair and threw it at the zombie, but the chair missed its mark and smashed into Nurse Hathaway, who fell hard to the floor. Screams pierced the small room as the zombie advanced toward the nurses. Nurse Hathaway dragged herself to a nearby utility drawer, grabbing a large knife. She scrambled to her feet and thrust the weapon into the zombie's back. It spun around and grabbed her by the neck, then squeezed until her eyeballs popped out of her head.

Nurse Ann jumped over the fallen nurse and ran for help. The remaining nurses cowered in a corner, all hoping that the abomination would just leave.

Maasai Milk:

Alicia watched her belly undulate as the life inside moved back and forth. Her stomach started to expand rapidly, and she shouted to anyone who would listen, "This can't be right! Someone help me!" The thing in her womb ripped at her soft tissue from the inside, and a rush of warm blood rushed from her abdomen and pooled below on the crisp maternity sheets. She managed to rip a leg out of one of the stirrups, but she was weakening quickly. She did not have the strength left to get the other leg down. A thought passed through her mind that she was going to die, and she swooned. A few moments later, she was shocked back into consciousness when she felt her baby's razor-like fingernails worming its way through her stomach. She panted, "Gotta be a nightmare." Monitor alarms wailed steadily. Seconds later, both of the baby's hands ripped open a large, jagged hole. Its head crowned and its chubby little arms spread the wound even wider. It gripped the fatty edges of the hole and pulled itself out, sitting on the ravaged remains of Alicia's torso, cooing pitifully. The heart monitor's high pitched tone continued non-stop. The baby scooted up a few inches and latched onto Alicia's breast, suckling noisily. After a few moments of gulping breast milk it was not satisfied, and began to chew on the nipple with its tiny, needle-like teeth. Blood mixed with milk and pooled between Alicia's breasts. The zombie's tiny black tongue lapped at the mixture until something interesting caught its attention. It clumsily climbed down its mother's dangling leg and cooed, "Gra, gra, gra!"

Hack Wounds:

The moving zombies resembled the forces of Death itself. Their awkward, lunging gaits made it appear as though they were struggling with heavy packs fastened to their backs; their boots created deep trenches in the ground. Distorted faces were highlighted by small growths that sprouted from their misshapen skulls. Some of the zombies had sustained gunshot wounds, while others had hack wounds from one type of blade or another. The oldest wounds had flies swarming along their blighted edges. The line of zombies stretched out for an eighth of a mile on the road, headed in the general direction of Baron Ranch.

Honolulu vs. Baron:

The Baron Ranch festivities were in full swing. The twenty-odd cowboys and cowgirls were practicing their riding, roping and shooting – the very epitome of good Texans. Even the professional cowboys appreciated the effort it took for these greenhorns to master all of those assorted skills in just one week.

Michael was dressed in the special outfit he'd bought for this important day. He wanted to look like an authentic cowboy while saddled up on his painted pony. The proud Texan trotted his horse around the corral, giving out courtesy nods to the others in attendance.

A small training bull received a firm slap on its rear end and bolted from the holding pen, entering the corral at full speed. Spotting the cowboy, it swerved sideways and darted in the opposite direction. Michael pulled the horse's reins hard to the left and yelled, "Yee haw!" The horse angled toward the young bull, hooves leaving a billowing trail of dust. As he twirled the rope above his head, Michael thought, *Gotta have the fastest time.*

Cora was intent on proving to her husband that she was a better shot than he was. There had been a friendly rivalry between the two since getting married three years earlier. She had grown up in Texas, while Kevin was from Oklahoma City. For Cora, it was time to put up or shut up. She unlocked her pistol's strap and took a deep breath. She positioned herself about forty feet from the black and white paper targets; she had ten seconds to get as many bull's-eyes as she could. In the event of a tie, each person would repeat the round until someone missed or beat the other's time.

Kevin was proud of his wife and really didn't want to see her fail, but she was so serious about beating him. He just had to prove he could out-shoot her. *Time to cowboy up!* His eyes drifted to her sexy body. *How'd I get so dang lucky?* He stood up in the bleachers and shouted, "Good luck honey!"

The cowboy staffer held up his stopwatch, waiting for the instant that her hand moved from its resting position. Cora stared at each target, sizing them up. *In and out, nice and slow.* When she was ready, she reached for her pink-handled pistol and – in rapid succession – shot the targets from left to right.

The timekeeping cowboy yelled out, "Eight seconds!"

Cora holstered the pistol and shouted an exuberant "Yee-haw!" She had hit every target, and could hear her husband yelling above the cheers of the bystanders, "Atta-girl, Cora!" Kevin proudly strutted to his wife, flashing a huge Texas grin. He whispered in her ear, "I've got that covered!"

Cora put both of her hands on her hips and sassily replied, "Well, if you're cowboy enough … take it."

Kevin whispered again, "Yes, I am!"

At the firing line, Kevin planted the heel of his boot into the dirt and slowly went through his breathing exercises. He took one last breath. *Each bull's-eye is another contract signed.* Exhaling, he quickly drew his pistol as the stopwatch clicked to a start. As each second ticked off the clock, more paper targets were shredded. Between the explosive rounds, he reveled in the thought, *I must win!*

The cowboy timekeeper was just about to yell out Kevin's time when all of a sudden, screams erupted from behind a nearby bleacher. Kevin, Cora, and the rest of the competitors ran to see what had happened. When they arrived, they found several people being attacked by grotesquely deformed humans. One man was already on the ground, with a bloodied zombie straddling his legs and ripping at his intestines. Kevin and Cora looked at each other. They knew they had to do something, and moved apart about twenty feet to create a crossfire zone. They fired their pistols, repeatedly striking the zombies in their torsos, but the rounds had no effect. The pair reloaded and released a second salvo of rounds as they moved closer to the carnage.

As the rampage continued, Cora shouted, "What in the world is going on?"

Kevin, trying desperately to hold on to reality, replied, "I have no idea, honey!"

Now standing side by side, husband and wife watched as the zombies advanced steadily toward them. They fired their weapons sporadically, but the rounds did nothing to stop the undead. Kevin gave his wife one of those looks. She didn't have to think twice about what his eyes meant. They retreated quickly, reloading their six shooters along the way. Zombies seemed to be everywhere they went.

Cora asked, "Why aren't they dying?"

Kevin replied, "Don't know. Just shoot at the heads." The couple hunkered down and unleashed a volley of head shots on the closest of the zombies, which fell to the ground, lifeless. Kevin checked his pockets and said, "I'm out of ammo."

Cora opened her pistol's cylinder and replied, "I have two left." They looked at each other meaningfully as Kevin said, "We need to hide somewhere fast!"

Moving quickly between buildings, Kevin and Cora paused to watch Michael and a few other guests work in unison to lasso a zombie. They dismounted their horses and managed to tie the zombie to a fence post. The small group did not see the other four zombies approaching at their rear. The husband and wife team yelled, "Watch out!" but it was too late. With superhuman strength, the zombies brutally dismembered the guests in the corral. Cora could not believe her eyes as she watched one of the horrors clutch someone's head in its hands and bite down. She screamed, "Oh my GOD! Oh my GOD!" and turned away.

Kevin took Cora by the hand and shouted, "C'mon, let's get outta here!" The couple ran past dozens of corpses. The air was thick with the sweet, gagging scent of blood. Kevin panted and said, "We really need a place to hide."

Cora, struggling not to vomit, pointed up. "Look." A dozen buzzards flew overhead and slowly started to descend. Kevin felt all of the pressure of the last thirty minutes and shouted, "Damn dirty birds!"

After running about one hundred and fifty yards, the pair reached a small building within sight of the main house and corrals. They ducked inside and Kevin shut the door, saying nervously, "I'm sure the police will be here shortly."

Cora gently reached for his hand. "Did you bring your cell phone?"

Kevin shook his head. "You know we can't get reception out here."

Cora peeked through a hole in the wooden-planked wall. "They all seem to be heading to Baron now."

"Great," Kevin sighed with relief.

The Baron Morgue and Hospital:

A few of the dead bodies in the old morgue coolers began to twitch. Burt, the morgue's technician, had been hired to clean up and keep an eye on things. While tidying up after a busy day of autopsies, he heard a noise in one of the old coolers. *Maybe it's that damn fan again.* He walked over to investigate, but as he approached, the noise stopped. He went back to wiping down the examination table, which was still covered with the last weirdo's bodily fluids. *My lucky night.*

The noise started again and Burt angrily muttered, "I can't go one freakin' night without that thing acting up." He was peeved about making minimum wage, and double peeved that he would have to pull the stiff out of the cooler, reach in, and hit the fan with a long stick. That was a trick he'd learned from the previous morgue technician. He pulled open the door and paused, letting the cool air caress his face. Two arms reached out from the bowels of the cooler and grabbed him. Frightened beyond belief, he felt as if all the blood had somehow drained from his body. He tried to run, but something had a firm hold on him and was pulling him inside. He fought back as best he could in the narrow space, but his arms were too big to fit completely inside the unit. Something was biting him and pulling him face-first into the darkness.

Jaws closed on his face, crushing his chin. He tried to scream, but the damage was too severe and he couldn't open his mouth. Instead, a loud wet moan erupted from his throat. The zombie's brain quivered at the noise; it became further enraged. It pulled Burt deeper into the unit and bit into a rib. He gasped for air. Seriously wounded and struggling to breathe, he pushed desperately against the attacker. He managed to free himself, dropping hard to the floor. The zombie's hands reached out of the cooler and grabbed the sides of the unit's frame. It freed itself with one tug and fell to the floor, flexing its jaws wide open like a snake. Eye to eye with the zombie and unable to move, Burt waited in agony for the final bite. Surprisingly, the zombie merely stood and shuffled toward the exit door.

Other zombies clumsily pushed the fridge doors open; they had been designed with inner safety release latches. The zombies dropped from the coolers like wet noodles from a bowl of pasta and stumbled toward the hallway that led to the street. Bleeding out and in shock, Burt spent his final seconds watching in disbelief as the dead walked again.

Hospital Lockdown:

Baron had become more and more like a scene from a horror story. Disfigured zombies shambled down streets and alleys, randomly attacking families in their homes. Corpses littered the nicely manicured lawns. Call after call to the police station went unanswered, and the chaos continued unabated.

Inside Baron Community Hospital, code black was in full effect, and the emergency lights continued to flash. Many of the on-call nurses and ancillary staff who had worked the previous shift were called back to work, but were not told the nature of the emergency. Department supervisors were only authorized to say, "Come in. No exceptions!"

The hospital's command center worked diligently to figure out exactly what had transpired. Nurses triaged the most severe wounds and lined patients up in the hallways. Doctors stitched and treated open wounds on the spot. Lab personnel hustled from patient to patient, taking blood samples. They were also tasked with getting samples from the corpses that lay strewn about.

The locked-down laboratory allowed only authorized personnel to enter or leave the department. Inside the lab, Doctor Kasay worked to analyze the blood samples as fast as he could get them. Unfortunately, the old light microscopes he was using couldn't match the power of an electron scanning microscope, and he was unable to determine the etiology of the unusual cells. He needed a second opinion, and called his senior lab technician over to his desk. "What do you think this is?"

The technician, truly puzzled, replied, "I don't know, Doc. I've never seen cell walls repair themselves like that ... ever!"

Kasay peered into the scope again. "Exactly! What in the world could be causing these cells to stay alive? They seem to keep regenerating, even after the heart stops. They just don't die."

The technician shrugged his shoulders and said, "This is definitely a job for the big boys. We just don't have the fire power."

Kasay went back to his work station. "I'm afraid you're right!" He took photographs of the slides, and gathered a few live samples. He packed it all up, including a flash drive that contained photographs of all the deceased. He called the hospital's courier to transport the package to the post office for delivery to the national lab.

Doctor Kasay faxed an URGENT note to Doctor Ludwig of the National Infection Control Center (N.I.C.C.). In the fax, Kasay explained:

"We have an unknown infection spreading in Baron, Texas. A code black is in effect, and the hospital is under quarantine. Infected individuals, presenting with tumors of some type on their scalp, are turning into homicidal maniacs. The fleshy tumors seem to affect the soft tissues and localized muscles of the head and neck, terribly distorting the anatomy and probably involving the brain. At some point, all of the individuals we saw died from this infection. (Remember I'm not crazy when you read the next sentence). They all appear to have reanimated after death and gone on a murderous killing spree, consuming their victims.

Other symptoms include: A walk that looks like a person struggling with rigor mortis, superhuman strength, and jaws that continuously open and close. Witnesses have confirmed that they saw the reanimated "zombies" disembowel their victims. They seem to bite with enough force to shatter large bones and appear to favor human brains, which they consume.

I've packed slides of the cells, and attached the files of our preliminary lab results. Also included are pictures of the "zombies" and photos of various victims' wounds. The package is being overnighted to you. Please inform us as to what this infection is and any treatment options. URGENT and CONFIDENTIAL REPLY REQUIRED!"

Old Man Higgins:

After twenty minutes at a nice pace, Higgins' hip started to bother him. *I should just sit here and rest a spell.* At the intersection of Pecos and Ranch Road, he sat on a flat rock for about ten minutes, massaging his hip. Before he continued on, he readjusted the authentic Cavalry hat that his grandfather had given him, wanting to be sure the wind wouldn't blow it off. He'd inherited the hat when he first learned to ride a horse. Back in his early days, boys learned to ride almost before they could walk. Higgins decided to take a left at Ranch Road, and tied his bandana over his mouth to keep out the dust he was kicking up. He patted the dust off of his trousers and began walking. He was hungry, thirsty and in need of a hearty breakfast. The ranches were good for a guaranteed meal. The cowboys always treated him right!

National Infection Control Center:

Doctor Ludwig read the fax and immediately picked up his cell phone and called Doctor Stockton of U.F.E.D. (United Front for the Eradication of Diseases). Doctor Stockton answered the phone. Ludwig leaned back in his swivel chair and said, "Doctor Stockton, this is Doctor Ludwig."

"What can I do for you, Doctor Ludwig?"

Ludwig took a deep breath and said, "There's a serious infectious outbreak developing in Baron, Texas. Doctor Kasay, working out of a lab in the local hospital, has sent me some interesting information that I'm passing along to you. He reported that people are dying, reanimating, and then murdering non-infected citizens. Yes, I know that sounds crazy, but please review the facsimile that I'm sending to you now." He pressed the fax machine's send button, and the machine sprung to life.

It took a few moments for the fax to transmit. As he waited, Stockton retrieved a book from one of his shelves and thought about how rapidly serious infections could spread and damage the human body. However, he had to scoff at the claim that people were coming back to life – that was pure fantasy, utterly ridiculous. He knew that these types of claims, such as the one from the doctor in Baron, were usually the result of professional paranoia. What *was* becoming the new normal was the discovery of new species of viruses and ancient spores, almost on a daily basis.

The fax appeared and Stockton read through it twice, adjusting his bow tie. He called Ludwig, and said, "These symptoms are very unusual and quite suspect, to say the least. Our lab will take a close look at what you're sending."

Ludwig, sounding harried, responded, "This is extremely urgent, doctor. Please inform us of your findings as soon as possible. By the way, I've just received another fax that says Baron's police force has been overrun with the same kind of infection. Its citizens are in serious jeopardy."

Stockton absently turned the pages of the book he had retrieved and replied, "We'll do everything we can to identify the pathogen, and recommend a cost-effective treatment plan. Thank you for calling, and

I'll talk with you soon." Ludwig tried to reply, but Stockton had already hung up.

After flipping through whole sections of the book, Stockton stopped at a couple of chapters on extreme cellular reproduction and started brushing up on this unusual subject.

Sporaton Works for a Solution:

Doctor Billings, founder of Sporaton Lab in California, was concerned that he hadn't yet heard from his Baron, Texas team following their recent trip. They should have faxed the preliminary reports to him by now. Expedition protocol demanded it. At a minimum, he should have received highlights and photographs within twenty-four hours of the team's return. The discovery of new spores would be huge for the company, and financially, just what he needed.

A self-made man, Billings took pride in the fact that Sporaton was a company with the most up-to-date technology. As such, each lab's conference room was wired to display any discoveries in three dimensions. The exterior of the buildings were also wired with security cameras. Billings waved over his longtime assistant, Rebecca, and asked her to set up a video link directly into the Baron lab.

After lunch, Billings returned to his office. Rebecca stood by with the secure link she'd created, and they both peered at his monitor. The camera gave a birds-eye view of the main area, but the normally busy lab was devoid of life. Rebecca flipped her auburn ponytail off her shoulder. Ever optimistic, and with electronic pad in hand, she said, "Maybe they all took a day off. You know how these expeditions can take a lot out of you."

Billings thought about his days in the field and nodded in agreement. "Yeah. I'm sure you're right. But it's odd that they didn't contact me before doing so."

Rebecca tapped a few more icons on the pad and a new area of the lab was displayed. Billings stopped pacing and tossed his pen onto his desk. The pen bounced and landed on top of a graph. He carefully scanned the other areas of the lab, then said with a grunt, "Highly unusual though. Keep me posted."

Rebecca replied, "Yes, Doctor!" as she walked out of the room. With a few additional taps of her finger, a continuous video feed of the lab was created. She carried the pad around with her and glanced at it occasionally as she busied herself with other duties.

Billings put his eyeglasses on and re-read briefs from his other labs. He fidgeted with his pen, but could not get his mind off of the empty lab in Baron.

Old Man Higgins:

Taking another break, Higgins sat on an old tractor tire propped against a barbed wire fence. The walk had taken a couple of hours so far, and his hip was definitely hurting. Although the doctor had ordered him to exercise it regularly, he had also stressed the need to take it easy for the first month. For five minutes, Higgins watched a single tumbleweed roll by. *It's funny how they miss everything in their path.* Once again, he got up, pulled the brim of his hat down, and dusted off his trousers. He raised his bandana over his mouth and resumed the last part of the walk.

A couple of fence posts further down the road, the old war veteran pulled the last granola bar out of his pants pocket. It had been hours since his last meal, and he chomped down on it like it was a juicy T-bone steak. As he continued down the road at a slow but steady pace, a car sped by, its back tires spraying him with small pebbles. He yelled at the people inside, mentally cursing them. *Dang kids ... why won't they give an old man a lift?* He daydreamed about his next meal.

Sporaton Lab, California:

Rebecca sat at her desk and took a bite of her apple. She thumbed through reports, scheduled meetings, and occasionally glanced at the video stream on her electronic pad. With each crunch of the apple, she wiped away any juice that dripped down her chin. Out of her peripheral vision, she caught a glimpse of something that moved across monitor three. By the time she had focused on the video stream, it was gone.

Doctor Billings knocked on Rebecca's door and walked in, asking for her help in putting together some materials for an important fundraising meeting that was coming up. He leaned over her desk, glanced down at the pad and asked, "Anybody home yet?"

She put her papers down and answered, "I thought I saw movement a while ago, but I'm not sure if it was just my imagination."

He replied, "Well, keep up the good work. If you can get that information to me by tomorrow, I'd really appreciate it."

She maximized the screen. "Sure thing, Doc."

<u>**Baron Police Station:**</u>

Garbled reports of attacks by crazed people blared through the station's overturned radio. A man's frantic voice broke through the static, shouting, "This is Mike … Jasper! Is anyone there? We need help. My location is 321 Cactus, behind the *Extra Mile* store." The vibrations from the speaker caused the radio to tumble to the floor. A lone zombie shuffled by.

Officer Randall, flagged down by a citizen, stood under the convenience store's lighted sign. It was the location of the town's latest victim. She was found in a fetal position, next to a dumpster. He dug into her purse and took out her driver's license, identifying her as Amber, a twenty-five-year-old female apparently on her way home from work. She had been mutilated; her arm had been completely ripped off at the shoulder. To be sure of a positive identification, he matched her driver's license with her bloodied face, and said, "Yep … it's her." Lacerations on her abdomen and chest seemed to have been made by some type of claw. Perplexed, he told his partner, "Make sure you report that her remaining hand and arm sustained defensive wounds."

The partner replied, "She looks like she didn't have a chance." At that moment, Randall received a call from another squad car. The mumbling, terrified caller barely made sense to the officer as he described his situation. A lab technician had been found mutilated in the town's morgue, and Randall thought he heard the caller say that all of the corpses were missing from the coolers. Randall thought, *How can that be? And why is a citizen making a call from a police cruiser?*

Randall glanced at the female victim one last time. He had seen traumas before, but none this severe. He left his younger partner behind to write the entire report, and hopped into his squad car, turned on his siren, and headed out to investigate the morgue mystery. A block later, he radioed back to his partner to be sure to note the large hole on the top of her skull.

His partner replied, "10-4."

As the squad car rolled to the new call, Randall thought about the recent rash of murders, wondering if they could possibly be the result of animal attacks. But there had been too many unusual reports during the past twenty-four hours, and the rabid animal theory just didn't fit.

Old Man Higgins; Meal and a Cot:

The old man had lost track of how many fence posts he had passed. He leaned against a weathered pole, squinted, and noticed a small group in the distance. He talked quietly to himself, saying, "Why, they must be drunk, or lost. Probably threw one humdinger of a party at that ranch." As they closed the gap, he thought he could hear moans come from their direction and said, "Wind's tricks … gotta be the wind." He resumed his trek, stopping again at a missing section of the fence. He turned his good ear to the sounds, heard honest-to-God moans, and was close enough to finally make out physical features. In shock, he raised his voice and said, "Holy Toledo! One of those fellas looks like the one that murdered my friend, Jay. But how in the world did he find me? Why is he coming from the opposite direction?" He lowered his voice and whispered, "It ain't normal, the way they're all moving." He counted three and a half fence posts between them and him, and turned quickly to head back to Baron.

The zombies continued to follow Higgins. Senses heightened, it made the hairs on the back of the veteran's neck stand up. The last time he had felt that frightened was during the war. He willed himself to move through his hip pain and did not look back. He prayed that he could out-walk them, and decided to head straight for the police station. They might think he was just a crazy old coot and throw him in jail for the night, but he had to tell them what he knew. *At least I'll have a hot meal and a cot for the night.*

Team One Comes Together:

When Nick returned from the Gulf War in the early nineties, he went back to work on the family ranch. After a few years of struggle with very little to show for his efforts, his desire to be a rancher had run its course. He decided to open *Unique Trophies* on Pecos Road. He had always liked earning trophies when he was in school. Now he wanted to be the guy that provided them for everyone else. The idea was based on a simple principle: hard work equals success. If all went well, he would expand the business into a franchise.

Nick's truck idled in the parking lot of his trophy shop. His buddy and employee, Ron, had gotten there early, but for some reason, the entire glass entrance was barricaded shut. Nick tucked his keys into his pocket and rushed over to the door. *What the heck?* Several rhythmic taps later, Ron poked his head up from behind the barricade. He looked like a meerkat on high alert.

Nick put his face to the glass. "Ron, what in the blazes is going on? You know we have to open the shop. Have you lost your mind?"

Ron looked frightened. He replied, "No, I haven't." He looked over his boss's shoulder and continued, "Something strange is going on. This morning when I was getting ready for work, I heard screams coming from my neighbor's house. Just as I got to the front yard, I heard gunshots, and saw my neighbor stumble out of her home covered in blood." He shook nervously as he continued. "She warned me to run, and call the police. I went back inside to call 911, but no one answered at the station. By the time I went back outside to get her, she was being eaten by some kind of weird zombie. It looked vaguely human ... I think it was a zombie!"

Nick could not believe the crazy story Ron was trying to feed him. He bared his teeth, pointed to the door and said, "Well then, let me in." He laughed aloud, "I promise not to eat you."

Ron moved toward the door and replied, "Okay, just let me move a few of these boxes."

Nick chose his next words carefully, in case Ron was in the throes of a nervous breakdown. He slowly said, "Atta' boy! You're alright now. We'll get to the bottom of this."

Charlene:

Charlene was standing at the stove getting breakfast ready for her husband, who had been on his way home. He worked the night shift mixing chemicals to make pesticides. She heard a loud crash come from the garage. She rushed outside and found that he had smashed the car right through the metal garage door. Panicked, she rushed to get him out of the car, climbing over drywall, bicycles, tools, and other items that had been scattered around the area. As she reached the car, the hideous sight of her husband's face and head with bumps all over it horrified her. He looked like he had suffered a massive stroke, but there was obviously something else going on. She thought, *Maybe it's a bad virus or a chemical burn.* The thing behind the wheel sneered and pawed at the car window to get out, glaring at her with murderous intent. She screamed for help and ran out of the garage. As she reached the midway point of the block, she heard other screams, followed by the sound of several gunshots. She saw other people on the street who seemed to be as disfigured as her poor husband, so she ran harder, as much to clear her mind as to escape the nightmare. She decided to run to her best friend's house. Hopefully, he would help her to figure out what was going on.

Charlene slowly replayed the scene in her mind as she ran. *Oh my God, it must have happened overnight. But how could something like that have happened so quickly?*

Joaquin:

Joaquin's name was airbrushed in block letters across the chest of his white tee shirt. *Class of 2013* was written beneath it. Only the day before, he had found himself wishing that the shenanigans of high school were over. Classmates would call him "Joke-heem" or "Jo-neen," and he hated it. He'd tried to school them a few times, punching them in the chest and shouting "You forgot the exclamation point!" but it would only work for a couple of weeks at most, and the teasing would begin again. Other than that, his girlfriend told him he didn't have many problems and was pretty well-adjusted. As he exited the bedroom, he thought about that conversation and laughed aloud. She was the only one who really knew him. She got him.

Lying on the floor of the kitchen in a pool of her own blood was Joaquin's mother. What remained of her facial features left little to mark her identity, and he could almost pretend it wasn't her, except for the distinctive tattoo on her upper arm: a baby picture of him. She was a mess. From a distance, Joaquin stared at her, glassy-eyed and on the verge of tears. He had never seen a real dead person. Something that looked a little like his father stood over the body.

When the zombie heard him, it snapped its head around, revealing a gaping mouth filled with blood. Joaquin scanned the zombie from the chest up. *That thing can't be my dad!* He was furious and panicked, and grabbed the hunting rifle that leaned by the fridge. Whatever the thing was, he was going to shoot it dead for what it had done to his mother. Finger squarely on the trigger, he aimed at the zombie's forehead, but his arms trembled. Sweat dripped from his brow and stung his eyes. He could not fire the weapon. He dropped it, but the impact caused the gun to go off, the bullet shattering a print of the 'Big Apple' that hung on the wall behind his mom. He yelled at the zombie, "How could you do this?" He ran out of the house and down the narrow streets of the trailer park, deciding to jog to his girlfriend's house. He took a few shortcuts between properties.

Five minutes later, Joaquin arrived at Lindsey's home. He squeezed between the rose bushes next to her bedroom window and knocked on the pane. She didn't answer, so he whispered, "C'mon Lindsey," and knocked again. Still no answer. He stepped around the bushes, careful not to crush them, and went to the front door. He straightened up his clothes and made himself yawn wide to tame any weird facial expressions; he didn't want to scare whoever might answer the door. Her parents were already upset that she was dating someone from the trailer park. If they found out that his mother lay dead on her kitchen floor, they would try to break them up for sure.

Joaquin rang the doorbell and waited for a response. After a few minutes of suffering from proverbial ants in his pants, he put his eye to the etched art-glass pane and looked inside to see if there was any movement. After another long minute, he heard a loud bang. He cleared his throat and waited for the door to open, until he heard something muddled that sounded like, "Come on in!" As he opened the door, expecting to be greeted by Lindsey's mother, he was instead overcome by the stench of rotted meat. He lifted his tee shirt to cover his nose and whispered, "Lindsey!" He walked to the den and saw both of her parents. They stood motionless for a moment, and then, as if a jolt of electricity had surged flowed through their bodies, began to slowly move toward him. Their joints sounded like stalks of celery, audibly popping and crunching with each step they took. He stared at them both in horror; they reminded him of the disgusting zombie his father had become. Unable to control his emotions he yelled at them, "Where's Lindsey?" They sneered through snapping jaws, and he turned and bolted toward his girlfriend's bedroom.

The zombies reached the door of the den just as Joaquin moved to the open door of Lindsey's bedroom. He heard their moans and the crash of knickknacks sent flying by their spastic arm movements. Not seeing his girlfriend, he ran back into the hallway. Red in the face and soaked with tears, he yelled, "Where's Lindsey?" Hearing no response from the zombies, and with no actual plan, he ducked into a spare bedroom and scrambled out of the house through a window.

Sam Green:

Sam Green ducked his head slightly as he entered the family hardware store. He was only the store's second owner; his father had willed it to him. Alone for the first time since the funeral, he sat in silence as fond memories rushed through his mind. He pictured himself as a boy, expertly navigating through the busy aisles and helping out wherever he could. Most kids measured themselves with a mark on the kitchen doorframe, but he measured himself by how high he could reach up on the shelves. As he scanned each aisle, he remembered his very first days, when he'd have to use a step stool to reach most things. Now, he could just pluck items with ease from the top of any shelf.

Because of his teenage growth spurt, Sam had played high school basketball with the Baron All Stars. His shot-blocking abilities were legendary. His dad told him his skill came from all those years reaching for merchandise on the tops of shelves, and he agreed. When he graduated from Baron High, he received an athletic scholarship for college. The only time in his life that he didn't work at the store was during those years in Dallas, when he played ball and dreamed of getting away from the small town. Unfortunately, during a playoff game in his sophomore year, Sam ruptured his anterior cruciate ligament. The injury ended his career, and had bothered him ever since.

As he walked to the register, he put away thoughts of the future he would never have, as he always did. He grabbed his name badge off the counter and pinned it to his shirt. Unexpectedly, he heard a loud clanging noise and walked to the back of the hardware store to investigate. The shovel rack had been overturned, but he didn't see anyone. *Maybe it was just cats. They like to hang out here.* He returned to the front of the store, then heard more noises. He headed for the stock room, scanning quickly, and saw the back of someone's head. He shouted out, "Hey you! Stop!" There was no response from the intruder. Sam picked up a fallen shovel and raised it, carefully approaching the stranger. The morning light shone through the tall windows and silhouetted the trespasser's head; he was not able to make out any of the person's features. When he was about twelve feet from the stranger, the man turned and faced him. What Sam saw made him reel backward from fright. He mumbled, "Mister ... can I help you?" The zombie said nothing, but snarled and lunged at him, its mouth opening and closing like a broken trap door. Sam dodged its grasping arms, but got tangled up in the pile of shovels that were scattered like pick-up sticks on the ground.

The zombie moaned loudly. "Dragaaa!" Its jaws strained to open wide.

Sam jabbed at the thing with the shovel. The blade connected with its neck, and small spurts of blood pattered onto its chest. Sam was shaken by the fact that the zombie continued to advance. He swung the shovel in a broad arc, striking the zombie at the base of its neck. The blow almost decapitated the zombie, and its head, barely hanging on by a few ligaments, tilted over onto one shoulder and then fell, landing face-up in a wheel barrel. The body dropped to its knees, and then fell flat onto the ground. Sam backed up shakily, reliving the scene as he tried to figure out who it could have been. He knew he had to immediately report the self-defense murder, and rushed to the front door. In a daze, he pulled out his cell phone and tapped in 911, but there was no answer. He tried to text someone, but received an error message and shouted, "Dang it!" For a split second, he thought he heard more noises, but could not will himself to go into the back again. The gruesomeness of what had just happened overwhelmed him. He spun around the *Closed* sign and shut and locked the door, then climbed into his pick-up.

Sam drove to the police station hoping to talk with the sheriff, a family friend he had known his entire life. He knew the old sheriff would be fair and understanding; he gathered his thoughts so he could get the story right the first time. In his mind, it was definitely a matter of self-defense. The bigger question was: what were those things on the intruder's head?

Sam reached into the glove box and pulled out his favorite Moon-Pie snack, tore open the wrapper and took a big bite. It tasted amazing and melted in his mouth; just what he needed to ease his anxiety. After this mess was cleared up, he figured he'd go back to Slidell, Louisiana during Mardi-Gras and stock up on his favorite goodies. Half the fun was catching the marshmallow snacks mid-air, as his favorite krewe tossed them out by the thousands to the jubilant crowd in Old Town.

With his cell phone clenched between his left palm and the steering wheel, and his right index finger on the electronic display, Sam continued dialing 911. At the intersection of Wagon Road, he dutifully stopped at a flashing yellow light, watching as another car began to slowly coast to a stop on the opposite side of the street. Something caught his eye in the rearview mirror. He'd just turned around to see what it was when he heard the distinctive sound of metal crunching on metal. He spun back around in his seat, and realized that the coasting car had never completely stopped, and had slammed into the back of a car sitting at the light. The driver of the rear-ended car got out, yelling and pumping his fist in rage. Sam thought, *Well, this is nice. What more will happen today?* He watched as the angry man walked back to the offending car and knocked abrasively on the side window, but there seemed to be no movement from within.

Now enraged, the first driver yanked open the car door, and Sam heard him shout, "Hey buddy! What's wrong with you?" The next thing Sam saw was an arm shooting out of the car and grabbing the first driver, pulling him violently inside the vehicle. The first driver struggled, trying to pry himself away from his attacker, but it was of no use. Sam rolled down his window and tried to listen to what the man could be saying, but all he heard was a gurgling scream. He got out of his truck and ran over to assist the hapless victim, but by the time he got there, the first man had stopped making noises of any kind. Sam watched as the zombie dropped the arm that it had been devouring and looked directly at him. Its eyes were surrounded by dark circles, like a raccoon's mask. He immediately saw the similarities to the man he had murdered earlier. The fact was, they both looked like death warmed over. The zombie started to squirm its way out of the front seat, but Sam did not wait around to see what would happen next. He bolted back to his truck.

A woman who had approached Sam's truck while he was across the street ran straight into his arms as he reached his vehicle. She screamed hysterically, "Oh my God! A man was just savagely attacked by this woman ... She tore into him for no reason. None at all! It was horrible, like she was on some sort of drug. The man screamed for me to get help, so I ran as fast as I could. That's when I saw you."

Sam peeled her arms off of his. "Okay, okay, calm down. Did the woman have growths all over her head?"

Out of breath, she replied, "Yes!"

Sam pushed her toward the passenger door. "Get into my truck. We're gonna go see the sheriff. What's your name?"

"My name is Yolanda ... and yours?"

He opened his door and answered, "Sam. Want a Moon-Pie?"

Sporaton Lab, California:

Rebecca tapped a pen on her desk as she scanned the expedition's expense report. She hoped that the scientists had found something of value. Lord knows the company needed a big breakthrough to stay in the black. She worried for her job all the time. The professional scientists could easily find research projects elsewhere, but finding another job of this caliber and pay grade would be a challenge for her, not to mention the fact that there were only a few other companies researching spores. She knew practically every detail about Sporaton's operation, and to take that knowledge elsewhere would be like stabbing a knife in the back of her friend, Doctor Billings. She picked up her mocha freeze, drizzled with caramel, chocolate syrup, and whipped cream, and slurped it loudly. She liked to do that when no one was around.

She glanced down at her tablet and caught a glimpse of someone moving quickly past one of the monitors at the Baron Lab. She tweaked the camera angle with a circular motion of her finger on the screen and followed the person. She noticed that the top of his head showed some sort of growths. She poked her head out of her office and urgently called Billings into the room.

"Whatcha got?"

"I have someone on monitor three. Notice the top of his head." She maximized the image on the screen and zoomed in.

Billings positioned himself behind her shoulder and stared into the electronic pad. He was glad that he'd had the security system put in from the get-go. "What is that? And why do I have a drunken scientist in my lab?"

Rebecca tapped her pen faster, then replied, "I don't know. It's strange." The man was roaming the lab and adjoining offices, seemingly without rhyme or reason. She added, "Look at how he's bumping into things with those jerky arm and leg movements. Maybe he's on drugs?"

Billings was intrigued. "Please scan the outside monitors."

She dropped her pen, then brought up monitors ten, eleven, and twelve. They peered at the screen and she said, "No sign of anything unusual." She tapped another icon and switched to monitor nine. From that monitor, they saw another man walking with the same unusual movements. This time they recognized his face, and Rebecca blurted out, "Jared Way! He was just hired as a field entomologist." Her eyes welled up with tears as she said, "It's Jared, Doc. What's wrong with his face?"

He rubbed his chin and replied, "I have no earthly idea! Please call the local police station and have them go out and take a look. Something isn't right out there."

Wiping the tears from her face, she answered, "Sure thing."

Rebecca sat back and dialed the number for the local Baron Police Station. She naturally expected someone to pick up, but instead got a recording that stated, "If this is an actual emergency, please hang up and dial 911. If this is to report a crime, please press two. If this is to speak with someone in the department, and you know that party's extension, please press three." She pressed buttons randomly, hoping to connect with an actual human, but no one ever picked up. Frustrated, she rolled her eyes, looked up and said, "No answer, Doc!"

Team One:

As she nibbled on her Moon-Pie, Yolanda's tension continued to build. Her hands shook, until Sam patted her shoulder and calmly said, "We're gonna get to the bottom of this real soon. We're almost at the station now." Less than a minute later, he stopped the truck at the corner of Buffalo and Cactus Streets. A half-block away, he saw a police cruiser that had crashed through the station's front door. Yolanda dropped her Moon-Pie and screamed, "Oh my God!" She tried to get out of the truck, but Sam put his arm around her shoulder and stopped her.

As he pulled into the police station's parking lot, he noticed a headless body sprawled on the ground. There was also a group of people milling around who had the same kind of disfigurement they had seen earlier. The zombies shambled toward the truck, and Sam whispered, "I have no clue as to what's happening, but we're gonna find out." Yolanda choked back tears and put her hand on top of his.

"Okay, Sam!"

Abruptly, a zombie they hadn't noticed smashed its arm into the rear of the truck. Sam peeled out of the parking lot, narrowly missing the horror come to life. He raced down Buffalo Street and tried to be reassuring. "My friend Ted should be off duty by now. He might be able to shed light on what's wrong with everyone."

At the intersection of Buffalo and Divine, he stopped at a red light and thought, *Funny how there's not many vehicles on the street.* Just then Yolanda screamed, pointing to a child with the same weird sores on its head. Its movements were as disjointed as the rest of the people they had seen. It was pursuing a man, but was as easily outrun as a newborn calf.

Yolanda wiped her runny nose and asked, "You think we should pick him up?"

"Don't think so. This has gotta be an outbreak of some sort."

The person who had been running from the small zombie returned with a four-by-four landscaping post and smashed the zombie across its head. The single blow removed the top of its skull, and its brain spilled into the street.

Sam and Yolanda drove on, but as they neared Ted's home, a waffle-chested zombie appeared and stumbled up to the passenger side of the truck. With a handless arm, it bashed at the window, which split its flesh even more. The force of the impact caught them by surprise. Yolanda yelped and scooted closer to Sam, who yanked the steering wheel sideways and, with a squeal of tires, fishtailed onto Main Street.

As he drove away from the zombie, Sam thought about how many people seemed to be affected with the disease. They noticed another kid ahead of them, approaching quickly. He appeared to be normal, and Sam pulled the pickup truck next to the curb. "Son, ya need a ride?" The kid didn't answer, but his steady, non-blinking stare changed to a dreadful glare.

Yolanda pulled even closer to Sam, asking, "Are you sure? What if he's like the people we saw earlier?"

Sam took a closer look at the kid and replied, "Look at his head, Yolanda. Nothing's growing up top."

"But, Sam, check out his eyes. They don't look right!"

He was torn about the possibility that she was right. "Well, I don't feel good about this." He pulled away from the curb, keeping an eye out for any more of the crazy people.

Sam made a couple more turns and accelerated slightly as he approached the home of his friend. He was relieved to see that a vehicle was parked out front; he pulled into the driveway. "That's Ted's car!" He turned off the truck and added, "If anyone knows anything, it'll be Ted."

Yolanda put her hand on his and asked, "Do you want me to come with you?"

He opened the door, put one foot onto the concrete slab, and replied, "Nah. I got this. You watch the truck?" His good vibes reassured her, and she pulled her hand back and replied, "Got ya' covered!" She added, "I hope he knows something. I'd like to go home."

Sam spotted a pipe in the bed of the pickup and said, "If you need a weapon, there's a pipe in the back." After he mentioned the possibility that she might have to defend herself, he immediately regretted it, because she started to freak out. He gave her a stern look, and she struggled to reel in her emotions.

She sucked it up and put on her game face. "Okay Sam!" Sam knocked on Ted's door for several minutes. Tired of the wait-and-see game, he jiggled the door knob and the door swung open. He walked into the house and called out for his friend; there was no answer, but he noticed that Ted's gun belt was on the kitchen table, and the pistol was lying next to it in several pieces. Gun cleaning supplies were spread out beside it. He called for Ted again as he walked through hallway that led to his bedroom. Though the air conditioner was off, he felt a shiver run down his spine; something wasn't right here. Voice cracking, he asked, "Ted? You here?" He fought back his fears, got to the bedroom, and saw that the room was empty.

As he turned from the empty room, he was startled to hear, "Rah-gra!" Though the voice was garbled, it was deep and had a distinctive Texas twang that Sam instantly recognized as Ted's. As he caught sight of the zombie that had once been Ted, he saw that it had those things growing around the crown of his head. Dark, dried blood coated its face. It lunged at him, but Sam ducked as it swiped at the air above his head. He ran to the back of the room, opened the bedroom window and leapt out, running quickly to the front of the house.

Yolanda screamed when she saw him and climbed out of the truck. She knew something had happened by the grim look on his face. As Sam headed back toward the front door, she said, "Oh crap! Why on earth are you going back in?"

He ignored her question and ran back through the door and into the kitchen. He quickly assembled the pistol that had been lying on the table, while keeping an eye out for the zombie. He finished the job and headed for the bedroom. The zombie was in the hallway, stumbling toward him. Sam kept his distance and cried, "I'm sorry, my friend!"

He opened fire. The rounds smacked into the zombie's chest, but it did not go down. Perplexed, Sam muttered, "Crap!" He extended his arms and aimed for the zombie's head. As the two bullets slammed into its forehead, the zombie's cranium exploded. Large chunks of gore splattered against the walls.

Sam backed out of the hallway and ran to Ted's rifle cabinet. He took the shotgun and all the shells he could carry. He ran from the house and back to his truck. "Yolanda, I need to go back to my house. You wanna come?" In actuality, he didn't have the faintest idea what he was going to do once he got there.

Still upset, she asked, "Yes, but can we go to my house first?" He didn't answer her, but she could read his thoughts. She tossed him a Moon-Pie and said, "Munch on this!"

Busy Street:

Charlene ran down Main Street and never once saw a normal person. Frazzled, she began talking to herself. "I need to call 911 again!" She stopped, and as she tapped the numbers on her phone's touchscreen, a grotesque figure stumbled out of a nearby business. It saw her and slowly began limping towards her, closing the gap between them. She screamed loudly and backed away, trying to make sense of what was happening. The zombie, badly injured, staggered and fell to the ground, but continued to slowly claw its way towards her. There was no answer from the 911 operator, so she clicked off the phone and clicked on her camera icon. She steeled her nerves and approached the zombie very slowly; she could hear strange gurgles come from it. She steadied herself and took a picture, feeling sorry for it as it strained to move. When she had seen enough, she turned to leave, but was horrified to find that another broken-jawed zombie now stood behind her. It was so close she could smell its stench, though she had never heard its approach. Both of its arms reached out to grab her, and without thinking or looking, she dropped her phone and bolted into the middle of the street.

Yolanda continued to look out through the closed truck window for anything that moved. In the middle of the street was a woman about her size, surrounded by zombies. She cracked open the window and yelled out, "We can help you! This way!" The woman waved her hands frantically and darted toward the truck. Sam slammed on the brakes. A second later, the woman stood at the front bumper, peering through the windshield.

Sam scanned her head; he could tell that she was normal. As a zombie clumsily stepped off of the curb and shambled toward them, he anxiously said, "Get in the back."

The woman passed the driver's side door and said, "Thank you!" She pulled herself over the wheel well into the bed of the truck, then leaned toward the window and said, "My name is Charlene." She got settled on the contoured wheel hump and tapped the side of the truck, yelling out to Sam, "I'm good!" The zombie extended its arms as it came closer to the truck. Sam peeled out, but the sudden acceleration did not faze Charlene. Sam watched from the rear view mirror as she balanced herself without difficulty. Amused, he knew she could not be one of those things, as she had coolly pulled a scrunchie from her purse, tossed her hair behind her shoulders, and secured it in a ponytail.

Unique Trophies:

Nick and Ron restacked the boxes against the front door. Nick finished his side, stood back, and spotted a sliver of light between a box and window. "Wedge 'em in good, in case one of those things drops by!" Ron showed off by ramming a small box in the tight spot.

When they had finished, Nick took up guard at the front door, while Ron checked on the back door. He jiggled the door handle to make sure that it was locked tight. Satisfied, he walked away and dialed his friend Wayne, who lived nearby. *Maybe he knows a thing or two about what's going on.* After a few rings and no answer, he yelled out to the front, "All clear back here, but still can't get anyone on the phone."

Dark Bloody Smear:

Sam looked for the nearest parking lot to pull into. *With whatever this is spreading faster than a Texas wildfire, we have to get away soon.* He was sure the two women's families would be worried about them, and assumed they would be better off home with loved ones than with a total stranger. On Pecos Road, he found an open parking lot to stop in. He needed to get the addresses where Yolanda and Charlene would want to be dropped off. At the last minute, he remembered that a friend owned a nearby shop. As he pulled a quick U-turn, he said, "Hold on y'all!"

A zombie was crossing Bull Road as they approached, and Sam drove toward it. Yolanda yelled, "What are you doing?"

He glanced at her and replied, "I want to see what'll happen!" He honked the horn to try and scare it, to gauge its response. It froze in its tracks, then turned toward the truck. Sam revved the engine, and the zombie moved toward the sound, looking confused. He revved the engine a second time. The zombie inched forward, so close that its spittle flung onto the hood of the truck. Then its body stiffened and it opened its mouth wider than humanly possible.

Yolanda also stiffened, straight as arrow. She screamed,

"Let's go! I don't want to see it anymore!"

"In just a second … I want to see what it's gonna do." He revved the engine a third time.

Charlene stood up in the back of the truck to watch what would happen next. The zombie convulsed, and its head unexpectedly exploded. Half of its face smacked into the windshield and slowly slid down, leaving behind a dark bloody smear. Yolanda gagged from the sight of all that gore, and rolled down the window to vomit. She heaved noisily and the wet mess splashed onto the street, including her recently consumed Moon-Pie which lay in partially digested chunks. Charlene sat back down in disbelief. Sam punched the accelerator, squealing the tires and rolling over the corpse. Other zombies were moving into the street, so he veered his truck onto the sidewalk to avoid them, knocking over a sidewalk sign in the process. He bumped back into the street. A few blocks further, he pulled into the Unique Trophy parking lot and honked his horn.

Nick recognized the truck's horn and stood up. He poked his head above the boxes and waved at them to come in. Sam got out of the truck, followed by Charlene and Yolanda. Without looking back, they hurried to the door.

A nearby zombie had heard Sam's blaring truck horn. Its enlarged head shuddered like a glitching video game. Its corkscrewed shin was twisted, causing its foot to face backward. One shoulder and part of its chest hung lower than it should have, partially crushed by a sport utility vehicle. A reddish-green viscous fluid bubbled from its mouth. With a stagger, it moved in the direction of the horn.

As the group entered the store, Sam and Nick shook hands, then Sam blurted out, "Nick, there's some weird things going on. I had to murder someone. He was horribly disfigured, and broke into my shop and attacked me for no reason. Do you have any idea what's happening?"

Nick walked to the customer counter and picked up his phone. He replied, "I'm not sure, but Ron has seen someone like that."

Ron added, "Yeah, my next door neighbor. It was wicked, man. That's why I barricaded myself in here and waited for Nick." He walked back to the window and added, "I tried to call the police, but there was no answer."

Charlene nodded her head and said, "Same here! No reply at the station."

Yolanda shrieked, "One of those things is outside right now." She pointed across the street. Everyone hurried to the door and gasped at the gruesome sight. Nick looked like a man without a weapon dropped onto a raging battlefield.

Sam picked up on his vibe and said, "I have a few weapons."

Nick, looking extremely relieved, replied, "Good! We'll need 'em, just in case that thing decides to come over here."

Memorial Park:

Joaquin continued to travel by foot, and eventually found his way to Memorial Park. The beautifully landscaped space was surrounded by wooden benches, with a fountain highlighting its center. The green oasis was located smack in the middle of the commercial district. As he approached the park, he figured his luck had finally turned. Just ahead was an abandoned Segway; he immediately hopped onto the platform. As he practiced maneuvering over a small bridge, he ignored the bodies of the people slumped over on park benches or scattered across the lawn. He spotted a zombie impaled through one of its eyes with a forked branch from a magnolia tree. That branch was wedged between the branches of another tree, and the corpse hung there, steel-toed boots barely touching the ground. Putrid brown fluids dripped from multiple orifices. Joaquin pumped his fist in the air. "Yeah! Somebody got one!" He scouted the rest of the park and noticed that other areas had large, bloodied smears where no bodies could be seen. *Where are they?* He drove along Baron and Main Streets, then turned onto Arbor. The hum of the Segway relaxed him as it echoed off of the buildings, so he drove around for a few minutes to gather his thoughts.

Joaquin accelerated toward a nearby mutilated body. Its arm had been ripped from the socket, but the hand still clutched a machete. The bloodied tendons and muscle strands of the arm were spread across the green grass. He leaned over and pulled the weapon out of the hand. A block away, he spotted three zombies. To gather his confidence, he rode the Segway in circles, then headed over to get a closer look. A few feet away from the zombies, he taunted them and bravely swung his new-found blade. The zombies looked like a macabre freak show as they twisted and contorted their bodies, trying desperately to reach him. He analyzed each one, and noticed that they had wounds only on their torsos; none of them had sustained any sort of head wound. Moving quickly and without thinking about it too much, he bent his knees, leaned to the right and charged them, twirling the machete like a ninja. The blade sliced cleanly through a neck. A head followed the arc of the blade through the air, and the body crumpled to the ground. Blood gushed from the neck stump like water from a fire hydrant. *Now that's the way to do it!* He let out a war whoop as he pumped the weapon in the air. Another zombie's head exploded from the noise, and he shouted, "Cool!" The third zombie had stopped to watch him, its jaws opening and closing like a dying fish, its arms spread wide apart. Joaquin leaned to the left and switched the machete to the other hand. He accelerated as he swung the weapon, but missed his intended mark. Instead, the blow gouged the zombie's right shoulder. In disappointment, Joaquin spun around and looked at the severely wounded wretchedness. *Better to leave well enough alone.*

<u>Baron, Quarter Mile Away:</u>

Higgins did not want to look back, but his instincts forced him too. Head half turned, he muttered, "Geez … those things are only 'bout two and a half posts behind me now." As he willed his legs to move faster, he thought, *All in all, the new hip's workin' purty well. If this had happened before surgery, prob'ly wouldn't be here right now!* Feeling a growing sense of urgency, he quickened his stride as he passed a road sign that read, "Baron: 0.25 miles." Determined not to end up like Jay, he focused on finding a hiding spot once he got to town. His stomach rumbled. He licked his dried lips, then whispered, "Good ol' short ribs would do well right 'bout now."

<u>Doctor Ludwig, National Infection Control Center, (NICC):</u>

Doctor Ludwig sat next to the lab technician, waiting for the preliminary results. Without waiting for the doctor to examine the cell count, the technician pointed at the screen and said, "Definitely not bacterial," then tapped a few icons. Two large, flat panel screens displayed additional results side by side.

The doctor gazed at the data set on one of the screens and said, "Plasma cell membrane is abnormal. No mitochondria. No nucleus. In fact, the architecture hardly resembles a human cell."

The technician nodded in agreement. The doctor continued,

"We have to get this specimen into a scanning electron microscope. Get a deeper, up-close look at it. Set up a courier for transport to the university lab. They have Mrs. Kravitz – that's what they call their electron microscope. She's a very nosy device; you can't hide anything from her."

The lab technician replied, "Yes sir, right away!"

<u>Unique Trophy Shop:</u>

Nick emerged from the back of the shop with a gun. It was the same pistol his grandpa had given him when he turned sixteen. He showed it off to the others. "1860 Richards-Mason pistol." He flipped it over and added, "Notice the original staple imprints on its butt. This, people, is the real deal! An original from the Old West, guaranteed to take down anyone or anything."

Segging:

Joaquin was gaining confidence with his riding ability on the Segway, and began jumping off small curbs. He started to imagine a crowd of people cheering his every move, and thought about buying one of the fun little machines for himself. At full speed, he bent his knees and braced for impact as he shot off the top of an orange mechanics' ramp. The Segway landed lightly on the dusty asphalt and peeled out. He shouted, "Yeah!" He drove toward a slow-moving zombie who was limping along not far away. As he approached, the zombie raised its head in a very curious manner, then clumsily continued on its way.

Hey Kid:

Nick stood in the parking lot just outside of the shop's door and aimed his heirloom at the approaching zombie. Just as he was about to pull the trigger, he turned and confidently said, "Watch as the head disappears from the shoulders!"

At that moment, Charlene heard a whirring sound and shouted, "STOP! Don't shoot!"

Everyone looked at her, and Nick asked, "Why not?"

As surprised as the rest, she pointed to the source of the whirring noise and said, "Someone's near it on a Segway."

Joaquin accelerated the upright vehicle to its top speed of 12.5 miles per hour. With machete in hand and right arm slightly bent, he sailed past another zombie and expertly removed its head with one swift blow. The severed head flew through the air and split in half upon impact with the street. This time, he got a little emotional, and choked up as he thought about his parents, his missing girlfriend, her parents, and getting even. He hoped that Lindsey was okay and that he would soon find her.

The group had exited the trophy shop and gasped as they watched Joaquin attack the zombie. Ron shouted, "Hey dude! I mean, kid, get over here! It's not safe out there!"

Joaquin stopped the Segway and looked over toward the voice. Then he drove over to the shop, and everyone moved inside and barricaded the door once more. Once they were all safely inside, Sam asked, "Kid, what's your name?"

Careful to pronounce it precisely so no one would mess it up, he answered back, "Wa-keen."

Sam played the inquisitive reporter and asked, "Do you have any idea what's happening, kid? What was that thing you just decapitated?"

"I don't know. But my dad looked like that, and my girlfriend's parents looked like that too – they had those same weird things on their heads. They tried to attack me."

Yolanda braced herself against a counter, feeling nauseated.

Charlene walked to the window and asked, "What about your mom? Is she okay?"

Joaquin replied, "My mom's dead … don't know about Lindsey."

Nick stood behind Joaquin, whose gaze was still frozen on a point across the street. He asked, "Have you tried calling the police?"

Without turning around, he answered, "Nope."

Although disappointed, Nick patted the top of his shoulder, empathizing with the kid. "We've all tried – with no success."

Joaquin said, "Maybe we should … naw … never mind."

Charlene asked, "What's that?"

Joaquin didn't turn around. He lowered his head. "Nothing."

Nick felt sorry for the poor kid, and could only imagine what a horror it must have been to watch his parents come to such a gruesome end. He said, "You're welcome to stay with us if you want, until help comes."

Grateful to be in the company of adults again, Joaquin answered, "Sure Mr. Nick. Thanks."

Nick sent Ron up to the rooftop to watch for more of the zombies. Ron ascended the ladder and positioned himself in a front corner of the building. He scanned the street. *Nothing out of the ordinary.* Then he went to the rear of the building and looked over a fence, where he could see into the next yard. Four zombies were spastically pushing at a gate, trying to break through. *Looks like a whole family.* He ran to the far side of the roof after hearing screams, and saw another zombie. It was clutching a man in its grasp, and the man was yelling repeatedly, "Let me go!" The zombie's head exploded all over him just as he broke loose. The unfortunate victim gagged and spat out the dark blood and brain matter that had gotten into his mouth. He wiped the goo from his eyes, yelled again, and screamed into the air, "Why? WHY?"

Ron yelled to him: "Come to the trophy shop, buddy!" The man was looking up, searching for the source of the voice, when another zombie came out of nowhere and attacked him from behind. It grabbed the man by the shoulders and pulled him backward, down to the ground. As he fell, he tried to pull the zombie down with him and succeeded in knocking it to its knees. He punched fiercely at its face and chest, trying desperately to get away, but it grabbed both of his arms and pulled him towards its mouth. Ron couldn't watch, and heaved at the thought of what was about to happen. He hurried down the ladder and back into the shop to report.

Sporaton Lab, California:

Doctor Billings called Rebecca into his office and asked, "Can you get us two tickets to Baron? We have to get there, ASAP." He glanced at his watch and added, "I hope you have your emergency suitcase here, packed and ready."

"Yes sir ... it's here." She logged onto the net and arranged for two flights in coach. Not keen on being a first class passenger, Billings always said, "Why pay double the money for a few extra inches of legroom and a rotten lunch?"

A short time later, Rebecca and the doctor left for the airport in his hybrid.

"Did you pack all of the records we'll need?"

Rebecca went over the list one by one. "Yes. I have the expedition's expense report, a list of all employees, and copies of the photo I.D.s of everyone who works at the Baron lab. I also have a summarized statement detailing what they were searching for. We have everything we need."

Keeping his eye on the increasing traffic, Billings replied, "Thank you. I've never seen a lab abandoned like that in my entire career. So unusual. Needless to say, I've never seen anyone with those kinds of things growing on their head, either." He paused a moment as he merged into the center lane, then added, "A few more miles and we'll be at the airport. I can't wait to get to the bottom of this mess."

Rebecca thought about what he'd said. When he got ramped up like this, it was best to keep her responses short. "Right."

Unique Trophy Shop; Crystal Pyramid:

Charlene paced the showroom floor quickly, although her gaze remained fixed on the scene outside the window. Yolanda chewed her fingernails as she slowly meandered along the length of the service counter. Coming to a decision, she turned to Sam and said, "I really need to go home. My family's there, and I'm just sick with worry. Can you take me?"

Sam nodded his head and replied, "I will. I promise."

Nick, worried for their safety, laid his pistol on the counter and said, "I wouldn't do that just yet. Let's take an inventory of any weapons on hand. You know, knives, guns, and hammers – anything we could use." He pointed to one of the shelves and continued, "Heck, even that three-pound crystal pyramid trophy isn't out of the question. By the way, I only have twelve rounds here."

Joaquin added to the inventory, muttering, "Machete." He waved it around listlessly.

Sam shrugged his shoulders and added, "I have a pistol and a shotgun, with a few rounds for each."

Ron jumped in and said, "We have some hand tools in the back."

Nick unlocked a glass showcase and pulled out his prized Louisville Slugger. He tapped it in the palm his hand and said, "I've got the wood, and I'll use it … but only if absolutely necessary."

Exhausted, Yolanda stopped her pacing and said, "Okay Sam, I trust you, but I'm not gonna wait here too long. I'll go on my own if I have to."

Nick eyed the Segway against the wall. He had only seen one on the Internet, and wondered how easy it would be to ride. He asked, "Hey Joaquin, you think you could show me how that thing works?"

Joaquin tucked the machete between his belt and pants, and said, "Sure, Mr. Nick." He walked over to the machine with the same "let's get down to business" mannerism that his dad would have used. "First, turn on the key." He performed the gesture slowly, then added, "When you want to turn left or right, just lean in that direction. To accelerate, turn the handle bar like you would for a motorcycle."

Nick stepped on the Segway and practiced leaning in each direction. After a few moments, he rotated the end of the handlebar to get the machine moving, and promptly ran smack into a plate glass window, nearly shattering it.

Joaquin laughed and said, "Take your time, Mr. Nick. Go *slow* at first."

Embarrassed, Nick pulled the Segway away from the wall and tried again. This time, he accelerated more slowly, and rode from one end of the shop to the other. Like a man test-driving a Cadillac, he said, "I like the way it glides. It's smooth and cool all at the same time."

Charlene walked to the middle of the showroom. She eyed the Segway like it was her first bicycle and said, "I wanna try it!" Nick steered it over to her and hopped off. She climbed aboard and seemed to get the hang of it quickly, practicing figure eights across the showroom floor. After a few minutes of watching, Yolanda and Ron each took a turn.

Finally, Joaquin said, "Okay guys. We should conserve the battery. We only have about six more hours on it."

Being the last to ride, Ron had the honor of parking it and said with a grin, "I want one of these for Christmas!" Everyone heartily agreed that it would be an awesome toy to find underneath the tree.

Old Man Higgins, Flashback:

The old man did not have time to look around or even give his sore hip a rub. He was frantic. By his estimate, they were maybe one or two fence posts behind. He walked as quickly as he could, but the zombies were still gaining on him. He thought, *"I don't wanna end up like poor Jay!"* As he passed the city of Baron's welcome sign, he flashed back to his time at war. He had been in the middle of his platoon as they walked into a small Korean town; dozens of kids ran up to ask for chocolate. As they'd marched down the main street, the enemy had been so close that he felt them breathing down his neck. He knew he had to find a spot to hide, and fast. He handed out the candy and blinked his eyes. As the flashback passed, he whispered, "I'm too old for this. I'm just an old man."

Classics:

Lindsey missed Joaquin, and wondered if he was okay. When she woke to find her mom had turned into one of those *things*, she started running as fast as she could. It was the fastest she had ever run in her life, and she finally understood what her biology teacher had meant when he said, "The fight or flight response kicks in when it needs to." All along her run, she saw many zombies that looked like what her parents had become. They were so gross, and she had nearly collided with one of them as she ran. She'd thought for a moment that it was her best friend; she even reached out and touched the back of its hair before realizing that it was a zombie. Periodically, she'd stopped running to catch her breath and send a text message or two, but none of her friends replied back. She wondered about them all, hoping that they had not been turned into those monstrous zombies.

She paused again, finding herself in front of a costume store where she had shopped in the past. The store was usually open year-round, but had been closed for a couple weeks because the owners were on vacation. At least, that was what the hand-written sign proclaimed. She needed a break, and smashed one of the front windows of the shop with a lead door stopper that had been leaning nearby. She climbed inside carefully, and dragged a large antique hutch in front of the door and broken window. After barricading herself in, she scoped out the first floor. She realized that there were too many windows to stay downstairs. On the second floor, she ran into a street-side room and looked out of the window. She saw an old man who seemed doomed, a whole herd of zombies following closely behind him. She screamed for him to come to the shop, but he didn't reply. *He mustn't be able to hear very well.* She averted her eyes, knowing that she did not want to witness the same horror and carnage that she had already seen many times.

Higgins glanced up for a second and saw a girl standing in an upstairs window, waving wildly. He knew that there was no way he was going to have the zombies follow him to her, so he continued on. Passing several bodies on the verge of reanimating, he tried to quicken his pace. As he looked back, he noticed some of the zombies trailing off in different directions. Most of the ranch zombies were still following him, though. He continued his half-walk, half-limp down Main Street, and saw a carry-out shop where he thought he could hide. *Gotta get these zombies to stop following me ... but how?* He remembered his lessons from boot camp; he'd been required to read a whole book on camouflage and diversions. He knew he'd have to come up with something pretty impressive to get them off his trail. *What can I do?* The zombies' awful moans had increased in intensity, sending shivers down his spine. He shrugged it off and went inside a nearby gas station, quickly finding a box of matches and some barbecue fluid near the entrance.

Quickly limping about a half a block away, Higgins squirted some of the fluid onto the hood of a newer-model car. As he threw a lit match on top of it, bright flames shot up into the air, luring the zombies like moths to a light. Higgins was proud of his diversion, and took advantage of the distraction to change direction and head to the Old Ice House. He hoped that no other zombies would be there waiting for him. His stomach rumbled again, and he also hoped that somebody had left food in the break room.

Doctor Billings and Rebecca Arrive in Texas:

Doctor Billings and Rebecca exited the passenger jet at the familiar Dallas airport. Billings pulled his own carry-on and without looking back asked, "Do we have a driver to get to Baron?"

Feeling slightly hurt that there was no faith in the simple task, Rebecca frowned and answered, "Yes! Of course we do."

Billings stopped, looked back and replied, "Good, then we can leave right away. I'll ring the lab once we're outside the terminal and can get better reception."

She smiled prettily, trying not to show her exhaustion and replied, "I'll call the driver."

Once outside the terminal, the hired car pulled up. The driver got out, opened the trunk, then asked, "Where to?"

Rebecca lifted her suitcase, but he grabbed it from her hands, and said, "I got this ma'am!" He placed the luggage in the trunk.

Rebecca replied, "Baron! Oh, and can you stay with us overnight? We'll need your services in the morning."

He flashed a big Texas grin, which showed his delight in making the overtime. "Yep … long as you pay the extra expenses."

Billings replied, "No problem with that." He tapped in the lab's phone number, but only heard the company's prerecorded message. They walked around to the opened car doors and he said, "Still nothing."

Now settled in the Lincoln's plush seat, Rebecca closed her eyes and nodded reassuringly.

Team One Investigates:

Sam and Joaquin lifted the Segway and placed it into the back of Sam's pickup truck. Nick stood guard at the back bumper, and Ron at the other. They waited for the girls to get into their seats. After the Seg was secured with bungee cords, Joaquin, Ron, and Nick climbed into the back. Sam got into the driver's seat, but realized he had forgotten his ammo. He asked Nick to get the rounds. While Nick complied, Sam turned the key and revved the engine.

As they waited, Joaquin spotted a zombie slowly closing in. As Nick exited, Joaquin shouted, "Hurry up! One across the street!"

From the shadows, a zombie lurched forward. Nick gave the go ahead bang on the side of the truck panel, and Sam peeled out onto the street. He narrowly missed hitting the latest threat with his truck. As they passed it, everyone gasped in disbelief at its appearance. Its right arm was ripped off from some trauma, and the stump looked like a pulverized sausage. But it still somehow managed to move. Joaquin let out his frustration, waved his machete in the air, and yelled, "Go to Hell! Freak!"

Nick could not help himself, sounded fatherly as he shouted, "Put that thing away, will you? You might hurt someone."

"Sure thing Mister Nick. But I only wanna hurt zombies!"

Ron, panicked at that statement, said, "Zombies! They are … aren't they?"

Nick shrugged his shoulders. "I don't know what else to call them."

With only about two hours of sun light remaining, Sam asked Yolanda for her address. He wanted everyone else safely back in the shop before dark.

After fifteen minutes of driving, and avoiding zombies everywhere, Sam finally said,

"We're here. We'll wait until you come back out, and give us two big thumbs up."

Yolanda happily replied, "Okay … and thanks for everything." She got out, and Nick hopped out of the truck too.

He planted his feet on the driveway right next to her, then said, "I'll go in with you."

She flashed a big, confident reply and said, "I'm sure they're alright."

Ever cautious, Nick drew his antique pistol from its holster, and added, "Just let me come in with you … to be sure."

She nodded her head because she was anxious to get inside, and knew he would not back down. Gun in hand; he held the pistol next to his ear as they entered.

Inside Yolanda's home, the zombies scuffed the parquet den floor as they moved forward. Her father's expression seemed to be stamped onto his face and belonged in a museum for the macabre. Her teenaged sister had a broken walking cane speared through the gut. Its forehead bulged outward from some traumatic impact, a flap of scalp twisted and hanging inside out. The flesh covered a quarter of its face.

Yolanda screamed the moment that she saw them. Nick, with fear in his voice said, "This just ain't right man." In a low growl, he hissed, "Get behind me!"

Yolanda was confused; even though she was terrified, she wanted to run to them and offer help. *Doesn't matter if I die now.* Nick felt her body brush against his as she prepared to bolt past him. He grabbed her arm with one hand and held on tightly. With the other hand, he shot each zombie in the chest, but the zombies absorbed the rounds like punches to a pillow. They smacked into the wall behind them, but clumsily regained their balance and momentum and continued to advance.

Joaquin started to jump out of the truck bed when he heard the gun shots, but Ron grabbed him by his collar and held on. Sam rushed to the door, but Nick got there first and pushed it open.

Yolanda flung herself through the door and collapsed into Sam's arms, crying. "Oh my God! They're like those things, those zombies! What am I going to do?" The men steadied her as her knees visibly buckled from the stress. They dragged her back to the truck, leaving the front door open. They spotted five more zombies a few driveways down, and as soon as everyone was back in the truck, Sam slammed the vehicle into reverse and floored the gas pedal. The tires burned rubber all the way out of the flat driveway.

The zombies streamed out of Yolanda's family home, lurching down the street as they tried to follow the truck's squealing tires. Suddenly, they stopped and switched directions.

A neighbor of Yolanda's burst through his front door with an overstuffed backpack slung over his shoulders, waving frantically at the truck. But it was too late – Sam and the others were already half a block away and moving quickly. Frustrated, he threw his arms up and shouted, "No. No. No!" as he kicked the side of his car, parked uselessly in the driveway with its hood up. Three zombies approached unseen from his rear. As they closed in, he sensed their presence and whirled around, managing to maneuver away from a small, advancing female. He grabbed it from behind and rammed its head into the engine compartment, finishing the kill by smashing the hood upon its head. He stepped back and watched as putrid fluids oozed between the grillwork of the car. While he was distracted, the other two continued to advance and grabbed him from behind. He panicked and tried to struggle free so he could retreat back into his home, but they dragged him to the ground. He looked like a topsy-turvy turtle as he lay on top of the bulging backpack, screaming and kicking as they ripped off his arms and devoured his flesh. His stomach was torn open, and his intestines were slung haphazardly over the driveway. More of the zombies arrived and joined in the feast. His last thoughts were of his family, as he looked toward Heaven.

Oblivious to the carnage behind him, Sam gunned the truck and ran down several of the zombies. Joaquin pumped the machete in the air and yelled, "That's three more zombies down! One hundred and fifty points for you, Mr. Sam!"

Nick shook his head, trying hard not to look amused.

Sam smiled at Joaquin's comment, and looked over at Charlene and Yolanda. He mouthed, "Zombies?" Only Charlene nodded her head in agreement. Yolanda just sat there, obviously in shock. He handed her a Moon-Pie to help calm her nerves, but she wouldn't take it. He asked Charlene, "You want it?"

Nodding her head eagerly, she took it and finished it off in three bites.

He Shot It Dead:

Sam stopped near the parking lot entrance to the Unique Trophy Shop. He stuck his head out of the window, looked to the back of the truck, and said, "We need to do something about this right now." More of the zombies had filled the street, and it was beginning to look like the early stages of a rock concert.

Nick replied, "I know what you mean," and unloaded the Segway. He climbed aboard, pointed to the machete, and in his best drill sergeant voice said, "Son, I need that now."

Joaquin, roused to defiance by the fatherly tone, replied, "Mr. Nick, I think I'm the one who should ride the Segway. I have the most experience."

Nick shook his head no. "I'll do fine. Now, hand it over."

The teen handed over the machete, grumbling, "Great, now I have no weapon."

Charlene and Yolanda watched from the truck's passenger side window as Nick started up the Segway and performed a few practice circles, then headed toward a group of zombies. He circled them slowly, careful to watch his back. After a moment, he swooped in on one of the zombies, swung the machete like a baseball bat, and chopped off its head in one stroke. Everyone shouted, "Yee haw!" He waved the machete in the air, then circled back for a second one.

Sam had the pistol drawn just in case something went horribly wrong. Again, Nick accelerated the Segway toward a zombie, steering it with one hand. Elbow loose, he held the machete with the other. Ten feet from his target, it lunged, forcing Nick to veer away. In the confusion, he fumbled the machete and dropped it.

Sam climbed out of the truck and trotted to Nick's aid, but slowed as more zombies closed in on him. Charlene scooted over to the driver's seat and put the truck into gear. She made a quick U-turn in the parking lot, then waited. Nick stood atop the Segway, preparing to charge through a small group of zombies that stood between him and the fallen machete.

Sam blasted three of the zombies with successive rounds. The pistol sounded like a cannon going off in his ear as he fired the first round, pulverizing the left side of a zombie's head. Grey, spongy brain matter splattered the street. The second round struck another of the zombies in the lower torso and the bullet smashed through its body, tearing through one hip. It struggled to stay upright for a couple of seconds, then fell to the ground. It tried to pull itself back up, but could not. The third zombie turned toward Sam and hurled itself at him. Before it could take five steps, Sam fired a round into its neck, nearly severing the head. He moved back to avoid the bloody fountain that continued to pump from its neck stump.

Meanwhile, Nick had retrieved the machete and was moving to attack another zombie who had wandered onto the scene. He circled behind the zombie on the Segway and brought the blade down in a sweeping arc. The force of the swing separated the zombie's arm from its shoulder. Strands of muscle fiber and pearl-colored tendons hung loosely from the stump. The body shook violently from the trauma, and then its head exploded from the sound of Sam's gunfire.

Nick rode over to his buddy and said, "Thanks for the help, man."

Charlene had once again positioned the truck near the shop's front door. She felt good about her decision to take over the driver's seat.

Joaquin stood at the passenger door and looked into Yolanda's eyes. He noticed that her legs were shaking so much she could barely get out of the truck. He offered his arm to balance her unsteady gait; he felt her hurt was like his own.

The group moved back inside the shop. In the break room, Ron prepared coffee and offered a cup to everyone. Joaquin wasn't interested in coffee, and remained in the showroom. As they sat around sipping the hot brew, the group tried to figure out what their next steps should be. While suggestions were being offered, Charlene tried dialing 911 again, but had no luck reaching anyone.

After the caffeine kicked in, the group got busy and helped stack boxes more securely in front of the shop's windows. Joaquin shouted from across the room, "Mr. Sam, there's only about five hours of battery life left on the Segway."

Nick was surprised, and said, "Crap. That thing sure came in handy."

Sam walked over to the teen and asked, "Are you sure about that, son?"

Joaquin flipped a display cover up and pointed. "Yes sir. It says so on the readout."

Charlene used Nick's cell phone to take pictures of the zombies who were still roaming around outside. Several of them had such terrible wounds that she wondered aloud, "How in the world can they walk?"

The conversation turned to the best way to kill the zombies. It was obvious that body shots had little effect, but blows to the head were very effective at stopping the zombies. Joaquin grunted and added, "Don't forget about decapitation by machete." He traced his finger across his neck and added, "I did five or six like that on the way here. They didn't get back up either." The men were impressed and nodded in agreement, but the ladies were repulsed and turned their heads away.

Yolanda slowly shuffled to the customer counter as if she were wearing lead boots. She said, "You know, you wake up in the morning, brush your teeth, and all of a sudden, things go completely sideways. Who would have believed that something like this could even happen?"

Her statement got Charlene's attention, who took a moment to reflect on her own day. She went over to comfort Yolanda and said, "That's pretty much exactly what happened to me, you know. I'm glad no one at either of the ranches had placed an order this morning, or I'd probably be stuck out there. I got lucky." Everyone agreed that they never could have believed their days could have turned out like this. Whatever was happening was definitely a game changer.

Fingertips:

The hospital was overrun with zombies. They roamed freely through the public areas, emergency room, patient rooms, and operating rooms. There was not a single nurse or doctor left to tend to anyone. Most of the ambulatory patients had gotten away with the help of family members. The patients with the misfortune of being confined to their beds now huddled miserably, still connected to the various life-saving devices that dangled from their bodies. A couple of the zombies, obviously patients who had been transformed during the attack, had metal halos screwed into their heads. Tumors had grown upward and corkscrewed around the various black rods that held the devices in place. Gaping mouths snapped at the contraptions in an attempt to break free.

In the past twenty-four hours, Officer Keaton had learned to be as quiet as possible. He carefully took his shoes off at the door and cautiously entered the hospital's emergency room, noticing the strobe lights that blinked every few seconds. The lights were disorienting, and he did his best to ignore them. His main objective was to find the department manager's office, as a panicked call had been made from that room. Slowly, he made his way through the corridors. As he turned a corner, he saw a slow-moving, elderly zombie dressed in a hospital gown. One arm was tangled in a haphazard ball of transfusion tubing. The end of the tube was leaking and left behind a thin bloody streak. The zombie's oversized neck veins bulged and pulsated. Keaton ducked behind a desk to hide, and almost puked when he came face-to-face with the dismembered body of a female nurse. He made the sign of the cross with the hand that held the Glock, then crawled from behind the desk and toward a nearby hallway intersection. As he neared the corner, he heard a scrape on the ground. He peeked his head around the corner and saw a greenish-colored dead man crawling slowly toward him. As it advanced, metal rods from an external traction device scraped the linoleum. Keaton white-knuckled the Glock; he wanted nothing more than to just get up and run, but instead, he scrambled backward and quickly duck-walked in the other direction. Something hit the floor behind him. When he turned, he spotted an IV pole that had fallen over, but no zombie. He shadowed the wall closer than ever, but his bulletproof vest kept him from being flush with it.

Moving safely away from the close encounter, Officer Keaton regained his confidence and stood upright. He spotted the office door he had been looking for and hurried over. He pushed the door open and whispered, "Is anyone in here?" No one answered, but he saw a large pool of blood on the floor in front of the desk. Dried blood spatters also covered the rear wall. He froze, hearing the same scraping sound as before, only this time it was much closer. He paused for a second to check his magazine to make sure it was fully loaded, and thumbed the safety off. A new sound was coming from the hallway. *What the heck?* He peered out and spotted a robotic medicine dispenser. The robot whirred along and stopped at each patient's room. Behind it, a zombie spastically careened into the walls, stopping whenever the bot stopped. *Dr. Denton, General Surgeon* was monogrammed above the pocket of the zombie's bloodied lab jacket.

Keaton heard yet another noise coming from behind the desk of a nearby nurses' station – the creaking of a swivel chair. A zombie rose from the chair and spotted him. The left side of its head was caved in.

Keaton was effectively cut off from the emergency room exit. *I have no choice.* He steadied himself and aimed the pistol at the zombie behind the desk, knowing that the other zombies would hear the gunshots. He pulled the trigger and the zombie's head exploded. An old-fashioned nursing cap flew through the air and landed atop a glucometer, somehow remaining pristinely white. The sound of the pistol fire reverberated in his ears; he did not hear the other zombie creeping up from behind. It grabbed his shoulder roughly but he pulled loose, spun around and fired. The bullet struck the zombie in the chest, sending its body crashing into the wall behind it.

On the move and already in the next hallway, Officer Keaton was confronted by several more zombies. As they closed the distance between them, he fired the Glock multiple times. He panicked as a green-tinted hand grabbed him from behind and ripped at his shoulder. The strength of its vice-like grip made him cry out in pain. He raised the pistol and turned to face the horror. As he did so, the zombie grabbed his firing arm. He dropped the pistol onto the ground and it discharged. He struggled to free himself and retrieve the weapon, but the zombie had him firmly in its grasp. Its jaws unhinged as it pulled him to its gaping mouth. He punched and kicked fiercely, still struggling to retrieve his Glock. He managed to break away and fall to the floor, but when he was merely inches away from reaching his weapon, a stray kick from another of the undead sent the weapon skittering across the hallway floor. Shaking and hurt, he tried to army-crawl his way to the gun, but just as he had it almost in his grasp, a nearby zombie dropped to its knees and latched onto the back of his ankles. It pulled him backward and he moaned. Then it moaned! A third zombie bore down on him. It was the former Doctor Denton, and it dropped to the floor and dug into his torso, exposing his liver. He screamed for his life, "No! No!" In one swift move, it yanked out his liver and started to devour the organ. Blood poured from his many wounds as more of the zombies zeroed in on the sounds of carnage. His once-strong heartbeat quickly faded. The last thing he saw was his service pistol laying a few feet away.

Nightfall in Baron:

The twenty-foot-tall neon cowboy sign across the street flashed the outline of a rope, back and forth, like it was twirling mid-air. As he took the last bite of his bologna and mayonnaise sandwich, Higgins peeked out a window of the Old Ice House. The sandwich was pretty good;

one of the employees had left it in the refrigerator of the break room, nicely labeled with the name "Larry" written on the sandwich bag it was stored in.

Higgins watched various tumbleweeds roll down the street. One of them smacked into a zombie, knocking the zombie off-balance and sending it to the ground in an awkward heap. It thrashed about for a moment and finally got back up, just outside the entrance to the Ice House. The old man wiped his hands on his pants and mumbled, "Dang thing is just outside the door. I need a weapon!"

The Baron Vista:

Doctor Billings and Rebecca arrived on the outskirts of town in their hired car. The driver, Bill, turned in his seat and said, "Here we are folks. Baron, Texas."

Billings gazed out at the vista before him, and said to no one in particular, "It only took us five and a half hours to get here."

Yawning hugely, Rebecca replied, "Let's check into a hotel tonight … please."

Billings quickly answered, "No. We have to go to the lab first and have a quick look around. Do you have your electronic pad with you?"

"Yes."

"Could you bring up all of the camera angles?"

She had already pulled the pad from its case and replied, "Sure thing, Doc!"

Triggers:

The trophy shop was on high alert as more and more of the zombies lingered in the street.

Nick looked over at Sam and said, "We're gonna need more ammo. And more coffee! We only have nine rounds left for this pistol, and there are more than nine of those things out there."

Reaching her limit, Yolanda cried, "Oh my God, what are we going to do?"

Charlene took her hand and said, "Don't worry … the guys will take care of everything. You need some rest. Come with me to the back and we'll take a nap."

Yolanda fought back tears and sighed as if taking her last breath. "My family, they're all dead. What's gonna happen to me?" Her knees buckled and she slumped against the counter.

Charlene put her arm around Yolanda's shoulder and said, "C'mon, let's go to the break room."

Sam leaned toward Nick and whispered, "How far away is that gun shop?"

Nick thought about it for a moment. "About two miles, I think."

Sam looked outside again and said, "We need to get some things. When was the last time anyone tried to call the police station?"

"About an hour ago. They must be totally overrun." Nick thought about that for a moment and said, "We've got to go. We can leave the Segway with the boy and Ron. Let's go and break the news."

Ron gazed out of the window. He watched the street as intently as a prairie dog. As he reached a headcount of fifteen zombies, he was interrupted by Nick, who patted him on the back and said, "We need you to watch over things here while we make a run to the gun shop. We need more ammo and weapons."

Ron heartily agreed. "Make sure you bring back plenty. I'm counting over a dozen of those things, with more showing up every minute."

Joaquin stood there for a second, feeling left out. He said, "I wanna go. You guys might need me."

Ron shook his head. "No, Joaquin. You should stay here and help me guard the shop."

Sam added, "We're trying to go as light as possible, son. We'll be back before you know it."

"Okay, Mr. Sam, I'll keep watch … but I'm keeping the machete." He retrieved the blade from where it leaned against the Segway and twirled it as if he were a Samurai warrior. The men were amazed at his abilities. "I know what to do with this," Joaquin said as he scraped the machete across the metal door handle. Sparks erupted from the metal on metal friction.

Although the pair had been quiet, the noise of the truck's door closing drew the zombies' attention; they advanced toward Nick and Sam. Inside the vehicle, Nick revved the engine and it rumbled as he quickly backed out of the lot. The right rear tire rolled over the large-bosomed chest of a female zombie, and its artificial breast implant popped out. It looked like a fumbled football as it bounced and skidded across the pavement. Nick looked at the implant and smirked. "That's kinda funny. Gross, but funny." Then the truck's front tire rolled over the zombie's bleach-blond head and flattened it into the concrete surface. Sam studied the body for a moment and said, "Hmmm. To think – I may have dated her once." They both giggled crazily, realizing that the stress was finally getting to them.

In a lucky stroke of comedic irony, another zombie stepped onto the gel-filled implant and landed flat onto its back. It looked like an overturned stag beetle as it flailed and struggled to get back up. Both men completely lost it, howling with laughter.

Finally regaining control of his emotions, Nick gripped the steering wheel tightly. Sam sniggered quietly next to him. A few blocks later, Nick turned on the truck's high beams. The focused light brought into stark relief the horror of their situation, as dozens of shuffling zombies came into view. Some of the zombies were dressed in Hawaiian shirts caked with blood, while others were in full cowboy attire. Nick shook his head in disbelief and said, "Crap … it's Honolulu! They're coming from the ranches now. It's gotten worse."

Further down the street, dozens of zombies feasted on their victims like chimpanzees at a banana buffet. Sam could only stare and say, "Look at 'em all! How did this happen to our town?" Nick shook his head. All he could do was plow through the horde.

As he reached the rear guard of the pack of zombies, he accidentally smacked into another vehicle's rear bumper as it tried to cross through an intersection against the light. The impact forced the smaller car to spin around and roll over, coming to a stop against a light pole. A zombie that happened to be standing nearby was struck by the spinning car, the force ripping it in half. Nick slammed on the brakes and looked to see if he could help the other driver. The severely injured man had managed to pull himself out of the wreckage, just as the half-zombie crawled towards him. It reached his legs and pulled itself up to bite into his thigh and tear out a chunk of thick muscle. The man screamed in agony, then fell silent.

The sound of the accident had drawn other zombies to the area. While the men were distracted by the gory scene in front of them, a long-haired zombie had moved in closer, and now stood at the driver's side window. As it pounded at the window with its fists, Sam grabbed the pistol from the floorboard, got out of the truck and ran to Nick's side. Point blank, he fired a couple of rounds into the zombie's head, destroying it completely. Nick's face looked distorted through the slimy goo left behind on the window, as he yelled, "Get back in the truck! They're getting closer!" Sam ran back to the passenger side and entered the cab of the truck. Nick floored the accelerator, fishtailing the vehicle and leaving behind a black cloud of burnt rubber.

Outside of *Trigger's* gun shop, a few zombies loitered near the front door. Sam squinted and said, "We're gonna have to try the back door. We can't shoot everything we see."

Nick nodded in agreement and turned off the headlights as he drove around to the back of the shop. At the loading area, the men got out of the truck and Sam shone his flashlight on the door. Nick noticed it had already been broken open.

"Look. See the gashes on the metal handle?" Sam nodded, and Nick continued, "Grab that other flashlight from the glove compartment, and let's go in quietly. If you need to shoot one, one shot only."

Together, they entered the gun shop. Sam shined the flashlight's beam toward the showroom. A noise that sounded like a rifle's butt being scraped along the ground startled them, and they crouched low between several metal racks. Nick noticed hunting weapons to his left and assault weapons to his right. He practically drooled at the thought of using an assault weapon to mow down dozens of the horrific zombies. The scraping noise grew louder, and they moved to a better hiding place. Just as they'd thought, it was a zombie, dragging a rifle along behind it by a broken strap. Sam thought for a moment and said, "Let's take this one out."

Nick replied, "Yeah, but it's my turn." He scanned the nearby aisles, then crawled on his belly to retrieve a compound bow with arrows. Steading himself on one knee, he knocked the arrow into place and made sure to put the yellow odd vane out for accuracy. Sam had the pistol drawn, just in case his friend missed. Nick squinted at the zombie and zeroed in on a head tumor, letting the arrow fly. It smacked into the back of the zombie's skull, sounding like an old-fashioned wood bat connecting with a fastball. Nick whispered "Bull's-eye!" as the zombie tumbled to the ground. He hurried over and, placing his boot between its chin and sternum for leverage, pulled out the arrow along with bits of brain. The zombie exhaled deeply and then stopped moving.

They scouted the store for other zombies, and finding none, they loaded up with several shotguns, pistols and a few assault weapons. They also packed multiple boxes of ammo and arrows into a shopping bag.

Cross-Cut Saw:

Before he could move, Higgins had to take a moment to massage his throbbing hip. As he did so, he pressed his forehead back against the window. Down the street, he could faintly see another zombie as it fell down motionless, its skull seemingly divided in half. A fountain of blood sprayed into the air. The old man lifted his forehead off of the window pane and saw that an oily imprint had been left behind. The distorted print caused his reflection in the glass to look like one of the zombies. He did not like what he saw, and quickly turned his head. To his right, a sexy pin-up poster was tacked to the wall. He rubbed his eyes and mumbled, "I need a weapon."

Higgins scanned the room. In one corner, he spotted a long cross-cut saw used for cutting through large blocks of ice. He hobbled over to it and lifted it, then tried to swing the saw. Its weight was too heavy and he dropped it, thinking that he was as clumsy as a drunken ninja. He picked up the saw again and held it with both hands by the dull side, the sharp edge pointing toward the front. He figured it was better than nothing, and with a wink at the bikini-clad pin-up model, he said, "Guess this'll have to do."

Try and Remain Professional:

As the sedan approached Sporaton, Rebecca raised her head to get a better view. She sleepily said, "There it is. Sporaton Lab."

Doctor Billings said the driver, "When we get closer, let's wait just outside of the parking lot. We need to be sure nothing out of the ordinary is happening."

Bill lowered the volume on the radio and replied, "Yes Sir!"

He parked the car near the lot's entrance, and the trio watched as a tumbleweed rolled by. Ten minutes passed with no sign of movement from the lab or its parking lot, and Billings decided to wait no longer. "Let's go, Rebecca."

They got out of the car and walked across the lot. As they approached the entryway, they looked around for the thing they had seen on the monitors, but there was nothing except for a cloud of swarming gnats. Rebecca looked over her shoulder at Billings and happily said, "So far, so good!"

Her boss replied, "Yes, but where is everyone?" as he swatted at a bug that had landed on his cheek.

Rebecca fished through her purse for her duplicate set of keys to unlock the lab, but Billings tried the door and found it wasn't locked. As they walked into the fully-lit lab, they immediately noticed a large pool of blood at the receptionist desk.

Billings exclaimed, "Whoa, this isn't good."

Shocked by the amount of blood, Rebecca averted her eyes, tried to remain professional, and side-stepped the coagulated mess on the floor.

As they ventured further into the lab, Billings shouted, "Oh, dear Lord!" Lying on the floor, chest-down, was a dead man with his head in pieces around him. Billings heaved a little at the sight and said, "Ugh, this is really disgusting, but I need you to look, too." Rebecca steeled herself and took a close look as he added, "See how the neck is intact, but the skull is broken into pieces? Also, do you see those weird growths on the remaining bits of its scalp? I've never seen anything like them." She peeked at the body as he added, "It looks like it could be the person from the video, but it's impossible to tell for sure."

Rebecca pressed her hands against her stomach and struggled to hold back the bile rising in her throat. She wanted to throw up, but knew it would only make things worse. She finally answered weakly, "Yes Doctor. I see," then turned her head away.

All Country, All the Time:

Bill turned up the radio while he waited in the car, listening to an all country swing station. He opened the sunroof and windows to let the breeze in, then settled back into the seat to rest a bit after the long drive. He did not notice as a zombie slowly approached the car from the rear.

Billings was starting to feel the strain of exhaustion. As he took a step into the darkened break room, his heel unexpectedly slid out from underneath him. He did a jerky little dance as he struggled to keep his balance, and as he twisted and turned, he nearly fell into what he thought might have been a pool of blood. Gathering himself and his thoughts, he shouted, "Dial 911!" as he reached for the switch to turn on the overhead lights.

Rebecca shouted back, "Yes Doctor … I'll try again."

He surveyed the room, seeing two more bodies that looked as if they had been partially devoured. Each body had large chunks of missing flesh. The ribcage of one of the corpses had been pulled apart; the other body was armless, its limbs ripped off at the shoulders. Flesh and bone lay scattered across the floor, and there was blood everywhere. *How could two people not get past one attacker? There's gotta be more than one.*

Meanwhile, back at the car, the zombie moved slowly and methodically, moaning softly with each step. Its right arm pressed against the car's dusty side panels, sliming them. Its jaws opened wide, then snapped shut with an audible click.

Bill had slipped into a twilight state; lights and fantasy images swirled in the fog of his tired brain. He dreamed about being with his new romantic interest back home, thinking, *Two weeks together, and things are going great!*

As the zombie approached the driver's side door, its head began to pulse from the noise of the radio. The disc jockey announced, "This is Country Al … bringing you Al country, Al the time." The zombie's brain vibrated inside its skull, and as the gelatinous mass begin to enlarge, it stood motionless for a moment beside the car door. Then it clumsily reached through the window into the compartment and grabbed the sleeping man by his throat, pinning him against the seat. Bill nearly jumped out of his skin, startled and panicked, and screamed, "What the heck, man! Let go!" The zombie squeezed his neck even harder, and Bill's vision blurred. He lashed out and screamed, "Why are you doing this?" as he tried to identify his attacker. But it was too dark, and he couldn't get a good look as he struggled. His whole body shook as the thing ripped and tore into his flaccid stomach with its free hand. As its fingers pulled at Bill's intestines, the ripe odor of feces permeated the air. The zombie raised the warm coils of flesh to its lips and began devouring them with relish. Bill's adrenaline surged one last time, and he punched at the fiend with all the strength he had left, moaning, "Please God, no," as his vision dimmed, then went dark.

Rebecca walked into the break room and said, "There's still no answer from 911." As she caught sight of the carnage, she couldn't hold back the contents of her stomach any longer and vomited violently.

Billings said, "Rebecca, I'm so sorry you had to see this," and grabbed a stack of napkins from the nearby table to help clean her up. He whispered soothingly, "I'll get you out of here as soon as possible. But first I need to grab any files related to that last expedition. Sit here and rest while I look around."

She looked away from the bodies, knowing that she couldn't spend another moment in that room, and replied, "I'm coming to help you find them; they're probably in Harrington's office."

Billings replied, "Sure thing, of course." as he handed her a napkin to wipe the last of the stringy vomit from her face.

The zombie pulled Bill head-first from the car and proceeded to devour more of his flesh. His bloated intestines were sprawled everywhere, some draped over the car's door, some tangled in a heap on the ground, and the rest on top of him. They looked like balloon animals from hell. When the zombie had eaten its fill, it left Bill's crumpled body next to the car and staggered across the parking lot toward the lighted entrance of the lab. A country favorite finished playing on the radio, and the disc jockey exclaimed, "Call now and give us that trivia answer! Don't forget, we play AL country, AL the time!"

Airborne:

Pacing back and forth behind his Segway, Joaquin thought about his mother as she lay on the trailer's linoleum floor. He could not get the image of his father out of his mind. He also thought about Lindsey, and where she might be. Tired of just looking at zombies through the window, he decided to do something about them. While the others were momentarily busy back in the break room, Joaquin mounted the Segway and drove out the door. He wanted vengeance. *I'm going to kill them all.* He patted the machete dangling on the side of his leg. He drove one-handed, and exclaimed like a boxing ring announcer, "Round two – ding, ding, ding!"

The first zombie heard the whirr of the Segway and started moving toward it. Joaquin yelled, "You're going down, freak!"

He raised the machete and accelerated to top speed. As he passed the zombie, he swung the blade hard and it connected cleanly at the base of the thing's neck and severed the head with hardly any resistance. He spotted another freakish nightmare nearby and said, "This one is for my girlfriend!" as he spun the Segway around. He hopped a small curb with an elegant movement, dropped his right shoulder, and swung the machete in a broad arc, catching the zombie in the torso. He forced the weapon upward into the chest cavity and pulled back. Blood ran down the length of the blade and into the palm of his hand. Even though the zombie had been hewn practically in half, it reached for him. Joaquin dodged, sped past it and finished it off with a clean chop to the back of its neck. The force of the blow caused its head to fall four feet behind its body, and the rest of it fell, draped over a curb. He shouted, "Yee haw!"

Ron, who had heard the commotion and was watching through the window of the trophy shop, said to the others, "The kid's got some balls. And some moves."

He yelled at the boy to get back inside, but Joaquin shouted back, "I'm going to get a few more, Mr. Ron!" He turned to chase down another zombie. He yelled, "This one is for Ms. Charlene's family!" and carelessly segged between two zombies. Both zombies reacted, and one reached out quickly enough to grab the back of his shirt and rip a hole in it. He nearly fell off the Segway. Embarrassed, he shouted to Ron, "That didn't just happen." He spun the Segway around to take out the two monstrosities. Within seconds he was upon them, bringing down the machete to split open the skull of the closest. Swinging around quickly, he closed in on the second zombie and swung the machete, burying the blade in its face. It reached up and grasped the blade, but Joaquin held on even as he fell from the Segway, and landed with the blade still in his grasp. Other zombies, hearing the noise, began to lurch forward toward the fallen boy.

"RUN!" Ron screamed, but the teen was surrounded and Ron had to race outside to distract them. Charlene and Yolanda ran to the door. Another zombie was closing in fast, within inches of grabbing the teen. In desperation, the boy swung the machete and severed the zombie's reaching arm. The limb hit the ground first, its fist slowly clenching; the body followed seconds after. With no time to spare, the excited but frightened teen ran back to the Segway.

Get in the Back, Boy:

As they approached the store, Nick peered through the windshield and pointed across the street. "Is that Joaquin out there?"

Sam glanced over to where Sam had pointed and replied, "I think so."

Nick quickly added, "Then that boy is in trouble! Get the AR-15 out of the bag and put a mag in it."

Sam said, "Already on it!" as he pulled the weapon out of the bag. A half block closer, Nick slammed on the brakes and Sam jumped out of the truck and started firing at the zombies, mindful of Joaquin's location. After each deadly head shot, Sam readjusted his position and continued firing until he could clear a safe path for the boy.

Seeing their chance, Nick yelled to Sam, "Get back in the truck! I'm going in for him!" Sam jumped into the bed of the vehicle as Nick started to accelerate. The truck moved to within a few feet of Joaquin.

Freaked out, Joaquin looked like a deer in headlights. In a tone that brooked no argument, Nick yelled, "JUMP IN THE BACK, BOY!" Joaquin didn't hesitate; he scrambled into the truck, abandoning the Segway.

Midnight at Sporaton:

The zombie shambled toward the lab's lighted entryway, still hungry for flesh. Its left penny-loafer scraped the ground, leaving a cloud of dust in its wake. Its stiffened right arm swung back and forth like an out-of-sync metronome. The entire front of its lab coat was caked in excrement and blood, and bits of flesh framed its lips. It moaned, jaws opening and closing on thin air.

Baron Canyons:

Danny turned down the lantern outside of the tent as Susie got into the sleeping bag. He knew she would be waiting for him with open arms. After six months of dating, this was their first time camping together. The relationship was finally where it should be, especially after her last boyfriend turned out to be a real jerk.

Danny swigged down the last of his energy drink. He knew it wasn't good for him, but wanted the extra pep it would give. Up above, the Milky Way shone brightly. *It's a beautiful night for this adventure.*

As he stretched his arms behind his back, he heard rustling in the nearby bushes. He picked up his new battery-powered lantern and let it dangle from his left hand, then went to investigate. *Maybe it's just a coyote.* He walked directly toward the sound and made abrasive noises. As he got closer, he heard a low moan and decided that it was not a coyote, but rather, a small wounded animal of some sort. An animal lover, he felt sorry for the poor thing. *Maybe it's just hung up in the bushes. I could help it.* Besides, he did not want it to moan all night when he was back in the tent.

Susie squirmed on the air mattress and coyly called out to Danny, "I'm in bed, Danny, come on."

Danny picked up a stick along the way, and beat the bushes with it. A dark shadow arose, and he was brutally knocked to the ground. Something jumped on top of him. He felt his head being ripped apart, and gurgled as the zombie bit into his skull repeatedly, removing a large portion of his scalp and ear. As his senses faded, he wished he had just gone into the tent.

Impatient, Susie brushed her hair out of her face and sexily called out, "Danny? Oh, Danny?"

The zombie let go of his head. Its mangled foot and boot spur dragged in the dirt. It spastically moved towards Susie's voice.

Susie heard the sound of shuffling boots, and became more and more excited. As the tent flap began to open, she lifted the sleeping bag off of her chest and said,

"Here I am, Danny boy!"

Swatting at Flies:

As midnight approached, the survivors inside Unique Trophy Shop gazed thoughtfully at the pile of newly-acquired weapons covering the counter. With his own choice of assault rifle slung over his shoulder, Nick told them, "No need to worry. Everyone will have their own weapon."

Sam reached to pick out a weapon and spotted a semi-automatic rifle. He shook his head and said, "This is one bad boy!"

Charlene chose a pistol, and Yolanda picked the bow. She had the most experience using one.

"In college, I was on the archery team and I was ranked number three. I can handle this … I don't need a gun."

Nick smiled and said, "No problem." Ron and Joaquin each picked up a shotgun and several boxes of shells.

Sam turned from the window and said, "We're all gonna need sleep. I suggest Ron and Joaquin get first dibs, since Charlene and Yolanda have already gotten some shuteye."

After Joaquin had moved into the break room to take a nap, Sam pulled Nick to the side and asked, "Do you have a thermometer? I'm not feeling well."

Ron, overhearing the question, said, "I think I have one in the first-aid kit."

In a lowered voice, Sam mumbled, "Good, I'm gonna need it." He followed Ron to the back room and retrieved the old-fashioned mercury thermometer.

Nick wandered over to Charlene, who was examining her new weapon, and said, "Just pop the clip in like this!" He also took a few moments to give her a quick lesson on how to aim and fire the gun.

Joaquin had been practicing thrusting the butt of his shotgun at a make-believe zombie. When he was done, he walked over to the pistol demonstration and excitedly asked, "Do you think we'll be able to keep these after whatever is happening is over?"

Nick smiled at the boy as he replied, "Ahh … young man, these are going back to the gun shop when everything is under control. We're only borrowing them for the night."

Joaquin rolled his eyes. "C'mon man!" He held a shotgun shell up to the light and added, "One of these to the head, and it's all over. It makes my machete obsolete."

Nick directed his attention toward Yolanda and asked, "Can you use the bow to plant an arrow in that poster on the other side of the room? Nail that middle star."

She replied, "No problem." She grabbed the bow and nocked an arrow. She drew her arm back steadily and firmly; when she had her breath under control, she relaxed her finger and let the arrow fly. It left the bow with a snap and made the trip across the shop with near invisible speed. It hit the star dead-center, and penetrated four inches into the wall.

Nick chuckled and said, "You're hired!"

Yolanda smiled, pretended to dust off her shoulder, and said, "Uh huh!" It was the first time he'd seen her smile since it all began.

Sam reentered the showroom and reported to the group that he had a temperature of 101.5.

Charlene sweetly said, "Well, then, I guess you're getting the couch!" No one disagreed with her, and she walked Sam back to the break room to get him settled. Ron followed, and lined up several chairs side by side. He stretched out on the makeshift bench and promptly fell asleep.

Joaquin followed suit, placing the shotgun next to him on the floor. He closed his eyes and tried to think about Lindsey.

The zombie roaming around outside the trophy shop was enormous. Nick measured the zombie against a nearby stop sign and figured it could be at least six foot six. Joaquin, who couldn't sleep, got up and stood next to Nick. They both saw the immense zombie moving slowly toward the shop.

"Look at its girth, son; that thing has to be at least two hundred and sixty pounds."

Joaquin was not keen on being called "son" by this near-stranger, and curtly replied, "Yeah, could be ... looks that way." He was about to tell Nick not to call him son, but in the back of his mind, he could hear his mom telling him to be polite.

The huge zombie's head and neck were cocked forward awkwardly as it moved. It did not look up; thick drool dripped from its mouth. It was dragging one leg, sending up little puffs of dust with each step. The other members of the group who weren't napping now stood at the front window, watching through peep holes as the giant zombie moved ever closer to the shop. It stepped off of a curb onto the fragmented remains of a crushed head. Its undamaged foot smashed through the torso of another fallen zombie, forcing pressurized body fluids to spray through the air. It dragged the carcass for several feet before its foot broke free of the mangled rib cage.

A smaller zombie collided with the giant. The giant flailed its arms wildly and crushed the chest of the little zombie. The mangled thing crumpled to the ground, but got back up on all fours and began to crawl. It looked like a prehistoric insect. Its head and neck moved rapidly out of control as it followed along behind the behemoth.

Joaquin turned to Nick and said, "I'm going upstairs to get a better count. I'm not sure if I'm seeing them all."

Not wanting to leave the front door, Nick replied, "Good idea, son."

The teen snapped his heels together military-style and said, "Yes sir!" before heading up the stairs. Once topside, he surveyed the surrounding area. He noted that each zombie seemed to have its own peculiar way of moving, depending on its wounds. He counted quietly, but the zombies seemed to hear him and began to move even closer to the shop. Joaquin finished his survey and came back downstairs, hustling over to Nick. He reported at least a dozen more zombies than he could see from street level.

Yolanda had been roused and was listening to the report. She began to pace, working herself back into a frenzy. Charlene moved to her side and tried to comfort her.

Nick said, "It might be a good idea to turn off all the lights." Without hesitation, Joaquin hurried over to each light switch and flipped it down. Impressed at the quick response, Nick said, "Thanks! Now that's how you take orders. In a couple of years, you'll make a great Marine!"

Yolanda followed Charlene back into the break-room. Charlene shone a flashlight next to Sam's face. Beads of sweat dotted his forehead, and muscles twitched all over his body.

Yolanda whispered, "I hope he doesn't give us all the flu."

Charlene turned off the flashlight and walked to the other side of the room.

Already panicked, Yolanda added, "Oh my GOD! I can't get the flu. I need to stay away from him."

Nick had just walked into the break room and asked, "Stay away from whom?"

In a hushed tone, Yolanda replied, "Him!"

Nick knew she was probably exaggerating and asked Charlene, "How is he?"

She looked him directly in the eyes and said, "He's definitely coming down with something, and needs as much rest as we can give him."

Crane and Divine:

"Three-twenty in the morning." Higgins opened the fridge to grab an extra soda and shoved the can into his pocket. Carefully, he placed the cross-cut saw over his shoulder, its razor-sharp teeth pointed away from his neck. He spit into a trashcan and grumbled, "Now where's that back door?"

Higgins crept like a cat burglar through the rear door, listening for any moans. Hearing none, he placed his back against a white stucco wall and sidestepped down the sparsely lit alleyway. At the end of the alley, he took a left onto Crane Street and winced when he heard bloodcurdling screams. *Dang place is like a horror movie!* Ever since the atrocities of the Korean War, he hadn't been able to watch those types of movies. As he stayed out of sight using the utility boxes and parked cars on the street, he reminded himself, *Don't make a sound.*

At the intersection of Crane and Divine Streets, Higgins decided to sit on the curb between two abandoned cars to catch his breath. He reached into his bulging pants pocket and took out the soda can, opening it with a quiet hiss of carbonation. At that moment, he heard a loud moan that turned into a grunt of agony, and his back was splattered with blood and brain matter. He spun around just in time to watch a zombie fall to the ground a few feet behind him. Shaken, he used the saw as a crude crutch and stood up. After he regained his balance, he took off his blood-saturated shirt. He used the dry area that had been tucked into his pants to wipe off the back of his neck and arms. Still thirsty, he leaned over to grab the soda from the curb, but as he moved it toward his mouth he noticed a small blood spatter on the can. He threw it down angrily and crushed it under the heel of his boot. It was useless to him now; he was sure it had been contaminated. He whispered, "Crap! Hope none of those critters heard that."

<u>Trembles:</u>

Sam's head was pounding, so he opened his eyes and asked Joaquin to get him some aspirin from the first-aid kit. Joaquin tried not to be obvious as he peered at the dark circles under Sam's eyes. *That's gotta be from lack of sleep.* He said, "Yes sir, Mr. Sam." When he returned, Sam opened his hand to take the tablets, trying not to let the boy see his hand trembling. He quickly popped the extra-strength meds into his mouth and chased them with water. He laid his head back on the couch and closed his eyes. Joaquin whispered, "Hope you feel better," and exited the room. Sam placed his trembling hand under the weight of his leg so it could not be seen, or fall off the couch while he slept.

The chairs Ron had been sleeping on separated unexpectedly as he shifted positions, and he fell through, butt-first. Startled, he opened his eyes and said, "Dang it," then stiffly stood up and stretched. He rubbed his tired eyes and walked over to Sam. For a moment, he just stood there watching his face muscles slightly twitch. He whispered, "I don't like this," as he walked out of the room to relieve Charlene and Nick.

With a shotgun now in the crook of his arm, Ron got an update from Charlene and Nick. He then took his position at the window as the pair headed back to the break-room. Charlene quietly pushed Ron's three chairs back together, careful to not wake Sam. She stretched out on the chair bed and was asleep in minutes. Nick leaned his chair into a corner and tried to relax. After a few minutes of listening to Charlene's manly snores, and with too much on his mind, he gave up and walked over to take a look at Sam. *Oh man ... I hope he's gonna be OK.*

From the oppressive darkness, the enormous zombie appeared again, followed closely by the insect-like zombie on all fours. They moved toward the main entrance and tripped the motion security light. The bright light flashed on and illuminated the giant, stretching its shadow to horrific proportions. It lurched along near a plate glass window, slowed by its injured leg. The shattered end of its ulna protruded through the skin of its arm and scraped along the window, leaving a snail-trail of viscous gore. Joaquin and Ron ducked behind a counter, but noticed that Yolanda had not – she looked like she was about to scream. As quietly as possible, they both whispered, "Shhh!"

Yolanda placed her trembling hand over her mouth. She could barely manage to hold in her terror. Ron had to creep over to her and push her head down. The monstrosity continued shuffling past the entrance and on to the parking lot. It weaved back into the growing horde of zombies and disappeared between two buildings.

Joaquin tried to take another head count, but as Ron walked over he said, "There are just too many out there – I can't see 'em all!" What he *could* see was the abandoned Segway, and knew he had to get it back. He figured he'd wait until daybreak and then ask Nick and Ron to cover him while he retrieved it.

Ron patted the teen on the back and said, "Don't worry about the head count right now – I'm sure everything will be fine." From the pat, he could tell that the teen was tense, and tried to reassure him by saying, "Really! Don't worry; we're gettin' out of here and we'll find your girlfriend!"

Joaquin replied, "Man, I hope so. It looks worse than ever out there!"

Sunrise, Sporaton Lab:

Rebecca killed the first zombie by herself. With a surge of adrenaline, she hoisted a heavy chair and smashed it into the zombie's chest. The hideous being stumbled backward and fell to the ground. While it struggled to get back up, she lifted a nearby metal trash can and forced it down over the thing's head. It thrashed about wildly for a moment, and then somehow managed to stand halfway up. She picked up the chair for a second time and smashed it down on top of the can. She heard an audible pop as the zombie's head exploded. Syrupy dark blood flowed from the inner sides of the can onto its body.

Billings had trapped a second zombie behind a large desk. Its thighs strained against the desk as it tried to walk toward him, but Billings pushed back and managed to keep it at bay. It repeatedly muttered, "Shar-ha."

Standing behind Billings and distracted by the struggle, Rebecca did not see a third zombie enter the room through an inner office. Billings gave the desk one last push and ran for the closest fire extinguisher. As he spun around to hit the trapped zombie with the heavy canister, he saw the approaching fiend behind Rebecca. He tried to warn her, but it was too late – the thing had already grabbed her by the scruff of her neck and jammed its claw-like hands into her shoulder. She screamed as it penetrated all the way to the scapula bone. The zombie pulled her swiftly to its mouth and took a huge bite from her head. She fell limp in its grasp. It bit her again and removed a chunk of flesh from her neck. Enraged, the doctor smashed the cylinder repeatedly into the head of the cowboy zombie. As it crashed to the ground, he turned his attention to the other zombie still struggling behind the desk. Holding the cylinder over his head, he ran over and smashed the ghoul squarely in the face. The butt of the extinguisher pushed its face through the back of its skull.

When Billings was sure it was dead, he returned to Rebecca and put his fingers to her neck, trying to find the carotid artery. She was without a pulse. The side of her neck, which had been torn apart, now only trickled blood. There was nothing he could do for her. Billings laid her body down on the couch in the break room and covered her with a silver fire blanket. The zombie that had done the damage lay on the lab floor, its head bashed in. Pulverized brain tissue, splinters of bone, and other unidentifiable bits of gore had coagulated into thick goo that covered the zombie.

Billings threw his lab coat over the grotesque body to keep it hidden from his view. Blood seeped through the starched white material and blurred part of his embroidered name; only the letters 'ill' were visible, and that was exactly how he felt.

He ran outside to alert Bill and get help. As he approached the passenger side of the car, he saw only an empty, blood-saturated seat. Trying not to panic, he walked around to the driver's side, and then saw Bill's horribly mutilated body on the ground in a pile of his own bloody intestines. He swooned a bit and had tunnel vision as he made his way back to the lab. Billings went into an empty office, locking the door behind him, and called 911 again. Alarmingly, there was still no answer.

Phoenix; Team Two Coming Together:

Phoenix had been driving around since the outbreak started. He occasionally passed other survivors as they hunkered down to wait out the crisis. He found that, like him, most people in these parts figured they could handle whatever it was that had happened. It was a Texas thing. He never ran across any of his friends or co-workers as he drove around, and wondered who was alive or dead. He called 911 multiple times, but no one ever picked up the phone. He tried the lab at Sporaton, but had the same luck. To simply abandon those he knew and leave town was not an option, and he knew it was time to take matters into his own hands. He was determined to find out what had caused this nightmare.

The two girls that Phoenix had brought home from the bar were dead – killed by him. He could now say with certainty that they were not normal, especially after all of the things he had seen on the street. Something had definitely happened in Baron, but he had no idea what.

He stopped the car and quickly scribbled his first journal entry: *What turned these people into zombies?*

He looked up and spotted a couple of figures moving up the street toward him. A dust devil whirled through and temporarily obscured his view, but after the mini-tempest passed, he could see that these two figures walked normally. He called out to them, but they quickly ducked behind a car. He shouted a second time, saying, "My name is Phoenix!" He received no reply. Not sure if he was wrong about their condition, he proceeded cautiously down the street.

Medical Discharge:

Garcia, thirty-nine years old and medically discharged from the Marine Corps, looked at his patrol partner and said, "I think he's okay." There was no way to tell that Garcia had been medically discharged, unless one happened to catch a glimpse of his high-tech Proprio Sensor rocker foot and prosthetic leg.

Like all Marines, Garcia was familiar with every minute detail of the M4 carbine he carried. After studying the stranger, and without looking, he flipped the safety back on. His partner, Nolan, waved the man over.

Phoenix parked the car and got out slowly, approaching the two men with his hands up. It was obvious that he didn't behave or look like a zombie; the men lowered their rifles and greeted him with handshakes, inviting him to come with them.

Granola and Cola:

After a breakfast of granola bars and cola, Phoenix went on his first "patrol" with the guys. As they slowly moved through the town, they took care to avoid the main entry points of any neighborhood. In the newer idyllic subdivision of Summer Plains, intermittent screams could be heard behind the green stucco security walls. It was obvious that zombies outnumbered the living in that subdivision. All three men wanted to rescue survivors with guns blazing; unfortunately, they didn't have the numbers to ensure their own safety and success.

Garcia raised a fisted hand. The trio stopped and squatted behind a sport utility vehicle. Nolan glanced at Garcia, then at Phoenix. They wanted to know how it had all started for him; Phoenix got the hint and began his story:

"I got out of bed after having some fun with these two girls I'd picked up in a bar. They had gone to sleep pretty quickly, and I was hungry for a slice of the key lime pie I had in the kitchen. I got up, cut myself a slice and got a cold beer out of the fridge. When I was done, I fell asleep on my sofa. In my slumber, I could hear weird moans coming from the bedroom. I didn't know what to think, but I was hoping for the best so I ran into the room and jumped back into the bed, right between the two of them. When I opened my eyes a second later, 'Double D' just stared at me with these blank, deep-set eyes. Dark blood dripped from her … I mean, *its* mouth. It tried to grab me, but its arms were trapped under the blanket."

Nolan shuddered and said, "Ugh. Sounds like a bad night, dude."

Phoenix continued, "The other zombie grabbed my arm so hard that pain shot through my entire body. I had trouble breaking free from its grip, but I reared up on the bed and I did. The first one snapped at me with its huge, dark mouth. I rolled over the top of it and off of the bed, somehow managing not to be bitten. I don't even know how I pulled it off, because these things were all mouth."

Garcia thought about his own recent experiences as he looked around the street for any movement, then said, "Yeah, man. That's seriously messed up!"

Phoenix went on. "This is where it gets even freakier, if you can believe that. I stood there in my skivvies, and the freaks tried to come after me. I still had no idea what was going on. Their movements weren't normal at all – it looked like their joints were rusted and hinged. They were really slow, which was my saving grace. I yelled at them to tell me what was wrong, but neither said a word."

Nolan asked, "Did you shoot them?"

Phoenix took it as a sort of test question about his manhood. Stone-faced, he said, "I ran and grabbed the biggest butcher knife I could find. The things had followed me into the kitchen, but I was still hesitant. About that time, I heard screams coming from next door; it seemed like everything around me was going loco. The faces on those things were really distorted because of some nasty tumors that pulled at their flesh. It gave me the creeps. They came at me, so I stabbed the first zombie in the chest, between the ribs. The other one slightly scratched me with its fingernails; it drew some blood. I swung the long blade like a sword and connected with its neck. I got lucky, and hit the jugular vein on the first try. Blood sprayed everywhere. I couldn't believe that those efforts didn't stop the things from trying to grab me – I knew then that I had to get out."

Garcia asked, "Where did you go?" Nolan pointed out a few zombies that had moved into sight down the street.

Phoenix continued quietly, "I wasn't going to run outside nearly naked, so I dashed back into the bedroom to scoop up my pants. I happened to see my field ax on the shelf in my closet and grabbed it. The zombies had followed me back to the bedroom and were standing in the doorway – I smashed the ax into the first one's head, which split into two halves. The brain looked like gelatin; there was blood everywhere. It was so disgusting, I almost threw up. The other one lunged at me and I swung the ax again as hard as I could, connecting under its chin and sending the blade straight up into its brain. I hit it so hard that the cutting edge of the axe protruded from the top of its skull." Nolan nodded his head. He was satisfied.

Phoenix glanced down the street, and then concluded his story. "There's not much more to tell. I took a minute to put on some clothes and got out of the house as fast as I could. I didn't want to leave without checking on my neighbor first, so I ran over and knocked. While I waited, I called 911 on my cell to report what had happened. The operator never answered the phone."

Garcia and Nolan nodded. Garcia said, "Same thing here."

Phoenix continued, "After I hung up, I figured I had waited long enough for someone to answer the door, so I just let myself in. I found three people already dead on the floor. Two were side by side, and the other was in the bedroom. None of the bodies had those nasty tumors growing on them. I breathed a sigh of relief and drove straight to the police station."

Garcia poked his head above the vehicle. The zombies that had been nearby had already moved on. He said, "Well, my story is a little different. One of the good habits I've always had is noticing my surroundings. I'm always checking people out when in public. I was at the Texas Paint Store picking up a few supplies when a man walked in wearing coveralls. It was obvious he wasn't feeling good. Out of the corner of my eye, I could see that his face was kinda puffy, and he had really dark circles under his eyes. You know, I've been there before, forcing myself to go to work when sick." He paused, looked around, and then continued. "As I waited for my paint to be mixed, I watched the guy pacing back and forth, holding his head between his hands. I should have known something was really wrong, but I didn't want any trouble, so I ignored him. He sort of bent over; I thought he had dropped something, so I walked past him to the checkout counter. Another customer entered the store and walked to the same aisle as the sick man to grab a gallon off the shelf."

Having heard the story before, Nolan scooted over to the rear bumper of the vehicle and surveyed the street. Garcia continued, "I heard someone yell, 'Damn no!' and the sound of a scuffle came from the paint aisle. I ran over to see if I could help. The sick man was in the process of biting a chunk out of the guy's calf. The customer screamed and cursed at the attacker, beating at him with a one-gallon paint can, but the dude was latched on really good. The can popped open and baby blue paint spilled everywhere. Blood pumped from the leg wound and mixed with the paint. I grabbed a can of something heavy from a nearby shelf and smashed it into the back of the sicko's skull, but he wouldn't let go for anything. I didn't know what to think. I clobbered him again with the can and he finally let go, rolling over and lying completely still. I checked for a pulse but couldn't find one. I helped apply pressure to the calf of the other guy, then put him in my car and drove him to the hospital. Before we left the store, the owner told me to come back later because everything would be on the house."

Garcia stopped talking and flexed hard on the prosthetic foot, then continued. "At the hospital, I told the triage nurse what had happened. She immediately called for a trauma surgeon and other staff, and wheeled the injured guy to a treatment room. As I left the waiting area, I noticed that a lot of people seemed to have the flu, so I covered my mouth and nose with my hand and hurried out. I drove back to the paint store to collect my supplies, and was really surprised to find that the police hadn't responded yet. That's when I got hold of Nolan, here."

Now that their stories had been shared, it was time for the men to make a plan. As the only military veteran, Garcia figured he should be in charge. He drew a map in the sand. "Guys, we need to set up a secure perimeter around this place until help arrives. We'll assist anyone we can, as long as we're all in agreement. Are you okay with that?" Phoenix and Nolan nodded their heads, and all three shook hands.

Phoenix said, "Okay, so every few hours we'll patrol the block, and assign any other healthy folks we might find to help with food and foot patrols. I've got a gut feeling this is gonna last more than a few days." The men spread out to resume the patrol.

Five minutes into the patrol, the three men ran into a desperate woman trapped in an alleyway, surrounded by several zombies. Garcia gestured for the men to stay low, then sprinted toward the woman. The curved prosthetic, aided by a tiny computer, adapted to the terrain with precision. With each step, the high-tech foot kicked up rock and sand. In full combat mode, Garcia pulled out his Glock and hammered the zombies with rapid pistol bursts. He continued sprinting toward the woman, then leapt from an overturned mattress. Airborne, he fired several more rounds, striking the closest zombies and knocking them to the ground. The woman was able to flee through the path created by the bloodletting.

Phoenix had never been involved in live combat, and was glad Garcia was there to lead the way. He made a mental note to add what he had just seen to his journal. The woman ran straight to Phoenix and Nolan, and hugged them both. Garcia backed up, then fired another burst of kill shots to finish off the rest of the zombies. He returned to the group, and the four hurried back to the paint store.

Daybreak at the Unique Trophy Shop:

Nick rubbed his fingers through his short beard and reluctantly said, "Okay Joaquin, it's a good idea, but let's check Sam first." They walked into the break room and stood at the foot of the couch. Sam's face was beaded with perspiration. Nick backpedaled to the doorway of the room and asked Charlene to give Sam more aspirin.

Joaquin snapped to attention and replied, "I'll give them to him, Mr. Nick," and turned to retrieve the bottle.

Charlene heard Joaquin, but told Nick that she would give Sam the meds anyway. She felt horrible about having to wake him. She walked into the room and shook his shoulder. He did not stir. She noticed how tortured his face had become and said aloud, "He's so stiff."

She picked up his hand and squeezed it as Joaquin said, "C'mon, Mr. Sam. Wake up and take this!"

Without opening his eyes, Sam muttered, "Leave me alone."

In her best Nurse Nancy voice, Charlene replied, "Sam, you're running a high fever. You need more medicine."

He opened his eyes, squinted, and closed them quickly, saying, "The light's too bright." Charlene noticed that his eyes were severely bloodshot. Sam reached out for the meds, but his hands trembled and he could not make them stop. Charlene had to place the tablets directly into his palm. Without reopening his eyes, he took the pills with a gulp of water. Satisfied that they had done everything they could, Charlene turned out the lights. The three left Sam alone in the room, giving each other worried glances.

Texas Paint Store:

Michael ushered Phoenix, Garcia, Nolan, and the woman they had just rescued into the store. A small group of people, found earlier by Garcia and Nolan, was gathered there. Someone barricaded the door behind them as the group came together to hear about the gunfire and rescue of the woman. Nolan walked over to the paint mixing machine and laid his gear on the counter. He gave a quick recap of her rescue, then asked, "Miss, I don't mean to be impolite, but what's your name?"

The thin thirty-year old replied, "Adele."

Johnny, one of the people who had been waiting in the store during the skirmish, walked to the front of the counter and asked, "How's your family?"

Adele sat down on a nearby stool, hunched forward, and replied, "My husband turned into one of those things while he was at home. He was out of his mind. I'm thankful we never had any kids." She picked up a paint color card that had been lying on the counter nearby and fiddled with it as she added, "I think that was about the time this whole thing began." Dora, who had been sitting nearby, thought about her own family. She looked over at Adele. *That poor lady is gonna need a lot of help.* She offered a hug, but Adele turned her back on her.

Vicki pulled her long brown hair out of her eyes, and with one well-practiced motion, clipped it back out of her face. She looked through the peep hole to check the street. Without moving her eyes from the small hole, she said, "Oh boy, one of those things is coming really close."

Ziggy, tall and lanky, stooped to grab his carbine and ran over to another peep hole six feet above Vicki. In a heavy Texas drawl, he confirmed the sighting.

"Yep … that thing is close by, alright! What y'all say? Do I pop it?" Garcia and the rest of the group gave him the thumbs-up.

Almost under his breath, Thomas said, "Why don't you let Vicki do this one?" Secretly, he thought she was a little soft and could probably use the practice.

Vicki turned and faced him. "Yeah, I'll do it!" She grabbed Ziggy's carbine and quickly pushed the rifle's muzzle through the firing hole.

Nolan moved in close and whispered in her ear, "Take your time, hold your breath, and squeeze the trigger when you're ready."

Though she had never fired a rifle before, she confidently replied, "Okay, I got it," and watched as the wretched zombie closed the gap. Deep down, she felt sorry for the thing. *Can't let anyone know.* She had been one of the lucky ones who had escaped from Baron Community Hospital. As a registered nurse, she had seen some of the first patients come through the door. In theory, she had no problem with the shooting of these zombies, but deep down wished she didn't have to be the one to kill them.

She readjusted her hair clip and squinted through the carbine's sight. The zombie had lumbered ever closer to their position.

Adele moved to her side and asked, "Well, how close is it?" Without answering, Vicki held her breath and squeezed the trigger. The end of the barrel flashed brightly, and the weapon's recoil pushed her backward. The round struck the zombie just above its left eye; the whole side of its skull disintegrated, spilling its brain onto the street. Vicki screamed – not from the recoil, but from the goriness of the scene before her. She had seen many traumas in the past, but never caused by her own hand.

Excited, Thomas blurted out, "Well, did you get it?"

She finally exhaled, and with a shaky voice, replied, "Yep!" He moved her gently to the side, peered through the hole, and confirmed the kill. Then he gave her a big high five.

Beginner's luck, thought Vicki.

Garcia called for everyone's attention, and reminded the group that they had a rescue mission to do. Dora, divorced and childless, grasped both of his hands and said, "Thank you so much." Not knowing the fate of her elderly mother and father was tormenting her. She clenched her teeth as she struggled to hide her feelings, a habit ever since her father had told her to never show fear. That long ago day, as she was placed atop a pony, she'd clenched her teeth and smiled.

Her father was now confined to a wheelchair; his poor health did nothing to help ease her mind. Even though he was a handful, her mother still lovingly cared for him. Dora had tried to convince her mom to put him into an assisted-living home, because she was clearly overwhelmed, but her mother would have none of that. She took care of him just as she had always promised on the day they spoke their marriage vows.

Garcia, Thomas and Ziggy stood at the exit, ready to head out for the rescue mission. Johnny grabbed the address off of the table and said, "Let's do it!" Garcia winked reassuringly at Dora and pushed the door open. They climbed into Ziggy's extended-cab pickup truck, with Ziggy in the driver's seat.

Garcia, squeezed between the other men, asked, "You know where this house is?"

Ziggy wiped the sweat from his brow and replied, "Yeah, it's just on the outskirts of town, not quite as far as those dude ranches."

Thomas, afraid but trying desperately not to show it, said, "When we get there, let's drive right up to the house. I don't want any of that 'parking blocks away' stuff to 'sniff out the place.' If we're going in, may as well go all in."

Ziggy shrugged and replied, "No problem, dude." He floored the gas pedal.

He navigated through the town, running over several zombies in the process. The zombies were obliterated upon impact with the large truck. Body parts and bits of gore clung to the windshield, and a foul odor wafted into the cab, forcing Thomas to open a vent. Unfortunately, that seemed to make the smell in the cab even worse, so he closed it quickly. Ziggy turned on the windshield wipers, but realized too late that he was out of the light blue windshield cleaning fluid. The wipers just smeared the gore into an arc. "Damn it!" To him, most of the walkers outside looked as if they had just ascended from the netherworld, but a few of them looked as though they had just gotten out of bed, teetering right on the edge of appearing normal. Only a few of the zombies had the bigger growths on their head, and they looked the creepiest.

Johnny tried to break the tension by saying, "Man, I'd do anything for a cold one right now!" The others chorused their agreement.

Thomas spotted an easy target and prepared himself to make a quick kill. As he lifted the weapon, Garcia pushed the barrel back down and said, "Whoa, conserve your ammo. Save it for action at the house ... if there is any."

Thomas snapped back sarcastically, "Got it, sir!"

Ziggy slowed the truck and tried to diffuse the situation. "Now c'mon boys, let's be grownups about this. Thomas, you know Garcia has combat experience."

Thomas rolled his eyes and replied, "Yeah, right. But does he have zombie fighting combat skills?"

The question caused Garcia to pause. Not wanting to make a big deal about his experience, he deflected the indirect question and said, "Just treat 'em like terrorists. I assure you they're not humans any longer. If her parents have turned, I'll kill them myself."

Ziggy weaved in and out of the empty vehicles that littered the road. Wherever they looked, the rescuers saw lots of blood but no bodies. As they passed the town's "welcome" sign, Ziggy's voice deepened. "'Bout eight minutes, people."

Garcia cleared his throat and said, "Let's pull into the parking lot of the old train station and talk a second."

Johnny replied, "Why? We're almost there. Action time!"

Ziggy ignored him and pulled into the parking lot as Garcia had suggested. According to a brass plaque displayed at the entrance, the building had been built in 1885. It was framed beautifully by the Caprock Mountains in the distance. The simple architectural design was reminiscent of the World's Fair of 1903: a beautiful red brick building with white wooden trim.

After a quick scan of the nearly vacant parking lot, Garcia said, "This is good. We'll talk right here." He sat forward in the seat and tried to maintain eye contact with each man as he continued, "This is going to be a two-man search and rescue. No sense in putting everyone in danger. So, it's gonna be Thomas and myself."

Johnny shook his head and replied, "Wait just a second. I'm coming, too."

Ziggy revved the truck's engine and said, "Me too – and by the way, it's my truck."

Garcia sighed with exasperation and said, "Guys, this isn't a U.S. military operation, but common sense dictates our course of action. I have the most combat experience, and know it's the right thing to do. That's why I've already made the decision for you. No sense in arguing. Get out of the truck and wait here. That's an order. If we're not back in twenty-five minutes, then hotwire a car from the lot and get back to the group." Ziggy and Johnny could not argue with his logic, and climbed reluctantly from the truck.

Johnny kicked at the dirt and said, "Yeah okay, man. If that's how you want it." As Thomas drove away, the two men who had been left behind slung their carbines over their shoulders and walked toward the large double doors of the station.

Ziggy pointed at the entrance and said, "Let's wait on those benches by the doors."

As the two sat down on one of the wooden benches, Johnny said, "I've always loved this station. My dad used to bring me here when I was knee-high, just to watch the trains roaring in. He'd buy us an orange push-up ice cream, and we'd sit on a bench facing the track, watching the people coming and going."

Ziggy shrugged off the bad memories of his childhood and replied, "That's cool, man. Wish I had a memory like that."

<u>Rescue:</u>

Garcia checked his ammo mag and addressed Thomas. "I hated leaving those two behind, but they'll be better off if we run into trouble."

Curious, Thomas asked, "Why did you pick me to go along? Not that I have any problem with it."

Garcia checked his backup magazine and replied, "Because I think you understand more than they do about what we're up against. You're more cautious and won't take any unnecessary risks. In battle, you have to be that way."

Thomas smiled at the praise, and replied, "It's cool. We'll get those old-timers out of there and be on our way. Military-like, right?"

Garcia smiled, double checked his safety and said, "Yeah. Military-like."

Thomas stopped the truck five feet from the steps of the obviously well-loved home. It was a ranch-style dwelling that Dora's father had built in 1969 – the same year the first man landed on the moon. It was nicely landscaped and had lots of squared-off hedges. Beautiful potted ferns hung from the underside of the porch roof.

Garcia locked and loaded his rifle, then switched the safety to the off position. He got out of the truck and quickly scanned the area. He turned to Thomas and said, "Okay, let's go – but keep quiet."

Thomas got out, leaving the truck door open, and the two walked forward and entered the house. Immediately, they could smell the aroma of burnt food. Thomas tapped Garcia's shoulder and pointed his thumb down. Garcia mouthed, "Yeah, but we have to have a positive I.D."

As they walked around the tidy home, Thomas noticed that it hadn't been remodeled since the house was built, and it had a nice Texas flair. Some of the rooms had planked wooden floors, while another still had the original orange shag carpeting from the 1970's. Thomas saw a picture of Dora on the mantle in the living room. She was dressed in her high school graduation cap and gown. Almost imperceptibly, he whispered, "Pretty."

Garcia made his way to the entrance of the master bedroom, Thomas following a few feet behind. They entered the room and saw the head of an eight point buck mounted on one wall.

Thomas asked, "Why on earth would they have that in the bedroom? Weird."

Garcia's nose started to twitch as he fought to hold in a sneeze. He whispered over his shoulder, "Never did like the smell of mothballs – we need to get out of this room." They checked out the rest of the house, but it was empty as well.

Thomas chuckled and said, "Let's go out to the barn and get you out of mothball alley."

The two men left the house and walked toward the barn, Thomas about twenty paces behind Garcia. When the vet reached the red and white doors, he stopped and waited. Because of the sun's glare, when he glanced up at the triangular-shaped roof, the building appeared smaller than it actually was. Reaching the entrance, Thomas tapped Garcia on the shoulder and said, "I'll go in first this time."

Garcia grinned, realizing that he couldn't take point all of the time and had to show that he trusted the man. He bent slightly at the waist like a loyal butler and with an elegant flourish said, "Be my guest, sir!"

Johnny and Ziggy:

To help pass the time as they waited for the others to return, Ziggy danced around like a Native American on the warpath. Johnny laughed at the birdlike movements as Ziggy lifted one leg, and then the other, adding a funny little hop in between. Eventually tiring of clowning around, he told Johnny, "Okay, now I've got to go to the bathroom."

Johnny grinned. "Not a problem dude!"

With one of his long legs, Ziggy gently pushed open the front door of the station. He kept a loose finger on his carbine, ready to mow down anything that looked even remotely like a zombie. With his back to a wall covered in Old West photographs, he crept down the hallway, passing a couple of corpses that lay on the ground. He didn't stop to examine them, but could clearly see that they had been gutted and partially consumed. The dead freaked him out; he especially hated funerals. He mumbled, "At least they aren't moving." He continued down the hall, not looking back. He slowly made his way to the bathroom as he listened for moans or other sounds. Not hearing anything, he entered the restroom and leaned the carbine up against the urinal. While he took a long leak, a rock song played in his head, and he made the yellow stream go up and down in time with the beat.

Johnny surveyed the parking lot through the waves of heat that rose from the ground, but didn't see any movement. He looked at the few cars parked there, and thought about which ones might be easiest to hotwire. He closed his eyes; the hot, dusty day was beginning to get the better of him. He daydreamed of an ice cold watermelon, and of eating it under a shady tree, a beautiful woman at his side.

By the time Ziggy saw the reflection of the zombie in the shiny tile, it was too late. The thing had come up behind him quietly, a long, antique rod impaled in its chest. Its head was a mass of freakishly large tumors and twig-like growths. Its enlarged neck muscles pulsated, and its intestines were looped several times below its waist, like a cowboy's rope. As it closed in on him, the rod actually poked Ziggy in the back, startling him. At the same time, a hand grabbed his head and slammed his face into the tile; everything went black. The impact was so brutal that his heart stopped beating before the zombie could take its first bite.

A shirtless, rotting zombie with a wicked snarl stumbled among the parked cars. Once a well-built woman, a single breast appeared as though it had been hacked off with a long blade. Its face was smashed in which gave it the look of a pug nosed canine. An exposed mandible showed a rotted row of teeth. A noise had drawn its attention, and it bumped into several vehicles as it searched for the source of the sound. It finally made its way onto the sidewalk, just shy of where Johnny dozed on the bench.

Johnny's head was arched back as he snored noisily. His carbine was in his lap at the ready. He was dreaming about feet. They were nice feet, toenails beautifully polished. He heard a strange moan and swam toward consciousness, He heard something moan again. *Am I still dreaming?* The zombie moaned louder as it closed in, spittle dripping from the corner of its mouth. Johnny woke in time to see the horror. He raised his gun and groggily fired off a couple of rounds, striking the zombie's body in several areas. It went down on one knee, then got back up and lunged forward. Blood and gore drenched the porch. Even though it was wounded and moving slowly, Johnny's fear and clumsiness evened the odds in the battle. When he finally managed to get up off the bench, he stumbled in the zombie's direction. It swiped at him and knocked the rifle out of his hands. Surprised, he yelled "Frack!" just as the thing slashed at him with its other hand, ripping open his gut. Johnny threw himself sideways and tried to retrieve his rifle. The effort caused his intestines to unravel, spilling them to the ground in a sickening heap. More worried about his guts than about crawling away, he tried in vain to push them back into the hole. The zombie grabbed him by the foot and yanked hard. Johnny reached at the same time to find something to hold on to, and miraculously, one hand found his fallen weapon. He pulled it up and fired several rounds at point-blank range, right into the zombie's head. The head exploded and splattered brain matter all over the zombie, Johnny, and the porch. Frightened beyond anything he had experienced since the outbreak began, he kicked out at the corpse with both feet and shouted, "You rotted piece of crap!" Then he looked down and groaned, "Oh my God! My stomach … oh, God."

Johnny tried to stand up, but instantly fell back toward the bench. He attempted to gingerly push more of his intestines back into the cavity, as if he were poking feathers into a pillow. He was petrified. Blood was pooling on the wooden porch – a lot of blood. He closed his eyes, not wanting to look at his guts or the bloody mess any longer, and yelled repeatedly for Ziggy's help. In between his pleas, he whispered, "Geez, how long does it take to pee?"

Point Taken:

Garcia made it a point to walk on the soft clumps of hay that were scattered throughout the barn. It felt better on his bad leg than walking on hard pavement. He stayed behind Thomas to give him the sense of leadership that he'd sought out in taking the forward position. They searched the entire barn, including the high lofts, but found nothing.

Walking back to the barn's entrance, Thomas turned and said, "Thanks for the point, man." He paused for a moment, thinking, then said, "You know, these old ranches usually have storm cellars. Maybe that's where they are, too afraid to come out."

Garcia gave him a congratulatory pat on the back. "Now that's a good point, man. Great idea! We'll just take a quick look inside, and then head back. We don't have much time before the guys leave us behind."

Thomas looked at him and asked, "Do you really think they would?"

Garcia shrugged his shoulders and replied, "With elderly people, I don't know."

Phoenix at the Paint Store:

Phoenix asked Dora to station herself on the rooftop and keep an eye on the street from above. Nolan kept watch at the barricaded windows. Vicki and Adele were taking a quick catnap. Satisfied that everything was under control, he grabbed his rifle and said, "Hey Michael – it's time for a block patrol. Wanna come?"

Michael put his burrito down, got up from the chair, and replied in his best "Igor" voice, "Yesss Master. Just let me get my stuff."

Watching horror and sci-fi movies had been Michael's preferred pastime. His favorite sci-fi scene of all time was the one where the creepy little alien burst from the man's chest. That one scene kept him sleepless for many nights. During those sleepless nights, he would stare up at the stars and fantasize about cool space adventures and defeating evil aliens.

As he followed Phoenix from the store, Michael began daydreaming about aliens and writing his first sci-fi book. As they patrolled, a zombie emerged from the Alamo Stationary door. It caught Michael by surprise, and in his confusion he reached out to the zombie, imagining it to be some sort of strange humanoid that he should make first contact with. Time stood still as it reached for his extended hand and yanked him towards its gaping mouth. It clamped its jaws onto his head and bit down hard.

Phoenix glanced back and saw the drama unfolding. He quickly dropped to one knee and squeezed the trigger of his weapon, just as the zombie bit into Michael. The bullet entered the misshapen head through its eye and created one large hole. Its jaws released Michael, who fell to the ground covered in spinal fluid and brains. Phoenix bent down to help him up, and saw that Michael's brain had been exposed by the bite. He ripped Michael's shirt from his teetering body and held it against the wound as a pressure dressing. Then he pulled the weakened man along and said, "C'mon, we have to get out of here."

Michael struggled against unconsciousness. Incoherent, he asked, "Wha ...?"

Phoenix replied, "You were bitten by a zombie, Mike. You tried to shake its hand." He half-carried, half-dragged the wounded man down the sidewalk, toward the relative safety of the paint store. "What were you thinking?"

From the corner of the rooftop, Dora saw them coming. She ran downstairs and blurted out, "Open the door! Michael's injured! They're almost here."

Nolan held the M4 at the ready and counted down, "Three, two, one," then swung the door open so Phoenix could drag Michael inside. Dora looked over Nolan's shoulder just before he slammed the door shut, and could see several dozen looming shufflers.

Frantic about their worsening situation, she said, "This really doesn't look good. I hope they come back with my parents fast."

Nolan, picking up on her anxious vibe, replied, "Don't worry. It shouldn't be much longer."

<u>Golden Delicious:</u>

"This will do, I guess," Higgins said, as he bent to pick up the tree branch that he planned to use as a makeshift cane. He was in a hurry, because several zombies now occupied the same street. His hip was throbbing, and he took a few practice steps with the new cane before heading off to find a hiding spot. He pushed his black-rimmed eyeglasses onto the top of his head and wiped his brow. *Dang critters been running me ragged. I need a drink.*

A zombie jolted into motion as it heard the sound of the branch being scraped along the ground and began to follow. Every few minutes, Higgins ducked behind a building, car, or tree to hide for a second and rest his hip. Ten minutes later, he happened on an open car door and an opportunity for a quick lunch. An apple was sitting pretty inside the car; he never could pass up a Golden Delicious. He put the heavy saw down, leaned on the branch, and reached in to pluck it from the dashboard.

Forty feet away, the zombie looked a little like an upright inchworm, undulating from the top down as it struggled to reach the source of the sound it had heard. Its soft fuzzy slippers made little noise as it somehow propelled itself across the lawn. It was lured forward by the crunching of the apple as the old man took bite after bite. Higgins, completely engrossed in his meal, plopped down on the curb and took the last juicy bites out of the apple.

Higgins' last few core-scraping nibbles took him all the way down to the seeds; he felt like Johnny Appleseed as he spit a few pips onto the dirt. Apple consumed, he tossed the hourglass-shaped remnant toward a tree, and pulled his saw and cane closer to his side.

Speckled with blood, the zombie now stood directly behind the old man. Its shadow was cast behind it, so Higgins had no idea that it was there. Thin, bloodied fingers extended and reached for his shoulder. As a small hand clutched him tightly, Higgins squeaked in surprise and tried to twist around to see who or what had grabbed him. Partially turned, he saw that the zombie was a young girl, still in her nightgown. *How can she be so strong?* He lost his balance as he tried to stand and fell directly on top of the small body. The fall had broken both its grip and its arm. The zombie's right arm now dangled useless at its side, but its jaws snapped wildly. Higgins rolled to the side and retrieved the saw, then stood up. Feeling sorry for the kid, he backed up against a car. Reluctant to do what needed to be done, he shouted, "Get back you … THING!"

The child zombie lunged forward once again. Higgins was petrified, and raised his saw as he said, "If you take one more step, I'll hit you with this! I mean it!" It did take one more step. With all of his strength, Higgins swung the saw and connected with the zombie's neck. The blade penetrated just below the ear, nearly severing its head, which now dangled. Blood sprayed the air, and the body fell to the dirt. Frustrated, Higgins wiped at his tears and shouted, "I told you to leave me alone, kid. Dang it!" Exhausted, he crawled into the car, locked all of the doors, and hid on the floorboard.

Unique Trophy Shop:

Joaquin jumped from the truck before it came to a complete stop, then ran over to the Segway, dodging a zombie that tried to grab him along the way. Amazed by the boy's courage, Ron shook his head and said, "That's one crazy kid!"

Nick swung his door open, propped his carbine on the rubberized seal of the window, then fired a two-round burst into the zombie's head. The head exploded and the body crumpled into a heap. He glanced at Ron and said, "That thing was gettin' too close to the youngster."

Joaquin turned the key on the Segway, but nothing happened. He yelled out to the guys, "It won't start!"

For a moment there was no reply, because Nick and Ron had been distracted when they saw something large starting to move toward Joaquin. Nick cleared his throat and yelled, "Then just leave it! That big zombie – it's back again!"

Joaquin shouted back, "No! I need it! I'm gonna put it in the truck!"

Nick targeted the zombie as it moved between the other zombies and vehicles. "I'm trying to get a clear shot."

Ron got out of the vehicle and aimed his rifle just beyond the kid, where another zombie was creeping up behind him. As it reached for the back of Joaquin's neck, Ron pulled the trigger. The bullet ripped through its shoulder. The impact spun the body around. He fired his rifle again and the round struck above the right eye. The deformed head exploded. Blood showered the street, and the zombie fell to the ground atop its own exposed arm bone. The fractured bone penetrated its flank and protruded through its back. Tired of trying to reason with the teen, Nick shouted, "You're crazy, boy. Get in the truck NOW!" Joaquin dragged the immobile Segway to the truck and loaded it into the bed singlehandedly. He hopped in beside it and leaned against the wall nearest the cab.

Back in the driver's seat, Nick gunned the truck and mowed down a handful of nearby zombies. Unexpectedly, a severed finger with a plain gold band hit the inside of the tailgate. Joaquin's eyes zeroed in on the ring, and he instantly thought about the promise ring he had wanted to give Lindsey. He picked up the finger and flung it back out of the truck. *Gotta get that ring for her. Maybe she'll stop singing that song.*

***

Charlene peeked outside from between a gap in the boxes. "I don't know if you guys have noticed, but there are a lot more zombies out there."

Stressed from their recent misadventure, Nick snapped, "Yeah, we noticed!" and walked over to a display case. Picking up a large, faux-diamond trophy, he tossed it like a baseball back and forth between his hands.

Ron turned to Charlene and asked about Sam. "Is he doing any better?"

She shook her head sadly. "It's not good. We should probably try for the hospital soon. Maybe a doctor can help him."

Nick practically dropped the trophy in his hand, saying, "We're all gonna have to pitch in to carry him. He's a big dude."

Over in the corner, Joaquin tinkered with the Segway, finding that a loose wire had been the culprit in its failure to start. He got a few tools and some duct tape from the storage room, and quickly fixed the problem. He turned it on and did a few lazy circles around the showroom, just to make sure everything worked. Nick, who had been watching Joaquin fix the Segway, turned and said to Ron, "That kid amazes me, but I swear, if he ever tries a stunt like that again ..." Ron nodded his head in agreement.

Sam was looking progressively worse as time went by. They all pitched in to carry him out of the break room, except Yolanda. She refused to touch him. Instead, she held open the front door for them, leaning as far away as possible to avoid even the slightest chance of contact. They laid Sam gently in the bed of the truck and put a cushion under his head. Nick felt terrible for his friend and was hopeful that they'd find help at the hospital. As he looked back at the trophy shop, he had a sudden premonition that he wouldn't be returning. Deep down, he figured the town would soon be put on quarantine or something like that, because for every zombie he shot, another took its place. Ron stood in front of the truck, shooting several approaching zombies. When the coast was clear, they took off for the hospital.

Throughout the ride, they saw many, many more of the zombies. Frustrated, Joaquin stopped counting. He threw his hands up and said, "Useless!" remembering as he did so that his father had used the same mannerism. He tapped the rear window and said, "I give up!"

Charlene scooted toward him and placed her hand on his. Looking into his eyes, she said, "You can't give up, hon. Hang on. I promise it'll get better."

The corner of his lip curled up in perfect teenage contempt as he said, "You don't understand – I was only talking about keeping a tally of the zombies."

Two Minutes to Go:

Thomas lifted the storm-cellar door and peered into the darkness, searching for the elderly couple. Garcia tapped him on the shoulder and said, "Let me go in first this time."

Thomas half-jokingly replied, "Geez, you still don't trust me."

Garcia tried to break the tension, and replied like a famous movie star from the golden age of Hollywood, "No, no, no, mon ami! It's not like that!" He grinned. "Okay, you go ahead."

Thomas smiled and shook his head, then descended the stairs. As he reached the floor of the cellar, he heard muffled noises coming from a darkened corner. Thomas whispered, "That must be her parents," and began to inch forward. His fingers drummed on the stock of the weapon.

Garcia's prosthetic crunched on the sandy cement floor. He whispered, "Take it nice and easy, and keep the noise down."

Thomas looked over his shoulder and smirked. "Really, man?"

At the far end of the cellar, they saw the back of a gray haired woman. She was covered with a blanket, and appeared to be trembling. At first glance, Thomas thought she looked like a typical grandmother, shivering in the cold, but he had to be sure. He whispered, "I'll go get her," as he advanced. Speaking to her as though she were his own grandmother, he asked, "Maw-maw? You okay?" She moaned. With the tip of the rifle barrel, he lifted the hand-quilted western blanket she'd been draped with. She turned her head toward Thomas, and he backed away in horror and disbelief, slamming into a shelving unit. Glass jars filled with nuts, bolts and screws shattered as they hit the ground. A bald zombie poked its head out from behind a deer antler coat tree, drawn by the noise. Its face was sunken, but its neck muscles were grossly enlarged. It staggered forward and groaned. "Nag-maw!"

The old woman stood and moved toward Thomas. He opened fire, bullets striking the zombie multiple times in the torso. Bloody craters pocked its body as it continued its advance. Again, he opened fire, and rifle bursts lit up the cellar with bright flashes. Most of the rounds missed and ricocheted off of the walls of the cinderblock basement. Both men ducked to avoid the flying shrapnel. Thomas was shaking so much that he couldn't make the fatal headshot. The flashes of light made the old female look like an unholy ghoul from the underworld. Realizing that Thomas was not going to be able to stop the zombie, Garcia stood tall and took the kill shot. Instantly, the zombie's head burst. Fleshy debris was strewn all over the small, confined space. Fragments of tissue dripped from the walls and oozed down a 1970's poster portraying a muscle car. Thomas freaked as the old dead male began to advance. It reached out for him like Frankenstein's zombie. Garcia fired on the walking corpse, but it grabbed Thomas's head and one shoulder. It shoved him to the floor and straddled his waist. Thomas struggled to get back up, but was entangled in a living hell.

Garcia hesitated to take another shot for fear of killing his partner during the close struggle.

Thomas screamed in terror. "He's got me! Do something!"

Garcia stepped forward and hit the thing in the back of its head with his rifle butt, but it was unfazed. Thomas continued to struggle and screamed again as the zombie's mouth latched on to his arm. The force of the bite nearly severed his limb; it hung by only a few muscle strands and tendons. The thing tried to bite him in the head even as Garcia continued to rifle-butt its skull, smashing it to a pulp.

Thomas was mortally wounded from the multiple bites; the old zombie's false teeth were imbedded in the last of his wounds. Garcia lifted the dying man's head and cradled it in his hands. He assessed the situation, careful not to put his fingers into the gaping hole in his head. Thomas moaned. His words were jumbled: "Tell car ... I ... that ... love them!"

Garcia sympathetically repeated the words he had often said to others during war time: "You're gonna make it!" He got up and grabbed a handful of old rags, and used them as a pressure dressing on the worst of the soft tissue wounds. He made a tourniquet out of Thomas's belt, tightening it above his shattered arm. He tugged at the lifeless limb; it severed completely. He wet a white towel in the utility sink and cautiously covered Thomas's brain to protect it. He lifted the injured man, cradling him in his arms as he moved up the stairs and out to the truck. He set Thomas gently on the passenger and seat belted him in. He looked at his digital watch and thought, *Two minutes to go,* as they left for the train station.

On the way back, Thomas's moans stopped and his head slumped to one side. Garcia knew that he had died, and made the sign of the cross. He finished the ritual by saying a short prayer for his new friend, something he had done far too many times in the war overseas. For a moment, he felt as if the war had come to America. He wiped his eyes dry. But this was different, and he knew he was in over his head. He didn't want to give in to his feelings of helplessness, and floored the gas pedal with his Proprio while he tried to figure out the best way to tell the others what had happened. *Just be as factual as possible … not too blunt. It's the best way.*

Garcia pulled up to the train station and saw Johnny slumped over near the bench, and another body lying on the ground near his friend. He got the willies as he tried to figure out what could have happened. He got out of the truck but left the engine running. As he approached Johnny, he saw the twisted mess of intestines and knew it was too late. He took Johnny's pulse anyway, more out of respect than actually thinking he could possibly still be alive.

"Sorry, buddy." Garcia shook his head, and added, "Gotta go find Ziggy." He walked through the double doors of the station and immediately saw several dead bodies. He also heard several moans coming from elsewhere in the station. He crept carefully forward and saw a zombie had emerged from the shadows. Its body was contorted and covered in blood. Garcia grumbled, "Crap." He called for Ziggy, but got no reply. He yelled out his name once again, but the zombie was quickly closing the gap between the two. *If Ziggy were still alive, he would have answered by now.* The zombie uttered something indecipherable. Instead of taking a chance and fighting the thing alone, Garcia whispered, "Only the smart survive," and hurried back to the truck.

Duck Shoot at the Paint Store:

Phoenix and Nolan alternated firing their M4's through the shooting holes. Each round that hit its mark produced massive head damage, leaving one less zombie to deal with. They high fived each other when they'd had enough, but soon heard rifle fire up above on the roof. Phoenix peered through another hole and shook his head in disbelief.

Dora reacted to the weapons fire below. She raised her M4 and let out a hailstorm of rounds, but the weapon went wild in her hands. As she accidentally blew out several windows on the opposite side of the street, she politely whispered, "Son of a fish!" She smacked the rifle's stock as if something were wrong with it.

Phoenix pulled back from the peephole and said, "Nolan, she didn't kill anything. Not a single headshot! Go and get her. I'll keep watch."

Vicki adjusted her hair clip as she ran with Adele to the front of the store. She asked, "What's going on?"

Adele stood with wide eyes, looking like she had just gulped a Grande Mocha Frappuccino. In a shaky voice, she asked, "Zombies?"

Phoenix, addressing them both, replied, "Michael was bitten while we were on patrol. Vicki, can you take a look at him? It's pretty bad."

She replied, "Will do," and rushed to Michael's side.

Vicki peeked under the field dressings to assess the wounds. Adele followed and tried to arrange her facial features into a positive expression. As she watched Vicki in action, she saw her in a whole new light; Vicki was obviously trained to respond to this type of emergency. She watched as Vicki hustled to retrieve the store's first-aid kit. Once back at his side, she removed the field dressings, cleaned the wounds, and reapplied sterile dressings. She saved the worst wound for last. "Okay, let's take a look at this." She peeled back the ragged cloth strips that had been loosely wrapped around his head. Hovering over her shoulder, Adele almost vomited at the sight of Michael's brain. The S-shaped lobes of the organ pulsated, and the worst of the bleeding had begun coagulating in thick clots along the jagged edges of his skull.

Vicki knew she needed more supplies. "Stay here, Adele. Please. Watch him."

Adele replied, "Don't worry, not going anywhere," then looked one more time at the horrible wound before turning her head away from the oozing brain.

Unexpectedly, Michael mumbled "Gonna … lay … right here."

Adele touched his shoulder and said softly, "You're gonna make it. You'll make it."

Vicki returned with more bandages and a black baseball cap that was embroidered with a golden fleur de lis. She pulled apart the hat's Velcro band, applied sterile, wet bandages, and used the cap to hold them on with light pressure. She looked up at Adele and explained, "I saw this trick on television. It'll keep everything in place." She leaned over to tell Michael something, but he had slipped back into unconsciousness.

Phoenix walked over to the two women and asked, "How is he?"

Vicki stood up and took a few steps away from Michael, just in case he could still hear. She whispered "He's not bleeding from the soft tissue wounds anymore, but his brain is still oozing and very swollen." She walked back to the windows, and then added, "I'm worried. I think this is what happened at the hospital when the initial outbreak started. A few people had checked into the E.R. with human bite marks. Some of the bites were so severe ... I mean, they not only left teeth marks, but had removed chunks of skin and muscle. Within a few hours, the patients became deathly ill, even after massive doses of antibiotics. Sometime after that, their monitors began flat-lining and all hell broke loose."

Phoenix thought for a moment, and then said, "But my two dates were never bitten, and they became zombies."

Vicki shrugged and replied, "We'll just have to monitor him for anything unusual."

Phoenix smiled at her and said, "Okay. Let's just keep this between ourselves for now – we don't want to alarm anyone until we know for sure."

Vicki nodded in agreement. "No problem, Phoenix."

Dora walked over to Phoenix and said, "Sorry about all of that commotion on the roof." She glanced over at Michael and added, "I'm glad I shot those things. They're worse than an infestation of rattlers."

Phoenix shook his head and said, "Well, you didn't get any head shots, so those things are still wandering around. Next time, wait until we're all together before firing. I wouldn't want you to accidentally shoot any of us normal folk."

Embarrassed, Dora looked out the window to avoid his gaze and replied, "No problem, Phoenix – I just got excited when I heard you guys, and wanted to help." With a voice full of hope, she added, "I can't wait for Garcia and the guys to return with my parents."

Garcia, on the Way Back:

Garcia zigzagged in and out of abandoned vehicles, just as he had through the streets of Iraq, back when he still had both of his legs. He mowed down any zombies that got in his way; as each body smashed into the front bumper, it caused the same type of damage that running into a small deer would have. The prosthetic device he was wearing was not the best thing to use when driving a vehicle, although the Veterans Administration had given him several attachments for different types of terrain. In an instant, his prosthetic became wedged between the gas pedal and the floorboard. He pulled his leg back hard and freed the device just in time to hit the brakes; he saw himself headed straight for a huge buffalo sculpture in front of a bank. The truck skidded but still ran head-on into the enormous brass animal. The buffalo wasn't damaged, but the front end of the truck was completely crumpled. Dazed, and with a bloodied forehead from the impact with the steering wheel, Garcia stumbled out of the truck, trying to steady himself to survey the damage.

He needed a tool to pop open the crumpled hood, and found one in the pickup truck's bed. With no zombies in sight, he pried open the hood with the crowbar. A large amount of steam shot up into the air like a geyser, enveloping the entire engine compartment. He jumped back quickly to avoid being scalded. "Damn! Radiator's busted." As he waited for the steam to disburse, he looked at the brass animal. Some steam appeared to flow out of the hollow buffalo's butt. *Great. I'm gonna have to hoof it now, or find a car to hotwire.* He dabbed his bloodied head with his shirt sleeve and spotted a '67 classic Ford a block away. The truck looked inviting, with its doors wide open, and he knew he could easily hotwire it. All he had to do was get over there safely and he'd be home free.

Doctor Stockton, UFED; No Guts, No Glory:

Doctor Stockton stroked his forefinger along the side of his smart phone and said, "It's not looking good in Baron. I think we should send in a medical military unit and get to the bottom of what Sporaton Lab was trying to accomplish. I'm not sure, but I think they may have found something we've never seen before. Have you noticed how the nerve cells were able to repair themselves?"

The aged voice on the other end of the line replied, "Yes, and it's quite miraculous. Well done, Doctor. That was quick investigative work and will certainly be acknowledged by your peers."

Stockton turned to the window and looked out at the sprawling assortment of buildings below. He knew the key department heads in each of the smaller brown buildings. "You know, I've never been in this field for the glory. But it would be especially nice to get a little recognition for this case."

"I understand," the voice replied, and promptly ended the call.

Stockton smiled at everyone present at the conference table. He had turned on the phone's external speaker during the call; they had all heard the conversation and now sat there, surprised. After all these years, it appeared that their mentor might get the recognition that he deserved. Perhaps it would not be long before they, too, received the same level of respect.

"Okay everyone – we've still got lots of work to do. Take a short lunch, and I'll see you afterward." The room emptied, leaving Stockton standing alone to ponder his future.

Garcia and His Proprio Crack:

Garcia nervously walked down the street with his right thumb tucked in his belt loop and his forefinger resting lightly on the M4's trigger. The semi-automatic weapon was positioned at his right hip, because he was going to bump-fire it, if needed. It was a technique he'd learned from an internet video; basically, you rocked the weapon back and forth to force automatic firing. He searched the abandoned street. *Those zombies won't know what hit 'em!* One of his eyelids twitched, but he kept a steady pace down the street. About twenty-five feet from the truck, he heard several moans and quickened his steps to get to the '67 – then he stopped cold in his tracks. Six zombies emerged from a nearby alley like a cluster of rotten grapes. They spotted him and began to spread apart, moving in his direction. He turned around to run, but found more of the zombies behind him. *Where in the heck did those come from?* He counted at least two dozen zombies, and they seemed to have some sort of primitive pack mentality. They lurched and shambled as they closed in on him. *They almost look like that music video ... dammit, now I've got that song stuck in my head!*

Garcia felt for the three ammo mags wedged between his belt and waist. *Use the first for the bump ... might scare 'em off, or at least force them back a bit.* Trigger finger at the ready, he continued to advance slowly toward the truck. The group of ghouls continued to move toward him; they had him completely surrounded. Almost at the truck, he fired a small burst of rounds. Several of the walking corpses ahead of him went down, but more emerged. Cold chills ran up and down his spine. He turned in a quick circle to determine the location of each zombie, and then unleashed his fire power. The deafening pop-pop-pop echoed off of the buildings. In between the rounds, he heard several heads burst, and said, "Look at that!" The bump technique had not worked as he had anticipated, but he had still scored a couple of kills. He now realized that only a bullet to the brain would keep the zombies down permanently. He continued to side-step toward the '67; he definitely didn't want to give up on his planned escape route. At that point, the tip of his Proprio lodged in a crack in the asphalt; Garcia went down hard. As his knee slammed into the road, he yelped in pain. He knew right away that it was fractured. With his rifle, he pushed himself up and hopped in a semi-circle on his good leg to test out his mobility. He fired off several more rounds to his left, but the zombies continued their advance. He limped the final few feet toward the truck as they closed in. *Just a few rounds left of my first clip.* He heard a voice calling from a second story window.

"Hey mister! Over here, over here!" He glanced quickly at the building and was going to head for it, but his path was blocked. He knew he had to stay with his original plan. *If all else fails, I'll lock myself in the truck and wait it out.*

"Behind you!" cried the voice. He planted his leg, turned and fired, but his rounds missed. A shock of pain raced through his fractured knee; it was already swollen to twice its normal size. One of the zombies grabbed him and he went down. He scooted backward while he switched magazines, aimed, and fired at the zombie's head, completing the kill shot. As he stood up and turned, he saw that more zombies had already flooded the street. In quick succession, he fired off round after round and eliminated three of the shuffling corpses closest to the truck. A gnarled hand grabbed him by the shirt; off balance, he fell again and landed on his tailbone. He could smell the thing's stench. He tried to get up, but his legs were numb and springy. He leaned to his side and fired a couple of rounds through the underside of the zombie's chin as it bent to grab him. From his angle, he could see the bullets exit the top of the skull, and briefly saw sunlight flood through the hole. Blood poured from the remains of the head. He rolled to avoid the zombie as it fell, and fired another burst of rounds. Several more zombies went down. *This is freaking me out ... too much like Iraq.* He struggled to keep his cool. He knew he had about a third of the mag left. He again used the rifle as a crutch, and then hobbled as fast as he could to the Ford, but his fractured knee was slowing him down considerably. With his back to the truck, he unleashed another salvo of rounds. Comically, he said, "Hot lead in your head!" He smiled briefly. *Now where did that come from?*

The voice from the window yelled, "Where ya going, mister?"

He fired a few more rounds and shouted back, "The Paint Store!"

The voice replied, "Be careful, mister."

"Thanks! I'll come back for you later!" Garcia pulled out his knife and moved to the driver's side of the truck. He knelt down on his good leg to get to the wires required for the fix. As he ducked under the steering column, he heard several zombies shuffling around on the passenger side. He popped back up and fired at them, but only killed one; still, it bought him a few seconds. He quickly stripped the wires with his knife, and then jiggled them. Sparks popped off the wires. The engine tried to turn over. *Just a little more and she'll be purring.* With another jiggle, sparks again popped off the wires and the truck roared to life. He shouted, "Hot damn!" and the voice from the window yelled at the same time. He looked up just as two of the zombies grabbed his legs and yanked him from the truck. His weapon slid from his hands. They descended on him like vultures, tearing into his flesh anywhere they could. He reached for the knife … the rifle … anything, but it was over in seconds.

The voice in the window screamed, "No! No! No!"

Sam Was a Man:

Nick drove faster than he should have, hoping that Sam's fever was caused by nothing more than an ordinary flu bug. He passed zombie after zombie but continued speeding toward the hospital until he heard someone pound on the roof. Ron leaned close to the driver's side window and shouted, "Stop the truck! We need to pick up some food!"

Nick slammed on the brakes just as Ron sat back down. He looked to the right and saw the Star Convenience Store. He leaned his head out of the window and said, "Okay, but just one of you goes in. Please be careful!" Hearing the word *food* made his stomach rumble.

Tired of sitting on the wheel hump, Charlene quickly volunteered. She yelled out, "I'll go!" and jumped from the back of the truck before anyone could argue. She sprinted toward the store and peered through the large front windows. She scanned as many of the aisles as she could see. *So far so good.* She pushed the door open slightly and stepped forward. A tiny bell jingled above the door and startled her, stopping her in her tracks. She half whispered, "Anyone here?" She edged the rest of the way inside and glanced around again to see if there were any visible signs of carnage. Seeing nothing, she grabbed a few plastic bags from the counter, and then stared hungrily down the aisles. Like a freight train, she started slowly and then picked up steam as she moved forward, snatching up cupcakes and chips. *This feels like a game show.* She went to grab some sodas and all of the premade sandwiches she could carry. She backed away from the coolers and a soda can fell out of an overloaded bag. It crashed into the floor and hissed as it burst open. She jumped back to avoid the soda bomb and shouted, "Damn it!" She bent over to clean up the mess, and then realized she really didn't have to. When she lifted her head, she caught a glimpse of movement through the stockroom door's small window. Weighted down with groceries, she crept toward the door just as another can tumbled from one of her overloaded bags and smacked into the ground. She jumped back to avoid the foamy spray as the can erupted volcanically, but it still coated the lower half of her body. She looked up, scanned the area, and saw another quick movement behind the stockroom door.

Nick tapped a country swing beat on the steering wheel for a few minutes before yelling to the back of the truck, "Can someone please go in and make sure she's alright?"

Equally worried, Ron jumped out of the truck and volunteered. He scanned the area for zombies and checked the safety on his shotgun. Before turning to leave, he looked Joaquin right in the eye and said, "Stay here. Don't come after me."

Joaquin held his machete up to the light and replied, "No problem, Mr. Ron."

Charlene propped the stockroom door open with a mop bucket, and entered the overcrowded space. It was filled with rows and rows of stacked boxes. She slowly pushed aside a shopping cart and stepped deeper into the room. She knew it was dumb idea, but she had to investigate the movement she'd seen. What if it was someone that needed help? *Just going to take a quick peek.*

Ron entered the store and called out for Charlene. She heard him, and her goose bumps disappeared, knowing that he was now in the store with her. She whispered, "Shhh!" He called her name again. She turned and said a little more loudly, "Ron … Shhh!" When she turned back around, a female zombie stood directly in front of her. It was missing an arm and had a huge gash across its chest. It was so grotesque that she dropped her bags into a previously unseen pool of blood. The soda cans crashed to the cement floor and exploded into a rainbow of sugary liquids. The liquids mixed with the blood, crushed chips and cupcakes and made the floor slippery. Charlene and the zombie both tumbled to the ground. Charlene sat up and pulled out her pistol. Ron heard the commotion and ran to the doorway. Charlene fired off a round, but the bullet only grazed the zombie's temple as it pounced on her. Ron reached the door just as its mouth bit into Charlene's abdomen. It lifted its head with a large chunk of her belly hanging from its teeth, her pierced navel clearly visible. Dazed and terrified, she fired the gun wildly, but the rounds only tore open boxes of laundry liquid. Charlene yelled in agony, and began to pistol whip its head as it came in for another bite.

***

Nick got out of the truck, walked around to the back bumper, and tapped Joaquin on the shoulder. "See anything unusual, son?"

Joaquin jumped out of the truck and glanced at the store one more time. "No … not a thing, Mr. Nick."

Yolanda ignored the two of them; she didn't even look up. Her head rested heavily in her palms. Nick looked at her, satisfied she was calm at the moment. He turned back to Joaquin and said, "This is a crappy situation."

Joaquin rotated the machete's handle around in his hand, and stabbed at the air a few times as if he were defending Lindsey's defense. He jokingly said, "For your honor, my lady!" Nick looked closely at the kid. He could tell he was trying to be funny, but his eyes gave away his teenage angst.

Nick exhaled deeply. "Okay, let's do this." Together, they walked toward the store's entrance.

The zombie in the bed of the truck lifted its head off the cushion. Its neck muscles were as huge as the ropes used to anchor large ships. Its tortured eyes bulged out a little as its mouth strained to open, producing a frothy ooze of saliva and blood. It gazed at Yolanda, who was sitting nearby and talking to herself. She wiped her nose with a palm, and said, "I don't know why she went in. Don't know why they had to follow, either. I should have just stayed at the shop."

***

Ron saw the zombie repeatedly biting into Charlene's now unconscious body. He grabbed a case of motor oil, too afraid to use his shotgun in close quarters. The thing saw him and muttered, "Rar-gra," then turned to continue its meal. With each beat of Charlene's heart, a shredded artery spurted bright red blood into the air. As Ron got closer, the thing reached out to grab him, but he smashed the heavy box onto its head. The skull, covered with small growths, was flattened and excreted jellified brain matter.

Ron looked at Charlene in dismay. "Oh my God!" He ripped open a box of paper towels and tore several feet from a roll. He wadded them and applied pressure to her abdomen. Shocked back into consciousness from the searing pain, she screamed in agony. With his bare hand, he wiped blood from her face and tenderly said, "Gonna get you outta here. Hold on."

She strained to look at her wounds. "I shouldn't have come in here."

He kept his cool and calmly replied, "Nonsense! You were doing what you thought was best." She passed out before he could even finish the sentence.

***

The zombie reached out violently and pulled Yolanda to its mouth. She attempted to scream, but its free hand ripped at her face and her mouth filled with blood. She could only manage a low gurgle. Enraged, the thing bit into her head and buried its free hand in her abdomen.

Walking toward the store's entrance, Joaquin heard a strange sound coming from the truck and turned to see what had happened. Not able to see Yolanda's back any longer, he raised his machete like a warrior. He wanted to charge the truck, but looked to Nick for direction. Without hesitation, Nick said, "Go help her. Kill it."

Confused, the teen replied, "But it could be Mr. Sam."

Nick paused for a moment as he thought about his life-long friendship with Sam. Feeling as if his whole world were crashing in on him, he said, "I know … but it might not be Sam anymore."

Joaquin ran to the back of truck and immediately saw the gory chaos that the zombie had created. It was hunched over Yolanda, feasting. He raised the machete overhead like an axe and brought it down on the zombie's head as hard as he could. As he pulled the blade out of its skull to strike another blow, the zombie rolled over and convulsed. When the thing's head lay in three separate chunks and its twitching had ceased, Joaquin jumped into the truck and pulled Yolanda farther away from the zombie's mouth. She was already limp.

***

Ron gently lifted Charlene into his arms and said, "I'm gonna get you out of here." He heard Nick calling out his name, and yelled from the stockroom, "I'm over here!"

Nick ran to the back room, and saw Ron with Charlene's limp body in his arms. The energy seemed to drain from his body as he moaned, "No! Not Charlene!"

Beads of sweat flowed down Ron's forehead. He said, "She's hurt badly, Nick. Grab some of those and apply pressure here."

Nick walked beside the two, holding the paper towels in place as Ron carried her out of the store. Nick grimly said, "Sam … I think he's turned, too. Pretty sure he attacked Yolanda when we were coming in to help. I let Joaquin take care of him."

Charlene went into a spasm at the door, her dangling legs kicking over a pottery display. The noise attracted several zombies who had been loitering by a dumpster at the rear of the store. Ron redistributed Charlene's weight and they hoofed it back to the truck. When they got there, they saw that Joaquin had shoved the zombie's body out of the truck bed, and had positioned Yolanda's injured body as comfortably as he could. Nick shouted, "Help us out with this, son." Joaquin went to their aid, helping to lift Charlene into the bed of the truck.

Ron gently shook her shoulder and tried to get her to talk, but got no response. "She's weakening."

Nick glanced down at Charlene. He did not want to seem inhuman, but knew he needed to say it. "If she turns like Sam did, don't hesitate, Ron. I don't want Joaquin to have to take care of another one of us."

Deep down, Ron wondered if Nick didn't trust him. "Don't worry, Nick. I promise, I'll take care of it."

Nick's mind was scattered, but he still wondered if Ron could really do it. After all, he hadn't even been able to protect Charlene in the first place. On his way to the driver's seat, he passed the zombie's crumpled body lying on the ground. He whispered, "Goodbye, Sam." A cold chill ran up the back of his neck.

Fire Blanket:

Doctor Billings sorted through the downloaded files of the Belize expedition and clicked on Doctor Phan's report. As he scanned the document, he found that the team had discovered a unique fungal super-spore. He traced his finger across the word 'Eureka', highlighted in red, then said, "This could change things!" He printed out the photographs that Kimball and Angela had taken. Although he was no Mayan-language expert, he wanted to at least try to decipher the glyphs. After some minutes spent organizing the photos, he separated the glyph stack from the fungal pictures, and then scribbled a few notes on his electronic tablet. He stretched his back. *I need a cup of coffee.*

Darkened rooms spooked Billings, just as funeral parlors always had. He stood in the doorway with pupils dilated wide, and backhanded the light switch to illuminate the room. He walked over to the coffee pot, set up the percolator, and plugged it in. The old-fashioned coffee brewer was one of the necessities that all of his labs had to have. He leaned against the counter and took a deep breath. Rebecca's body still lay under the silver blanket, but her arm had slipped off the couch and now dangled, swollen to twice its normal size. He couldn't look at her like that and picked up the stiffened, bloated arm, placing it back at her side. *Poor girl, already getting the mortis.* Curiosity overtook him, and he lifted the blanket off of her face to get a closer look. She still had that agonized look of pain and horror. He felt terrible, a guilty, hollow feeling burning in the pit of his stomach. As he tenderly covered her back up, he wondered how he was going to explain the death to her family.

The zombie's gait was aberrant, even for a shuffler. It would stop, shuffle, stop, and then heave its chest outward. Its torso undulated over its hips. It had found its way through a delivery door at the back of the lab, and stood motionless just inside. After a few minutes, it started moving again. It heard the cheerful bubbling of the old-fashioned percolator and advanced slowly, struggling against the traumatic injuries it had sustained.

Exterior security monitors showed no sign of zombies, and Billings thought, *Good! Maybe there were only two of them.* He relaxed a bit as he sipped from the mug emblazoned with Sporaton's logo: a picture of a single spore elevated over a line grid. He breathed in the comforting aroma of the coffee as it wafted to his nose. Studies had proven that coffee helped improve work productivity, and in the lab, the scientists appreciated the finer New Orleans blend. Coffee was the one thing he did not want to be cheap about. He rubbed the back of his aching neck and slumped deeply into the black chair. He closed his eyes for a moment and thought, *Sooner or later, somebody from the lab will show up and I'll get to the bottom of this mess.*

With labored breathing, the zombie continued its slow, stop-and-go progress toward the break room until it stood in front of Billings, who had his eyes closed. He was just about to doze off when the zombie's raspy breathing startled him awake. As his eyes flew open, he caught a glimpse of the new horror in front of him. It shocked him so much that he knocked the cup off of the table. He stood up; the zombie took a swipe at him. He leaned back to avoid the blow and fell hard onto the corner of his chair. His lower back screamed with pain and his legs went numb.

The zombie's brain began vibrating violently. It shook in place, the tumors on its head pulsating out of sync like defective Christmas lights. Billings struggled to rise, but his back was speared with pain and he stumbled backward, crashing into the cabinets. The zombie's body stiffened. It made a beeline straight for the doctor. It swiped at him again, and this time connected with his scalp. His hair line filled with warm, salty blood, which dripped down into his eyes. Unable to see, he cried out in fear and pain. He managed to stand halfway up, but the zombie attacked again, swinging its claw-like hand at his stomach, connecting with an ugly tearing sound. The doctor's soft abdomen popped open like a can of biscuits. As he fell to the floor, he pleaded, "LORD! Help me!" He held out both of his arms in self-defense, but he was no match for the strength of the beast. It pounced, landed on top of him, and bit full-force into his face. The bite crushed his cheekbones and removed his entire nose. He struggled to breath as air and blood bubbled from the jagged hole. He could feel himself drowning in his own fluids; he could taste his blood. The zombie sloppily chewed, and Billings heard the cartilage of his nose crunching in its mouth. The zombie continued its meal as the doctor, in shock and fading fast, closed his eyes for a much needed nap.

Old Man Higgins:

Higgins watched in horror as one of zombies peered into the car. Its eyes were nearly buried in darkened sockets, and the inside of its mouth was black and vile. When it lazily snapped its jaws at the air, dark spittle rained onto the window. The old man thought, *What on Earth?* He squeezed further down onto the floorboards. Eye to eye with a yellow "Old Time" burrito wrapper, he could smell the seasoned meat and salsa residue left behind. He was tempted to lick it, and thought, *If the war didn't kill me, this probably won't*, but quickly abandoned the silly idea when the large zombie started rocking the vehicle. Higgins tried to reposition himself, and accidentally pressed the horn, which let out a loud, "Ah-OOOO-ga!" Some of the zombies froze in their tracks, while a few others' heads exploded. The car was pelted with small bits of brain matter, skull, and matted strands of hair. The old man felt helpless.

The Texas Paint Store:

As the wall clock chimed, Phoenix leaned forward and whispered, "They've been gone almost an hour now. We need to do something."

Nolan nodded and whispered back, "What do you have in mind?" He reached for his leather gloves.

Phoenix looked around at their dwindling snacks and replied, "How 'bout we go and see what's happening with them. We could use some real food and a better place to hunker down."

Nolan quickly put the gloves on and pushed each finger through the cutouts. Out of the corner of his mouth, he asked, "What about everyone else?"

Phoenix was sure about one thing – no one got left behind. He replied, "Everyone goes. We'll use the store's delivery van. Can you get the keys from behind the counter?"

In a disappointed voice, Nolan replied, "No problem, dude," then went to retrieve the keys.

Phoenix gathered the rest of the group together. Without beating around the bush, he said, "We gotta leave. Get your things."

Adele piped up, "Well, it's about time."

Dora put her hands together, looked up to the heavens and said, "Amen!" No one put up an argument about why they should stay; instead, they hurried around, collecting their gear. When they had everything together, they lined up single-file at the rear door. On the count of three, Vicki opened it up and led them toward the store's van. It featured a large paint can purposely tipped over on the rooftop. Multiple streaks of color seemed to flow from the cans and dribble down the doors, creating the store's logo.

Adele had Michael's legs and Phoenix took his shoulders as they carried him to the vehicle.

Nolan hopped into the driver's seat and started the van, letting it idle as the others got in. Adele and Phoenix entered through the double side-doors of the van and laid Michael down. At Vicki's request, Adele elevated Michael's legs atop an old painter's tarp, then scooted to the back doors and peered through the rear window. Without looking toward the front, she said, "We'd better hurry – several zombies are approaching." Nolan caught a glimpse of the zombies in the side mirror and revved the engine in acknowledgement.

Adele shouted to the others, "Hurry up guys, they're almost here!"

Three zombies in tattered utility uniforms approached, practically in formation. She noted the peculiar way that each one moved. One of them had such severe burns that its flesh hung off of its body in long bacon-like strips. A fourth had a medical-halo device bolted into its head. Its arms were raised to form a hoop.

Phoenix tossed the last of their supplies into the van, then turned to Dora and asked, "Which way, D?"

She replied, "Take a left, right up there at the corner."

Nolan zoomed out of the parking lot and up the street. Dozens of zombies meandered nearby, seemingly without rhyme or reason, until they heard the van.

Phoenix clutched his M4 and, winking confidently, said, "I'm gonna take a few out." Nolan stopped the van a short distance from the nearest zombies, and Phoenix hopped out and went down on one knee next to the front bumper. He zeroed in on the closest and shot it in the head, then continued to fire on several others that were blocking the street. He was a decent shot, and each zombie's head exploded like watermelons during target practice. Phoenix stood up as the last shell casing bounced between his legs and shouted, "Did you guys see that? Some exploded, even though I didn't shoot them." Everyone nodded and watched as dozens more zombies began to move on the van.

Nolan revved the engine and shouted, "Get back in! There are too many of them!" Without waiting for a second invitation, Phoenix hopped into the van and held his hand up for a high-five.

The van drove right over the bodies of the fallen zombies. The corpses tumbled under the length of the van, sounding like a couple of tennis shoes bouncing around in a dryer. Grossed out but satisfied, Adele watched the broken body parts fly from beneath the rear of the vehicle. The gore was perfectly framed in the squared windows. It gave her a weird sense of satisfaction unlike any she had ever experienced when watching the fake gore of the low-grade horror films she loved. She congratulated Nolan on his driving skills, and then teasingly added,

"You guys really don't wanna see this," as she went on to describe the scene in detail.

Dora ignored the vivid monologue and kept her eyes on the road. After a few minutes, she spoke up. "That's it. Take a right."

Phoenix turned in his seat, looked back at Vicki and asking, "How's he doing?"

She leaned in toward Phoenix and murmured, "Not too good. He's mostly in and out of consciousness."

He tried to reassure her. "Don't worry; we'll be there soon."

She lifted the edge of the dressing that covered his head and shook her head. "His brain is swelling so much."

Phoenix turned around in his seat, and Nolan glanced at him, trying to ignore his dour expression. Dora said, "Take the next right." Nolan turned the steering wheel and found himself on a commercial street loaded with shops. Zombies haphazardly roamed about.

Exasperated at seeing more of them, Phoenix said, "Just floor it." Nolan gunned the van, and they smacked into several more bodies, sending them flying. A fast-moving car entered from a side street, and Nolan had to swerve to avoid ramming another vehicle. He slammed on the brakes, stopping just shy of a fire hydrant. Adele opened the rear doors and jumped from the back of the van. She was immediately surrounded, but fired the M4 like a mad woman on the edge of sanity. Phoenix jumped out of the van, grabbed her by the shirt collar and pulled her back into the vehicle. He yelled, "Are you crazy?"

She looked at him, not embarrassed at all, and replied, "I just couldn't take it anymore. Had to pay 'em back for what they did to my husband."

Many more zombies were bearing down on them. Nolan strained to see through the bloodied windshield, and pulled a lever down to spray the window with solution. The wipers cleared an arc through the nasty fluids, which allowed small fragments of tissue to accumulate at the bottom of the windshield. Nolan backed up, turned the wheel, and peeled out toward the outskirts of town. He said to no one in particular, "That's better."

They had gone about a mile when Vicki caught sight of a prosthetic leg lying on the side of the road. She yelled, "Oh my God! Is that Garcia's leg?"

Nolan quickly stopped the van and said "We'd better take a closer look."

Phoenix glanced over to where Vicki was pointing and spotted the device. He replied, "I'm not sure. It could be."

Nolan slowly drove the van to within a few feet of the prosthetic and stopped again. Vicki, Phoenix and Adele got out and hurried to the leg. Phoenix flipped the bloodied, well-crafted device over with his rifle barrel, getting sticky residue for on the end of his weapon. He said, "There it is. The manufacturers label. He was the only one around with a Proprio."

Saddened, Adele bowed her head. "Poor dude. He was a good guy."

Phoenix tapped the rifle on the toe end of the prosthetic. It rocked back and forth. He continued, "Let's look around for his tags. Garcia told me that he always wore them." He pointed to an imaginary perimeter with his finger, while he scanned the area.

Vicki wiped away her tears and said, "Good idea."

A dozen or so feet away, Adele spotted a glint of light. It looked like a stray coin or two, but she wasn't sure. *Worth checking it out.* She hurried to the spot, yelling, "Hey guys – over here." Phoenix and Vicki ran to where she stood and gazed upon the twin metal objects in her hand.

Phoenix grimaced and said, "Those are his tags, alright. That's his name." Vicki's eyes filled with tears, seeing the tags up close and knowing what that meant. Phoenix put a hand on Vicki's shoulder and said, "I don't know if you two knew it, but he was a Gulf War hero."

Nolan leaned his head out of the van window and shouted,

"Well? Is it him?" The girls nodded. At the same time, he could see several bloodied zombies ambling toward their position. The hairs on the back of his neck rose.

Phoenix tucked the tags into his pocket, then said, "We better get out of here – we've got company." Vicki had already started running toward the van, peppering the walking dead with round after round. *Payback!*

Adele lowered her rifle and shrieked, "I'm gettin' some of that!" She sprayed the area with half a mag.

Vicki looked over at Adele and saw the sparkle in her eye. She stopped firing and said, "You're doing it out of fun, aren't you? I'm doing it out of necessity!"

Adele answered, "Don't be so sure, Vicki."

Caught in the middle, Phoenix smiled. *Maybe we'll be okay after all.* Before he could say it aloud, he realized that they did not need any more encouragement. After several of the closest zombies fell dead, Adele forced a high-five out of Phoenix, and they all jumped back into the van.

Phoenix smacked the dashboard and said, "Let's go!"

Nolan floored the gas pedal and the van shot forward, "Where to, now?"

Phoenix looked toward Dora. He could see that she was a nervous wreck and replied, "Just keep driving to her parents' house."

Dora looked up, and then humbly added, "Thanks, guys."

On the Way to the Hospital:

Tired, hungry, and in a trance-like state, Joaquin sat on the wheel well. His thoughts focused on Lindsey. *If she's alive, I'll prove that I can take care of her. GOTTA BE A MAN!* He clenched a fist tightly and whispered, "I have to."

Ron scooted forward until he was kneeling next to Charlene. He lifted her dressing and shook his head in disgust. Joaquin cocked his head and asked, "You want me to hold pressure there?"

Ron thought, *This kid never ceases to amaze me.* As he gently laid the dressing back down, he smiled and answered, "No, Joaquin; I have it."

In between flashes of memory about his mom and girlfriend, Joaquin gazed at the corpse-littered streets of Baron. No longer able to contain his turbulent emotions, he leaned forward on the wheel well, breathing quickly. As he eyeballed the shuffling zombies with growing anger and disgust, Ron leaned over and said, "Go ahead." The teen smirked, picked up the M4, and knelt on the bed of the truck to steady himself. He opened fire, quickly killing several of the freaks, and continued blasting away until Nick shouted for him to stop.

About a quarter of a mile from the hospital, Joaquin's heart pounded. He demanded, "Stop the truck! Stop now!" The truck screeched to a halt, and he tried to keep a steady voice. "I need more ammo."

Without asking any questions, an arm was thrust out of the truck window with a magazine in hand. Nick trusted the teen. If Joaquin were his son, Nick would consider him to now be a man. Joaquin inserted the fresh clip and opened fire, taking down as many of the zombies as he could. The barrel was smoking hot when he tossed down the empty M4 and picked up his machete. He made a move to leap from the truck. Ron saw a blur and yelled, "What in the ...?" He reached for the Joaquin, but completely missed as the teen vaulted over the side of the truck bed.

Ron followed Joaquin with shotgun in hand as the teen ran toward a large horde. He tried to stay close, but was cut off by the advancing zombies.

Rifle at the ready, Nick got out of the truck and positioned himself with his back against a headlight. Zombies swarmed to his left and rear, and he fired at them to make sure they didn't get any closer.

As he ran ahead of the truck and deeper into the horde, Joaquin screamed, "Lindsey, Lindsey!" The zombies had encircled her, but some of them turned at the sound of his voice and staggered toward him.

Lindsey was hysterical and yelled, "Oh my God! Joaquin, help me!"

As Joaquin ran through the group of zombies to rescue Lindsey, Ron lost sight of him. Trying hard not to take any wild shots, Ron aimed carefully at the closest zombies. The shotgun did little damage at that distance. Horrid figures closed the gap as the teen zigzagged in and out between the putrid walkers. Joaquin ignored the fact that they were attracted to sound and yelled as loudly as he could. "Mr. Nick! Mr. Ron!"

Nick repositioned himself ten feet in front of the truck and killed several more of the undead, but there were so many he could not take them all down. He noticed that he was low on ammo and yelled "GET BACK HERE, SON!"

As he ran, Joaquin slashed at anything he could reach with his machete, decapitating the closest zombies. Fountains of blood shot into the air and darkened the ground. Lindsey screamed and giggled hysterically, her emotions a jumbled mess. She was terrified watching her boyfriend come close to being bitten so many times. Joaquin had become completely overwhelmed, and yelled again for help. The space between Lindsey, himself, and the zombies shrank. One of them latched onto her arm and pulled her spastically towards to its gaping mouth. Her humerus was crushed instantly by the force of the grasp. She shrieked and almost blacked out. Her painful screams sounded like his mother's had the morning before. Her voice sent chills down his spine. He spun around at the last second to avoid another swipe, and then raised his bloodied blade to chop off the arm that held his girlfriend. He missed! The zombie's mouth was now mere inches from her head. He swung the machete with all of his strength, and cleaved the zombie's head in two. Blood sprayed Lindsey's face, and she gagged as she pried the rotting, filthy fingers from her arm.

Nick scanned the area, and could not believe his eyes when he saw the six foot six behemoth zombie come out of nowhere. In fear, he shouted, "Ron, look!" Ron turned and saw the familiar zombie standing head and shoulders above the rest. It maneuvered itself clumsily into the horde. Both men sent out a volley of shots that sounded like a Fourth of July fireworks display, but while several zombies bit the dust, the giant was unscathed. The horde continued to swell around the teen-aged couple. Some of the zombies looked like they had just left the gym, while others appeared to have just crawled from their graves.

Joaquin grabbed Lindsey's sweaty hand and hacked his way toward a thinned-out section of the horde, pulling her along. They made little progress as new zombies filled the gaps. The crawling, insect-like zombie grabbed Lindsey by the ankle and yanked her legs from underneath her. She lost her grip on Joaquin's hand as she fell flat on the ground. The zombie lunged at her; Joaquin slashed it across its back while she rolled out of the way. Ron and Nick saw her go down, and in desperation, fired round after round into the area of her screams. Joaquin squatted, hacking wildly at the crawling thing. Now other mouths were within biting distance.

The two teens scrambled to their feet at the same time. All of a sudden, the behemoth was behind Lindsey. Its jaws unhinged like a giant python; it easily slipped its mouth around her neck and shoulder and bit down. Her body crumpled to the ground, but her head remained attached by a few strands of the thick sternocleidomastoid muscle. A river of blood flowed from her massive wound and filled a depression in the ground at Joaquin's feet. Tears poured from his eyes as he screamed, "NOOOOO!"

Ron ran back to the truck to get the Segway. He positioned Charlene's rifle on its steering column and used it as a tripod. He barreled through the outer perimeter of the zombies while he fired the weapon. Nick followed him on foot. Joaquin weakly swung the machete. Another muscled horror grabbed his arm and pulled it backward, causing his shoulder to dislocate with a loud pop. He screamed in pain and terror, and then dropped the machete as he fell to his knees in the middle of the horde. Ron accelerated, fired, and killed several more. Nick anticipated his next move and yelled, "No! Don't do it, Ron!"

Joaquin's screams were now completely drowned out by the ravenous zombies and Ron shouted, "I gotta!" They both unloaded their remaining ammo into the crowd. Many in the horde turned and careened after the men. Unexpectedly, the Segway stopped; the patched wires had loosened again.

Nick let loose with a bellowing, "RUN!" With absolute despair, the two men turned and ran back to the truck, leaving Joaquin, the Segway, and Lindsey behind.

HeLa Cells:

Hanging on the wall behind Doctor Ludwig was a beautiful poster telling the story of Henrietta Lacks' famous cells, dubbed "HeLa" by the medical research community. It described how her cells had been the first to ever be cultured and kept alive outside of a human body. It also listed many of the more famous experiments the cells had been used for since the 1950's. These studies included the effects of zero gravity on human cells while aboard the International Space Station, and a multitude of life-saving pharmaceutical developments. The poster also included a small portrait of Mrs. Lacks as a teenager, acknowledging her contribution to science. In spite of the fact that these cells had made millions of dollars for the companies that had used them, neither Henrietta nor members of her surviving family were ever paid for her important contribution to science.

Ludwig switched between images of the HeLa cells and the cells collected in Baron. His favorite graduate student, Rosie, entered the dimly lit room. Thrilled to see something new, she asked, "Is that the unusual Texas specimen I've heard about?"

Ludwig smiled and replied, "It is. Wanna take a look?" Rosie rushed around the desk, double clicked a camera icon, and studied the two images side by side.

She said, "I don't know, Doctor. It doesn't make sense for a cell to reproduce itself perfectly and not have any defects from the original."

Ludwig pushed his eyeglasses further up the bridge of his nose and answered, "Yeah, I know. Normal cells generally develop some sort of defect as they replicate themselves throughout their lifecycle. But these cells seem to be the exception to the rule." Rosie set the computer mouse down and stood up as he continued, "These cells obviously function at a higher metabolic rate, even at the end of their long lifecycle. Accidental or not, this could be a major breakthrough."

She excitedly asked, "Can you e-mail a photo of the slides and video to me? I'd like to feature them in a presentation I'm giving at next week's lecture."

"No problem, Rosie." He glanced at her arm and asked, "Oh, is that a new tattoo?"

On her way to the door, she flexed her arm and replied, "Yep, it's a pinup girl with a broken heart! I've always loved hearts, broken or not. Don't forget to send the e-mail."

Ludwig was convinced that Sporaton was close to a new and startling discovery. He asked his secretary to charter a flight to the nearest airport to Baron, and to make sure that Rosie and Gene were on that flight. The secretary replied, "Okay Doc, will do!"

***

The small jet sat fueled and ready to go on the tarmac at Aviation Field. Rosie had never been on a sanctioned mission, and was excited and definitely over-packed. Sarcastic to the point of being funny, Gene counted each suit case and said, "Wow, girl, you *really* know how to pack light."

Rosie grinned as she replied, "This is just for tomorrow!" They both laughed, and Gene settled into his seat, pulling out some research papers that he had brought along.

While the threesome waited for the tower to clear the jet for takeoff, they briefly went over the trip's itinerary. Ludwig talked about the types of files they could use more of, and newer samples that still needed to be collected. After a good ten minutes, the pilot interrupted the conversation via intercom and stated, "Ladies and gentlemen, in just a few minutes we'll be at cruising altitude. A few hours later, we'll arrive at your destination. Please enjoy the flight and thanks for flying with YouGo Charters."

Ludwig stretched in the comfortable leather seat. Gene and Rosie unbuckled their seatbelts and huddled in front of him. As they continued to discuss the finer details of the specimens, Gene stated, "Maybe it's a freak of nature, a one-time occurrence."

Ludwig held up a hand-written report and tapped it with his forefinger, saying, "In addition to the research we've done and the outside reports you've already seen, I've got an eye witness who said that the dead were coming back to life all over Baron. That person is a medical doctor."

Rosie shook her head and replied, "No way!"

Gene pulled a research paper from his folder and added, "Maybe they're doing some sort of weird, hybrid stem cell research out there."

Ludwig shook his head and said, "No, that can't be. Sporaton is a spore research facility. Their experiments are focused on manipulating spores and finding better ways to use them naturally."

Slightly embarrassed, Gene sat down and replied, "Oops. Sorry Doc, I didn't know."

Rosie sat between the two. She put her hands on her knees and very seriously said, "Listen, there's nothing I know of that can cause reanimation of dead tissue. Nada!"

Ludwig punctuated his next word with a click of a pen. "Exactly! That's why we need to get to the bottom of this!" Rosie and Gene sat back down in their plush leather seats and all three sipped coffee from their YouGo courtesy mugs, which were emblazoned with a small, stylized jet.

* * *

The chartered jet taxied to the small airport terminal, where a clerk with a rental car awaited them. Gene signed the contract and said, "Okay, everybody. All done."

Ludwig pulled his cell phone out his pocket and turned off airplane mode. Another tap on the touch screen brought up his most recent calls. He tapped again, and waited for Doctor Stockton to answer.

"Stockton speaking!"

"This is Doctor Ludwig. I'm with my assistants at the airport. We're getting ready to head to the Baron lab."

Stockton readjusted his grip on the phone. He could hardly believe what he had just heard. "What do you mean you're at the airport? I wouldn't have gone just yet. We don't know what we're dealing with!" Ludwig threw his bag into the trunk of the car. He smiled at the tiny screen as if he were in FaceTime mode and said, "Don't worry. We'll take all precautions and use the lab's DECON suits if necessary."

Stockton motioned for an assistant, then replied, "I'm going to send a crew to help you."

Ludwig wanted to get going, and did not have time to sit around chatting. He tapped a few icons on his phone as he replied, "What's that? Your call is breaking up."

Stockton replied, "I said …!" The connection encountered some electronic static and the call abruptly ended.

Stockton stood up slowly and addressed his assistant. "We need a team down in Baron, Texas. I think something miraculous or horrific is happening – I can't tell which."

The assistant nodded in agreement and said, "Yes, sir, and your arthritis medicine is in the cabinet."

Old Man Higgins:

After an unexpected nap, Higgins woke up sprawled out on the car seat. It was absolutely quiet. He sat there, stretching and yawning. He looked around and, seeing nothing, opened the car door as stealthily as possible. About a block away, he spotted one of the zombies. It stood motionless. With his saw in hand, and using it as a crutch, he crept out of the car. Quickly remembering that the zombies were attracted to sound, he placed the saw over his shoulder. He limped toward the paint store that his old friend owned, hoping his buddy would know what had happened to the town. Along the way, he kept low and peeked through windows, not wanting to be ambushed by any more zombies.

Doctor Ludwig Arrives at Sporaton:

Gene drove the car into the parking lot, pulling right up to the front entrance of Sporaton. They all got out and walked up the steps of the building. Ludwig turned to Gene and asked, "Would you please check out the vehicle at the end of the parking lot?"

Happy to stretch his legs for a moment, Gene replied, "Sure thing, Doc."

Ludwig then turned to Rosie and asked, "Will you come with me?" The pair entered the building and immediately started smelling the stench of death. Rosie cupped her hand over her mouth and nose as if it were a surgical mask and said, "Crap! I don't like this." The doctor just shook his head. Rosie propped the front door open with an office chair before they moved deeper into the building.

A little further inside, Ludwig and Rosie saw a body with a small garbage can smashed over its head. A large scab of viscera was caked on the body; it reminded Rosie of dried candle wax. Struggling to maintain her composure, she yelled, "What the heck?" Ludwig shushed her, and they continued to the main work area of the lab. They looked at each other in shock after seeing another bloody pool. She turned to Ludwig, and asked, "What's going on, Doc? Who could've done this? And why?"

He stood back from the dried, coagulated pools of blood. "I have no earthly idea."

At the threshold of the break room, Ludwig and Rosie found another horrible mess. They entered the room, and Rosie immediately went over to the couch. She lifted a silver fire blanket, which revealed dried, bloodied seat cushions. In a shaky, frightened voice, she said,

"Someone was here, too." Ludwig walked around the dried pools of blood on the floor, and scooted around shards of broken glass. They tried to connect the dots like forensic investigators, but the scene was just too much to behold.

Finally, in disbelief, Ludwig stated, "Yeah, it looks like there was a huge fight, but a very important piece of the puzzle is missing – the body."

Gene entered the building and found Ludwig and Rosie in the break room. Seeing the amount of carnage, he nearly vomited. "This is just too much!" He heaved again as he stepped into a bloody smear on the floor.

Ludwig felt sorry for him and said, "Go ahead and get some fresh air."

With both hands holding his stomach, Gene said, "Good idea!" He quickly and gingerly stepped out of the room.

Ludwig went back into the main lab and squatted down next to a fire extinguisher. He looked up at Rosie who had followed and said, "Judging by the amount of blood, this extinguisher wasn't used to put out a fire. Look at the marks on the ground. They were hitting something pretty hard!" He got back up and they walked around the rest of the lab, but did not see anything out of the ordinary. He leaned against a desk and said, "Doesn't look to be a robbery." Rosie agreed, and headed for the inner offices. Ludwig moved toward an opened laptop and double-clicked a few files and their attachments. Gene reentered the lab, but this time held a cloth over his nose. Ludwig looked up and saw that some of the color had returned to his face. He asked, "Gene, will you see if you can get the Baron Police on the phone? We need to report this."

Gene replied, "Yes sir!" After a minute of receiving no answer at the station, Gene said, "No one's picking up, Doc."

Ludwig shook his head and replied, "Just our luck."

Rosie heard strange noises come from an inner, smaller lab. She was hesitant to investigate on her own, but her curiosity got the better of her. She figured the danger had already passed. Intrigued by the sound, she thought, *Maybe it's an experiment, a caged animal of some sort.* She slowly moved toward the darkened room. At the threshold, she paused and looked around. Hearing nothing, she walked into the middle of the room and realized just how dark it was. She squinted in an effort to see more clearly. Once again she heard the strange, lower-pitched gurgle. She felt the hairs on the back of her neck rise. "Phlaw-gla!" She turned to her left and saw the zombie. Its arm bone protruded through its sagging green skin and brushed against a table. It limped badly. The zombie now stood almost motionless, directly in front of her. At the top of her lungs she let out a high-pitched scream, and tried to make sense of the coal-black eyes that stared at her. As the zombie began to lift its arms, she screamed again and almost urinated on herself.

Ludwig dropped his papers and shouted, "Holy crap!" as he heard the terrified screams. He and Gene ran toward the small lab and froze in terror when they saw the zombie. It was reaching for Rosie, who had backed up against a metal lab table. Through her terror, she noticed that its leg was bent backward at the knee, and she thought, *How can it still move?* Phlegm speckled her face as it came closer and muttered, "Phlaw-gla!" Without looking, she nervously reached behind her for something to use as a weapon. She quickly grasped a heavy microscope and smashed the zombie's face with the U-shaped base. The impact created a horseshoe-like imprint below its eye. Amazingly, it ignored the whack to its head and lunged again, wobbling precariously on its twisted leg. It lost its balance, and she took advantage of the situation by kicking the zombie in the gut. It tumbled to the ground.

Rosie spun around as she heard other shuffling feet. She thought, *Finally!* but quickly realized Gene and Ludwig were not making the new sounds. A second zombie came lurching out of a darkened corner. Frog-like, it murmured, "Cra-ga! Cra-ga!" Strips of pectoral muscle hung from its chest like a flesh necklace, and its abdominal cavity appeared to be hollowed out. A deflated lung protruded from under a name tag that identified it as Bill. She screamed again, just as Ludwig's paralysis broke and he reached to turn on the lights. He shouted at Gene, even though Gene was right next to him. "DO something!"

Gene grabbed a computer monitor from a nearby desk and heaved it at the zombie. It was a good toss; the monitor smashed into its chest.

The fallen zombie snarled and rose slowly to its feet. It moved toward Rosie, who was frozen with fear, and grabbed her by the arm, yanking her roughly toward its snapping jaws. Ludwig looked desperately around and grabbed a fire axe off of a nearby wall. A raspier sound erupted from the zombie's mouth as it moaned "Craaa-gaaaa!" and bent to take a big bite out of Rosie's shoulder. She tried to scream from the searing pain, but her throat was hoarse and dry. The zombie bit into her shoulder again, and she shook violently from the trauma, losing her footing and falling to the floor. Somehow, she managed to turn over onto her back and kick the thing in its chest. It flew backward and landed in a contorted heap. She crawled to Gene; she felt as if everything was happening in slow motion and gave out at his feet.

The doctor was enraged. He circled the zombie and screamed, "Rrhah!" He took a deep breath and attacked it with the axe. The dull blade connected with the back of the thing's head. It split one of its large lesions in half, sending thick, black fluid splattering everywhere. Brains oozed from the wound as well; the zombie fell to the ground and writhed in convulsions.

In all the mayhem, no one had noticed that the zombie with the twisted leg had pulled itself back upright. It wobbled over to where Rosie was laying and fell on top of her with a grunt. Before she could even scream, the abomination bit the back of her head with incredible force, tearing away a large chunk of her skull. Grey matter swelled and protruded beyond the edges of the traumatic opening. The zombie flung the flap of bone and hair from its mouth and started to consume her brain. Her mind was filled with a symphony of flashing lights; she no longer felt any pain.

Ludwig screamed, "Help her!" Gene kicked the zombie in the face, and then grabbed Rosie by the ankles and pulled her out of the room. The zombie tried to follow, but Ludwig blocked the door with a metal cabinet before it could reach them. It slurred indecipherable sounds as it pummeled the filing cabinet.

Sweetheart Memories:

Higgins stopped dead in his tracks when he saw a very loud moaner advancing on him. Its head was caged by a medical traction device; it looked like a magician trying to twist out of a straightjacket. Its eyes were as dark as roofing tar as it twisted and contorted its neck to try and break free. Higgins watched as one of the four rods loosened from its skull, and realized it could bust free at any second. He lifted the saw and shouted, "Dang it!" He positioned the broad metal band in front of his waist, business end out, to use a barrier. He walked as quickly as he could toward the closest store, but another zombie had just wandered out and stood on the sidewalk, much too close. He needed a quick hiding place, and caught sight of the sign above the door which said "Busy Bees." He whispered, "That's Delores's quilting place." He feared what he might find if he went inside, but thought, *I've gotta take a risk*. The zombie with the traction device had moved closer, and now two of the zombies stood between him and the shop, with more closing in. He mumbled to himself, "Gonna have to kill 'em." He inched forward, holding his saw tightly. He addressed his next comment to all of them: "Alright you things, I don't know what you are, but I'm getting through that door!" The zombie with the cervical contraption leaned to its right, and then made a beeline for him, screeching "Haaich!" The freakish sound increased in volume as it closed in. A gust of wind blew dust into Higgins' face, so he raised his bandana to cover his mouth. As the zombies tightened the circle around him, he brandished the big saw over his head and shouted, "Just stay there you … you THINGS! Just stay right there!" One of them continued crawling toward him, so he swung the saw at its back, the jagged teeth of the weapon carving a trench all the way from its sacrum to its neck. He backed his way to the quilting shop, thrusting his saw, then quickly slipped inside. He pushed a large hutch in front of the door to block the fiends from getting in. As he backed away from the door, he heard a grunting noise, like someone clearing their throat. He shouted, "Delores? Is that you?"

Tangled up in yarn, the old zombie moved from behind the front counter and shuffled toward him. Higgins sobbed, feeling completely defeated as he recognized the woman he once had such a crush on. His mind flashed back to the one date they'd shared in high school. He took a deep breath, looked at the ground, and shook his head. "Oh, Delores! Not you too!" He moved toward the zombie and did what needed to be done. He swung the saw as hard as he could; the blade penetrated just above its ear. He could feel the vibration of the blade as he pulled it back and it cut even deeper into the bone. He used all of the strength he had left to pry it out. The zombie fought back and tried to lunge at him, but a cracked segment of bone fell to the floor, followed by a cascade of blood. He recalled what a pretty face she'd had as a teenager, and whispered, "Delores, I … I didn't want to do it." The zombie fell to the ground and rolled onto its side. Gelatinized brain bubbled out of the hole in its head. He watched its arthritic fingers twitch as if it were knitting a scarf. He stepped over the stream of blood and headed for the back door, saying a short prayer. He left the shop with one final thought about the single kiss they once shared.

Barricade and Research:

Gene pulled Rosie into the break room. He lifted her thin, lifeless body up onto the already stained couch, and then covered her lower half with the silver fire blanket. With his forefinger, he gently opened her eyes to see if her pupils were fully dilated. He felt for her carotid pulse and got nothing, as expected. He pulled the rest of the blanket over her head, then hustled back to the hallway to help the doctor.

Ludwig pulled his cell phone from his pocket and tried 911 again. The trapped zombie followed him along the window of the small lab; when he turned to look at it, it surged forward and hit the window with a splat. It bounced backward, and then repeated the movement. Ludwig fumbled his phone, but Gene, now at his side, caught it. The doctor stared at the gooey residue that remained on the window and noted how green it was. He asked,

"Do you see that Gene?"

Gene nodded his head and asked, "Would you like a swab of that stuff?"

Ludwig thought about the data he had compiled and replied, "Maybe later, if it calms down."

Gene patted his back and replied, "Thanks Doc. I was gonna tell you to get it yourself if you wanted it now." They barely cracked smiles as they watched the zombie paw at the window.

The zombie had moved back to the door. Its weight was pressed hard against the file cabinet, rocking it back and forth. The sound of an unbalanced washing machine echoed throughout the hallway as it repeatedly smashed into the door. Gene tapped out 911 but still received no answer. He shook his head in disbelief. Ludwig asked,

"Where's Rosie?"

Gene took a deep breath and said, "Sorry, Doc. No pulse. I covered her up in the break room."

The news was a huge disappointment, and the doctor leaned on the wall for extra support as he tried to wrap his mind around the horrors of the tragedy. He looked through the window at the deformity in the room. With compassion he said, "This is horrible ... that poor girl."

To distract the doctor, Gene asked, "What are those things on its head?"

Ludwig shrugged and replied, "I don't know, but I've gotta get back to those files to see what Sporaton has discovered. Stand guard here, and if it gets out, sound the alarm and run!"

Gene assured him, "You don't have to say it twice, Doc!"

"Is This the End of the World?"

His reflection in a store window revealed Higgins' true exhaustion. He looked and felt sorry for himself. "I'm an old man ... too old for this." His knees hardly bent as he slowly shuffled his feet, shadowing the walls of the buildings that he passed. He heard a loud explosion coming from about a block ahead, followed by the crash of debris as it rained back down onto the street. He looked up to the sky and asked, "God, is this the end of the world?"

What just blew up? He sat down and scooted his butt back against a wall. After a few minutes of rest, he used the saw as a crutch to push himself back up. At the end of the building, he turned right and relaxed his hold on the wooden handle, letting it scrape along the ground.

A freshly-turned zombie rose to its feet from behind a parked car. It shambled toward the sound of the explosion, followed by many others. Some of the followers had huge tumors all over their heads, which looked like turbans. The others had hulking, oversized necks, and they all moaned horridly.

Doctor Stockton, M.M.H.U.:

Doctor Ludwig spread out the hieroglyphic pictures and said,

"Yes! I'm looking at the glyphs right now. I can't read ancient Mayan, but there appears to be an oddly shaped human head on one of the stones."

Doctor Stockton doodled on a yellow writing pad, then picked up a remote control. He replied, "Okay, I'll have an expert decipher the images."

Ludwig asked, "Have you sorted through the data on the cells yet?"

Before he answered, Stockton put his phone on speaker. He continued, "We have! That's the main reason I've phoned you. The nerve cells are able to regenerate themselves. Doctor Kasay of Baron Hospital stated that deceased patients were able to reanimate without any sort of medical interventions. Patients who were immobile or paralyzed were able to walk again, albeit slowly. We're talking paraplegics and quadriplegics. Needless to say, this could be a fantastic medical breakthrough."

Ludwig agreed and asked, "What about a working heart? How does their blood circulate?"

Stockton pushed a button on his remote control, and an image of a muscle cell appeared on a video screen. He answered, "The cell's regenerative process is turning the entire musculoskeletal system into one giant heart. Every movement, no matter how large or small, causes blood to pump, and I think bone marrow stem cells are morphing into heart cells." Stockton listened for a surprised response, but got none. Instead, he heard things crash in the background, and asked, "Are you okay?"

Ludwig nervously replied, "Yes, Doctor. But you should know these reanimated things are incredibly aggressive!"

Stockton's eyes widened in shock, as did those of the other scientists that sat at the conference table. He asked incredulously,

"It ... as in a reanimated person? You have one of them in the lab with you?"

As plainly and calmly as he could, Ludwig stated, "Yes! We have one of them trapped in a small room. The other one we found has already been killed my assistant. It's dead, along with a few lab workers, including Doctor Billings. These zombies are extremely dangerous!"

Stockton glanced at the people in the conference room, who squirmed in their seats. He replied, "That's awful news! I'd keep an eye out for your student, just in case of reanimation."

Ludwig flipped through some additional images and added, "We'll be vigilant, but don't forget about the glyphs. I believe one of Sporaton's finest was onto something."

Stockton quietly motioned for his assistant to come over, and then reassured Ludwig, "We won't forget, Doctor. Take care!" He ended the call, and then said to his colleagues, "The situation is worse than I thought. We're going to send a team to Texas. Alert the Medical Military Hazmat Unit."

His assistant asked, "What's that? I've never heard of it."

The doctor picked up an already prepared order and replied, "They're special forces, trained for both medical field work and combat operations." The assistant nodded in understanding, and Stockton continued, "They can perform biological testing and maintain security at the same time. They're the only team in the world that has this capability. Even Navy special ops can't mobilize like the M.M.H.U."

The assistant replied, "Wow, I had no idea."

Stockton handed the written order to his assistant and said, "Dispatch the team right away. When you contact the General Appropriations Office, use the code on the order. Afterward, shred the paper."

The assistant sharply replied, "Yes sir, Doctor Stockton!"

Caprock Canyon State Park:

The dusty road was lined with metal windmills and ranch homes. In the distance, towering wind turbines dotted the horizon. Dora excitedly exclaimed, "There it is – see that sign that says 'Simmons'? My daddy welded it together when I was a baby. It was my job to chip off the old paint and refinish it every year. That's where I grew up … broke a lot of horses out there."

Phoenix pushed his blond hair off of his face. "I think only Nolan, Adele, and I should go in. You two ladies stay put and keep guard out here, just in case."

Dora pleaded, "Phoenix! I'm going in too. I have to see for myself."

He shook his head and said, "No, Dora, please stay out here. I promise if your parents are inside, we'll bring 'em out."

Vicki reached out and grabbed her hand, giving it a squeeze to reassure her that it would all work out. Dora squeezed back and replied, "Okay, Phoenix. You're probably right." She accepted the truth of the matter, and popped a full mag into her rifle. Nolan pulled through the gates of the manicured, acre-sized front yard.

Phoenix gazed at the pool of blood that was now haloed around Michael's head. He leaned slightly toward Vicki in case her patient could still hear. She leaned forward at the same time, and they bumped heads. They rubbed their noggins and Phoenix whispered, "He's looking a lot worse." Vicki answered,

"Oops! Sorry about that. I know – I'm getting really worried about him." Adele watched the two of them and thought, *Oh Lord!*

At the foot of the porch stairs, Phoenix, Nolan, and Adele checked their weapons. When they were all ready, Phoenix looked into their eyes and said, "Okay, let's do this!"

Nolan and Adele followed as he took the lead and entered the front door. They carefully checked each room.

After the inspection, Nolan happily said, "Well, no signs of anyone."

Adele, with her back against an open door, scanned multiple rooms at once. The only thing visible was the tip of her rifle's muzzle. A little antsy, she stepped into the open and replied, "Yep, that's a good thing … especially for the zombies." Phoenix and Nolan breathed a sigh of relief.

The threesome exited the house slightly more relaxed, standing a few feet from the back door. They surveyed the picturesque landscape, taking in the sights—including a barn silhouetted by Caprock Canyon State Park.

***

Increasingly anxious about her beloved parents, Dora struggled with the idea of having to stay outside. She distracted herself with childhood memories of sleepovers, riding horses, and the occasional snowfalls they would get. She pictured herself riding with friends through the glistening snowflakes. Afterward, they would build a snowman and top it with an old beat-up cowboy hat and bandana. A sing-along, complete with hot chocolate and marshmallows, always awaited them when they returned.

Vicki mentally multitasked while she dangled her legs outside of the van. She kept an eye on Dora, who paced back and forth, and wondered if the hospital would even be functional once they got there. She pictured the layout of the emergency room in her mind, remembering the exact locations of transfusion tubing, antibiotics, and steroids. She was sure Michael was also going to require surgery, and hoped that a neurosurgeon would still be around. Absently, she traced her finger along several grooves on the M4 and noted that the safety was on. She glanced over at Dora again. Concerned that she might decide to rush the home, Vicki patted a make-believe seat next to her and said, "Why don't you come over here and sit with me, honey?"

Dora replied, "Nah, I'm good sweetie!" without taking her eyes off of the front door.

***

Phoenix said, "Let's check out the barn." His partners followed. Halfway to the building, he pointed to an eight foot long diamondback rattlesnake that had crossed their path and said, "Whoa, look at that zombie!"

Adele raised her rifle to take a shot at it, but Nolan quickly pushed the muzzle down, saying, "Adele, save your ammo!" Disappointed, she kicked dirt and rock toward the beast until it slithered away.

A few moments later, Phoenix entered the barn, followed by Nolan and Adele. They examined every nook, cranny and stall, and found no signs of life. The barn had not housed livestock in about twenty years, ever since Dora's father had gotten too old to care for the animals. Everything appeared to be exactly where it should have been. Nolan speared the ground with a pitch fork and said, "Maybe they're hiding out with other folks somewhere safe."

Phoenix replied, "Yeah … maybe. But I think they would have locked up the house when they left."

Adele descended a ladder from the loft and shouted, "There's nothing up there!"

Phoenix waved her over and said, "C'mon … we gotta go."

Nolan put his rifle back on safety and said to Phoenix, "People out here leave their doors unlocked all the time. It's not like the big city."

Phoenix replied, "True dat. It's something I need to get used to. Let's look around the sides of the house for a storm cellar."

Nolan nodded in agreement, saying "Cool, never thought about that." They walked out of the barn and headed toward the left side of the house. Adele spotted another snake and shot at it. The head vanished and the body curled into a tight ball.

Phoenix yelled, "Why did you do that?"

She flashed a sinister smile and replied, "I couldn't help myself. There must be an infestation around here."

He wrapped his arm around her shoulder and said, "From now on, stay close to me."

***

Dora, getting frantic, decided to wait no longer and snuck into the house while Vicki's back was turned. She searched each room until she spotted a favorite portrait of her mother sitting sidesaddle on a horse, her dad leading the Palomino. Dora's heart was filled with loving memories as she stood in front of the photograph and whispered, "Momma … Daddy." She broke out of her trance-like state when she thought she heard something outside. She was desperate to find her parents, and then remembered the storm cellar.

***

Intent on being the first down the steps, Nolan looked over his shoulder and politely asked, "Mind if I take point?"

Phoenix replied, "Not really. Feel free." Nolan lifted the heavy wooden door by its knotted rope handle and descended the stairs. He immediately smelled the worst kind of stench and covered his nose with the bend of his arm. At the bottom of the ten steps, he unhooked a flashlight from a wall and aimed the beam at a far corner. Phoenix and Adele were close behind. Nolan traced the wall with the beam of light until he saw two bodies. Phoenix tapped him on the shoulder and said, "Shine it on what's left of their faces." After the beam zeroed in on the two mutilated heads, he added, "That has to be her parents."

Before they could say a quick prayer, the cellar door rattled and startled the three. They spun around like hardened soldiers ready to prove themselves, but the sunlight's glare momentarily blinded the two closest to the door. Phoenix shouted, "Hold your fire!" He quickly directed his next statement to the intruder, "You shouldn't be here!" But then he realized who it was and somberly continued, "I think we found your parents."

Dora rushed halfway down the stairs and said, "Oh my God! My parents?"

Adele turned ice-cold as she said, "It looks like they didn't make it, sweetie." Dora felt the blood drain from her face. She struggled to get past Nolan and Phoenix; she needed to see them for herself.

Nolan grabbed her by the shoulders, and whispered, "They're gone, but you have to go on."

She burst into tears. "No, it can't be!" Her voice had a hollow, empty sound as she asked, "You're sure they're dead?"

Nolan and Phoenix each took one of her arms and, without answering, ascended the stairs and brought her up into the light. Vicki, who already stood at the top of the steps, had come to tell them about Dora. After she saw the distress in everyone's faces, she held off. Adele backed up the steps. Once at the top, she lifted the heavy doors and dropped them into place.

Back in the van, Nolan tried to give Phoenix a look that projected confidence, but internally, he was a mess of squishy nervous energy. He faced him and asked, "Where to now, boss?"

After thinking about their options for a moment, Phoenix replied, "Let's check out the old train station and then head over to the hospital to see if we can get some help for Michael."

"No problem!" Nolan stomped hard on the accelerator, causing the vehicle to fishtail on the dirt driveway.

Sitting between Vicki and Michael, Dora continued to sob. Vicki held her hand and tried to console her. She said, "You've got to try to remember your parents as they were, not as they are now."

In between sniffles, Dora wiped away her tears with a napkin and replied, "I know. But … I love them so much! They meant everything to me."

Vicki put her arm around her shoulder and said, "I know, honey." Out of habit, Dora gritted her teeth.

Without warning, everyone was jolted forward as the van's brakes were applied. Then they were all forced backward as the van reaccelerated. Adele felt a thump against the side of the vehicle. When she peered out of the double windows, she noticed a female zombie limping along in tight circles. It had sustained a glancing blow. A couple of seconds later, the zombie widened its circle, and ended up staggering in a zig-zagged line. Watching this pitiful spectacle, Dora's emotions got the best of her. She tried to choke back her tears but couldn't. They flowed freely.

Vicki held both of her hands and said, "I know. It's gonna be hard, honey."

Under her breath, Adele muttered, "Shoulda' finished the dang thing off." *Those two will never shut up.* She pulled the mag from her rifle, counted the rounds, and reinserted all except one. Looking at it closely, she memorized each and every detail, then kissed it and slipped it into her pocket.

Vicki looked down at her patient while she reassured Dora once again. "Don't worry. The police will get to the bottom of what's happened, and things will settle down."

Dora used her right arm to steady herself against the back of the driver's seat. She stared blankly at Michael's brain, noticing increasing twitches in the dull mass. At that moment, one large bubble of brain protruded from the hole in his head. His arm tightened and, with amazing speed, he grabbed Dora's left arm and yanked her off her knees. She lost her balance and fell on top of him.

Vicki screamed, "Oh my God!" She tried to pry his hand from Dora's arm.

Dora shouted, "He's hurting me!" and quickly rolled to her side to break his grip.

Adele turned from the window. She took aim and was about to pull the trigger until Vicki yelled, "Stop! He let her go! The fever probably caused a spasm. That's all."

Phoenix turned and looked directly at Adele. "Okay, everybody. Let's chill out. Please." Adele could not look him in the eyes. She turned her attention back to the rear windows and watched a group of zombies feasting on a corpse.

Dora slumped against the passenger seat and asked, "Do you think he's going to turn into one of those things?"

Vicki never replied. Instead, she thought about the steps she would need to take in the emergency room.

Nolan, in his best Nicholson voice, announced, "Ladies and gents, we're here!"

Phoenix said, "Pull right over to that sign. I see somebody over by the bench." Seconds later, the van screeched to a stop and Phoenix got out. He scanned the immediate area, then checked his rifle's safety. A three-story cowboy sign towered above his five foot eleven frame. He walked cautiously towards the body, and stopped when he realized that it was Thomas. He waved Nolan over before he continued any further.

When Nolan saw the bodies, it was his last straw. He ran up to the dead zombie and fired a couple of rounds into it point blank. Unsatisfied, he blurted out, "I gotta shoot more of these things!" Then he exhaled deeply and started looking around for other targets.

The comment startled Phoenix, whose mind was racing. He replied, "Yeah, this isn't good. I'll have to go inside and see if Ziggy's in there. But this time, you stay out here. I'll ask Vicki if she wants to go in." His voice deepened when he leaned forward and whispered, "Keep an eye on Adele. Don't let her get trigger-happy. She could take us out with friendly fire." Nolan was stunned with the decision, but accepted his babysitting fate.

Phoenix waved Vicki out of the van and popped the question. Still feeling as though she needed to prove herself, she replied, "I'll go in with you, Phoenix. No problem."

Nolan got back in the van. Embarrassed, he said, "Yeah, I'm sittin' this one out." It did not sit well with him.

Phoenix got down on one knee and pointed, whispering, "Do you see the stains over on the floor? I hope that blood isn't Zig's." In that brief second, Vicki sized up the stains. *At least several liters of blood here. Way too much for any one person to be alive.* Phoenix stood back up and they carefully stepped to the left of the blood pools.

Every few seconds, Vicki whispered Ziggy's name. They passed a vending machine and Phoenix checked his pocket for fifty cents, for powdered donuts, but found nothing. Before long, they heard some moans and crept closer to investigate. Moments later, they made their way into the men's restroom and saw a partially-eaten body, face down. Blood spatters covered the walls. The back of the corpse's skull was missing along with a few strips of flesh from its left arm. The right arm was bent oddly at the elbow. Phoenix turned the man over. He forgot to whisper when he said, "It's Zig." The abdomen looked like a high school dissection gone wrong. Bloodied streaks on the floor led to a bathroom stall. Phoenix and Vicki looked at each other.

Phoenix had just started to whisper something when a deep, guttural sound emanated from the stalls. "Rog-gra," was followed by a loud bang as a stall door slammed open. The power behind the swing tore the door from its hinges; it crashed into the opposite wall. A blood-soaked zombie staggered out. Its thick neck merged with its head in a straight line. Its eyes bulged beyond their sockets as it mumbled, "Rog-ra! Rog-ra-ra!" Phoenix and Vicki opened fire simultaneously, but Vicki's weapon jerked wildly and her bullets strafed the wall above the zombie's head. Debris from the popcorn ceiling rained down. Phoenix's rounds penetrated the body from the groin up. The sound of air hissing from a puncture in one of the zombie's lungs was followed by an audible pop. An explosion of gore soaked the checkerboard black and white tiled wall. The sudden gush of blood stopped just short of their feet, but the ceiling above now rained red. Phoenix and Vicki did not wait for the headless body to crash to the floor. They bolted out of the room and back to the van.

Doctor Ludwig and the List:

Ludwig called Gene from the hallway. Happy to be away from the zombie even for a second, he hurried over to the doctor. Ludwig thumped a stack of paper files along with some photos and said, "These are the key to what's happening here. The photos *must* be a clue to what the team discovered in the jungle. Can you look up names and addresses of the scientists on the expedition?"

Excited to do something other than guard the crazed zombie, Gene replied, "Okay Doc, will do." He retrieved a laptop and a rolling chair. He placed the computer on the chair and rolled both down the hallway, out of the direct line of sight of the trapped zombie. *Don't want to agitate it any more than need be.* He sat down and began to scan the bright screen. He lucked out and quickly found an icon which, when clicked on, listed all of the Belize team members.

Ludwig spread out photos and unedited notes on the table. After a quick scan, a single word circled in red by Doctor Phan caught his eye: "*Ophiocordyceps!*" He looked up the unfamiliar word and wrote down its definition. Then he remembered a paper-folding technique he'd learned by watching a television documentary. He grabbed one of the photos of a glyph and folded it until a new image emerged, then rough-sketched the new pictogram onto a sheet of paper.

Gene printed the list using a nearby wireless printer, then walked the document over to Ludwig. Curious, he asked, "Are we visiting these people?"

The doctor put down the newly-created glyph and said, "Thanks! We are."

Gene looked down at the hand-drawn glyph and asked, "What's that, Doc, someone's notes?"

Ludwig shook his head. "No, this is a trick I learned from a television show."

Gene replied, "That's really cool. I gotta say, though – this assignment is definitely creeping me out." On his way back to his chair, Gene stopped at a beautiful poster which highlighted various types of spores. The Sporaton logo was emblazoned at the bottom of the large, copyrighted paper. A simple definition of a spore was written on the poster. It stated:

Spore - a walled, single to many-celled organism, capable of giving rise to a new individual, either directly or indirectly; courtesy of dictionary.com.

He stood there admiring the pictures of the spores and thought, *Wow, even the ones photographed in black and white look beautiful.* Their shapes reminded him of primitive flowers, or even naval warfare mines. Then he heard a sound coming from the room where the zombie was confined. Curious, he put his back against the poster, slid across the wall to the window, and peeked in to get another look at it. The zombie was standing near the window, completely still. Its tumors had grown noticeably larger. Gene ducked to crawl beneath the window so he could look in from the other side, but he banged his knee on the wall. When he stood and looked back into the window, he was terrified to see that its gaping mouth was mere inches from the window. Its eyes were so dark that Gene couldn't tell where the eye sockets ended and the face began. It stared directly at him, gnawing at the plate glass. Completely freaked out, Gene swallowed hard and stumbled backward. He nearly wet his pants, and promised himself that he'd be manlier the next time he came face-to-face with something terrifying. He called out for the doctor.

Ludwig dropped the photograph he was holding and ran to Gene's aid. He pointed to the new smear left behind on the window and asked, "What happened?"

Gene moved further down the hallway and answered, "I'd been peeking at that thing through a corner of the window, and moved to reposition for a better look. When I glanced back into the room, it was standing right there and tried to bite me through the glass."

Ludwig patted his back and said, "Alright, just hold tight. We'll be leaving shortly."

Gene raised his eyebrows and asked, "We're not just gonna leave that thing in there, are we?"

The doctor playfully responded, "Are you proposing that we take it with us?"

Gene replied, "Of course not … but, don't you think we should do something about it?"

Ludwig shrugged and asked, "You mean execute it?"

Gene nodded vigorously. The doctor pointed to the blocked door and said, "Well, you can be my guest. But, judging by what happened a few minutes ago, I wouldn't if I were you." He patted Gene's shoulder and added, "We'll put things on hold here while we investigate the addresses you gave me. I promise, we'll come back later and you can take care of it. Does the rental car have GPS?"

They walked away from the window, and Gene took the car keys out of his pocket. "Yeah, Doc. It does."

Back at his workstation, Ludwig glanced at the list that Gene had given him, recognizing most of the names. John Kimball, Angela Smith, Phan Nguyen, Oscar Remmy, Max Honoree, Phoenix Holiday, and Jim Knocks. There were a few others, too. *Just concentrate on these for the time being.*

Gene's stomach rumbled continuously as he walked over to the doctor's workstation. "I'm gonna raid the fridge. Do you want anything?"

Ludwig replied, "No, not right now. I don't think I could eat."

Gene walked into the darkened break room, opened the fridge door, and pulled out everything he saw that didn't look spoiled. He glanced at the couch. The light from the fridge reflected off of the foil blanket, and it appeared to glow. He felt sorry for Rosie, and was tempted to peek under the blanket, but decided against it. The thought of her lifeless body lying there gave him the heebie-jeebies.

Gene and Ludwig headed out to the car, and Gene programmed Angela Smith's address into the GPS unit. As soon as the data was entered, Ludwig said, "Let's get out of here." Gene pulled out of the parking lot and followed the prompts from the GPS's robotic female voice. Motivated more than ever, Ludwig scanned the list and said,

"Let's find out what's caused this outbreak. I just hope everyone is alive and well—and that they can give us the answers we need."

Gunfire in the Distance:

Higgins had a flashback as sporadic gunfire went off in the distance. He ducked behind a large tree, then army-crawled to a pile of old lumber. *Where's the enemy?* He stood straight up without any soreness at all. He looked around, and the glare of the hot sun transported him back to Baron. He shook off the flashback and whispered, "Wonder where those shots are coming from?" He continued on his way, keeping out of sight as best he could.

Higgins walked for blocks, hoping to find the shooters. He knew that the zombies weren't using guns, and figured there was a group of normal folk out there somewhere who could lend him a hand. Out of the blue, a platoon-sized group of zombies emerged from a side street. Before they could hear or see him, he found another car to hide within. He placed his saw against a side panel, opened the door, and climbed in quietly, closing and locking the door behind him. He squeezed under the dashboard as far as he could. He remembered the basic lesson his drill sergeant used to bark out repeatedly: "If you can find cover, use it. Stay alive to fight another day, Marines." He felt for his saw, but realized that he had left it outside. He whispered, "Dang it!" The stress of the event triggered another flashback, this time to a bitter cold day and the foxhole that he had lived in. Even his canteen of water had been frozen. He exhaled warm air onto his hands and rubbed them together as he relived the bitterly cold day in his mind.

Five minutes later, the roving band of zombies had moved past the vehicle. He snapped out of the flashback and remembered that he was in a car, and cheerfully thought, *They didn't find me.* He prayed he could find the people that had fired the weapons, and opened the door. He retrieved his saw and continued down the street toward the gunfire. Thirty minutes later, he spotted a small group of people shooting down a crowd of zombies. As fast as his hip would allow, he circled around to the backside of the group and approached very carefully.

U.F.E.D. Team Lands:

A secret desert location somewhere in the United States housed the United Federation for the Eradication of Diseases team, U.F.E.D. It was funded by a coalition of seven countries, and each country supplied the best of the best. The team loaded their personal gear onto the special operations aircraft in a well-rehearsed maneuver only used in dire emergencies. They had most recently been dispatched to handle the bird flu scare and Hurricane Katrina. Katrina had unleashed all sorts of toxic chemicals and diseases into the flood waters of New Orleans; they were sent in as a precaution against some weird outbreak. They wound up staying for months longer than expected to help out at a local hospital as needed. The upside was that they got to live on a first-class cruise ship docked in the port of New Orleans, disguised as health workers. Housing was funded by F.E.M.A. and the American taxpayers.

Colonel Caster, M.D., was the last of sixteen to climb aboard the aircraft. Everyone else sat back and relaxed into the comfort of the plush leather seats. Caster buckled himself in, then leaned into the aisle and gave a thumbs-up to the pilot. The plane immediately taxied down the tarmac and prepared to take off. Cruising at 528 mph, the two hour flight would be quick and painless. Caster tried to merely concentrate on the mission, but the report about human reanimation had him worried. He could not wait to get to the bottom of this mystery.

Phoenix's Team Tries to Save Michael:

Back in the van, Dora sat and stared into space, her mind lost in childhood memories. Phoenix was chatting with Vicki, keeping his voice low-key to avoid alarming anyone. He said quietly, "I can't believe the extent of this outbreak."

Vicki nodded in agreement, "I know. There wasn't any mention of it on any of the news stations, or in any directives sent to the hospital."

Phoenix stretched his stiff left shoulder and replied, "Yep. It's just so strange."

Vicki went on. "I had the department manager's ear and would have been the first to know anything had there been some sort of precursor event."

Phoenix stretched his other shoulder and mused, "Where do you think we should go?" He thought for a few moments, then answered his own question. "I guess we should just keep moving until we find a suitable hideout, or until the military comes marching in."

Vicki said, "Let's not forget about Michael. He needs a hospital."

Adele, sarcastic and uncaring, glared at Michael and replied, "He's as good as one of them things. We should do him now and save ourselves the trouble later." She roughly slapped the stock of her weapon and said, "Man, I just want some action. I really wanna fire this thing."

Phoenix shook his head and replied, "Don't worry! I believe you'll get your chance. Next time, you're gonna take point."

Unexpectedly, Dora chimed in, "I want in on the next one! I wanna kill some too."

Phoenix knew he would have his hands full with the two women and replied, "Ladies, we're all going to get our fair share. Just look around."

Phoenix's stomach growled and he tried to lighten the mood. "Okay, time to get some food! We should head over to the Big Texas Roadhouse for some ribs. I could go for a truckload of those fall-off-the-bone baby backs right about now."

At the mention of food, Adele noticed her own hunger pangs. "Yeah, I could really go for some baby backs too."

Phoenix pulled out his note pad and wrote: *"On our way to the roadhouse … several dead, one injured."*

Michael moaned deeply, but no one said a word, save Vicki. She waited for someone to say something sympathetic, but realized that the others had given up on him. "We really need to get him to the hospital. Maybe the police have secured it by now."

Phoenix kept his eyes on the road and replied, "Yep, that's right! We're gonna drop him off at the hospital, then go get the food."

Nolan agreed, but noticed that the streets were growing increasingly crowded with zombies. As he carefully navigated the van, he said, "Look around. They've definitely increased in numbers." He ignored the strong urge to just drop Michael off on one of the street corners. *Maybe soon we'll have to.*

Adele stiffened her body so much that she looked like a palace guard. Over her shoulder, she yelled, "Stop here!" then turned her baseball cap backward and pointed behind the van. "Look right there! Easy targets. Let's go and shoot 'em up."

Startled by her outburst, Nolan slammed on the brakes. Phoenix and Vicki scooted toward the rear window and gazed outside. Eight zombies had staggered onto a nearby lawn.

Vicki replied as if she were scolding a child, "Let's not. We have a sick patient here. We can't waste any time."

Adele pointed to her left temple and said "If something like that happens to me, just drop a bullet right here!"

Dora sat still and ignored the others. She casually flipped the rifle's safety off and then back on again. She placed her free hand on the door handle, trying to curb the building urge to jump from the vehicle and just run. Phoenix looked at Adele and said, "Just chill out, please!

You're gonna get plenty to shoot at soon." Dora gripped the door handle tighter. The urge to jump out was strong.

Adele sat back on her heels and thought about the way that her husband had died. She shook her head and replied, "I'm just ready, man! You know, I just need some action." Dora pulled down ever so slightly on the door handle and instantly felt the building pressure leave her body.

Nolan turned and faced Adele, saying, "You're gonna have more chances than you can handle here pretty quick. The streets are crawling with those things." He punctuated his comment by sideswiping another of the walking dead. It careened at an angle away from the van, then split into two.

Nolan added, "Let's just keep on keepin' on … for Michael." Phoenix's sixth sense told him something was about to explode in Baron, and that all hell would break lose. He looked down at Michael, then over at Vicki, and said, "For Michael!" Dora slowly released the door handle and meekly said, "For Michael."

Warm Beer:

Higgins moved along the exterior wall of a building that jutted out onto a sidewalk. The moans he heard down the street were just another setback, and he decided to play it safe. With his back against the wall, he whispered, "I'll just let them wander by like before." He looked up and saw an old beer sign. *Wait one second. That's Joe's bar next door. I'm gonna have a drink … on the house!*

The front door of Joe's bar was partially blocked by a juke box, so Higgins had to push hard against the door to get it all the way open. He quietly stepped across the tiled threshold and immediately smelled a putrid stench. The stink was almost unbearable. Several corpses were sprawled out on the floor. Instinctively, he turned back toward the door to make a quick exit, but a zombie rose from the corner where the juke box had been pushed. It now blocked his path. He suddenly felt strong, as if his body had grown six inches taller, even though he knew it had not. He shouted loudly, "Get away from me!" The shout caused the zombie's enlarged, tumor-ridden head to explode; the lifeless body fell atop a nearby table. The shredded neck stump pumped out blood like a beer tap from hell. He gagged at the sight and spat, hoping none of the infection had gotten into his mouth. Before he left, he snatched a bottle of beer from the bar. Outside, he used the edge of a brick to pop off the bottle cap. He took a swig and swished the warm golden liquid around in his mouth, then spit it out. Satisfied that any nastiness was gone, he grimaced and chugged the rest of the beer. When the bottle was emptied, he whispered, "Never did like warm beer, but it'll do." He gingerly set the empty bottle down on the sidewalk.

He listened for moans, but did not hear any and started walking back down the street. As he reached the corner, a zombie's arm awkwardly swiped at him from his blind spot, connecting with the brim of his Cavalry hat. The hat flipped and tumbled through the air, landing directly on top of his empty beer bottle. He grasped the saw by one of its wooden handles and swung hard, knowing it would be all over for him if another one of the zombies showed up. The blade connected with the zombie and ripped the shirt and flesh away from its rotting chest. It was heavily damaged, but it continued to lumber toward him. *Dang it! How can it move?* The old man swung again, and the saw connected with the thing's shoulder. When he pulled back, strands of flesh and tendons hung off of the toothy blade. Thick blood trickled down its damaged arm, but it still continued to advance. Higgins burped loudly and immediately felt better. The warm beer buzz energized him, and he swung the saw again as the zombie moaned, "Cra-gaa!" The saw connected right between its macerated lips, and nearly sliced the head in half just above the lower jaw. Its tongue remained attached to the floor of its mouth, and stiffened as if the last nerve had been severed. The body crumpled to the ground, motionless. The old man walked over to pick up his dusty blue hat, then slowly walked away, muttering, "I need another beer."

U.F.E.D Arrives in Baron:

Once the military flight was on the ground, the pilot taxied the large plane to the unloading area of the tarmac. Several M-925 cargo trucks were parked nearby, waiting to be loaded up. About twenty lower-ranking Marines were already there to load the crates into the reconfigurable oversized vehicles. The crates contained special gear for their mission—everything from weaponry and ammo to advanced medical equipment and MRE's that would last for two weeks or more.

After a special numeric code that meant, "All clear and on the road," had been texted back to base via his secure smart phone, Colonel Caster and his team took off for Baron. As they drove, he re-read the report and scratched his forehead. He tapped his finger at the word "reanimation." *Walking dead people … crazy at best.* He turned away from the driver so he wouldn't see him crack a smile.

A couple of hours later, the cargo trucks pulled into a large parking lot just inside the city limits of Baron. Colonel Caster got out of his truck and made a few hand signals, and the team began to set up equipment. To deploy their uniquely-designed inflatable tents, all the soldiers needed to do was open the box, hook it up to a compressor, and step away. The flexible, lightweight solarized material would quickly expand into a full-sized tent and provide all of the power that they would need.

Colonel Caster twirled the ends of his mustache, then motioned for the Commander of the hazmat team to meet with him. Cummings walked over and snapped to attention at his side. Caster casually said, "I'd like your team to go out and scout the area. See if you can find a specimen or two of those 'reanimated' bodies that the Baron medical doctor mentioned. Get started on this right away."

With a perfectly executed hand salute, Cummings replied, "Yes, sir!" He turned sharply and started barking out his own orders.

Cummings walked over to his busy team of eight, and gestured for everyone to fall in. He walked their line, then moved back to the middle and explained, "This looks like it'll be a clean sweep operation," then leaned in and whispered, "I mean, dead people coming to life? This has got to be a drill of some sort to test readiness. Don't unpack everything just yet. Put on your hazmat suits; make it look good for the colonel." The small group replied with a collective, "Yes sir," and began the process of opening crates and helping one another get into their bright orange hooded suits.

Despite being designed for comfort, the bulky suits compounded the problem of collecting samples, and were anything but comfortable. Before pulling the hood over her head, the last team member switched on her built-in internal cooling fan. Without the fans on such a hot day, the mission would be impossible.

Caster stood in the middle of the newly-created compound, surrounded by the rest of his team. He addressed them soberly. "We're in go mode. Everything we do from here on out will be scrutinized. We'll take any specimens the hazmat team gathers, whatever they may be, and process them. If all goes well, we'll be gone from here before midnight. I want this deployment to be perfect, and I want a perimeter guard out front and one in the back. The rest of you can finish setting up camp."

Bartholomew and Jake gathered their weapons, exchanged a few pleasantries, and talked about the rumors they'd heard from other team members. Jake smirked and said, "This has to be a drill."

Bartholomew pointed at his rifle and replied, "Just in case it's not, stay on your toes, man. Take it seriously."

Jake, always cocky and absolutely sure the whole thing was a set-up, replied, "C'mon man! Dead people? Maybe you're in on it." He walked away, a smirk on his face.

Phoenix's Team, Taking Point:

When they pulled up near the hospital's emergency room entrance, Nolan jumped out of the van and followed Vicki as she hustled through the automatic doors. Before they advanced much further, they paused to listen for signs of either survivors or zombies. After taking a few more steps forward, Vicki tapped his shoulder, shaking her head in disappointment. He understood what she meant; judging by the disarray of things, there was not much of a chance that anyone could still be alive.

Vicki moved to place her back against the wall. Emergency strobe lights flashed continuously. She sidestepped a severed hand; the sight of it almost caused her to burst into tears. Blood spatters and smears covered the walls, the privacy curtains and the waxed floors. She pulled her M4 tightly against her chest and said,

"The entire department is totaled!" Switching the safety of her rifle to the off position, she slowly moved past a triage room and added, "I don't like this."

Nolan, walking backward directly behind her, mumbled, "Uh huh!"

Vicki's heartbeat began to keep pace with each flash of strobe light. Secretly, she wondered if she were having heart palpitations, then sucked it up and put the feeling on the back burner. "We're going to get what we need, but before we turn back, I wanna make sure no one else needs us here." Happy to be out of the driver's seat, Nolan agreed and followed her.

***

Dora sobbed as she sat in the van, monitoring Michael. She figured she got the job because the others saw her as an emotional wreck. She closed her eyes and thought, *Okay, no problem. I can do this.* After a minute, she opened her eyes and noticed that Michael's partially-exposed brain now pulsated with each of his breaths, not just sporadically. His eyeballs darted back and forth under his lids, as if he was having a horrific nightmare. *Did the same thing happen to my parents?* In

167

confusion, she pointed the end of her rifle at the bloody, wet towel that covered his brain. She was tempted to pull the trigger but fought back the urge. *If he's NOT turning into one of those things, I'd be murdering someone.* With all of her willpower, she pointed the barrel of the weapon at the floor of the van, then looked up to the heavens, asking for guidance.

Leaning on the front bumper of the van, Phoenix stared at the entrance to the emergency room. Adele stood next to him, her rifle site pointed at the entrance. She wiped the sweat off of her brow with the crook of her arm. Two full mags were in her oversized pants pocket. *It'll have to do.* She watched the American and Texas state flags lightly flapping in the breeze, then said aloud, "God, I'm thirsty!"

Phoenix replied, "Yeah, I am too, but do you think you could keep your voice down?"

***

Vicki shushed Nolan, then paused. She gestured for him to hit the deck and he did so. She squatted low, looked into a corner mounted mirror, and saw a single zombie laboriously move past a hallway intersection. It was dressed in a hospital gown that only covered the front half of its body, revealing the light green sagging skin of its rear end. Vicki made bunny ears with her fingers behind her own head to signify something was on top of its head. Nolan shrugged his shoulders. He couldn't figure out what she meant by the gesture. The zombie shuffled past the intersection and she whispered sharply, "Stalks … close call."

She moved forward, but Nolan hadn't understood what she had said and asked, "What did wiggling your fingers over your head mean?"

As seriously as she could say it, she replied, "Stalks! It looked like the one I saw earlier." Nolan's expression was priceless and reflected what he thought. *Impossible!* She turned and faced him, adding, "What feels really weird is that there are no 'normal' people here, and only one zombie. By the way, let's not forget the meds."

***

Figuring her time had finally arrived, Adele refocused her line of sight, took a controlled breath, and released the round. A single bullet struck the zombie squarely between the eyes. Its body arched backward and crumpled to the ground behind a dumpster. Her muscles relaxed enough to reposition for another kill, but she felt the rifle become heavier.

Phoenix latched onto the middle of the weapon and yelled, "Dammit, Adele!" A slight tug-of-war ensued, but she rapidly lost control of the weapon. He leaned it against the van away from her, and angrily said, "C'mon, we already decided not to shoot these things. What's wrong with you?" She gave no reply.

Panicked by the sound of the shot, Dora jumped from the van. She seemed to come out of the fog she'd been in, and asked, "Are they here yet?"

Phoenix shook his head and answered, "Nope. And things are about to get a little hairy."

***

Vicki and Nolan stopped when they heard Adele's single gunshot. The sound seemed to echo throughout the empty hallways. At that moment, the zombie they had previously seen appeared and wobbled in their general direction. Its joints were a symphony of pops and grinds, and as it uttered, "Cha-ra," Vicki clutched Nolan's hand. They had remained as quiet as possible, but it was too late. It stopped, pivoted, and looked directly at them. A plastic nasogastric tube hung from its nose. Nolan bent at the waist and scooted to a nearby I.V. pole. He grabbed the pole, stood up, and swung it so hard that one leg of the wheeled base imbedded in the zombie's forehead. The former patient fell to the floor. Nolan stomped on the other side of the pole's base, causing a spinning wheel to protrude through to the other side of its skull. Blood spattered his boots and gushed from the zombie's mouth in a thick, syrupy stream. Vicki motioned for him to keep moving, and they continued down the hallway. They both thought, *Won't follow us again.*

At a computer charting station, a uniformed zombie moved into view from their left side. Its spine protruded through several areas of missing flesh, and it appeared to have taken a serious beating at some point. As it began to slowly follow them, Vicki pointed and said, "Let's go this way. We can circle around the operating rooms, and that will lead us back to the E.R."

Nolan nodded. "I'm right behind you."

Shoulder to shoulder, they stayed close to the wall and hurried along, listening for additional moans. Twenty-five feet later, another zombie appeared at the end of the hallway. They ducked behind a bloodied gurney, pushed it forward, and switched to another hallway. That stretch of hallway featured artwork of tiny babies as they held onto the fingers of their parents. At the end of the hallway, Vicki whispered, "Look – these doors lead to the operating rooms and back to the E.R." She pressed a metal wall plate, and the double doors opened.

As they walked through the authorized personnel only entrance, Nolan whispered, "I feel funny walking back here – I've never seen the inside of an operating room."

They continued, but kept a low profile and crossed over a red line on the floor. Nolan poked his head into operating room number one and said, "It looks like the inside of a space ship. Look at the fancy machines and that robot."

Vicki knew that he was awestruck, which would only delay them further. She patted his back and said, "Okay, we've got to keep moving."

He ignored her and whispered, "I'm hearing lots of moans right over there." He moved forward so quickly that she could only clutch her rifle and follow. Together, they peeked through the observation window of operating room number five and saw a patient on the table. Medical monitors blared and flashed non-stop. Several scrub-clad zombies were covered in blood, hovering at the head of the bed. They had cored out the patient's brain leaving only an empty shell. Another body lay dead on the tiled floor. Its head had been impaled with a large pronged surgical instrument. As zombies jockeyed for position, they separated, exposing the patient on the table. A metal horseshoe-like device was screwed into the patients head. It was obvious that brain surgery had been taking place before the catastrophe. Surgical instruments were scattered all over the floor, and a heavy microscope was turned over on its side. A nurse with a fire ax in his hand lay dead against one wall.

Nolan whispered loudly, "Oh my God, that's Derek. I know that dude. He must've died defending his patient."

The intensity of the scene overwhelmed Vicki, and she lost her cool. Sobbing, she asked, "Why is this happening?"

Nolan grabbed her by the shoulders. "Let's run for it. No more stopping. When we get to the E.R., just grab the meds."

Vicki nodded, and said, "The faster we're out of here the better I'll feel." Her hospital was no longer a place for healing; it belonged to the living dead.

***

Adele's single gunshot had attracted dozens of zombies. They were in various states of decay and had strangely lined up. Instinctively, they turned from the old strip mall a few blocks away and shambled towards the noise.

Phoenix focused his attention on the approaching ghouls. He darted from the back of the van to the front, then tossed Adele her rifle and said, "I'm counting three to the right, and seven to the left."

Adele's resentment against Phoenix quickly faded, and she clicked the safety to off. Her adrenaline surged like she'd just pounded down five energy drinks. As she dropped down to one knee and prepared to blast them, she replied, "I've got five behind us."

Dora locked and loaded her M4, then added, "I think there are a few on the left side of the hospital."

Phoenix said, "It's time. Adele, you have rear. Dora's got the left, and I'll clear the hospital entrance."

Adele shouted, "Yee-haw! Now we're talking!"

***

Vicki slung her rifle behind her back and waved her hand over the multi-drawer machine like a game show hostess. She said, "Here it is — the drug dispenser! I just have to gain access." She placed her forefinger on the electronic security pad. Nolan stood guard and hoped that she would be his nurse if he ever got sick. The lengths she was willing to go through for the health of her patient amazed him. Multiple drug drawers opened, and Vicki retrieved a handful of pain meds, steroids, and antibiotics. She closed the drawers and grabbed sterile gauze, a bottle of saline and some peroxide from a supply shelf.

Nolan heard a wicked little coo, and with his back to hers, whispered, "Did you hear that?"

She replied, "Yeah, but I'm done. Let's get out of here."

As she turned, she saw a large baby scooting on its butt toward them. Nolan saw it and could not believe his eyes. He shouted, "Good God!" and stood transfixed.

Vicki's motherly instinct took over. "Oh, no! I have to help him!" The tiny zombie stood up. She ran over to pick him up, but with a good look at its pudgy face, she immediately backed away. It bared its needle-like teeth at her, its jaws unhinged. She fumbled for her rifle; the zombie stumbled forward and nearly latched onto her leg. She kicked at it, and it slid across the room. The zombie baby screeched. Its neck muscles bulged, and it clumsily crawled toward her. She aimed her rifle and fired. The bullets riddled its tiny body and slammed it back into a wall, where it cooed one last time. Nolan and Vicki ran toward the exit with tears in their eyes.

***

Adele's mind raced with an inner, healthy fear. She wiped the sweat from her brow and said, "I got this," and repositioned herself at the base of the flag pole. She stood there, weapon at the ready. For some reason she felt patriotic. *If I go down, at least it's for Texas.*

The zombies continued to move toward the van. Phoenix was giving Dora a quick pep-talk. "We really need your best shots, hon. Make sure you aim for their heads."

She sighted in a target, then replied, "I will. I will." He had no way of knowing that her father had taught her how to shoot like a pro by the time she was ten years old. This was her chance to get back at the zombies, once and for all. *This is for you, Mom and Dad.*

Adele fired a round. Her target reeled backward and went down with a gaping wound in its neck. *Cool ... I'll take it.* Again, she aimed her rifle and fired. The bullet struck a zombie in its temple. A large chunk of bone blasted away from its head, exposing a large cavern, and it collapsed face down. Two rounds later, two more zombies had dropped to the ground.

Phoenix killed all five of his intended targets without a hitch. Not hearing much gun fire from Dora, he ran to her position at the back of the van. Excited, she confidently said, "I got three!" He looked at her with surprise, but had no time to celebrate her kills as he popped another mag into his rifle. She lowered her weapon and said, "I need to check on Michael. Can you take care of the rest?"

He sighted in on an approaching zombie, pulled the trigger, then glanced up at her and said, "No problem." As she entered the van, he thought, *Glad she got something.* He started firing three round bursts as more zombies swarmed into the area.

***

The exit doors of the emergency room were blocked by several milling zombies. Aggravated but confident, Vicki said, "Don't worry, I know this place like the back of my hand." At that moment, they heard more of the zombies moving inside of the building, beyond their line of sight.

Ready for a fight, Nolan cracked his knuckles and said, "That sounded like it came from just a couple of hallways away."

Vicki ducked behind a computer station, then pointed to the exit doors. She said, "That's a lot of gunfire out there. They must be under attack."

Nolan poked his head around the closest corner. "It's clear this way."

Vicki stood up. "Okay! Follow me!"

The emergency strobe lights continued to blink eerily as Vicki and Nolan picked up their pace. He recognized one of the hallways, tapped her on the shoulder, and casually asked, "Mind if I take point?"

She answered, "That's a longer route. I think I should stay in front." She loved being the "point man," and really wanted to prove something to herself. She also liked how it made her feel. In the hospital environment, she could handle almost anything nursing had ever thrown at her, from a life or death situation to a simple wound dressing. Right now, she wanted the challenge for her sanity.

Nolan shrugged off her refusal and said, "Okay, Vicki, after you." Sensing that they were being trailed, Vicki stopped just shy of the end of a hallway. She looked up for a safety mirror, but found none, and quickly turned the corner. She immediately collided with a zombie. Its wild arms knocked the M4 out of her hand. As soon as the rifle hit the ground, it fired several rounds, shattering a ceiling light. Pieces of plastic and glass rained down on Vicki when she fell backward into Nolan's arms. She shouted, "NO! Not you too!" The zombie was one of her dearest friends.

Nolan put his arm on her shoulder and said, "Pull yourself together and get your rifle!" She dove for the weapon, picked it up one-handed, and scooted back against the wall. The former human resources worker, dressed in a three piece suit, bounced off the walls on its way to the feast, a necktie still tied neatly in place around its throat. It shook as it moaned.

Nolan advanced and fired on the zombie. His rounds impacted its back in a tight cluster, leaving a deep hole. Blood poured from the wound, but the zombie turned and started lurching toward him. Vicki shook her head in amazement. She had seen her share of gunshot victims; none could have survived something like that. She aimed her rifle and fired a three-round burst. Once again, the impacts only knocked it back. The partners looked at one another, then fired their weapons in unison. The body took the impacts like a ground meat package being hit with a hammer. Its head exploded, and slushy debris splattered them. An eyeball bounced and rolled toward Vicki's hand; she scooted sideways to avoid touching it. The corpse hit the deck, blood gushing from its multitude of wounds. Nolan and Vicki looked at each other in shock, knowing that they had survived a close one. She extended her hand, and he helped her to her feet. They edged around the headless corpse and, finding themselves near an exit, ran out of the building.

***

Phoenix stopped firing and yelled, "There they are!"

Adele sprinted over to them, grabbed Vicki by the shoulder and said, "C'mon, we gotta get out of here!" All three ran past the flag pole and back to the van. Dora shot several zombies with a skill that Phoenix finally noticed. He shot down several more zombies that started to encircle them.

Before Dora entered the van, she stood next to Phoenix and fired on another horribly disfigured zombie. She said, "That's for my parents!" With her remaining rounds, she unloaded on a cluster of zombies and added, "And this is for Michael, Garcia, and the rest!"

Back in the van, Vicki administered five milligrams of the pain medicine to Michael and prepared the antibiotic. She also gave him one hundred and twenty-five milligrams of the steroid. As she lifted the damp towel to change the dressings, Dora glanced over and nearly passed out. Michael's brain protruded from the wound by at least three inches and had flopped over onto his temple. It pulsed with each of his heartbeats. Vicki said, "Don't look. It takes some getting used to." She replaced the soiled cloths with wet sterile gauze and a head wrap.

After the dressings had been applied to his head and other wounds, Adele blurted out, "He's gonna turn on us. I can feel it!"

Vicki looked up with less confidence and replied, "We don't know that for sure. Right now, he's still a human being. Remember, I'm a registered nurse, and I'm not going to give up on him until I have to."

Nolan turned and added, "I'm with Vicki. The only thing we're gonna do right now is bring him with us."

Phoenix got out of the front seat and squatted next to Michael. He looked at the bulging dressing and said, "It's our responsibility to save lives. Right now, we don't know if he's infected. If we leave him, it's a definite death sentence. With us, he still has a chance."

Vicki looked into Phoenix's eyes and said, "I'm glad we're on the same page."

Dora smiled. "I agree with Vicki and Phoenix."

Adele raised an eyebrow, scooted to her position at the back of the van, and muttered, "Yeah, okay. We'll see how it goes."

Phoenix turned to Nolan and said, "Let's get out of here. There are at least a dozen of those things headed this way." He pulled out his notepad and scribbled a journal entry. Nolan revved the engine, squealing the tires, then pulled out of the parking lot.

Taco:

Higgins put the second empty beer bottle down on top of the car's hood. Sporadic gun fire continued in the distance, so he resumed his walk in that direction. Though the soreness in his hip persisted, he was easily able to duck behind a mailbox as three zombies lumbered past him. When they were gone, he got up and walked past a small taco stand. A Spanish-accented voice whispered, "Hey, you! Right over here, Meester." The old man turned and stepped up to the counter, and saw a man taking a bite out of a soft taco. The freshly-shredded cheese fell onto the counter. The taco vendor said, "Hey amigo, you need to get off the streets." Higgins eyeballed the taco and smacked his lips. Jose, the taco vendor, felt sorry for the old man and said, "You want one too?"

Higgins rubbed his belly and replied, "Si!"

Jose pulled an already-prepared soft taco out from under the counter and said, "Here, Señor. Take it!"

The old man looked him directly in the eyes. "Thanks, Mister!"

The kindly taco vendor smiled and said, "You need to hide somewhere, Señor. I'd invite you to stay here, but there's not enough room for two." He gestured with his hand at the confining space, and continued, "Just be as quiet as you can." Higgins ate the taco in two huge bites, then dug deep into his pocket. In his younger years, he would have come up with a whole handful of coins. Jose saw the old man come up empty and said, "Señor, I didn't want your money. These tacos will go to waste anyway. Now hurry! Go hide." Higgins nodded, turned, and resumed his walk. He heard Jose whisper, "Hurry up, Señor, they're coming."

U.F.E.D. Camp:

Colonel Caster booted up his laptop and entered the time of arrival and names of the team members who had made the trip. When he was done, he double checked each stenciled crate against an attached inventory list and his master list — a well-practiced routine. Satisfied that the unit had all that it needed, he surveyed his surroundings.

***

Jake walked to the end of the parking lot and leaned against a brick wall, surveying the area. He pulled out his smart phone and cranked up his industrial music. He loved it. Before he zoned out, he thought about the plausibility of people actually coming back to life. *No worries here.* He shuffled to his favorite song.

Dozens of zombies were staggering toward the sounds of the specialized camp. One of the walking dead was barely covered in a bullet-riddled team jersey. Its throwing arm had been reduced to a dangling piece of meat, held there by only a few tendons. Its mind was consumed by uncontrollable flashes of light and hunger. An arrow was lodged in its oversized neck.

Another zombie, clad in a once-fashionable yellow polka dot party dress, lamely crawled along on its knees. An automobile tire print ran up the side of its body and had split the dress nearly into two, exposing the mincemeat flesh underneath. It continuously mumbled, "Maa-gra! Maa-gra!"

Jake removed a cigarette from the flimsy pack. A wide assortment of synthetic drum beats blared in his ears. He was about to light up the smoke when he remembered that he was supposed to quit on this mission as a surprise for his girlfriend's birthday. *Dang habit is costing too much anyway.* He gazed at the soft pack, and the images of people wracked with cancer ran through his mind. It grossed him out. *Today's the day. I'm gonna quit for ME.* He made up his own lyrics on the spot; in a mad, punk rock-styled voice he shouted, "I'm gonna quit for me … for me … for me!"

Zombies were moving ever closer to the new non-smoker. He was oblivious as he concentrated on crushing the unlit cigarette with the tip of his steel-toed boot and making up more inspiring lyrics to share with his girl later.

***

Colonel Caster monitored the quick construction of the camp. Several of the mobile tents were already up and running, but he had the nagging feeling that he was forgetting to do something. Then he snapped his fingers and said, "Call Pookie." Just before he tapped on her picture icon, he stopped and decided to text instead. He wrote: "Just here for a few days. Talk to you soon. Forevermore, I send my love! :)"

Worse Than I Could Have Ever Imagined!

Doctor Ludwig and Gene were stunned by the number of reanimated that shambled around town. To make matters worse, dead bodies littered the street. As Gene slowed the car to turn corners, many of the zombies would unexpectedly change direction and veer into their path. Although terrifying, this gave the pair a good opportunity to study their features up close. They noticed that some of the walkers had well-defined tumors, but some had very few or none at all. They passed a group of zombies that were on their hands and knees. Underneath the cluster was a human body. They were in the process of devouring the victim like a pack of ravenous wolves. Gene asked, "Do you see that, Doc?"

Ludwig nodded his head, but had to put his fisted hand to his mouth to keep himself from throwing up. He spoke through his clenched fist and said, "Yeah ... let's go."

Gene gathered his thoughts for a moment, and said, "Doc, there's a name for this condition, but it's fictional."

In disbelief, the doctor shook his head and asked, "Well, what's the condition?"

Gene replied, "It'd be safe to say that these people are zombies."

Ludwig could not believe a word like that would come from the mouth of a graduate student. He lowered his hand to his belly and laughed. "ZOMBIES?"

Gene remained steadfast in his assessment. He stopped the car in the middle of the street and said, "Yes, Doc! They fit the popular definition very well. Reanimating flesh eating corpses"

Ludwig was intrigued by the theory, but the scientific voice of reason won out. He replied, "You've put forth an interesting hypothesis, but I doubt they're truly what you describe. I mean, that's the stuff of science fiction." Gene sighed, feeling as though he might get an F for this mission after bringing it up. The doctor was right; to think that zombies were real was preposterous.

Gene accelerated the car over several lifeless forms sprawled out on the road. He cringed at the sound of their breaking bones. A block later, he slowed down to avoid several other bodies on the road, and watched in horror as one of them wobbled to its feet. The flesh on the left side of its face and neck was completely shredded, exposing its lower jawbone, rotted teeth and trachea. A ghoulish grin was permanently stamped onto its hideous face. It tried to follow the car, but was woefully slow. The doctor checked the door and said, "Thank God it can't catch us. Let's get outta here!"

Another man half limped, half ran towards the car. Gene gunned the vehicle, but as he looked into the rear view mirror, he wondered if the man was really contagious.

Ludwig pondered a decision to stop and help, but ultimately, he said, "Just keep going." Several zombies ambushed the man. Ludwig turned his head from the mirror and said, "This is worse than I could've imagined." He clutched his stomach as a wave of nausea took hold.

Angela's Apartment:

Doctor Ludwig and Gene got out of the car, looked around, then picked up whatever they could find to use as weapons. They approached the apartment cautiously and rang the doorbell. After a few seconds of silence that seemed to stretch for minutes, they decided to walk through the small alley to the back door.

Angela's rear patio was nicely landscaped and very tidy, except for the shattered sliding glass doors. Intrigued, but frightened at the same time, Ludwig said, "We'll need to take a specimen, but I forgot my bag in the car. Can you get it?" Gene did not want to leave the doc alone, but knew that groundbreaking research was about to begin. He could not let him down, so he sucked it up and just smiled. *Show no fear – just run and get the bag.*

"Be back in a jiffy."

Out of the corner of his eye, Gene saw someone stagger from a nearby home as he reached inside the car for the bag. He poked his head above the door for a better view and saw its enlarged, distorted face. It showed no humanity whatsoever. He lifted his scavenged weapon to eye level, shook his head, and thought, *This branch isn't gonna work. I need something heavier.* He looked around for a better weapon.

After a brief scan of the area, he spotted a pile of plumbing trash and whispered, "Perfect." The zombie was much larger in person than any he had seen as he passed them on the street. He gathered his confidence, rushed the zombie, and impaled a three-foot long lead pipe through its forehead. The pipe sticking out of the forehead looked like a mythical unicorn's horn until blood poured from the end. The zombie convulsed, then fell face-first onto the ground. Upon impact with the street, the pipe was forced through the back of its skull. Blood poured from the top of the pipe and onto the street like a nightmarish fountain.

Thirty seconds later, a more confident Gene arrived back at the apartment and said, "Doc, here are your things." As he handed over the bag, he thought about the kill. He felt that he could do it again if need be, but really did not want to. He was not a killing machine.

With seven-inch long dissecting tweezers, Ludwig pulled a bloodied glass shard from the frame of the door and placed it inside a plastic baggie. Then he retrieved a strip of flesh in the exact same way. Gene squatted next to him and asked, "Doc, do you think that's from Angela?"

Ludwig said, "I don't know. I hope not." Gene stood up and scoped out the rest of the den. He called out Angela's name, waited for a reply, and got none. He called out several more times, then heard a faint moaning. The zombie's body was wretched, and was dressed only in skivvies. *Must be her boyfriend or husband.*

"Hey, Doc, We need to get out of here, fast."

Ludwig put all of his tools back into the bag, one piece at a time. A zombie advanced on them from a hallway, its low-pitched moans becoming louder.

"Hurry, Doc," Gene said as he backed up to the sliding glass doors.

A microscope slide fell to the ground and cracked under Ludwig's penny loafers. Ludwig fumbled inside the bag and pulled out a tool. Gene tried to pick up the specimen, but the doc said, "Leave it – it's ruined," and quickly tried to retrieve another strip of flesh from the door jamb.

Gene looked up. "Hurry, Doc!"

Ludwig retrieved the replacement specimen in time to see the zombie skirt around the couch. Gene knew he had to stop its advances, and grabbed a barbeque utensil from the patio. The zombie lunged at him, but only managed to scratch his arm before the double prongs were forced deep into its rib cage. Gene had reached his limit, and as he backpedaled away from the zombie he shouted, "Doc!" It teetered, but continued its awkward, clown-like advance. It seemed completely immune to the pain it should have felt.

Ludwig wished that he had more time to take samples, but instead appeased his assistant as he said, "Got it! Let's go!" He scurried back toward their car, Gene right on his heels.

Back inside the vehicle, Ludwig programmed the address of Max Benini into the GPS unit. Gene glanced at the display and said, "Good, we're only about seven minutes away."

Smoke-Free Zone:

Medical school had been one of Jake's options, until he found out that he was squeamish about the sight of blood. While on one of the many training maneuvers he was assigned to, a soldier had ripped his arm open on a piece of barbed wire fencing. Jake had fainted at the sight of the man's blood. It was then and there that he decided to forget about medical school. Since he had a high aptitude for anatomy and physiology, and because he was a first-rate marksman, he was chosen to be the first non-medical grunt assigned to the special unit. He had strict orders that prohibited cell phone use on missions, but figured a little game play every now and then was okay. He turned his back to base camp, hiding his smart phone from the view of the colonel. He opened up his favorite game application with a few taps and got started.

Five zombies closed in on Jake as he was engrossed in his alien war game. They had zeroed in on the sound effects coming from the phone and were within just a few yards of Jake as he reached level ten of the game. He thought he heard something strange, but didn't want to look up from the game and risk being killed by the "Shriekers." It had taken him nearly two weeks to get this level. All of a sudden, something blocked the sun's glare and Jake could see the screen much more clearly. He rapidly tapped on the touch screen with his forefinger and pummeled the alien ship with smart bombs and missiles. A sense of pride overwhelmed him when the boss ship exploded. At that moment, a zombie grabbed him by the collar and yanked him off-balance. It speared its hand deep into his stomach and pulled back a fistful of intestines. Jake's pain was amplified by the smell of his own feces combined with the rotten stench that surrounded him. He vomited and dropped his phone, then somehow managed to get his hands onto the fully automatic rifle that hung from his shoulder. He squeezed the trigger. Stray rounds sprayed a couple of pieces of military equipment.

A few of the zombies were also hit, but none of them had suffered kill shots. Each of the closest shufflers grabbed a body part; they pulled and ripped at his flesh hungrily. He dropped his rifle, completely overwhelmed by the strength of the real-life zombies, and screamed.

Colonel Caster heard the weapons fire, followed by several other bloodcurdling screams. He yelled at the top of his lungs, "We're under attack! Grab your weapons!"

Bartholomew ran from the back side of the camp, firing off rounds as he came to Jake's assistance. The rest of the soldiers quickly opened up weapons crates and retrieved their rifles.

The zombies let go of Jake as they saw the approaching soldiers, but the pain was too much for him to handle. He fell to his knees and struggled to get away. His movements attracted them once more; they ripped at any part of his body that they could reach. He was about to lose the fight and knew it. He yelled as loudly as he could. "HELP!"

Rifle rounds from other positions began to pummel Jake's attackers. A zombie dropped to the ground. On its hands and knees it wrapped its mouth around Jake's tibia. Jake screamed, but before he could pull his limb out of its mouth, he felt his bones shatter. Blood poured from the traumatic wounds to his torso and leg. In agony, he kicked at the zombie with his other leg. It fell backward. While it was distracted, he grabbed his rifle and fired off another round at point-blank range. A single bullet exploded through the zombie's head.

Further down the street, zombies that were attracted to the sounds of gunfire and screams advanced on the camp unhindered.

Colonel Caster barked out orders: "We need to flank the zombies. You four go that way, and you four that way. Everyone else, follow me." On the run, the soldiers locked and loaded their weapons.

Bartholomew continued to fire off rounds on his way to Jake, but only managed to impact a few of the zombies in the torso.

Jake tried to perform first aid on his leg, but his fingers simply wouldn't obey his commands. He was in shock. The music still playing on his fallen phone became just a hollow background noise. His pack of smokes now lay crushed under the feet of the busy shufflers. During his last remaining seconds of consciousness, images of his girlfriend filled his mind.

Commander Cummings knew the weapons fire had come from Jake's direction, and immediately ordered his group to get into combat positions. As he quickly approached the young soldier, he fired a few rounds that took down some the zombies that had surrounded Jake, but more of them advanced from nearby. *This really is no joke.* He got into a firing position and scored chest shot after chest shot. Confused, he wondered why some went down and others did not.

A flank of soldiers let out a barrage of rounds at the newer incoming zombies. Caster sprinted the last few yards toward Jake, and unleashed a full magazine. Unprecedented gore prevailed as body parts came undone and dropped to the ground. Bartholomew caught up with the Colonel, and with a fearful expression, yelled, "We're gonna need more troops!"

As the zombies continued to surround the soldiers, Cummings shouted, "We need help over here!"

Over his shoulder, Caster shouted, "Hold your position!"

Max Honoree; "You Are Here":

At the home of Max Honoree, Ludwig rang the doorbell. There was no answer. This time they did not wait to let themselves in; they quickly entered and walked to the kitchen. There, they found a bloody mess, and once again called out Max's name. Hearing no reply, they searched the rest of the home and found the room where Max kept his fungus specimens. Ludwig said, "I'll get these. You can collect the blood samples from the kitchen."

Gene smiled, happy to be doing real research and not killing zombies. "Yes, sir!"

After collecting all of the samples that were needed, the scientists got into the car and took off.

Relieved, Gene said, "Strange we didn't find any dead or undead bodies."

Ludwig nodded his head and entered Phan's address into the GPS. The monotone female voice said, "You are here." The stress of the day brought out a big laugh from the men, as they realized the address was right next door. With no time to waste, they got out of the car and stood at the door of Phan's home. They yelled out for him, but got no reply and had to kick the door in to enter the house. They were greeted with a now-familiar rotten stench. Both men gagged, and lifted the bottom of their shirts to make crude masks and block the putrid aroma. Then they heard a horrible raspy sound. "Shak-a-ra!"

A zombie entered the room they stood in. Gene stepped in front of the doctor to protect him and said, "Stay back. I'll take care of it." He grabbed a heavy oriental dragon lamp and struck the older, slow-moving female zombie on the side of its head. Its tumors drained vile, puss-like fluid. It reeled sideways and spun around from the impact, but it quickly regained its balance and lunged forward again. Its head shook violently as it swiped at Gene. This time it nearly succeeded in slicing open his abdomen with stiffened fingers, narrowly missing only because he had sucked in his gut. He raised the dragon lamp again and bashed at the head of the monstrous thing, which fell over and stopped moving. The impact had caused the dragon's tail to break off; it tumbled to the floor.

Gene turned and said, "Done! But let's hope I don't have to do THAT again."

The doctor looked at the thing lying on the floor; he could barely face the facts about what was going on and what had just happened. He turned his emotions off and let the scientist in him come forward. With a blank expression, he replied, "Alright. Good job." On the way out of the room, he accidentally knocked over a terrarium full of fungi, and added, "Let's collect more samples, and look for any notes he may have left behind. But don't spend too much time searching. We don't want to end up like that one." After a few more minutes of note taking, Ludwig gathered his field bag and unfolded the list of names. "Okay, Gene. Time to go."

John Kimball:

They got back into the maroon vehicle and Gene zig-zagged through the carnage on the streets. Ludwig noticed that the amount of dead bodies seemed to have multiplied everywhere they drove. At the two-story home of John Kimball, they pulled into the driveway and saw a lawn that was littered with corpses and a couple of stationary zombies. Gene shifted the car into reverse, drove up on the neighbor's lawn, and backed into a zombie. It became wedged under the back tire and moaned horribly; not because of the pain that it was in, but because of the feast it could not reach. Ludwig could not take the horrid sounds, so he jumped out of the car and stomped the zombie's head into the ground. He wiped off his shoe in the grass and waited for his assistant. Gene was proud of the doctor, and when he met him at the front door, he said, "Nice one, Doc."

Ludwig shrugged off the compliment and replied, "Didn't wanna to do it, but it seemed to be suffering."

At the bottom of the staircase, Ludwig and Gene stopped momentarily to gaze upon a large, dried-up blood stain. A severed arm lay in the middle of the mess. Gene stared at the arm and said, "This is so bad, Doc."

Ludwig walked past the arm and replied, "I know. I can barely look at it. Let's check the kitchen."

On the kitchen table, Ludwig found a stack of photographs. He picked them up and said, "These look like they're from the expedition. No doubt the mycologist took these." He thumbed through the photographs and lifted one up, adding, "This is a beautiful picture of a fungus. I think we've found what we came for, but let's get a few tissue samples from the arm before we leave."

Gene stood at the doorway and replied, "That's cool, but I think we've been here far too long – I'm already beginning to hear moans."

The two men continued down the list, gathering as much data as they could from each scientist's home. Ludwig took a deep breath, held the list taut and said, "Just one more name." Phoenix Holiday was last on the list. He programmed the address into the GPS and said, "Let's get this over with." He tried not to show how terrified he really was; all he wanted to do was to get back into his own lab. Ultimately, he wanted to leave zombie killing to the military, who would undoubtedly be arriving at any moment.

Phoenix Holiday:

The GPS voice blandly said, "You have arrived." Ludwig and Gene got out of the car, but left the engine running this time. After they ascended the stairs, they walked into the wide open apartment. They quick surveyed their surroundings, and Gene walked into the kitchen. Ludwig immediately squatted down and sprayed a solvent onto the various blood stains that covered the floor. He waited for the solvent to do its job, and watched his assistant pace back and forth like an expectant father. A minute later, he swabbed the various stains, then, smeared the stickiness onto the microscope slides for later analysis. He packed up everything and closed his field bag. Gene stopped pacing and leaned against the kitchen counter, gestured at the blood. He summed up the situation: "Judging by the amount of blood, it looks like there were two victims."

The doctor shook his head in agreement. He was impressed and replied, "I just hope Holiday's blood is not in the mix."

Gene replied, "I don't think the stains belong to him. It looks like it might have been two females, or children, judging by the smallish bloody footprints."

Ludwig scratched his head. "Good deduction, Mr. Watson. I agree with you one hundred percent. Now let's get the heck out of Dodge."

<u>More Weapons:</u>

After the attack died down, Nick and Ron regrouped at the hood of the truck. Nick tried to keep his cool and only half-shouted, "Okay, Okay, Okay!" He took a deep breath, but his anxiety got the better of him. "We gotta get outta here!" He sidestepped to the driver's door and got into the truck.

Ron followed him, looking over his shoulder for zombies the whole time. "Yeah, but where we gonna go?" He now backed up to the passenger door.

Frustrated, Nick said, "We have to find another place to hide and wait for the police, the military, F.E.M.A., or even N.A.S.A. Hell, I don't care, as long as someone helps us." He topped off his plea by putting his baseball cap on, then started the truck.

As the truck accelerated past the zombie horde, they could not help but look back; maybe Joaquin had somehow escaped. What they saw was so gruesome they didn't want to believe their eyes. Lindsey's intestines were scattered about, limbs were ripped from her body, and she was slowly being consumed. The flesh was missing from her face. Then they caught a glimpse of Joaquin, who was obviously dead. A few of the zombies held an arm or a leg, and dragged his body away from the scene of carnage. They were trailed by others trying to get a piece of him.

Ron stuck the rifle out of the window and pulled the trigger, but all he heard was a hollow click. He sobbed broken-heartedly, and said, "Man, I can't believe I couldn't help him." It was the first time Nick had ever seen his emotions in that way. In a shaky voice, Ron continued, "He called our names ... they brought him down ... devoured him ... I should've done more."

Nick wiped away his own tears and tried to console his friend. "You couldn't have stopped him. He ran so fast. No one could have saved them."

Nick pulled the truck over to contemplate what their next move should be. "We're gonna survive this. The zombies are really slow, and we'll be able to pick them off easily. We definitely need more weapons and ammo, though."

Ron tossed an empty mag to the floorboard and replied, "We should go back to the gun shop, restock, then come back here. I really wanna take down the ones that got him." An unseen zombie abruptly crashed into the truck, and Nick jammed his foot onto the accelerator,

185

causing the truck to fishtail and barrel through several more walkers just ahead of them.

Through the rear view mirror, Nick looked back into the truck bed to make sure Charlene was still there. He said, "She's still unconscious, and she looks like hell." He took another hard right to avoid a zombie collision, and Charlene's body rolled over from the momentum. Pointing over his shoulder with his thumb, he continued, "We have to get her medical help. We can try again to get to the hospital, but judging by what we've just seen, I don't know."

Ron wiped his tears away with his sleeve and decisively stated, "I know what we should do. Gun store. Definitely." He knew that he had to pull it together fast.

Doctor Stockton:

Stockton's assistant nearly tripped into his office, and had to catch his breath before he relayed the urgent information. He gasped, "The emergency team …" He had to stop to take a deep breath.

Stockton raised his eyebrows, ticked that the man had run into the office. He put the phone receiver down. "Spit it out!"

The assistant calmed himself and said, "One man is dead, and the colonel is pleading for backup."

Stockton picked up the receiver and started tapping numbers into his desk phone. "We can't do anything yet – I need to see the field report first. You're dismissed for now." He spoke into the handset and said, "Anything new?" Three feet away from the office, the assistant overheard, "Okay, okay, I'll elevate this outbreak to the next level."

Nick and Ron; Leverage:

The truck slalomed down Main Street with Nick at the wheel. He then drove up onto sidewalks at breakneck speed seeking out any zombie he could smash. Vengeance was the only thing that would sooth his anger. He gunned the truck toward their destination, swerving to avoid several stalled cars, until Ron shouted, "Over there!" The vehicle swerved toward the rotted flesh that stood in the road. The ensuing impact caused the decaying heap to catapult over the truck and hit the road with a wet smack. Bouncing and rolling several times like a skipping stone, it left behind bloody strips of flesh where it landed on the street. When the heap clumsily stood back up, it wobbled forward like a drunken pirate until its head expanded rapidly, then exploded.

Nick spun the steering wheel around, braked hard, and nearly slid the vehicle into a utility pole. He revved the engine and shouted, "Did you see that head?"

Another zombie moved toward them. Nick jammed his foot down hard on the gas pedal and plowed into the emaciated walker. Its body was quartered on impact, and the truck left the pieces behind in its dust. Nick was still was not satisfied, so he reversed course, then asked, "Another one?" Ron nodded in agreement, but unexpectedly Nick stopped the truck to size up the approaching horror. Large pulsing tumors on its face oozed a gooey, viscous material. Various sized tendrils grew from its head. A matured tendril completely covered one of its eyes.

Ron had had enough, and said, "I'm getting out!" He hopped out of the vehicle and ran over to an aluminum street pole that had been knocked over. He grabbed the pole, and with a running start, used it as a jousting lance and rammed the weapon through the zombie's head, just above the bridge of its nose. The forehead was lifted by the impact; the thing's brain looked like a spoiled can of black beans.

Nick got out of the truck and said, "Ron, look at its brains."

Ron dropped his makeshift jousting lance and looked down at the hideous zombie. He asked, "What the heck is growing on its head?"

Nick stared and replied, "I have no earthly idea."

Back in the vehicle, Nick plucked a single bullet from the floor and handed it to Ron, who loaded it into his gun and fired as another zombie shuffled toward them. The round struck the zombie between the eyes and blew out the back of its skull. The mangled horror fell flat onto its face, exposing the roots that had penetrated deeply into its brain.

Ron got out of the truck and surveyed the damage to the zombie's head. He then jumped into the bed of the truck, putting two fingers to Charlene's carotid to search for a pulse. He spoke loud enough for Nick to hear: "She's still alive ... but for how much longer, I don't know." As Ron climbed back into the cab, he said "If we can get her some help, she might make it."

Nick knew it was just an empty platitude and fought the urge to be a pessimist. "Yeah, she might."

Taxi Driver:

The sun's starburst pattern reflecting off of the windshield caused Nolan's head to throb. He squinted deeply, which gave him the look of a lonesome cowboy on the high plains. The van accelerated forward and plowed through a pot hole. *Dang it! Didn't see that one.* The sudden jolt caused Nolan's head to pound ten times harder. With one hand he took the first right turn possible and proceeded to the roadhouse, angrily wondering why he had the duty of being the taxi driver. Without looking back, he said, "We're on our way," and applied pressure to his temple with the other hand.

Though he fought waves of hunger and exhaustion, Phoenix addressed the group, saying, "Okay, we need food and protection. First stop is food. I think my stomach is starting to eat itself." Just the mention of food caused Dora and Vicki's stomachs to rumble, as if they were part of a Pavlov experiment; they replied in unison, "Agreed!" Vicki reapplied fresh bandages to Michael's head. Phoenix glanced at Nolan and said, "I hope Big Tex has a pile of ribs ready – I'm starved!"

Adele mock-pumped her M4 as if it were a shotgun and added, "Yeah, and maybe we can kill some zombies for dessert!"

At that moment, Michael tried to sit up. His involuntary action startled everyone in the van. Vicki pushed his shoulders back down, and blocked Adele's view as much as possible.

Once again, Adele tried to state her case for killing him. "He'll turn into a crazed, ravenous zombie." Phoenix sternly said, "No, Adele!" She turned her back to him and thought, *He's not gonna keep treating me like that.* Her husband had sometimes treated her like a baby and she hated it.

Vicki carefully placed the tympanic thermometer in Michael's ear, checking to see if his fever had gone up. A few seconds later she said, "He's at 104 degrees. Definitely hotter." She fanned him with a piece of cardboard, wondering if it wouldn't be better if they just left him somewhere. What if he turned into one of those things?

Nick, Ron, and Charlene:

Nick studied the broken axle and noticed a long, linear crack that ran the length of the outer casing. Thoroughly disgusted, he pushed off on the underside of the truck and said, "Well, it's busted. Must've happened when I ran up on that curb."

Ron knew a laugh would help diffuse the situation, and said, "Hey Nick, remember when we hijacked Ted's truck? We need to do that again."

Nick stood up and chuckled. He replied, "Yeah, well that's an idea, but I'm hungry and the Road House is just around the corner. We really need to stop and reboot."

Not quite sure if he had heard everything clearly, Ron slapped a boot and replied, "I don't need boots. Got two here."

Annoyed, Nick replied, "No! I mean refresh."

Ron held back a snort, feeling silly. "Oops. Sorry, man." His emotions turned on a dime, and Ron got a little choked up as his thoughts turned to the horrors of their battle earlier in the day. "I still can't get over what happened to Joaquin. He was a good kid ... didn't deserve to die like that."

Uncomfortable about expressing his emotions in front of a friend and employee, Nick turned his face away from Ron's to hide a tear. He replied, "I know, Ron. He was a really cool kid." He wiped his face with a sleeve, looked back, and added, "Those moans are getting closer, and we only have a few blocks to go. Let's get out of here."

Ron shook his head and asked, "What about Charlene?"

Nick hopped into the back of the truck and cradled her head with one hand while he felt for her carotid with the other. He said, "She's burning up; barely has a pulse. Probably wouldn't be a bad idea to just leave her before she turns."

Frustrated, Ron smacked the side of the truck with his bare hands. "I know! But it's a shame we can't do more for her."

The Zombie:

The enormous zombie struggled like a newborn calf to control its arms and legs. It was covered with evidence of multiple traumas. Strips of flesh hung from its body. Flakes of dried blood were caked around its mouth. Its brain, swirling with a constant flux of flashing lights, caused it to lurch forward a few inches at a time. Eventually, it slammed into the side of a sport utility vehicle, tearing off the side mirror. Crazed with hunger, it moaned and flexed its jaws, muttering "Braw-gla! Braw-gla!"

A Game of Luck:

Higgins plopped down in the black vinyl seat of an abandoned wheelchair and thought, *That's better. Too bad I didn't find this thing hours ago!* The gunfire that he had heard earlier in the day had since stopped, and his new plan would take him back to Jay's work. With the bloodied saw lying across his lap, he grasped both wheels and pushed down. As the chair began to roll down the sidewalk, it clicked sharply. After a quick glance at the wheel, he saw that playing cards had been mounted on the spokes of the bicycle-like wheels, so he stopped the rolling chair and whispered,

"A prankster." He pulled each card off the spokes and pocketed the nine of diamonds for good luck. Decades earlier, he had won a beat-up pickup truck with that card. He resumed his roll, and turned left at the end of the block. With his bandana in hand, he wiped the sweat from his forehead. *Where are those dang snickety things?* Then his stomach growled loudly. *I need food ... food!* He craned his neck, but because he was sitting so low, he couldn't see well above the numerous parked vehicles.

Tag Team:

Nick and Ron were amazed. The hair on the female zombie's head looked like a poorly-combed Einstein wig. Greenish, loose skin covered its thin, frail body. It was covered with open wounds, and wore western-style slipper boots. It followed their every movement. The men quickly split up, and Nick pulled the cleaver from his waistband. He raised it like an insane butcher, then counted down, "Three, two ... one!" Without hesitation, they rushed the monstrosity from opposite sides. Ron connected first with a long skewer, shoving it into the back of the zombie's neck. The tip of the skewer lodged deep within its cervical bone, and he fought to control the flailing zombie. He managed to push it forward, and yelled, "Now, Nick!"

Nick aimed for the head, but missed. Instead, the blade of the butcher knife dug into the thing's clavicle and partly separated the arm from the shoulder. Its other arm lifted like it was doing a wild country wave, and bellowed out ungodly sounds. Thick blood gushed from both wounds. Again, Nick raised the cleaver, swung with great force, and struck the zombie between the eyes. When he pulled back on the cleaver, built up pressure was released from the skull, causing blood to spray him in the face. The thing dropped to the street. Ron stepped on its upper back, grasped the skewer, and yanked it out. He shouted, "Good one, Nick!"

Nick mumbled closed lipped to avoid getting blood in his mouth. "Uh-huh." He took off his shirt, using the back side to wipe the blood from his face. Between wipes, he spat numerous times making sure nothing had gotten into his mouth. When he had gotten it all off, he exhaled and said, "Okay, let's double-time it to the bar." He threw his soiled shirt on top of the zombie's head, and tucked the butcher knife between his waistband and belt.

<u>Living on a Prayer:</u>

Gene rushed through the front door of Sporaton. He carried the field bag, and was followed by Ludwig. The doctor tapped him on the shoulder and said, "We need to get the blood and tissue samples under the microscope ASAP to determine if anything matches up with the scientists' observations."

Gene replied, "Okay, Doc. I'll start setting everything up." He moved to the doctor's workstation and put the test tubes and slides into plastic dividers. Next, he placed the whole rig into the refrigerator, and started setting the microscope.

Ludwig retrieved additional supplies. When he'd finished, he took a short break.

Five minutes later, Gene entered the break room. The doctor sat straight up and cordially said, "Have a seat. Rest while you can. I'll let you know what I find."

Gene settled into the chair, then looked over toward the dead body on the couch. *Poor girl ... hope I don't end up like that.*

It didn't take more than a couple of minutes for Gene to become restless. He crept to the barricaded room, stood at one corner of the window, and peeked inside. The zombie stood silently, but its head growths seemed to be larger. He took a picture with his cell phone and thought, *This'll go viral.* After the picture was saved, he walked away, confident that the room was still secured.

He reentered the main lab, and asked Ludwig, who was now hunched over the microscope, "Hey, Doc, how ya' doing?" Ludwig mumbled something that sounded like, "Huh?" Gene continued, "I'm gonna go clean up the break room, if that's alright with you." Ludwig did not reply or raise his head from his work.

Gene tried to break the silence and added, "I took a picture of the zombie."

Ludwig finally grumbled, "I hope you didn't disturb it."

Satisfied that the doctor was okay, Gene trudged to the maintenance room at the other end of the lab and retrieved what he needed. He rolled the squeaky mop bucket right up to the dried blood, but did not notice that the fire blanket now hung halfway off of the couch. He started mopping in a figure eight pattern, getting into a rhythm.

One by one, Ludwig pulled out the labeled samples in the order that they had been collected, and noted the locations they had been taken from. He cross-checked the samples against the medical records of the expedition scientists. ABO typing would determine the blood types for each member. He carefully mixed the blood samples with the specific antisera, which contained antibodies for A, B, and Rh antigens. Then he waited to see which antigen the sample clumped with, which would determine its blood type.

Gene rinsed the bloody mop out until the strands were clean. He wanted to clear his guilt-ridden mind with a short nap, and thought, *Maybe I could have done more ... gotten there a little faster*. He then vigorously washed his hands at the sink, and replayed the scene of Rosie's death. While rinsing, he did not notice the fire blanket was now on the floor, and didn't hear the very faint sound of "Cra-hish!" As he lathered his hands one final time, the zombie moaned again, but the running water splashed in unison with its moan. "Cra-Hish!" Gene snatched brown paper towels from a dispenser, dried his hands, and turned off the faucet. It was only then that he heard a deeper "Cra-HISH!" Goose bumps erupted all over his body as he realized it was Rosie's raspy voice. He dropped the paper towels in terror. The zombie stood right behind him, and as he spun around to face it, its arm swung with such power that the uppercut to his chin knocked him completely out. He laid unconscious, bright red blood pouring from a jagged laceration. The zombie dropped to its knees and lifted his head. Its jaws unhinged and clamped down on a large portion of his skull. It feasted on his exposed grey matter in pelican-like gulps.

Hearing the crash of tables and chairs, Ludwig ran into the break room with a fire axe in hand. The zombie repeated, "Cra-hish!" A hellish goatee of Gene's hair surrounded its mouth. Bits of brain had dribbled onto its shirt. Ludwig raised the axe, and with all his might, slammed it down upon the former student's head. The log-splitting force of the axe embedded so deeply, it separated the skull into two halves. Only the wooden end of the handle was visible. The zombie arched its back to the breaking point, then slowly stopped moving.

Ludwig nervously ran his fingers through his salt-and-pepper hair. He could not believe what had just happened, but knew Gene had to be dead, judging by the extent of his wound. He frantically thought, *Gotta check on that other zombie*. When he got to the room, it immediately lunged at the window. Startled by the jarring impact, Ludwig smacked into the wall behind him. The collision knocked the wind out of his lungs. He gathered his composure, ducked down, and jiggled the door handle to make sure that it was still locked. Now satisfied, he crawled past the windows, and went back to Gene's side. Hoping for a miracle, he felt for a pulse, even though the trauma to Gene's head would have made it impossible to survive. He said a prayer, covered both bodies with the fire blanket, and went back to work.

Nick and Ron at Big Texas's:

Just inside the parking lot of the Big Texas Road House, Nick and Ron cautiously peered above the hood of an extended cab truck. They did not like what they saw. A zombie's clothes were tattered and bloody, and it appeared to be guarding the door. Nick whispered, "I haven't seen any of them do that before."

Ron whispered back, "Me neither!" The skinny zombie stood quite still, looking like a mime in the French Quarter of New Orleans. Its skin was greenish tinted, and it had a head full of tumors. The two men crept over to the next truck, remaining crouched the entire time.

Nick said, "As best I can tell, it's a woman."

Ron nodded in agreement. "Yeah, I think so, too. Not that it matters!"

Nick chuckled. "Okay, say it with me." In unison, they whispered, "Ribs and beer!" Nick stood up slightly. "Okay, for real – let's go for it."

The two hungry guys stealthily maneuvered between the parked cars and trucks. They positioned themselves as close to the door as possible. Their plan was interrupted when a large zombie burst through the doors and stared right at them. It was followed by a couple of others. The trio of zombies shoved through the door and moved toward the parking lot. Nick clutched his ax with a death grip. He knew what needed to be done but grimly said, "We may have to eat somewhere else."

Confident and hungry, Ron replied, "I think we can take 'em!" Visions of juicy, slow cooked baby back ribs danced in his head. He looked around at the other vehicles and half whispered, "Look at that truck over there. The shotgun is still in its rack. I'm gonna try and get it."

Nick looked around and replied, "Okay man – I've got your back."

Ron raced to the truck, keeping the gun rack in his sights. The zombies tracked Ron. Nick whispered loud enough for Ron to hear. "On second thought, this might not be such a good idea."

Ron turned back and replied, "No worries – I've got this." One of the zombies moaned and started to advance, albeit slowly, in Ron's direction. The larger one also started to move, coming around Ron's left.

Nick blurted out, "C'mon – see what they're doing? Hurry up!" Ron ran the rest of the way to the truck, and then pulled up on the door handle. He shouted, "Dang, it's locked!" while kicking the side panel.

C'mon Ladies:

The front end of the van, now coated with a thick layer of bio-matter, looked like hell. Phoenix jotted an entry into his journal, until he heard two powerful rifle blasts. He looked up just in time to see a man duck down on a rooftop and said, "Hey – I just saw the shooter."

At that moment, the man stood back up at the roof's corner and fired two more times, Adele shouted, "A couple more zombies down!"

Her shouting caused Michael to squeeze Vicki's hand hard enough that it made her yelp in pain. Adele quickly scooted to Vicki's aid and slapped the hand hard enough that it broke his grip. Vicki angrily said, "Adele, don't do that again." She graciously added, "But thanks."

Nolan immediately took a left onto a one-way street and gunned the vehicle.

Adele resumed her position at the rear doors. She thought about her kidnapping when she was a child and being forced to live in a box. Her captors had told her that if her parents did not provide all of the ransom money, they really didn't love her, and she'd wind up in the box permanently. Over the days she'd been a prisoner, her masked captors taunted her whenever they were in the room. On the tenth day of the kidnapping, her captors were killed during a police raid. The gunfire and carnage overwhelmed her so much that, from that point on, she became a much more rebellious child.

She continued to watch from the window as another zombie mutilated its victim, but did not say a word. She knew she needed to wait for the right moment.

<u>Nick and Ron at the Roadhouse:</u>

Ron turned and shouted, "Toss your axe over here!" Nick threw the axe with the skill of a lumberjack, and it embedded in the side panel of the truck. Ron yanked it out and began to hack at the door handle. Between hand jarring whacks, he added, "Nice throw!"

Nick ignored the complement, but yelled, "Hurry up!"

After one last whack to the handle, Ron was able to kick the door open. He retrieved the shotgun from the gun rack, then grabbed a box of shells off the seat. "Thank you, Jesus." He ran back to Nick as he loaded the weapon.

When the zombies were about a car length away, Nick stepped to the side and said, "Okay, shoot 'em." Ron pulled the trigger on the double barrel 12 gauge, and its full fury was unleashed. The head of the first zombie was blasted off completely; shredded arteries erupted like bloody geysers. The larger zombie continued to advance.

Not wanting to be outdone, Nick grabbed the shotgun and said, "With that thing, anyone is a marksman!" He shot the larger zombie in the face. The buckshot exploded through the back of its head and pinged nearby vehicles. The corpse landed on a car and was hooked by its hood ornament. A large streak of blood painted the hood, as though someone had applied a gory racing stripe. "See what I mean?"

Ron shook the shell box vigorously, adding, "We have about a half box left. I love Texans – always prepared!"

Nick felt his stomach churning. "Dang, did you hear that?"

Ron replied knowingly. "Yep!" Instinctively, he clutched his own stomach.

Nick smiled and said, "We're gonna have to barricade the door. C'mon, let's get our grub on."

<u>Rapid, Faint Pulse:</u>

Phoenix readied his M4 after hearing weapons fire. "Hey, did you guys hear that? Maybe it's coming from the bar."

Nolan slowed the van to a crawl and whispered through a raging migraine. "And ... we're still going?"

Phoenix took a deep breath and looked around. "Yes, but I'll scout the area before we go any further. I know it pretty well."

Nolan nudged him with his elbow. "Just let me drive us a little closer."

Phoenix placed his hand on the door handle. "Nah. Just keep the engine running."

Vicki assessed her patient. "I don't think he's got much time. His pupils are nearly fixed and he has a very faint pulse!"

Phoenix stepped out of the stopped van, then cocked his head back through the window. "Just do what you can for him. If anything out of the ordinary happens …"

Vicki quickly read his mind, and frowned. "I know, I will."

Tired of being left out, Dora rose to her knees, then blurted, "I'm ready for anything." She watched Phoenix hustle behind a tree.

Phoenix scanned the area. Spotting no zombies, he advanced quickly. *I gotta find whoever is shooting and get everyone to safety.*

Deciding that she wanted the passenger seat, Adele patted Dora on the way up to it. "It's about time, missy!"

After hearing several more gunshots, Phoenix hustled to the corner. He took a knee and listened intently to what sounded like a shotgun.

Head Piece:

Humming nervously because it was hard to ignore the dead bodies in the break room, Ludwig drew a red line through each of the scientist's names that did not match. *How will I explain all of this to their families? What about the hieroglyphics?* He tried to hold his emotions in check. After a while, his eyes tired from looking through the microscope, and his mind became foggy. He stood up and stretched, then picked up a bunch of photographs. He flipped through the stack and stopped at a glyph of a Mayan prisoner, who had a guard stationed on each side of him. The prisoner appeared to wear some sort of elaborate head piece. He wrote in his notepad: "Why would a prisoner be dressed like that?" The photograph also showed three men on the ceremonial platform of a stepped pyramid. Continuing through the stack of photos, he picked up another one that showed a strange-looking plant attached to the trunk of a tree. It was circled in red. The last photograph was of a cracked clay tablet. It was missing segments, but showed some sort of crude insect mandibles.

Convergence:

Ron and Nick entered the bar and scoped out their immediate surroundings. Nick grabbed tables and chairs, and shoved some of them to Ron. Together they barricaded the heavy doors. After it was completed, Ron shook the homemade barricade. "I think it'll hold." Nick nodded, and they carefully made their way to the kitchen. Along the way, Ron told the story about the night he rode the mechanical bull.

"Hey Nick! That's a mean one over there. Remember the night I paid five bucks for a shot at it? At first the hostess went easy on me, until I gave her thumbs up. Big mistake! As soon as the power was increased, I was tossed off and landed on my shoulder. The next day, I couldn't run the injector machine. Remember that?"

Nick laughed. "Yeah, I remember that day. You couldn't do much of anything. By the way, you don't have the balance to ride a bull like that. Still don't."

Ron smirked at him. "Ten bucks says you can't either."

Nick punched him lightly in the shoulder, saying, "Ya got a bet there, my friend, but first – let's eat."

The two men entered through the swinging doors of the kitchen and immediately raided the stainless steel refrigerators that were stuffed with food for the next day's lunch rush.

Ron stretched, arching his back, and said, "I'll take some ribs and beans, please."

Nick opened the containers and spooned out a heaping amount of beans. He then put the entire spoon into his mouth and licked off the remnants. Ron replied, "Cute. Now slide it over."

Nick slid a white plastic container over to Ron, and they both ate directly from them like there was no tomorrow. Without any additional conversation they chugged down an ice cold bottle of beer to let off steam.

Drive-By:

Phoenix reached the edge of the parking lot and hid behind the roadhouse sign. He observed a few zombies hovering near the entrance. *We can take those out.* After a few more minutes of observation, he ran back to the van to tell the others his plan to get into the bar.

The deteriorating zombie stood completely still behind a tree. A construction helmet hid most of its tumors, but it could still hear Phoenix's heavy breathing. It stepped out in front of him. Phoenix practically ran smack into it, but dodged and sidestepped it at the same time. It took a large step forward; its arms narrowly missed him again. Phoenix heard another one moving in from the rear. The helmeted zombie lunged forward, and Phoenix raised his gun and released a spray of bullets. The rounds struck the zombie from the chest up. One round destroyed the nametag that said Billy, and another penetrated the skull and exploded through the back side of the plastic yellow helmet. The helmet spun around on its head as a torrent of blood flowed beneath it. With a final brain flash, the zombie's consciousness faded into nothingness. After death, what was left of Billy floated out of his body and followed a beautiful, luminescent tunnel of light.

Phoenix spun around and fired off several more rounds, but missed the second zombie. It moved in quickly and connected with his forearm, opening a small laceration. Stunned, Phoenix fired the rest of the rounds in the clip. Its body seized as each round penetrated its torso. Riddled with holes, it looked like the victim of a drive-by shooting as it held its arms wide open. Several rounds had found their sweet spot, and the thing collapsed. Only half of its head and face were still attached. Phoenix ripped a piece of cloth from the bottom of his shirt and wrapped it around his injured arm, then ran for the van.

Nolan got out the van and sprinted to Phoenix's location when he heard the gunfire. He met him at the halfway point and asked,

"Was that you, man?"

Excited, Phoenix replied, "Yeah, I took out two of them on the way back. I had no choice. We're gonna have more action though – the bar has more of those things right outside the front door."

Through his lessening headache, Nolan looked a little more relaxed and asked, "Think we can take 'em?" Phoenix nodded his head. Nolan added, "Great, let's go back and tell the others."

Ten Dollars and a Bull Ride:

After he finished off his last rib, Nick said, "We have to secure this place. Let's go back outside and take care of the rest of those things."

Ron loosened his belt a notch, and with fresh vigor replied, "Okay, I'm good to go!" He pushed through the swinging double doors of the kitchen and eyed the mechanical bull. "Hey, don't forget our bet!"

Nick replied with a big laugh, "Oh, I won't," pulling out a ten dollar bill and slapping it down on top of the bar. He continued, "When we get outside, we'll move together, but stay about a car length apart. After we sweep the area, we'll come back in and secure the rest of the doors and windows. Then we'll settle that bet. How many shells you have left in that box?"

Ron looked at the ten dollar bill and answered, "Uh, 'bout ten … like that bill over there."

Nick replied, "Well, depending on how many are outside, we might use all of the ammo, so be prepared for a little shish kabob action with that skewer."

The two men quietly opened the bar doors and slipped into the parking lot, spotting zombies to their left and right. They ducked down and Ron shrugged his shoulders, saying, "Really not too bad."

Nick scooted forward and pointed. "Let's take out those two over there, and the rest right over there." They continued to observe the movements of the zombies as if they were linked with ESP. Without saying a word they used parked vehicles as barriers and weaved slowly between them. Nick gestured, and Ron nodded his reply. They stalked the closest zombie carefully, but it spotted Nick with its one remaining eye. Its other eye had already been gouged out. The cracks in the tumors on its head were filled with glistening green goo. Ron crept up from the rear, making sure other zombies did not see him. He checked Nick's location, then positioned the shotgun and carefully fired. Instantaneously, the zombie's head disappeared. Nothing was left above the armpits – even its collarbone was vaporized. The body slammed into the gravel, and a cloud of dust rose above it.

Ron reversed course and said, "Dang, that's so disgusting." Nick never looked back, for fear of throwing up his baked beans.

Unseen by the men, several dozen former gravel-pit workers had moved in on the bar like characters from an apocalyptic movie. Each was still clad in a blue denim work shirt. The company logo above the pocket spelled out "Rock Star Gravel Pit." The lettering was surrounded by a big white star. One of the zombies had a chain embedded in the mangled flesh around its forearm. As it lurched forward, it flailed the chain back and forth like someone spastically swatting at a fly. Meanwhile, Nick and Ron regrouped and focused their attention on their next targets.

Off the Record:

The Hazmat team looked down at Jake's mangled body. Colonel Caster shook his head, then pulled the bloodied dog tags from around the soldier's neck. He stared thoughtfully at Jake. "We're gonna need the hospital's resources for this mission. I need someone to take my vehicle to recon the facility. Cummings, disperse your team to collect blood and tissue samples from the corpses."

Cummings snapped to attention, saluted the colonel, then sharply replied, "Yes sir. Got it covered!"

Caster tucked the dog tags into his pocket and walked away. Cummings signaled for his team to get into half-circle formation. The group quickly formed, and he addressed the men and women of the small sub-unit. "We definitely have something weird going on here." He lowered his voice and continued, "Reanimated dead people … gotta be a first of its kind. No one has ever documented a single case. This is definitely one for the 'weird but true' books. Now, let's go get those samples."

Without hesitation, the group snapped to attention. They replied with a shaky confidence, "Yes, sir!"

One of the female Hazmat team members asked, "Is everyone ready?" Several thumbs up later, the team began to spread out. Each member carried a white specimen collection kit as they combed the area, looking like Apollo moonwalkers. Around their waists they carried extra ammo mags; slung over their shoulders were M4 carbines.

As they approached the first downed zombie, the hazmat team took defilade positions, which allowed two members to safely acquire samples. One of the collectors kneeled down and removed a number ten scalpel blade from his kit. The other positioned himself near the zombie's head, holding a sterile specimen container. The first team member positioned the surgical knife on the zombie's scalp and pressed down hard into the tissue. Ooze the color of black licorice immediately erupted. He carefully incised the area, cutting gently around the outside edge of one of the tumors and removing it neatly. He placed it in the specimen container, and the team proceeded to the next corpse and repeated the process. Eight bodies later, they had enough samples and moved to Jake's body.

Caster called Lieutenant Commander Dagrepont over to the command tent and asked if he would be willing to recon the hospital. Gung ho, the newly appointed lieutenant commander replied, "Yes, sir!" He hesitated a moment, then added, "Off the record, you know I have this, sir!"

Caster was proud of his new appointee, and made a mental note to write a letter of accommodation when the mission was over.

"Good. Here's the address. Use this handheld GPS unit and take my personal vehicle. Bring a weapon and extra rounds. I don't want you to get lost, especially after what just happened."

Dagrepont appreciated the trust the colonel had placed in him, and replied heartily, "Yes, sir! Will do!"

With his gear stowed in the back of the vehicle, Dagrepont proceeded out of the parking lot; he caught sight of several zombies staggering toward the camp and wondered if he should still leave. Not wanting to lose his new commission and the trust placed in him by his CO, he obeyed the direct order. *They should be able to handle a few without me.* He pressed hard on the gas pedal and followed the prompts of the GPS's guiding voice. Several blocks away, he heard the distinct sound of M4 rifle blasts.

<u>Fourth of July at the Roadhouse:</u>

Nick and Ron blasted through the remaining zombies methodically, until a large zombie managed to get between them and the door. Ron asked, "Do you think that's the same one from outside the trophy shop?"

Nick replied, "Kind of looks like it. See those longhorns mounted above the door? The top of that thing's head is almost level with them. It's gotta be close to seven feet tall. I don't know many people in Baron with that height." He then tiptoed forward for a better view.

With a pained smirk, Ron followed. "Ya think that's Big Tex?"

Nick faced him, then shook his head. "I'm not sure."

Ron jiggled the shell box and thought, *Well, whoever it is, this is my chance to get it.*

As they paused for a moment to regroup, the men heard several moans coming from their right flank. Nick pulled the axe from his belt loop and practiced a few chopping motions with it. Several dozen zombies approached and he said, "We should thin 'em out; can't take the chance of even one getting inside."

Ron reloaded the rifle and tucked the extra rounds into his pocket. "We're definitely gonna need some rest after all this. A little shuteye without the worry of being eaten alive would be nice." As he separated from his partner, he added, "Let's use the same plan as before. I'll go this way, and you flank 'em."

Nick shouted, "Wait, don't forget the shotgun!" then tossed it.

Ron caught it, then excitedly pumped the weapon one-handed. "It's gonna be a turkey shoot."

Nick whispered, "Wait a sec ... let them get just a little bit closer." As they approached, he saw the logos on their shirts. With a pained expression, he said, "Damn, Ron, look. They work for Rock Star."

Ron shook his head sadly. "Crap, this is so out of hand. We made trophies for the gravel pit guys last spring for their annual baseball game. I honestly don't know if I'll be able to kill them."

The parked vehicles had forced the zombies to split up. Nick looked back over his shoulder and saw the giant again. It stood stationary, about five feet from the door. Its head was almost completely covered in matured stalks. Its fractured arm had rotted off completely. Nick lowered his voice, waved his axe-wielding hand frantically, and said, "Ron, will ya' please start blasting 'em?"

Ron weaved in and out of the vehicles to get into definite kill range. He said, "This one is for Yolanda!" as he aimed at the closest zombie and pulled the trigger. Its head was pulverized, but he did not wait around for the results of the blast. He hurried over to take aim at the next one, whispering, "This one is for Sam." The zombie moaned and tried to swipe at him.

Nick beat the axe on a car hood to distract it, then shouted to Ron, "You're too close!" The zombie bellowed "Cra-ga!" as Ron pulled the trigger and blasted its skull to bits. Ron was splattered with debris, but ignored it and scooted over to the next target. His mind was racing with contempt over the death of his family and friends. As the zombie moved toward him, its arms and legs were a contradiction in fluidity. Ron gritted his teeth and murmured, "This one is for Joaquin." He forcefully pulled the trigger. The shotgun blast seemed deadlier as a flame shot from the end of the barrel.

With a little more gusto and a grunt, he aimed at the last zombie in the group and said, "And THIS one is for Charlene!" Just as he was about to pull the trigger, he slipped on an empty beer bottle, and the blast went wild. He pulled the trigger again, but it just clicked. He reached for his skewer, then ran toward the zombie, jamming it into its decayed head. After twirling it around, he shouted, "Oh, NASTY!"

Nick laughed hysterically and had to wipe away tears from his eyes. He caught his breath. "Let's go get the others, Mister Zombie Slayer."

Ron wiped the sweat and gun powder residue from his face. "Not so fast. The big one is still here."

Nick caught sight of it. "Well, I'll head this way to distract it. You can go around to the other side and take the shot. You have more shells, I hope?"

Ron checked his pocket. "Got three left." As he turned and began to circle around to get into position, the chain-wielding zombie shuffled forward from behind a big rig. Its arm ratcheted forward, and wherever the chain hit metal, sparks flew.

Nick shouted, "Watch out, Ron!"

As Ron spun around to look, another zombie closed in and blocked his escape route. He jumped atop a car's hood, pulled the trigger, and killed it instantly. The giant advanced toward the sound of the weapons fire. Ron reloaded the shotgun with the second-to-last shell, then turned to shoot. Nick couldn't get into a position to help him, but he yelled, "RON! BEHIND YOU!" The chain-wielding zombie swung, and the chain uncoiled from around its forearm and struck Ron in the back. He fell to the ground, his back imprinted with links. He rolled over and wailed in pain, then desperately pulled the trigger. The blast missed, and buckshot blew out a nearby car window. Another less tumorous zombie moved in on him, cutting him off from Nick. The chain-wielder swung the chain again. Ron tried to dodge it, but the thick links smashed into the side of his head. He could barely catch his breath as each link ground against his skull. He managed to pull himself up and leaned against a car like a crooked tower. The chain lashed out again, and this time smashed him square in the face. The momentum of the impact rolled him across the side panel of the car, and his bloodied shirt got caught up on a broken antenna on the vehicle's hood. A newly turned zombie on the other side of the car reached for him, so he tore off his shirt and dropped to the ground in agony to avoid its menacing hands.

Nick knew he had only seconds to act. He got down on one knee and peered under the cars that separated him from his friend. All that he saw were the legs and feet of zombies, causing the hair on the back of his neck to stand up. A zombie blocked his path, so he stood up and buried his axe into its forehead. Like a superhero, he leapfrogged over several car hoods, then slid around the front of a bumper and saw that the chain-wielding zombie had his buddy pinned. It did not look up as it devoured Ron's brain. With a cry, Nick snatched up the fallen shotgun, aimed, and pulled the trigger. Completely overwhelmed by the hollow click of the empty gun, he leapt into the air and smashed the butt of the weapon into its skull. The head broke into several fragments. He carefully dragged Ron over to the side of the roadhouse and leaned him against the wall. He whispered quietly, just in case his buddy could still hear him, "I'm gettin' us out of here."

Nick spied the shell box that had fallen from Ron's pocket. He picked it up and shook it, and heard a lone shell rolling around. He quickly loaded it into the rifle as he was backed against the wall by another zombie. He rifle-butted the thing in the forehead; it reeled backward and fell to the ground. Nick took aim and shot it in the neck. The thing's head was decapitated by the blast and rolled under a truck. Nick used the empty shotgun as a crutch to steady himself as he pulled Ron around the corner and into the doorway of the roadhouse. At the same time, a van barreled into the parking lot and screeched to a stop right in front of him. Several people leapt out.

Phoenix and Adele jumped from the van and moved quickly to their right. Nolan and Dora did the same, but moved to the left. Vicki stayed behind to attend Michael. As the horde of zombies advanced toward them, the team unleashed a volley of rounds. The firepower sounded like an unsynchronized fireworks display. Adele purposely moved forward, firing every few seconds at the center of the mass of decrepit, foul-smelling zombies. As if in a game of whack-a-mole, each one that she shot dead dropped to the ground from the explosive head shots. Several heads exploded before she could shoot them, much to her dismay. Their macabre death poses made her smile.

Phoenix used the diversion that Adele had unintentionally created. He advanced toward the entrance of the bar, where two strangers huddled, one obviously injured or dying. Turning to his left, he saw Nolan and Dora methodically moving forward after each of burst of rifle fire. Out of the corner of his eye he saw another group of zombies appear on the road in front of the bar, and at the top of his lungs, screamed, "Vicki! Get out of there NOW!"

Vicki's back had been turned from the action. Michael had just become pulseless, and she wished that she had defibrillator paddles, but there was nothing she could do. She heard Phoenix call out her name and grabbed the M4 just as a huge arm smashed into the side of the van next to the open sliding door. She lost control of the weapon, dropping it. The zombie moved toward the opening and tried to grab Vicki by the foot. She desperately felt behind her for the fallen weapon as the thing dragged her out of the van. At the last possible second, her hand found the butt of the weapon and she grabbed it, swinging it forward to fire. Her rear slammed into the gravel as she pulled the trigger. The gun had tipped down, and the rounds ricocheted off the ground and impacted several vehicles just in front of her. She pulled the M4 back up and fired; the new burst of rounds struck the zombie in the legs. It crashed to its knees, but now hovered directly over her. She desperately rolled sideways, hoping to evade its grasp.

Phoenix had run toward her, unable to get a clear shot head shot. Vicki rolled back over and sat up quickly, leaning against the door of the van. She fired her weapon once more at the zombie. This time, the rounds struck it in the chest and shoulders. Blood sprayed into her face and stung her eyes. Just as she was about to take the head shot, an arm reached out of the open door, yanking her back into the van. Phoenix heard her desperate shrieks and closed in on the vehicle. He fired at the behemoth still kneeling at the side of the van; several rounds tore into its back and one round exploded into the base of its skull. As it fell to the ground, he looked to his left and screamed, "NOOO!" Dora and Nolan turned and ran back to Vicki at the sound of her agonized scream. Adele locked and loaded another mag into her M4 and provided cover fire for the team.

Just inside of the van, Michael held Vicki by the back of her head, his fingers entwined in her hair. He lifted her with ease. She tried to elbow him in the face just as he bit into the back of her skull. She could not utter a single word as her eyes opened wide in shock. The newly-created zombie shook its head rabidly, revealing a mouth full of skull, hair and brain. Phoenix raised his weapon and aimed carefully, firing the round directly into its mouth and shattering its upper skull. It dropped Vicki, and Phoenix fired a second round that blasted it into the far wall of the van. Vicki lay motionless, sprawled half-in, half-out of the vehicle. As the team gathered around Vicki, several zombies continued to advance, but Adele, now frenzied, killed them all. Nick ran closer to the group and waved them to the bar.

Milliseconds:

The sounds of the all-out assault transported Higgins back to the multi-tiered rice fields of Korea. In the throes of the flashback, he rolled over to the side of Big Texas Road House and stopped. His arms and legs twitched as he sat in the wheelchair and relived the scene. He saw himself climbing into a foxhole for cover, and it took him a few seconds to come back to reality as he heard a female voice say, "Stop! Don't move a muscle!" He emerged slowly through the flashes of light and artillery smoke that surrounded him, and opened his eyes. Time stood still when he saw Adele's weapon pointed in his direction. He quickly shut his eyes again and waited for the end. A loud pop and a thud later, a zombie lay on the ground behind his wheelchair. The woman calmly said, "You're a lucky old man that I'm pretty good with this thing."

Higgins opened his eyes, then turned in his seat to see a zombie sprawled on the ground with a hole in its head. With much gratitude, he replied, "I am too, Missy!"

Phoenix and Nolan slung their rifles on their backs and gently lifted Vicki. Dora stayed about three feet in front and provided cover as they all moved toward the roadhouse's entrance. As they got closer to the door, they heard a faint noise and paused. Dora dropped back and

205

whispered, "Y'all here that?" They nodded yes, and gently laid Vicki down. Nolan knelt next to Vicki to stand guard, and Dora and Phoenix moved to investigate. Something slurred, "Shar-ha! Shar-ha!"

Phoenix crouched low to the ground and pointed his rifle in the direction the noise had come from. Dora did the same. A zombie finally came into view, lurching around the far side of the roadhouse. It propelled itself forward with an agonized gait. The little bit of skin left on its face gave the zombie a sickening permanent smirk, and its tongue dangled out of one side of its mouth. The zombie's chest muscles were huge, disproportionate to its undersized lower body. Phoenix's errant shot impacted the gut. It fell to the ground, and appeared to gasp for air like a fish out of water. He had seen many of these zombies repeating the same behavior, but knew it was only a reflex; it was simply trying to bite whatever it could reach. He fired another round that put the zombie out of its misery once and for all.

He tapped Dora on the shoulder. "Let's get Vicki inside." They jumped to their feet and were back at her side in seconds. The rest of team pitched in and they all carried her inside of the bar.

Adele looked at the old man and said, "Follow me, sir!"

Higgins rolled the chair forward and replied, "Yes, ma'am!"

They barely noticed the dead man lying against the wall just a few feet away.

Doctor Ludwig and Doctor Stockton:

Even though he could have spoken from across the room and still been heard clearly, Stockton leaned forward and spoke directly into the speaker phone. "We have a team on the ground right now, Doctor Ludwig. The first report from Caster was that they were blitzed as soon as camp was up and running. One casualty and they're asking for backup. This is a very peculiar situation."

Ludwig surprised him by saying "I understand. I'm seeing it first-hand in the field and at the lab. Both of my assistants have been murdered, and I have one of the zombies still locked up in one of the small labs. Send more troops – better yet, send more troops with bigger guns, so I can get my work done."

Stockton scribbled notes and backed away from the speaker. "We can't send back-up until we get a handle on exactly what we're dealing with. I wouldn't want to come across as an alarmist – it would be embarrassing."

Without any hesitation, Ludwig replied, "I understand that you're trying not to alarm the general public. The last thing we need is a panic on top of everything else. But these things are all over town. I need help. You need to do something right away – especially the back-up part."

Stockton, sensing the man's desperation, wanted to throw a life preserver and answered, "Tell you what, I'll send a man from Colonel Caster's team to pick you up. You can work with him."

Ludwig smacked his leg hard enough to make him wince. "Thanks – I think that's a great idea!"

Stockton picked up a photograph and read the attached note. "Before I hang up, I have to tell you something. A few of the photos have been deciphered. The glyph in photo number one says 'Tu Lak'in,' which literally means 'after death.' Do you have any idea what's going on? It almost sounds like this whole thing could be related to the Mayan calendar. Maybe your team was on to something after all. I'll relay the rest of the results as soon as I can."

Ludwig thought about his stack of photos and replied, "One of the glyphs showed what looked like a prisoner with some sort of weird headdress on. It was definitely one of the oddest ceremonial hats I've ever seen – it looked like it was growing right out of his head. I'm not sure, but I think the priest might have been trying to leave a message in that cave."

Stockton moved away from the speaker phone and looked at his copy of the photo being discussed, muttering, "Ah, I can see it here."

Ludwig gathered up his papers and replied, "Okay, I'll pack up my things and be ready when the soldier gets here."

Stockton ran his finger over the photo and replied, "Alright, take care. Just stay alive!"

Lt. Commander Dagrepont; Hide and Seek:

Dagrepont ignored the beeping two-way radio on the seat and turned quickly to the right in response to the GPS's directions. After the turn, he picked up the radio and answered. "Dagrepont here!"

Colonel Caster finished placing a specimen under the microscope and said, "I need you to pick up Doctor Ludwig at Sporaton Lab. I'll text the address to you. You can do that right after you recon the hospital. The doctor should be ready and waiting by the time you get there. Oh, and kill the zombie he has locked up in one of the labs."

Dagrepont swerved to right in response to another voice prompt from the GPS, and acknowledged, "Yes sir, copy that!"

The GPS informed Dagrepont that he had reached his destination. He pulled into the parking lot and immediately saw the remains of dead zombies littered all about the grounds. He looked at the GPS screen and asked, "Really?" as he removed the keys from the ignition and laid them on the front seat. He looked up and noticed a zombie lurching through the facility's automatic doors. It was dressed in a hospital gown, and had a large bandage wrapped around its head. A bloodied plaster cast dangled from its right arm. He grabbed his semiautomatic rifle and aimed at its head, while cautiously walking forward. After seeing it struggle, he had a change of heart. He felt sorry for whoever it was and decided not to kill it.

Unexpectedly, Caster's voice crackled once again over the walkie-talkie and Dagrepont backed up to his vehicle and picked up the radio. Weapons fire could be heard in the background. The colonel practically shouted, "Dagrepont, I need you to hurry back here ASAP. The zombies are multiplying like rabbits all around camp. How much longer will you be?" Dagrepont realized he had a more immediate concern at the moment; the zombie near the automatic doors had turned and started to careen his way. He thought, *So much for leaving it be.*

He glanced at his black wristwatch and replied, "Don't know, sir. I'll get there as quick as I can." He tucked the radio under his arm and flipped the rifle's safety to off, firing a three round burst. All of the rounds pummeled the zombie's head; only small fragments remained atop its shoulders. He saw another zombie heading his way, and blasted it with a second burst, dropping it easily. He stood near the doors, contemplated not going in at all, and thought, *This is going to be a challenge.* He knew he had to complete the mission, though – an order was an order. He heard Caster's voice come through the radio once more, as he replied, "Okay, son. Complete the recon and get back here as quickly as you can."

Dagrepont stepped across the threshold and walked over the body of a lifeless zombie. It was stiffened into a pose reminiscent of the ash corpses of Pompeii, and was missing about half of its head. He wondered if the scrub-clad victim was a nurse or doctor. Not able to resist his inner scientist, he pulled a pen from his shirt pocket and used it as a surgical probe. He peeled back the greenish-hued skin at the edge of the zombie's head wound and looked into the gaping hole. *Dura matter of the brain obviously inflamed. Not a surprise there.* He proceeded to remove the pen and push it through a sticky tumor. The tumor released a green, musky-smelling viscous fluid.

Dagrepont was startled by a voice from behind. "Za-ca, za-ca!" In one motion, he dropped the pen and swung the M4 around. He swept the zombie with a volley of rounds. It absorbed the rounds, falling over a wheelchair like a clumsy clown. Dagrepont stood up and sprinted deeper into the lobby, determined to carry out his mission.

Inside the lobby it was eerily quiet, and there were no other bodies in sight. *Maybe they evacuated.* He moved through the hallway with his back against the walls, peering into a handful of open doors, seeing signs of struggle here and there. His confidence began to dwindle a little when he heard several screams down the hallway. *This'll have to be a quick recon.* Moving forward, he eased into a small security room where he quickly scanned the monitors. Joystick in hand, he manipulated cameras A, B, and C, and what he saw made him feel extremely lucky that he had made it that far. He whispered quietly, "Crap! This place is infested!" As he was preparing a getaway, he looked into one of the monitors and noticed another zombie near the café. It limped about in big fluffy slippers, a clear plastic endotracheal tube sticking out of its mouth. From the tube, phlegm and blood dripped to the floor. *Gotta take care of this one so I can finish my recon and get out of here!*

A few hallways farther down, he rolled a silver transport cart into the gut of a malnourished senior zombie. He didn't have the heart to kill it. The smell of burnt food permeated the air and caught his attention; he followed it to the cafeteria. Something nearby made a sound like a breath taken through a snorkel. *Gotta be what I saw in the monitor earlier.* He hid on the side of a large food display case, and hoped the humming motor would mask his own breathing. While he waited for it to come into view, he was reminded of when he used to play hide and seek with his siblings. When he sensed that the zombie was about fifteen feet away, he stepped out from his hiding spot and unleashed a half-clip of firepower. The bullets pierced its torso, but it continued to struggle forward. He realized more problems were now gathering to his rear.

With his escape route blocked, he faced the tubed menace, which was swinging its arms wildly. With another squeeze of the trigger, he planted a few rounds in its head, which promptly burst open. The tube flew into the air and stuck into a ceiling tile, leaking blood. Dagrepont hurried past the fallen zombie and made his way out of the hospital. He ran around the building to the front parking lot, hopped in the Jeep and started it up. He entered Sporaton's address and waited as the device loaded the results. He thought about Caster's last words, and the zombies he had just killed. As he drove out of the parking lot, he smashed into several zombies that had blocked the way.

Under his breath he mumbled, "This is unbelievable!" He jumped out, shoved a severed arm off of the hood and resumed his mission.

Big Texas Road House:

Phoenix and Nolan stood guard at the bar's entrance while everyone else moved into the interior. Adele rolled Higgins inside, which really got his goat. The old man stated, "That's alright. I got it, young woman." He was embarrassed over the sudden loss of his independence, but managed a half smile. She let go of the handles, and he wheeled himself the rest of the way in on his own.

Phoenix walked inside and said, "We have to secure this bar. Nolan and Adele, check out the kitchen. Dora, guard Vicki. I'll take the storage area and the restrooms."

Instead of being happy, downtrodden Nick addressed the group. "My name's Nick. There's lots of food in the kitchen; grab a bite while you can." He followed Phoenix to the storage room and said, "I have something I need to tell you."

Still hyped from the recent battle, Phoenix looked at the blood-speckled man, then reached out to shake his hand. He quickly said, "My name is Phoenix. Were you here all alone?"

Emotionally drained, Nick's face crumpled. "No, I was with my buddy Ron. He's out front, dead. I'm the last of my group." He paused and leaned against a stack of boxes. The reality of the day had set in firmly, and he took a deep breath before continuing, "If you don't mind, I'd like to check out the restrooms with you. I need to wash the blood from my face anyway."

Phoenix nodded. "Sorry about your team, man. I'd be happy to have your help. First stop, restrooms."

***

Adele and Nolan peeked through the doors of the industrial kitchen. They didn't see or hear anything, so they entered and maneuvered around the stainless steel prep counters and walked over to the sinks. Adele grabbed a wash rag from the counter and wiped the sweat and blood from her face. At the end of the room were the double doors of a large walk in freezer. Nolan pointed and said, "We should check that out. Maybe someone is waiting for rescue inside."

She slapped him on the back and replied, "No problem. Let's get it done."

Nolan took a shooter's stance, saying "You pull the handle. I'll shoot if anything comes out."

Adele jokingly replied, I see you've done this before," and counted down, "Three ... two ... and one!" She quickly pulled on the door's handle, but it slipped out of her grasp. Nolan furrowed his brow at her. She grabbed the handle and was able to yank the door wide open. A wave of freezing air enveloped them, and she scooted to the side. Nolan peered into the misty freezer looking for any signs of movement.

Not seeing anything obvious, he walked past her and said, "Stand here," then entered the freezer.

Inquisitive, she whispered, "Well? Anything?"

He shrugged his shoulders and answered, "Naw, don't think so," and disappeared deeper into the freezer.

A couple of seconds later, she anxiously whispered, "Anything?" He purposefully did not reply as he eyeballed all sorts of food items. His stomach growled loudly. *I could eat a horse!*

At her wits' end, Adele put her finger on the trigger and whispered, "What was that noise?"

He advanced deeper into the walk-in. "Just my stomach." At the far back wall of the unit, he saw a single glass jar sitting by itself atop a shelf. It was filled with a maroon-red liquid and was labeled, "First sauce; 2002."

***

Nick put his rifle down next to the bathroom sink and looked into the mirror. He wiped off specks of dried blood with a damp paper towel and watched Phoenix as he rifle-butted each stall door open. At the last stall, Phoenix turned and asked, "Are you finished yet?" Nick did not answer the question at first. Instead, he dropped a bloody paper towel into the sink. He wet a new one, and asked, "Hey, how long has your group been together?"

Phoenix walked to the sink and replied, "About a day and a half, but I wasn't the first in the group. We've lost some good people, and I don't intend to lose any more." Phoenix put his hands into the running water and asked, "Can you take care of the entrance while I check the ladies' room and the rest of the storage areas?"

Nick dropped the last of the bloodied napkins. "Okay, will do. But are ya sure you wanna go into those rooms alone?"

Phoenix looked into the mirror. He thought about it a second and replied, "You know, you're right. On your way to the front, why don't you pop into the kitchen and ask Adele to meet me back here when she's done."

Nick looked surprised and didn't understand why Adele had been chosen over him. He tried to appear indifferent. "Okay, will do." He walked out of the room.

Lieutenant Commander Dagrepont:

Whenever he had to slow down for a turn or a road blockage, Dagrepont worried about being pulled out of the open-topped Jeep. After a few near misses, he stopped the Jeep in front of a horde of zombies that were blocking the road. In a mere ten seconds, he neutralized fifteen. Unfortunately, there were more than he could shoot, and as one of them fell, another took its place. They lurched forward, without rhyme or reason, either gnashing their teeth or murmuring. *Can't figure out why some of their heads explode for no apparent reason.* He knew it would be foolish to try and shoot them all, so he pulled a U-turn and accelerated. The GPS screen chimed in and the voice said, "Rerouting."

About twelve minutes later, Dagrepont pulled up to the lab with his M4 in hand. He took a deep breath and opened the front door of the building ready for anything. Once inside, he called out for the doctor. "Doctor Ludwig, Lieutenant Commander Dagrepont here."

Hearing him enter, Ludwig picked up his kit and shouted back, "I'm back here!"

Happy that the doctor was still alive, Dagrepont rushed to shake Ludwig's hand and said, "Great, glad you're safe."

Ludwig said, "I just need to transfer these files to your vehicle." and started stacking folders, then pointed to the area that held the zombie. "The thing in there is really giving me the creeps."

Dagrepont pushed his weapon's safety to off. "I'll be back. Gonna take care of that thing for you."

The doctor stopped in his tracks. "No! No! Maybe we can save it at some point. No sense in destroying it now. Just put a sign up at the entrance to warn people of the danger."

Dagrepont had his orders, but the doctor made sense. "Okay, I'll make the sign." He grabbed a jumbo-sized felt tip pen and wrote on a piece of paper, "CAUTION: FLESH EATING ZOMBIE INSIDE! ENTER AT YOUR OWN RISK!" He taped it to the front door of the small lab. Dagrepont then helped Ludwig grab the last of his files and specimens, and loaded them into the Jeep. When they were done, they climbed into the vehicle and Ludwig asked, "Where to, now?"

Dagrepont explained everything that had happened at the hospital and added, "We need to get back to base camp. The colonel said they were seeing more of the zombies. As a matter of fact, I need to check in with them now." He pressed the radio's rocker button and spoke directly into the mouthpiece, but got no reply. Figuring the colonel must be busy at the moment, he put down the radio and turned to Ludwig, asking, "Can you tell me about your research? Any info would be greatly appreciated."

Ludwig shifted in his seat and said, "It's just speculation, but I think the infection might have something to do with a recent scientific expedition. A Sporaton team working in the Mayan jungle found some hieroglyphics depicting what we think might be a ritual sacrifice. One stone glyph had some sort of strange plant carved into it." He thumbed through chemistry results and added, "The blood samples collected from the team members who 'turned' are equally as strange; they uniformly show a rapid increase in cell growth and restoration. There's no obvious kick starter or death mechanism, and they seem to be long-lived like HeLa cells."

Dagrepont stopped him and asked, "You mean these cells are as virulent as HeLa cells?"

Ludwig nodded emphatically. "Yes they are! And after all these years, we still haven't identified the mechanism that keeps THOSE cells alive! We definitely need to determine the etiology of this disease, or the country will be in a world of hurt."

Dagrepont said, "I'm going to try base camp again." He radioed, "Colonel Caster, this is Dagrepont." No one replied. He waited a few seconds, turned up the volume on the radio, then tried again, "Colonel Caster, this is Dagrepont. Come in." He heard a loud crackle of static. More concerned than ever, he said, "This isn't good. We need to get back to base camp ASAP!" He floored the accelerator of the Jeep and peeled out of the parking lot. Under his breath, he muttered, "Damn! I hope everything's OK."

<u>Big Texas Road House:</u>

The group sat at the hand-varnished tables and ate like it was Thanksgiving, except for Nick, who guarded the front doors. Between bites of ribs, beans, and mac and cheese, they let off steam by sharing stories of their recent trials.

Higgins rose out of his wheelchair and everyone froze. They stared at him like they had seen a ghost, so shocked that he could stand up. He acknowledged the expressions by saying, "Hope y'all didn't think that I was THAT old and decrepit!" He reached for a plate of ribs and sighed contentedly. "I've been waiting for this for hours!" Everyone tried to hide their surprise and chewed their food quietly.

The old man sat back down, and talked about his young friend Jay, who had worked at the roadhouse until being killed by a zombie. He set his plate down and said, "He was a good kid and a good friend, always nice to this old man." He took a bite out of a rib and swallowed hard. He added, "When this whole mess started, he was out back – worked cleaning up here, ya know – when he was killed by one of those shufflers."

Phoenix, who was sitting next to the old man, patted his arm and said, "I'm sorry to hear about Jay. I agree … he was a nice kid."

Bewildered, Higgins put down the rib for the first time and asked, "You knew Jay?"

Phoenix nodded. "Yes sir – I'm pretty much a regular here, and I saw him all the time."

As he stood leaning against the front door, Nick was tempted to run outside and start shooting zombies again, but kept himself in check. He just had to accept the fact that everyone he knew was probably dead, and his new group needed to save ammunition for whatever the future held. *It might be a while before help comes.* He cracked open the door and could see Ron's body sprawled next to the wall. Just then, a wave of heat, followed by an electrical shockwave surged through his arm. His hand involuntarily cramped into a fist. *Can't let these people see this. They'll think I'm changing into a zombie.* He stuck the fisted hand into his pocket, but he understood that there was nothing to be done but wait and see what happened next.

Behind Nick, off to one side, Vicki's body lay in a pool of blood. Her upper torso had been covered with a red and white checkered table cloth.

Nick put his frustrations aside, turned to the group and shouted, "So far, so good – it's pretty quiet out there."

Dora looked over at the lone stranger, feeling that he'd been left out. In her best Texas cowgirl drawl, she replied, "Well, darlin', barricade that door and sit with us!"

He smiled and replied, "Thank you, ma'am; I think I will." His fist released itself, so he grabbed a metal chair and wedged it under the door handles, nice and tight. He walked over to the tables and dipped a rib into some sauce. With a mouth full of meat he mumbled, "Not really hungry, but these are darn good."

After everyone had eaten, the group gathered around the mechanical bullpen, which was encircled by a mishmash of tables and chairs. The pen was designed to look like a professional arena and sported various advertising banners to promote local businesses. Phoenix leaned on the bull in the middle. Not wanting to come across as overbearing, he asked their opinions on what the next move should be.

Adele entered the pit and sarcastically said, "Why don't ya tell us what YOU want us to do!"

He laughed and put his hand on the bull's foam horn, then replied, "I don't roll like that!"

Fired up and needing to draw a reaction, she added, "We need to get out there and shoot 'em up. That's my choice!"

Fed up with her antics, Dora shook her head and said, "All you wanna do is shoot 'em up. Phoenix is trying to help us figure a way out of this crazy town. Just hush and listen to him." Adele crossed her arms and glared at Dora, then sat down.

Phoenix added, "I'd be happy to draw up a plan we can all agree on."

Nick stood up with his hand in his pocket and added, "I'm with Phoenix. Anything he thinks of … I'm for it." He was happy to not have to think about anything. Nolan agreed as well.

Relieved, Phoenix happily said, "Okay, now we're making progress. The floor's open for dialogue."

Adele unexpectedly said, "We need to stick together. But you won't be coming to the ladies room with me. My DEAD husband wouldn't appreciate that." She thought, *Now why on earth did I just say that?*

Dora looked over at her and asked, "You need to go, Adele? I'll go with you."

Adele rolled her eyes and replied, "Nah, I don't need a babysitter, I've got this right here." She slung the M4 around to the front of her body, then checked it in front of the group. She felt sick to her stomach, but didn't want to say anything.

Phoenix stood tall like he was a general at a war conference and addressed the group. "Just like Adele ... firepower first." Then he drew a quick sketch on a piece of butcher's paper. Rooms, hallways and the bull pen quickly appeared. He added, "This is a diagram of the bar, and we're here. This is where all of the exits and windows are."

Nolan moved over to the map. He lifted a corner of it and said, "But how are we gonna defend all of this space, with only six people?"

Phoenix gestured like a car salesman and replied, "Good question. We're not!"

Adele jumped back into the pit and shouted, "What in the world?" She spun the newly created map around.

Not wanting to rattle anyone's feelings, Dora asked, "Is that a good idea, Phoenix?"

Nick studied the map, traced his fingers along the lines. "Settle down. I see what he's done. We'll defend only a portion of it, and block off the rest. Good idea." Phoenix's confidence grew as he drew additional arrows and boxes on the map. In the back of his mind, he thought, *Remember to include everyone.* He continued to explain, "This will be our holding ground. We'll have two ways out, and use tables and furniture from the bar to block off the windows and exits. Everywhere else will be off limits ... oh, except for the bathrooms. We'll go in pairs when we need to."

Adele resigned herself to the plan and said, "Great."

Glad to be around other people, Higgins added, "Good plan, young man. I'm all for it." Then he bit into another baby back rib.

That's a Direct Order:

Colonel Caster crawled to his radio. He struggled to press the button, while holding a picture of his Pookie. He was severely wounded, and bled from multiple bite sites. The entire team had been overwhelmed, and they lay dead or wounded amongst the zombie corpses. Nearly breathless, the colonel grimaced in pain, then pressed the radio's rocker button and spoke. "Dagrepont, Caster here. Do you read me?" He waited for a reply, but knew death was imminent as his breaths became shallow. He was in agony, and the field bandages that protected his bloated intestines were falling off. He dropped Pookie's picture so he could have a free hand to adjust the dressing, then he heard an excited, "I hear you Colonel!"

Caster clicked the radio's button and ordered, "Don't come! Many dead ... I'm wounded."

Puzzled, Dagrepont thought, *How in the world could the medical equivalent of a Navy Seal team have been overrun that quickly?* He replied, "Dagrepont here … I'm on my way with the doctor. We'll pick you up and any other survivors and get you to safety."

As sternly as he could muster, the colonel replied, "No … don't … don't wanna contaminate … direct order."

Dagrepont shook his head and turned to Ludwig, who was utterly in shock. "This IS going be a rescue mission. I'm not following those orders. We have to go!" He heard the colonel gasp for air, then floored the gas pedal. At the same time, he spoke into the radio, "Colonel? Colonel? Colonel, are you there?"

Ludwig reprogrammed the GPS unit. The voice prompt immediately gave directions, and they sped off toward base camp.

Ludwig said, "This is definitely getting out of hand." At every turn, the zombies had multiplied. There were little skirmishes going on everywhere between the normal Texans and the zombies. Ludwig wanted to stop and pick people up, but before he could say anything, Dagrepont read his mind and firmly said, "We just can't take a chance … it's too dangerous. We've gotta get back to the colonel. He's only wounded."

Ludwig shook his head. "He's probably already contaminated. I watched my assistant get bit and become one of those things in just a matter of hours."

At that moment, Dagrepont noticed that they were becoming surrounded, and said, "Doctor, I highly recommend that you take that rifle into your hands and shoot anything that gets in front of the Jeep." He flinched as Ludwig clumsily lifted the rifle and grazed his temple. "Careful, it's loaded. Check the safety!" Ludwig pretended to know what he was doing and fumbled around for the switch. Dagrepont pointed, "Right below there, Doc."

Ludwig snapped, "Alright, alright, I got it!"

Dagrepont weaved between cars and said, "Just start shooting, will ya?!"

Door of Death:

Stockton took one last glance at the newest data set, then pressed the icon for the speaker phone function. He said,

"So, it looks like one of the scientists from the Belize expedition could be immune to the infection. You'll need to find him if he's alive, and get me some blood samples."

Ludwig held the door tightly as the vehicle accelerated, slowed, and quickly turned to avoid a large group of zombies. He spoke through his handset and asked, "Did you say someone might be immune?"

Stockton replied, "That's what we've gotten from the data. How bad is it over there?"

Ludwig rubbed his temple and replied, "It's all happening so fast. The numbers just don't add up." The GPS voice chimed, "Rerouting!" Ludwig repositioned the rifle's barrel between the side mirror and the door of the Jeep. From his perspective, the rifle looked as big as a bazooka.

"Do we have a name yet?"

Stockton flipped his reading glasses down from the top of his head. He replied, "Phoenix Holiday."

Ludwig said, "Good, we've already been to his apartment and taken samples." He nodded to Dagrepont, who had given him a quick glance.

Stockton gave quick thumbs up to someone in the room and replied, "Perfect. Get them to me ASAP! But be careful. You're going to have to be our eyes and ears on the ground out there."

Mumbling, Ludwig replied, "Will do! Talk to you soon." He ended the call, then nervously placed his finger on the rifle's trigger, and aimed at a nearby zombie.

Dagrepont calmly said, "According to the GPS, we're about two miles away." Ludwig pulled the trigger on the rifle, but had forgotten to exhale. The rifle kicked upward and several bullets slammed into a large metal Savings and Loan sign hanging on a nearby building. The chains that suspended the older sign gave way, and it fell to the sidewalk, cutting a zombie in two. Eerily, the upper half of its body began to crawl away and Ludwig shouted, "That's incredible!" Just ahead of them, the door of a sport utility vehicle was shoved wide open, its hinges cracking with the forcefulness of the motion. Two powerful but spastic arms emerged from the driver's side, followed by a ghoulish body.

Dagrepont swerved, but they were too close and the Jeep crashed full speed into the door, which became firmly wedged in their front bumper. The force of the impact spun the Jeep sideways, and they watched in horror as a very large zombie emerged from the vehicle they had just hit. Dagrepont gripped the steering wheel and shouted, "Shoot it. Shoot for the head!" Ludwig fumbled the rifle, but managed to aim and let loose a barrage of bullets. Not one of the rounds penetrated its head. A dozen more of the shufflers began moving toward the Jeep.

"C'mon man … just shoot for their heads! Hurry!"

Ludwig ignored the voice, took a deep breath, and pulled the trigger. The end of the barrel looked like a cinematic special effect as a blast of flames spewed from its end. The rounds peppered the body, and the zombie's arms flailed like badly controlled nun chucks. Totally by chance, one of the rounds struck the zombie's head, and it exploded like a grenade inside of a watermelon. The body dropped to the ground.

Ludwig yelled, "Let's get outta here, man!"

Dagrepont straightened the Jeep and sped away, the door still attached to the bumper and positioned in such a way that he could see well enough to steer. He smiled at the thought. *Maybe I could use it as a zombie plow.*

Ludwig grimaced at the sounds the zombies made after each body was cut down by the plow. It gave him the heebie-jeebies when a severed hand bounced up on the hood, grabbed on to a windshield wiper, and would not let go. He looked at Dagrepont and said "Yep, we're definitely gonna need the military."

Dagrepont found a macabre humor in the unorthodox weapon. Tongue-in-cheek, he said, "I'm gonna call it, 'Door of Death,' our newest weapon of mass destruction."

Scissors in Hand:

Adele paced the floor while waiting for the effects of the soft candy to kick in. *Isn't peppermint supposed to be good for a stomachache?*

Dora noticed Adele pacing and walked over to her, asking, "Anything wrong?"

Adele told Dora, who now stood right in front of her, about the night her husband turned.

"It was a little bit before midnight, and I rolled over to snuggle with him. When I realized that he was not in bed, I got up and saw him standing in front of the dimly lit bathroom mirror. I stood in the doorway and sleepily asked, 'What's wrong, honey?' He trembled in place, but did not answer or turn around, so I flipped the light switch to brighten the room. The glare of the bright lights caused me to squint, but I could see that the back of his tee shirt was covered in sweat. I inched forward to stand next to the man I love, and to look directly into his eyes. He did not turn or say a word, but in his reflection, I noticed that his eyes were black and deep set, making his face appear to have none at all. Blood and vomit stained the front of his shirt. I panicked and said, 'You're throwing up blood, honey. We've got to get you to the hospital.'"

"Next, I moved to take his arm, but he turned and reached for my head, entwining his fingers in my hair and yanking hard. I yelled, 'Stop it, honey! You're hurting me!' and fell to the floor. As he loomed over me, saliva from his mouth dripped onto my hair and face. He yanked me towards his mouth and I screamed, 'Stop it! You're hurting me!' He mumbled gibberish and tried to bite me, but I turned my face away just in time. His breath had a musty, rotted swamp smell, and his skin was tinged green. I shoved at his chest to get him to back off, and he lost his balance and smacked onto the ceramic tiled floor next to me. I was cornered against the tub, but he still had a firm grip on my hair. I tried to break free, screaming, 'Are you out of your freakin' mind?' I remembered the antidepressant he had started taking recently was known to have some serious side effects, including homicidal tendencies. I could barely move, but managed to reach into the drawer of the nearby vanity and grab a pair of scissors."

"As my husband pulled at me again and again, he tried biting my neck, but I shoved off against his chest and defensively stabbed at his arms. He wouldn't let go, continuing to snap at me like a wild, rabid dog. He got to his knees and threw himself down upon me with his full body weight. I had been holding the scissors pointy side toward him, and as he fell onto me, the blades pierced through his neck, soft palate, and deep into his skull. His full body tremors caused the blades to wiggle back and forth, scrambling his brains."

Dora said, "I'm so sorry, Adele," and leaned in to give her a hug, but Adele refused.

Dora stepped back to give her space and continued to listen.

"I had needed to push him off so I could get up. As he landed flat on his back, I broke down in tears, but still had enough presence of mind to get up and call the police. Oddly, no one at the station answered. Frantically, I pondered what to do next, and decided that the best thing to do would be to go to my parents' home around the corner."

"Walking inside of my parent's home, I immediately saw them lying on the floor dead. Dizzy with fear, I backed out of the house and ran for my car. I turned the ignition and decided to drive straight to the police station, but the ride was a complete blur. Minutes later, I choked back tears after seeing the crashed police cruiser. I put the car into reverse and spent the next hours just driving around, sobbing hysterically, and trying to avoid the crazy people. That's what happened."

Dora leaned in to give another hug, but Adele refused again. Dora walked away, because she now had her eyes on Phoenix.

In spite of the pain in her stomach, Adele was furious. In her heart, she knew she had to go outside and avenge her husband's death. *If I kill enough of those things, I won't hurt so badly.* In her mind, it was that simple.

Dora loomed over the chair that had barricaded the door. She finally removed it and cracked open the door. Surveying the situation outside, she did not see Adele grab her rifle. Adele waited for the right moment for Dora to move back inside. Before Dora could replace the chair, Adele squeezed past her, bursting through the doors and ran from the building. She opened fire on a group of zombies who had been standing nearby in the parking lot, and managed to hit several of them before Phoenix and Nolan ran after her. They yelled for her to come back inside, but she yelled back, "No! I have to do this!"

Nolan tried to block her from fleeing while Phoenix pleaded with her. "Please, you have to come back inside." Another gut busting cramp seized her, causing Adele to clutch her stomach and back up hard against a vehicle.

She yelled, "I'm doing this," and expertly lifted her rifle and unleashed another volley of rounds at a group of zombies. A bullet whizzed by Phoenix's ear. He could feel its heat. A zombie fell just behind him. She moved to her left and yelled, "Go back inside!" then ran deeper into the parking lot. Determined to not lose her, Nolan and Phoenix followed. All of the sudden, a set of arms reached out from a nearby car and tried to grab her. She spun around and crashed to the ground, but managed to fire off the M4. The rounds went wild, and one carved a groove into the side panel of the car that Nolan was standing next to.

Adele's gunfire had drawn more zombies toward the three. Nolan and Phoenix rushed to reach Adele, but before they could get there, the zombie in the car opened the door, grabbed her, and pulled her quickly toward its waiting mouth. It bit an enormous chunk from the top of her head, ripping a large, bloodied drape of flesh from her scalp. It bit again and again. Her brain instantly ballooned in size. Without thinking, Phoenix aimed his rifle and shot both Adele and her killer dead. He looked over at Nolan and said, in a cracking voice, "We don't want her coming back again."

Nolan, confused and hurt by what had just transpired, took a few moments to respond. "No! We don't." He couldn't say anything else. They used up their remaining rounds to cut a path back to the door, then retreated inside and stared into the faces of the disbelieving group.

Nolan felt numb and dropped his empty weapon. Dora slammed the door shut and barricaded it tightly, but noticed as she did that a few dozen more zombies were converging on the bar.

After the door was secured, Phoenix addressed the group somberly from the bull pit. In his most reassuring voice, he said "Okay guys, we just lost Adele. I don't wanna lose anyone else. Do any of you have anything you wanna get off your chest before you go all Green Beret on us?" No one said a word. They just stared at him, glassy eyed.

Phoenix continued. "We need to stay focused if we're gonna live through this. We also need to get some rest. Mr. Higgins and Dora, you two sack out first?"

Higgins tipped his hat and replied, "Don't mind if I do."

Dora thought that sleep would be a welcome respite from the waking nightmare they were all in. She looked around for a place to bed down as Phoenix continued his pep talk.

"We have to seal off the part of the bar that Adele has been guarding."

Nolan jumped out of his chair, picked up a can of soda, and said, "I'll get right on that."

Nick added, "Hold up there. I'll give you a hand."

Phoenix smiled and replied, "Good! At least we're working together."

Dora placed a few chairs side by side to create a makeshift bench, then opened a checkered tablecloth for Higgins to use as a blanket. He refused it, saying, "Why don't ya keep that for yerself? I've been to Korea, ya' know, I got no problem sleepin' rough." She put the finishing touches on her own impromptu chair bed and stretched out.

Dagrepont and Ludwig:

Like caped crusaders, Dagrepont and Ludwig jumped out of the Jeep in front of the colonel's tent and ran among the contorted bodies searching for him. Ludwig scanned the bloodbath, cleared his throat and said, "It looks like they were overrun and tried to escape."

Dagrepont's eyes gave away his internal terror. He stood there speechless, almost at attention surveying the bodies of his friends and fellow team members. Most of the dead lay with their heads pointed towards the center of camp. Some were only half-clothed, and appeared to have been trying to struggle out of the cumbersome Hazmat suits.

Ludwig rolled over the nearest body. A large wound punctuated the side of her head, and her Hazmat suit was dotted with coagulated clumps of blood. He pulled a few cotton swabs from his nearby kit, dabbed the wound edges, then placed them into the sterile specimen containers. He plucked a loosened tooth from a second corpse's mouth, and placed it into a separate container. He quickly scanned the area.

In a whisper, Dagrepont said, "He's over there!"

They ran over to Caster's body, kneeling carefully to avoid the bloated, smelly bowels that were spread out along the ground. Dagrepont checked for a pulse, but his facial expression spoke volumes about the colonel's condition. He picked up a sleeping bag and covered him with it. Ludwig walked around checking for palpable pulses, but found no signs of life.

Their work was interrupted by moans from inside a tent, followed by the walls being pushed outward, as if it had been overfilled with something. Dagrepont knew better than to investigate. He looked nervously over his shoulder and saw the zombies they had spotted on their way into camp getting closer.

Ludwig tapped Dagrepont's shoulder and said, "Look, we need to get out of here."

Dagrepont stood up and evaluated the speed of the approaching zombies. He replied, "Yes, but we'll need more supplies. Grab those MREs over there. I'm going to get more weapons and ammo."

Ludwig felt as if he were on a military mission, and followed the commands like an obedient soldier. Within just a few minutes, they had gathered what supplies they could, the samples taken on the scene, and climbed back into the Jeep.

Ludwig asked, "Where to now?"

Dagrepont put the Jeep into drive, then replied, "Frankly, I have no idea."

Doctor Stockton:

At a secret location somewhere in Nevada, Stockton addressed the group of men and women at his conference table, saying,

"The situation is even worse than we could have possibly imagined." He looked over at a long-haired linguist and asked, "Were you able to decipher any of the glyphs?"

The linguist replied, "Yes sir, I was." He clicked a remote control in his hand and an image was projected onto the wall of the dimly-lit room. He continued, "If you look carefully at this image, and the way it has been folded together, you can see that it creates a new image. A new story emerges. Notice how the figure now seems to be wearing an ornamental headpiece. Prisoners of the priest would have actually had their heads *bared* as they were prepared for sacrifice. From other research projects I've been associated with, I've determined that the things on his head are probably some sort of growths; possibly a plant of some sort." The attendees in the room gazed at the screen. He flipped to the next slide and continued.

"If you noticed, the sun was present in the glyph on the first slide, but it disappears when images are combined and a serpent's head appears. This is the point where the glyph's true meaning emerges. Using the Mayan counting system, you can see that an incomplete number also appears on the side of the glyph. The number could be twelve, thirteen or fourteen. In other words, maybe the dates relate to the legendary prophecy about the end of the world or a new beginning."

Stockton motioned for the projector to be turned off and sat back down. He made eye contact with each person at the table, and said, "This is a serious situation, folks. A research team from Sporaton Labs appears to have been infected by something. Likely, it was transferred from spores in the air, or via direct injection caused by an insect's bite. They could have also brought back something – possibly a plant or fungus – that serves as a host for the infectious substance. We've already determined that the team had a chartered flight, and probably bypassed international customs."

Stockton stood up with both hands on the conference table and continued. "If you turn to page thirty-three of the handout, you'll notice that we could be dealing with a mutated form of the virus that causes meningitis." Sounds of pages being turned filled the room. The scientists nodded as they considered the data.

Stockton walked around the table patting each person on the back and continued, "I want each of you to spend the next few days at the lab. Inform your families that you'll be occupied with groundbreaking research, and you won't be able to go home. We are going to recommend a total quarantine of Baron and the surrounding towns, and we need solid data to back up that decision."

The researchers got up and filed out of the room. Stockton waved over his senior researcher. He clicked to a new slide and said, "Look at this one. See the inflammation in the meninges, but the cells are still multiplying at an exponential rate." He took a sip of coffee, then flipped to a new slide. "This one is from an older specimen we collected. Notice how the cell counts are quadrupled – and there may been only a few hours' difference between the two."

The senior researcher replied, "I see. That's extraordinary."

Stockton lowered his voice and said quietly, "We need to send another medical team to Texas. They'll have to secure additional specimens. This time use a dedicated military team to provide security."

The senior researcher replied, "But maybe the other team is still active."

Stockton turned to the window and looked to the horizon. "Let's hope so."

Silence:

Nolan patrolled the area in front of the restrooms and did whatever he could to distract his thoughts from the travesty of Joaquin's death. He kicked a wadded paper ball between two chair legs and whispered, "Score!" while trying to ignore the reemergence of his migraine.

Nick wanted to eat again, but distracted himself by listening to Higgins' wake-the-dead snores. He walked over to the old man and could see rib sauce on his chin. He headed back toward the bathrooms and told Nolan, "He sounds like a sputtering chainsaw!"

Nolan listened intently, then replied, "Yeah, that sounds like an old '52."

Nick chuckled and said, "No, I meant Higgins' snoring."

"Oh. Oh yeah. Right." Nolan walked over to the old man, gazed into his opened mouth, and wondered if he could kick a paper ball into it.

Nolan played bartender as the men took a five minute break. Phoenix sat hunched over on a bar stool, and snagged a sliding mug that was bee lining toward him. He swished a mouthful of the purple liquid across his taste buds, then swallowed. It burned going down, but he had no problem gulping down more of the exotic concoction, it tasted so good. He asked, "You're sure this is alcohol free? Sure packs a punch!"

Nolan replied, "I'm sure, Phoenix. No alcohol." He gestured at the ingredients laid out on the bar.

Phoenix took another sip and smacked his leg as the spicy liquid hit the back of his throat. He said, "Dang good … but it's got a lot of heat!" He leaned back and added, "You know … I just came back from an expedition to South America. I wonder how the rest of my team is doing."

Nick was surprised at what Phoenix said and asked, "So, you're working for that lab down the road?"

Phoenix replied, "Yep … almost a year now."

Nolan wiped down the mess he had made and asked, "What was Sporaton doing down in South America?"

Phoenix brushed his hair out of his face and replied, "Our mission was to collect spore specimens from exotic plants. Sometimes, we experiment with the spores ourselves. But mostly, we just sell the samples and data to other labs around the world, which reduces the amount of work and expenses they'd incur if they had to mount their own expeditions."

Nolan pushed the leftover drink ingredients into a trash can. He realized that his headache was subsiding and added, "Oh, so you would gather the data …"

Nick finished his sentence, "… and have nothing to do with who purchased it and what they did with it? What if that data was used for some sort of bio weapon?"

Phoenix shook his head and said, "Specimens are collected and sold to labs all over the world every day, by all sorts of companies. That's how progress is made. It's cost effective."

Frustrated, Nick opened his arms and replied, "But the same mistakes seem to be repeated over and over from this type of thinking."

Phoenix rubbed his forehead, then looked at both of them in the eyes and replied, "Think of it this way. Imagine two different guys, working for two different companies, trying to achieve the *same* results. It's twice the effort to gain the exact same outcome. It's just not cost-effective, don't you see?" The two men nodded, agreeing with the rationale. Phoenix continued, "At Sporaton Labs, we put in all the effort to gather specimens and basic information, so other specialty labs don't have to. They can focus their efforts on developing what we give them. It's a simple matter of teamwork."

Nolan, feeling better now that his headache had gone away, backpedaled figuratively. He replied, "Oh, I wasn't trying to blame you guys at Sporaton. Just trying to understand what y'all are doing."

Nick realized that Phoenix looked uncomfortable, and didn't want him to think they were making him shoulder the blame for the scientific blunders of the world. He chuckled and said, "Yeah, man, this isn't the Spanish Inquisition. You're alright by me. But I'm ready for some shuteye. Can we wake those two and get some chair time? It's been a while."

Phoenix nodded and said, "Yep, sounds like a good idea." He stood up, but instantly felt a weird bubbly sensation in his head. He thought, *Wow, what the heck was in that drink?* He grabbed his rifle and hurried back to the windows.

Nick quietly made his way over to where Dora and Higgins were sleeping, then yelled, "ZOMBIE!" The two sat straight up. Dora reached for her M4 and brought it to a firing position in a flash.

Nick had to force the barrel back down as he hollered, "Whoa! Whoa! You don't need that thing yet!" His voice sounded high and squeaky as he added, "It was just a little test."

Higgins stood up and grumpily shouted, "Young man, I don't need a test – been tested all my life. That wasn't funny, dang it!"

Dora was silent, but if looks could kill, Nick would have been incinerated on the spot.

Nick, realizing he'd made a huge blunder, said, "Really guys, it was just a joke. I'm sorry I startled you. But it's your turn to guard this place."

Dora stood up, slung the M4 over her shoulder, and said, "Lucky for you, I'm not Adele." She rolled her eyes as she walked away.

His head feeling fuzzier by the moment, Phoenix asked Nolan, "Man, what was in that drink?"

As he stretched out on his chair bed, Nolan garbled his words, as if he were hiding something. "Berry juice ... lemon, touch of honey, cinnamon, baking soda, and water."

Phoenix scribbled a few notes into his journal.

Nick tried to forget his bad joke, and quickly asked, "Phoenix, you sure you don't want to catch a quick nap?"

Phoenix put the notepad back into his pocket and answered, "Yeah ... I'm alright." Then, so only Nick could hear, he added, "I wouldn't pull that kind of stunt again."

Still red-faced, Nick replied, "Okay, I promise, I won't."

Higgins walked over to Phoenix, and patted him on the back. He said, "Young man, you're doing a fine job here."

Dora came up behind them and added, "He's doing an awesome job with this whole situation." She had the beginnings of a crush on him.

It had been a couple of years since her boyfriend's untimely death. They had been in a five-year relationship that tragically ended at the junction of 70 and 256 in a head-on car collision near Baron. His death was bittersweet, because he was an organ donor. A month later, she received a letter from the donor organization that said his donation had helped to save the lives of seven people in the area. One of the patients was a twelve-year-old boy with a failing heart. He was now able to play baseball with his friends.

Phoenix couldn't help but notice Dora's glances. He chose to ignore them for the present, and instead said, "You two are survivors! Together, we'll get out of this mess." He walked them around their duty stations, pointing to the changes that had been made while they slept. "If we become overwhelmed, we'll take positions in the bull pen. I don't believe going back outside is a good idea. It's swarming with zombies."

Glad he didn't have to make all of the decisions anymore, Higgins replied, "Okay, young man. If that's what you think we should do, I'm all for it."

Phoenix pointed to the M4 and asked, "Do you know how to use that thing?"

Higgins replied, "Young man, I'm a Korean War vet. I took out several of those creeping zombies with just that ice saw. I can handle myself, I promise."

Phoenix saluted and replied, "I meant no disrespect; just asking." At the same time he thought, *He's just like my grandpa.*

Higgins looked down the sight of his M4 and said, "Okay. No problem, young man." He checked his rifle thoroughly, and after the somewhat meticulous display in front of Phoenix, moved to his position near the bar.

Dora shyly asked, "Where would you like me again?" Phoenix pointed to the barricade of tables and chairs near the bathroom area.

He added, "I'm taking the front doors. It's our weakest spot, and also our best chance of escape if needed. But, like I said, we shouldn't go back out."

They both agreed and quietly moved to their respective areas. Phoenix passed Vicki's corpse, and tried to divert his eyes away from the body, but still looked to make sure she had not moved an inch.

Turkey Beats Tofu Any Day:

Surprised and disappointed at the same time, Dagrepont slowed down, and said, "Hey! That's police headquarters." His voice trailed off as he continued, "What's a cruiser doing crashed … through … the … entrance?"

Ludwig glanced to his right and said, "Well, that explains why no one ever answered the phone. I don't know about you, but I'm not investigating."

Dagrepont responded more as a buddy. "Yeah, you're right. You know this town more than I do. What ya suggest we do until then?" Wait for reinforcements?

Ludwig grinned and said, "Well, I suppose we could ride around running into zombies until the cavalry arrives or hide somewhere."

Twenty-five minutes later, an obviously nervous Dagrepont tightened his grip on the seat as Ludwig, who was now driving, plowed into another zombie. The oddity hurled through the air. Its guts, unraveling by the millisecond, looked like a kite with a tail.

An impressed Dagrepont said, "Nice take down! Even the door is still attached."

Ludwig laughed. "Yeah, I got those skills delivering packages around my college campus. If I wasn't on time, I wouldn't get paid."

Dagrepont spotted another zombie on the sidewalk. With the precision of a trained marksman, he aimed and pulled the trigger. The zombie dropped to the ground like the number one pin on bowling league night. Behind it, another in a traffic vest hobbled forward. A whistle somehow hung outside of its abdomen through a gaping wound. He pulled the trigger again, and it fell atop the first. Ludwig slowed the Jeep as a more hideous zombie crossed their path. Its head was covered in tumors and stalks, and its body was quartered from the left shoulder to the kidney. Without a second thought, Dagrepont shot it, but its jerky body movements caused the round to strike the neck instead of its head. It continued thrashing toward the Jeep. After a few expletives, he muttered, "Dang! How could've I have missed that one?" Ludwig sped the Jeep forward and crushed it into a stalled car.

Still elated from the previous takedowns, Ludwig yelled, "Yeah, but the first two were spot on!

Dagrepont added, "Just sloppy work on my part. By the way, what's the population of this town?"

Ludwig pulled a stat sheet from his top pocket, glanced at it, and replied, "About fifteen thousand." Then he backed the Jeep up and pulled away from the mangled corpse.

"Then you'd better start conserving ammo."

A few blocks away, Ludwig tried out the door again. He crashed into another zombie, but it was only knocked off its feet. Dagrepont got out of the vehicle and ripped a piece of metal from the "Door of Death." He quickly walked to the fallen, thrashing zombie and bashed its skull into pulp. Brain and skull fragments splattered the surrounding area. He wiped the gore from his forehead and said, "Okay, I'm satisfied."

For the next hour and a half, the two men scouted the town, looking for survivors and taking down zombies wherever required. As they headed down a street in the town's small business district, Dagrepont pointed and said, "Look, we're in luck. There's a gun store ahead. We should resupply again like you suggested."

Ludwig glanced down at the gas gauge. It had about an eighth of a tank left. He added, "Yeah, and we need gas too."

After restocking with ammo at the gun shop, the pair continued searching for survivors. Dozens upon dozens of zombies staggered along Seventeenth Street. Ludwig stopped the Jeep for the biggest horde they'd seen since arriving in Baron. Puzzled, Dagrepont asked, "Hey, did you see that one's head explode? I didn't shoot it."

Ludwig scratched his chin and asked, "I know you didn't, but who did?" They looked at each other in shock. Ludwig cautiously backed the Jeep away from the huge crowd of oncoming zombies.

The GPS chimed, "Rerouting."

Dagrepont scanned the area, realizing it might be hard to spot a shooter from their position in the Jeep and not get shot. "Maybe someone is sniping them – or worse … us."

Ludwig partially lifted his butt out of the seat and craned his head to back up. At that moment, another zombie's head exploded. He said, "I definitely heard it that time."

Dagrepont sought out the source of the explosive round. "Yeah … sounded like a high powered M40A3 Marine Corps-issue … Sniper rifle."

Ludwig glanced around nervously and said, "No way I'm going that way without knowing who's firing that rifle." He made a left at the first opportunity and headed down a side street.

The GPS chimed, "Rerouting."

A block farther along, another large group of zombies stretched across the street. Ludwig asked nervously, "Are they possibly organizing? This is getting ridiculous." His hands visibly shook as he turned the steering wheel for a U-turn. Seconds later, they were heading back to where they had just been.

The GPS chimed, "Rerouting."

Dagrepont thought about how the last zombie had fallen. He said, "I think the sniper is on a rooftop."

Ludwig ignored the comment. Instead, he replied, "We're blocked on three sides now." Yet again, he reversed the Jeep's direction.

The GPS chimed, "Rerouting."

Clearly frustrated at the mechanical voice, Ludwig added, "Will you just shoot that dang thing?" Dagrepont looked at Ludwig as if he were a military officer, and smartly replied, "If you insist, Chief." He then fired a round into the head of an older, decayed zombie. The explosive impact caused a spray of dark blood to mist the air. The corpse smacked into the ground and draped over a hedge bush.

Semi-serious, Ludwig pointed at the device on the dashboard and said, "I really meant the dang GPS."

Ludwig continued to drive down Turkey Street and spotted a large, multicolored tin sculpture. It was a turkey decoration on someone's lawn. A mutilated body lay at the turkey's feet. The arms were bent behind their back and stuck, as if they were going to be ripped off. Ludwig thought about what he'd been through with Rosie and Gene, then said, "Looks like that fellow doesn't have much to be thankful for today." Out of the blue, Dagrepont said, "Turkey beats tofu any day!"

I Second That:

Normally, Higgins would not have been able to see Dora's blushing cheeks from across the room, but as she gazed at Phoenix, he was glad he could. While rubbing his hip he thought, *Better have some manners and leave those kids alone.* He snatched a soda from a bucket of ice, flipped the tab, and started to drink. In a rested but strong voice, he asked, "Anybody else want a soda? I'll bring it to you."

Dora yelled out, "Yes sir, I could go for one."

Phoenix noticed Dora's flushed face and replied, "Yeah, me too, Mr. Higgins"

As he leaned against the table, Phoenix wondered how Big Tex was doing, and where he might be hiding. With a final tilt of the can, he drank the last of the soda. Then his thoughts shifted to the old man and he asked, "Mister Higgins, how did you come to find us?"

Higgins told his story: about Jay's death, his walk to the ranch, and his various encounters with the zombies. He told them how he had killed several of the zombies with just an ice saw. He told of the many times that he was almost eaten, but managed to escape by hiding in cars and buildings. He told them about the taco vendor, and about how he had followed the sounds of gunfire to the bar. He ended his story with, "Today, I just got lucky. I'm awfully glad to be here, young man!"

Dora stood next to Phoenix and patted his arm. As if they were a couple, she said, "Well, we're happy you found us."

Phoenix echoed the sentiment, but stepped away from the advance. He knew she had something up her sleeve, but couldn't figure out why.

Dora held out her hand. "I want you to have this 'Big Texas Road House' t-shirt, Mr. Higgins. I found it in the back."

Higgins reached for the t- shirt and said, "Well, that's awfully nice of ya!" and quickly pulled it over his head.

"No. You're Not Crazy.":

After driving another half mile, Ludwig turned to Dagrepont and said, "You're right, we need a place to call home. Have any ideas?"

Dagrepont spread his arms like he was commanding the Red Sea, and replied, "Yes ... something easily defensible."

Ludwig smiled and said, "You know, if we're going to shack up together, I should at least know your first name. "What is it?"

Happy to be rid of military protocol, Dagrepont replied, "It's Carl. What's yours?"

Ludwig slowed the Jeep and answered, "Ben." Then he squeezed between a few stalled cars and added, "Short for Benjamin. But you can just use Ben." He stopped the vehicle and revved the engine, looking at a small group of zombies walking on the road ahead of them. "Hold on, I'm gonna drive right through!"

Dagrepont braced for impact and said, "You sure you wanna do that again?"

Ludwig grimaced and said, "I'm sick of trying to maneuver around them. I'm gonna use the Door of Death and wipe em' out!"

Dagrepont nervously fumbled with the rifle as they plowed through the horde. One of the zombies managed to latch on to the top of the door as it mowed the rest down. It pulled itself across the hood of the car toward them. Face to face with the wretchedness, Dagrepont flicked the safety off and fired at it just as its arm reached the top of the windshield. Three rounds obliterated its skull cap, exposing the still-intact gelatin-like brain. It bared its bloodied teeth and said, "Raahrr-gra!" He noticed that several stalks had started to emerge from the brain itself.

Ludwig cried, "Do you see that? Look at those stalks!" He slammed on the brakes and cut the steering wheel hard to the right, sending the body catapulting from the hood. It landed in a heap, brainless.

Ludwig said, "As ludicrous as it might sound, maybe that thing had a plant-related infection."

Dagrepont responded, "You know, I'll have to admit, I thought the same thing. But I didn't want you to think I was off my rocker."

Ludwig reversed course and accelerated rapidly. He added, "No, Carl, you're not crazy. After what I've seen today, anything is possible. Let's go find a hiding place."

Dagrepont pointed forward. "Alright, let's head west."

The GPS stated, "Rerouting."

Beans, Broth and Blood; Gut Check:

After using the restroom, Phoenix walked quietly past the two sleeping men, thinking, *I'll let them have a little more, then it'll be my turn.* He covered his mouth for a huge yawn, then turned toward Dora who was busy pacing back and forth. "I'm gonna peek out of the window and see what's happening. Can you help me move the barricade?"

Dora snapped out of her daydream like state about Phoenix and all that he'd done. She asked, "Sorry, what was that?"

Phoenix courteously repeated his request. Dora only responded by hurrying to the windows. He lifted a case of beer bottles, the empties clinking together like wind chimes, and placed them on the floor a little bit away. She thought, *Well, at least this will break the monotony ... and give me a chance to talk with him.* She lifted another box and placed it on top of his, then walked over to stand next to him at the window. Phoenix pressed his face against the window pane and looked to the right. Shockingly, a zombie threw itself against the exterior of the window, right in front of his face. The force of the impact bowed the glass inward, nearly shattering it. A glowing neon beer sign hanging nearby crashed to the ground. Electrical sparks lit up the corner. Phoenix jumped back, but the zombie continued to press its single bloodshot eye against the window, greenish goo dripping from its pulsing tumors and down the pane. The enlarged tumors looked as if they would explode. Dora screamed, and Phoenix shuddered and said, "That thing scared the crap out of me!" With his adrenaline surging, he used the burst of energy to quickly restack the boxes in front of the window.

Dora regained her composure and asked, "How many do you think are out there?"

Phoenix took a deep breath and replied, "I'd say about fifty." She heard the answer, but the mixture of adrenaline and relief coursing through her body made her snort as she was gripped with a hysterical

233

sort of mirth. It turned into a giggle, and then a full-blown laugh. Phoenix couldn't understand her laughter, but caught a little of the hysteria and started to chuckle, too.

With his back to the front window, Higgins ignored the commotion as he tried to make out the noise at the rear of the bar. While the man and woman whooped it up out front, he decided to investigate, and moved toward the sound. He heard the whispering-like noise again, but the stress of the situation caused him to flash back. Deep in enemy territory, with the past and present mingling freely in his mind, he covertly pushed aside the tables and chairs that formed a barricade. He glanced back at the young soldiers who were still laughing over by the window; he would reprimand them later. He proceeded forward, and his eyes darted back and forth as he searched for the source of the weird sound. Then, he heard it again. "Crrr-jaa!"

Higgins investigated the low-lit area. He had come to know the familiar sound, but the horrors of war and the smoke of the battlefield distorted his perception. He asked, "Is that you, Corporal Tommy?"

A zombie moaned louder and closer, "Crrr-jaa. Crrr-jaa."

Higgins popped to attention and shouted, "What's the password, soldier?" No reply. Again, he shouted, "Password, soldier?" He could feel sputum hitting him in the face. He lifted his rifle and took another step forward, but slipped on something and fell onto one knee. The enemy appeared underneath a flare. He could see its face and was confused. "Jay … is that you? What ya' doing in Korea?" The enemy soldier stopped. It dryly uttered, "Crrr-jaa." Then it moved forward.

Knee pain caused Higgins to snap back into reality, but it was too late. The zombie lunged and swiped at him. He fell hard onto his back. It shuffled forward. Higgins yelled, "NO! It can't be." Without looking, he switched the rifle's safety off. The zombie leaned forward and swiped at him again. This time, its fingernails connected with the thin skin on his hand and tore it open. Confused, he tried to reason with it as he pushed it back with the rifle's barrel. "No Jay … it's me, your friend." A split-second later, it swung again and ripped open a zigzagged laceration on his scalp. Using his uninjured leg, Higgins pushed himself away on the concrete floor, and created a little distance. He pulled the trigger. A three-round burst lit up the area, followed by a second burst, and the zombie landed headless at his feet; its body bleeding out thick dark blood.

Nolan and Nick awoke sleepy eyed, and although confused, hustled behind Phoenix and Dora. They all bolted towards the sound of the gunfire. Everyone was locked and loaded by the time they arrived at

Higgins' side, and could clearly see that the zombie was dead. Dora leaned her rifle against the wall and squatted next to Higgins. She gingerly assessed both of his wounds and said, "Just skin tears, he'll be okay. But we'll need some bandages and tape."

The four looked at one another with passing glances. Secretly, they all thought about the worst case scenario. *What if a small laceration was all it took to become one of those things?* They did not speak of it, and tried to hide their internal panic.

Nick slapped Phoenix on the back and said, "I'll go get it." He needed a couple of minutes alone to puzzle about how the zombie had gotten inside. On his way to the kitchen, he spotted a full mag and thought, *Maybe I should just bug out now.*

Feeling responsible for the attack, Phoenix looked down. He let his emotions get the better of him. "Why didn't you call us?"

Clearly defiant, Higgins replied, "Young man, I told you I can handle myself." He pointed to the zombie that lay at his feet.

Nolan agreed and said, "You've certainly got some moxie for an old man." Then, he walked over and kicked the corpse for good measure.

Phoenix kept his cool, but wondered if he had been responsible in some way for Adele's killing spree. *Maybe I should have gone out with her, let her get it out of her system.* He took out his journal and wrote an entry.

Nolan squatted down beside the corpses' body. He poked at a tendril with his rifle muzzle, then his headache came back with a vengeance. He stood back up and almost fainted.

Nick ran back to the group and handed Dora the first-aid kit. She opened the plastic box and applied antibiotic ointment and gauze to his wounds. Everyone watched as she taped each one securely.

Phoenix stated, "Well … we have a bigger problem now." He pointed to the dead zombie and expanding pool of blood on the floor. "We need to look around back there and figure out how it got in."

Dora felt queasy on the inside, but feeling protective of the old man, gently grasped his forearm to tried and lead him away. She wanted to shield him from the horror, but also thought, *I wanna show Phoenix I can handle myself.* She said, "C'mon Pops – we gotta get you away from this mess."

Higgins said angrily, "Just one cotton pickin' minute, Missy. I'm just fine, and I can walk by myself." Embarrassed, Dora let go of his arm and turned away so that her man could not see her blush with embarrassment.

Higgins stretched his arms behind his back like a young man, then followed behind Nolan and Nick as they headed to the back room to investigate.

Phoenix politely said, "Mister Higgins, you don't need to go back there with us. We'll be okay. I promise." Frazzled, but feeling better than usual, Higgins replied, "I'm alright son!"

With a spasm at the back of his neck shooting intermittently into his head, Nolan angrily said, "Old man … just stay put. You've done enough."

Higgins did not argue, but momentarily flashed back to his boot camp drill sergeant, who was prone to yell for the slightest infraction. He turned around and, with slumped shoulders, followed Dora.

Phoenix moved forward, gesturing for the men to spread out and follow him into the large stockroom. He shushed their low whispers when he spotted a beam of light at the farthest door. He pointed to it, then mouthed the words, *"We have to check that out."*

Only Nick followed, because Nolan had heard a faint gurgle in a far corner. He tried to get their attention, but they were fixated on the door. He reversed his tracks to check it out.

***

A figure suddenly blocked the light and caused Phoenix and Nick to grip their M4's even tighter. Phoenix braced himself against several kegs of beer, and Nick braced himself against a pallet of soft drinks.

Nick was curious about who or what was on the other side of the door. As he waited, the figure moved back and forth past the sliver of light, creating an intermittent beam that seemed to tap out Morse code. He quickly glanced over his shoulder to find Nolan, but at that moment the figure crashed into the door, commanding his full attention. He whispered, "Oh crap!"

Phoenix continued to stare at the narrow opening, realizing that they needed to quickly secure the door. He took off his shoes and put them atop a beer keg so he could advance without making a sound. He headed to the door, the weapon in his hands feeling as if it weighed a hundred pounds. Ten feet from the door, he listened as it creaked heavily, then watched as it exploded open from the strength of two dozen flailing arms.

***

Meanwhile, Nolan had followed the faint sound until he caught a glimpse of the zombie. He reversed his path and circled around tall metal racks stocked with one-gallon cans of beans. He knew that he needed to be situated just right so he could take a shot that would not endanger the other two. He repositioned himself between racks of plastic silverware and take-out boxes. He thought, *It's all about position.*

At the same time that the door burst open, Nolan already had the zombie in his sights. Abruptly, the menace jerked sideways, slamming into a tall rack. As if in slow motion, one rack fell into another like a set of dominoes. Before Nolan knew it, he was pinned underneath a rack, flat on his back. His migraine eased when his head smacked into a fallen shelf. Various contents of cans had spilled all over the floor and splashed onto his lips. A bit irrationally under the circumstances, he licked his lips and thought, *Not too bad.* He tried to get up, but could not move his legs. *Maybe they're shattered.* Grimacing in pain, from his low vantage point he scanned for the zombie, but didn't see it. A large can of beans fell from an upper shelf and splattered on the concrete inches away from his head. Pinto beans burst from the can and splattered onto his face. He tried to pull his legs out from under the shelves, and heard a wobbling sound. He looked straight up and saw a one-gallon can of chicken broth teeter at the edge of a shelf. He turned his head at the last second to shield himself, but the lip of the heavy can connected with his temple, creating a huge, bloody crater.

***

Phoenix and Nick fired their weapons with gusto at the zombies that had burst through the door, but were forced to retreat behind stacks of pallets. After thirty seconds of holding the door crashers at bay, another zombie was able to get between them. Nick asked, "Where did that one come from?"

Phoenix replied, "Not from the doorway … must have others in the room with us." They retreated once more, but this time Phoenix climbed a ladder. Nick stood tall right below. Together they reduced it to a pile of indistinguishable fleshy pieces.

Dora and Higgins stood at the doorway of the stockroom and unleashed a volley of rounds on the foul-smelling monstrosity that had hunted Nolan. After felling it, Higgins side stepped the still twitching corpse, carefully avoiding its entrails and put a bullet in its head. Dora hugged his shoulder and smiled.

Higgins replied to the kindness by saying, "Like I said earlier, Missy. I can handle myself."

A second zombie startled the old man, causing him to trip on a stray can and fall amongst the tumble of downed shelves. Dora glanced at Higgins' face and for an instant saw her dad laying there. *My poor dad!* She knew she had to protect him and stood between him and the advancing zombie. She placed the rifle at her waist line and strafed the shuffler.

Now deep inside of the stock room, Phoenix and Nick backed into Dora, who noticed the stress on their faces when they turned around. Phoenix looked down and said, "Nick, grab Higgins." Nick pulled the old man to his feet, wrapped his arm around a shoulder, and ushered him out of the room. Phoenix took a shooter's stance at the doorway, and shot the closest zombie right between the eyes. Its head broke apart. Only raw, meaty remnants from the chin up were left behind. The nearly headless body fell to the ground. Dora ignored the gore as she watched Phoenix's every move, transfixed. Filled with pride, she thought, *He's just awesome!* She wanted to give him a hug and a kiss, but decided to follow Higgins and on his way to the bull pen. Nick went back to Phoenix's side.

Phoenix hovered over the corpse that he had killed and told Nick, "This looks like a newer infection. See how the growths are less severe than on some of the others?"

Nick replied, "Yep. Gotcha, but let's get outta here." Another zombie stopped without warning, then its head exploded like Gallagher's watermelon.

The rapid firing of machine guns interrupted their few seconds of peace, so they bolted into the main area of the bar. Dora and Higgins were already firing at the front door, because zombies had breached the barricade. They looked to each other in disbelief. Several corpses now blocked the entrance. Dora and Higgins scooted behind the mechanical bull and continued to fire upon them.

As Nick got into better position to defend the entrance, Phoenix glanced behind his back to see a zombie breach the karaoke stage door. Low on ammo, Phoenix rerouted to the stage to grab a wireless microphone and ram it into its mouth. The garbled, gagging sound of the zombie echoed throughout the stage area from the live microphone. Phlegm and blood flowed from the corners of its mouth. Cracked teeth fell to the stage as if there were too many marbles in its mouth. One broken chair later, it lay sprawled on the floor with a splintered wooden leg impaled through its head.

A front door of the bar was completely off of its hinges and the other teetered as zombies careened awkwardly through the entrance. The team peppered them with a hail of bullets, but they just seemed to keep coming and coming. The one-eyed zombie seen earlier muscled its way through the mass of death and destruction. Somehow it entered the bull pit and nearly blindsided Dora as she had to pick off individual zombies that were now to her rear. She turned just in time, then fell to her knees, crawling under the bull.

For fear of striking Higgins or Dora with an errant shot, Phoenix ran to the pit and set the mechanical bull to maximum action. Dora rolled several times to her right as the bull began to swing around wildly. Its butt smashed into the backside of the zombie, flinging it across the pit, but it practically bounced back up on the cushy mat. Although it had one crazed eye, it haphazardly lunged at Dora again.

Higgins, bouncy-legged, got to her first and grabbed her by the hand. One armed, he pulled her to her feet. He noticed how his bicep muscle flexed; it made him feel young again. Phoenix spun the joystick around like he was playing a video game, and the rear end of the bull smacked into the zombie's head, which exploded all over the matt.

Dora backed up to Phoenix. With much gratitude, she kissed his cheek and said, "Thank you, Hon!" She looked at Higgins and said, "And thanks to YOU, Dad."

The fallen second door had created a teeter totter bridge as it lay atop the freshly dead corpses. Zombies staggered over the bridge and into the bar. A few more heads exploded, littering the entrance with considerable gore. A cacophony of sounds emanated from the zombies that had made it through, and they made a beeline to the bull pit.

Higgins exited the pit and bore his full body weight onto his somewhat swollen knee. *Strange.* The pain in his knee had stopped as he led Dora by the hand. "Follow me, young lady." She felt comfortable with her hand in his, and followed without question.

Phoenix followed Dora and Higgins and shouted, "Nick, we need you."

Nick hurried over, and the small group made their way to the long bar. The stench in the room was overpowering, and they had to cup their hands over their noses.

At the bar, Higgins picked up more ammo and said, "Here, take these!" He tossed a couple of mags to Dora, who caught them and tucked them into her waistband. Breathless, she said, "Thanks, Dad."

Phoenix grabbed a couple more mags off of the bar and tucked them into his pockets.

Nick did the same, but then broke away from the others. He whooped and hollered to lure the closest zombies away from the trio, then shouted, "I'll catch up to you. Get out of here." Other zombies continued to pour through the entrance. He shot and killed the ones that had followed him, imagining himself in the Louisiana bayous shooting at gators. A zombie managed to corner him in his state of mind, so he jumped atop a movable bar and bashed its head in with the butt of his rifle. Several more tried to grab his legs. To conserve ammo, he ripped a plastic beer banner down from a wall. He wrapped it around a massive neck, then he jumped over the body, pulled the banner backward, and snapped its spine. The others continued to reach out for him as he raced to join the group.

The lingering smell of gunpowder wafted out of the bar and into the parking lot as Phoenix knelt down and checked out the bodies that surrounded them. His earlier observations confirmed the multiple stages of zombie transformation. *Maybe three stages, total.* Some had little or no polyps. Others had polyps that had progressed into small tumors, but the third stage had large to super-sized tumors. *Looks eerily like a fungus.*

Dora, once again in a fog of complete denial, asked, "Where's Nolan?" The three men looked at her and shook their heads. Nick said a quick prayer, and everyone whispered, "Amen."

The zombies outside seemed to have been refocused by the sound of gunfire coming from the roadhouse, and they advanced on the group. Phoenix stood up and fired at their flank, while Nick moved to the middle of the parking lot to provide crossfire. Higgins and Dora stood side by side and made sure none of them exited the bar.

Above the gunfire, Phoenix said, "Let's get to the van."

Dagrepont and Ludwig:

Jubilant, Dagrepont readied his rifle and said, "More gunfire ... I love the crackle of M4s!"

Just as excited, Ludwig thought, *Yeah, maybe we can finally get some rest.* Not to be outdone, he added, "I'm liking that sound, too."

Dagrepont looked at the GPS map. More as an order than a request, he added, "We should head that way."

Ludwig smiled, then rolled through a stop sign. He slapped the steering wheel, and added, "This feels good, Carl."

Dagrepont looked at him like he had gone insane and asked, "What feels good?"

Ludwig replied, "Liberation! Not having to read street signs or stop at red lights. My whole life, I've followed the scientific method. Now, I can let go a little."

Dagrepont opened his arms wide, gesturing at the town, and said, "Careful, Doctor, we have a critical patient before us. We need every man on board!"

Ludwig slapped his leg again. The sting took him out of his momentary euphoria, and he confidently replied, "No worries, Carl … I know what I'm doing!"

Hordes of zombies streamed toward the direction of the gunfire. Intrigued and impatient, Dagrepont said, "Hurry up, Ben! They're swarming like army ants."

Ludwig thought back to the photos in his briefcase, connected some dots, and said, "I agree. I have a photo of a hieroglyph that shows an insect. It did look like an ant. But the glyph wasn't complete. Other photos showed a prisoner with a fancy headpiece, but I no longer believe it to be a ceremonial headdress. Look at the zombies we're seeing – the one with stalks growing out of the top of their skulls. The picture looked just like that."

Dagrepont shook his head and said, "Never mind that, look over there. That's where the gunfire is coming from."

Ludwig scanned the large building. The sign read, "Big Texas Road House." As he scoped out a place to pull into, he asked, "How many people are out there?"

Dagrepont counted carefully, and said, "Well, if you don't count the zombies, I'd say about four normal … and they sure do need our help. They're outnumbered!"

Ludwig spun the steering wheel hard to the right. The tires squealed, and he added, "It'll be a challenge, but I'll pull as close as possible."

***

Phoenix popped another full clip into the M4 and said, "Cover me while I get the van."

Out of breath, Dora squeaked out, "Be careful, Hon." She tried to caress his hand as he hurried away.

Higgins and Nick protected his flanks and laid down cover fire. Together, they mowed down several zombies, but steadily lost ground.

Higgins' bandage dropped into his eyes, and several of his rounds went wild. The rounds ruptured a pickup truck's gas tank and the truck

241

exploded. Fire and smoke formed a mushroom cloud in the air. The intensity of the explosion and crackling flames caused zombie heads to explode. Higgins lifted the gauze from his eyes in time to see the fiery spectacle. The shock wave blew out nearby windows and knocked everyone back. The heat of the blaze caused his head laceration to twinge.

Nearing the van, and over the crackle of fire, Phoenix remembered that he wanted to do something inside of the bar. Halfway back to the roadhouse a trailing zombie stepped between him and the building.

Nick advanced to help Phoenix as a wild-haired female zombie crawled toward him, unnoticed. Part of the horde now surrounded Nick. In desperation, he jumped atop the hood of a car and fired his weapon at the growing cluster. He took out the closest walkers, then jumped down. Without a sound, the crawling female zombie stopped just shy of his legs. It then grabbed him by his shins. The ensuing yank pulled him completely off of his feet, and he hit the ground face first. With his nose crushed, he turned onto his back and moaned in agony. Blood mixed with mucous bubbled out of his mouth and nose. He was delirious as he pawed away the tiny bits of gravel from his eyes. Stunned and dazed, but able to see, he looked into the female's eyes and said, "Vicki?" Sitting on his butt, Nick jabbed at the zombie with his rifle. On one lucky jab, he managed to wedge the stock of the weapon squarely in its mouth. When he pulled back, teeth and blood poured out of the gaping hole. It continued to thrash about until he kicked the muzzle and forced the stock out the back of its head. Trapped between two vehicles, additional zombies moved in to rip at his body. He shot and killed them with the remainder of his rounds. He tried to crawl his way over them, but his hands sunk deep into the foul smelling, rotted bodies and thought, *Oh my God.* As if in slow motion, each time he moved forward, his hands pulled out various densities of bloody, debris. He looked up, and realized that he was boxed in; rapidly losing blood from his injury. Other zombies fell to their knees and savaged his body. He screamed for help.

Phoenix leapt from vehicle to vehicle and yelled, "Nick. Hold on!" At the car next to Nick, he noticed movement under the pile of killed zombies. He jumped down and pulled the corpses off of his friend and said, "Hold on, buddy." Lightning fast, a clawed hand reached up and nearly grabbed him by the throat. One-handed, he put the tip of the barrel under its chin and pulled the trigger. The muzzle flash lit up the inside of its head like a Jack-O-Lantern. Smoke and blood poured through the hole. He lifted Nick's head, but knew that he was mortally wounded; too many areas had been torn open. Phoenix raised his rifle and placed it against Nick's temple. He knew now, without a doubt, that his friend would become one of them. It was just a matter of time.

Nick struggled to speak, feeling the muzzle against his temple. He whispered, "Do it … Don't wanna be … *them.*" His tears fell into the bloodied gravel. Phoenix glanced down at Vicki's once beautiful face among the tangle of corpses. He made the sign of the cross, and fired a single round into Nick's head.

Higgins reached Nick's ravished body. The shock of his death caused another flashback. With a blank expression, he said, "Not you too, young man." He pulled Phoenix up by the scruff of his collar and firmly added, "He's gone! Grab his tags, soldier."

Phoenix wiped Nick's blood and his own tears from his face. The single blast to his new friend's head had left little features to identify him with. Nick was gone and he would want the same treatment if the shoe was on the other foot. He finally stood up and swept his own matted hair out of his eyes. He spotted a Jeep approaching and said, "Okay, Mister Higgins. Let's go see who this is."

The old man, still in the throes of the flashback, replied promptly, "Atta-boy, soldier! See, Sonny, we have reinforcements now."

Dora could not bring herself to go over and look at Nick's body. Shocked, she turned away in time to watch Ludwig and Dagrepont pull up with a screeching stop. Zombie after zombie became M4 fodder from their barrage in the Jeep, but dozens more swarmed from the sides of the building. For a full minute, Dagrepont and Ludwig's fire power alone punched the air with blazing lead.

They got out the vehicle and ran to the group. Ludwig tossed full mags to the trio, while Dagrepont held off the rest of the horde with rapid-fire shots.

After quick introductions, all five people let loose another barrage of firepower at the undulating line of zombies. Phoenix was closest to the van and said, "Let's get out of here." He sprinted towards the vehicle.

Dagrepont yelled, "You can join us if you'd like."

Phoenix, trying not to sound disrespectful, replied, "Sir, we have this van; provides more protection from those zombies."

Dagrepont thought about their many near misses and replied, "Good point!"

Dora plopped down on the bumper of the van, sobbing uncontrollably for Nick, Adele, Nolan and Vicki. She could barely ask her question. "What are those things?"

Ludwig felt as if the question were aimed directly at him, and replied somberly, "I really wish we knew, but we just don't have enough information yet."

Shocked at his reply, Phoenix asked, "You know something about this?" He really wanted to find out what had happened at Sporaton.

Ludwig tried to backpedal for a moment, then shrugged his shoulders and replied, "No ... not exactly ..."

Higgins pointed down the street and said, "Y'all may be younger than me, but I can see pretty good right now. We need to get out of here."

Dagrepont quickly scanned the area, and realized Higgins was right.

As they readied the van, Dagrepont said, "I guess if we're leaving in this thing, we need to get our supplies."

Surprised, but not wholly disappointed, Phoenix said, "You're more than welcome to join us!"

Ludwig and Dagrepont nodded to one another in agreement, then hurried to the Jeep to retrieve their supplies.

Phoenix said quietly, "Wait right here – I'll be back." He then ran back to the bar before anyone could react, M4 cutting a path before him.

Dora screamed, "No Phoenix, don't!"

At the Jeep, Ludwig tapped Dagrepont's shoulder and pointed toward Phoenix, saying, "Look at him ... going back inside. He might be crazy. Carl?"

Dagrepont answered, "They're survivors, and mighty lucky to have made it this far. They could have been pushing daisies by now if we hadn't arrived."

Ludwig nodded and replied, "Yep, they are lucky ... aren't they?" He thought about his own mortality, because his last words crushed him like a ton of bricks. He grimaced from the sudden urge to throw up, and turned his face for a moment. The two men grabbed the rest of their gear and met the others at the van.

After stowing the supplies in the back of the vehicle, Dagrepont stated, "I thought Phoenix would have been back by now."

Dora replied, "Don't you worry about my boyfriend. He can take care of himself."

Just inside the entrance of the roadhouse, Phoenix stood atop the bullet riddled door, and aimed at cluster of propane tanks that he had seen earlier; a dozen zombies angling towards him. He lined up the white tanks in his M4s site and fired one round. A huge explosion of flame and shrapnel leveled the walkers and also blew him back out of the door. He stood up, dusted himself off, and then ran back to the van. The roadhouse burned intensely behind him.

Phoenix hopped into the driver's seat, turned around, and without missing a beat, asked Ludwig, "What did you mean when you said ... wish we knew?"

Ludwig, careful to give out as little information as he could get away with, replied in kind, "I was sent to investigate Sporaton Lab. When I got here, all of this had already started."

Stunned, Phoenix replied, "Wait a second. I work at Sporaton!" At that moment, a zombie pounded its fists on the side of the van. The large hands rocked the vehicle and left imprints in the sheet metal. Phoenix pressed down hard on the accelerator, the van fishtailed wildly and everyone in the back was knocked to the floor. More than a dozen zombies were left behind as the van sent up a spray of flying rocks and dust.

Ludwig rubbed his head and quickly sat back up. He had a moment of clarity, and blurted out, "Then you're my missing link! You're the last one left alive from the Belize expedition."

Phoenix screeched the van to a stop; he had had enough. Filled with sorrow he said, "I'm the last one?"

Everyone listened attentively as Ludwig continued, "Yes! And I'm so sorry." Phoenix frowned as the truth of the matter sunk in. Ludwig held back a grimace when he was besieged by a painful stomach cramp. He collected his thoughts, then went on with the facts. "I've seen all the photographs, the specimens, and the general conclusions of the scientific team. I have a preliminary hypothesis."

Phoenix pulled himself together and said, "Go on." He thought, *I want a concrete answer now.*

Once again, zombies approached the van. Feeling nauseated from the cramps, Ludwig caught sight of the zombies through the rear window and replied, "We should just get out of here."

Higgins barked out a reply to an imaginary lieutenant. "Yes, sir! Area secured, sir!" He watched as headquarters burned.

Epilogue: Flight 1622:

Paramedics waited for the sick pilot to exit the jumbo jet's cabin. The airport's administrator was already on the tarmac at the Hong Kong Airport, in response to their mayday.

No one exited the plane.

A couple of ground crew workers were dispatched to climb the steps and investigate. They knocked on the exterior door, waiting for one of the flight attendants to open it up, but no one answered. Again, they knocked but got no reply.

Chen and Jing were perplexed. They knew the paramedics needed to urgently treat the pilot, so they felt extra pressure to get inside. The men knocked again and waited, but still received no answer. The looked at each other and shrugged their shoulders in disbelief. This had never happened to them before, but they knew they had to have permission to enter the cabin. They radioed the supervisor and in their native Mandarin dialect asked, "Sir, do we have permission to open the cabin door?"

The supervisor dryly replied, "Permission granted."

The men began to unlatch the door, and Chen pulled up hard on the handle. The door slowly opened. A foul smell quickly engulfed them, and they both reached into their pockets for their light blue medical masks.

Chan shouted through the open doorway, "I need to speak to the head stewardess." There was no reply. Then they heard indecipherable words coming from the cabin. They looked at each other with alarm. Chen did not like what was going on, but nudged his partner to follow him inside. Both men crossed the threshold of the jumbo jet. When they got to the first class cabin, they pulled back the curtain and stopped dead in their tracks. The carnage was unimaginable, and both Chen and Jing immediately added to the horrific scene by projectile vomiting.

A zombie reached up from its seat and grabbed Jing's arm, pulling him into its lap. Jing struggled against the hideous zombie's strong grip. Others moved toward the sounds of the struggle. Still buckled over from retching, Chen reached out for his partner. Multiple hands pulled him deeper into the cabin, and bit chunks of flesh from his torso and arms. Screams of terror filled the cabin as the two were literally torn apart by the voracious zombies.

Their radio crackled on the cabin floor. "What's the pilot's status?"

No response.

"Come in ground crew 1622. Ground crew 1622!"

Zombies now clumsily exited the plane, stepping and falling over each other.

By then, additional ground crews had arrived to assist the flight crew, but stopped in their tracks. The paramedics at the foot of the stairs were shocked by the screams they had heard. As the full scope of the situation unfolded, they began to retreat, but security officers ran forward and shot at the advancing horde. When the zombies did not go down they were confused. How could the bodies have survived the multiple gunshots?

The zombies continued to exit the plane, and trailed off into multiple directions. A few of their heads spontaneously exploded from the noise of the nearby jet engines.

Too curious to think clearly, the airport supervisor moved in for a closer look and snapped a picture. His boss would require a full report in the morning, and he wanted to be prepared. All at once, he found himself surrounded. Frightened beyond belief at their gnashing mouths, he called for additional security on his walkie-talkie, but was wickedly yanked off of his feet from behind. A reply came back just as his neck was bitten. "This is the airport security. What seems to be the problem?"

About the Author:

Derrick LaCombe was born and raised in New Orleans, La. At an early age he was exposed to Mardi Gras, the arts, a unique culture, and great food. All of these things and many more have shaped his creativity and passion for life. He puts these spices into the things he writes about, whether it's zombies, Christmas, or mysteries, and creates an awesome literary gumbo. Join him on the many adventures you'll take as he explores the rest of his imagination.

If you would like more information on any of his books, contact him at:

derricklacombe@hotmail.com
www.facebook.com/zombieauthor
www.moniquehappy.com/derrick-lacombe

John 11:25, Jesus said to her,

"I am the resurrection and the life; he who believes in ME will live even if he dies."

DERRICK LACOMBE